VOIDWALKER

Also by S. A. MacLean

The Phoenix Keeper

VOIDWALKER

S. A. MACLEAN

First published in Great Britain in 2025 by Gollancz
an imprint of The Orion Publishing Group Ltd
Carmelite House, 50 Victoria Embankment
London EC4Y 0DZ

An Hachette UK Company

The authorised representative in the EEA is Hachette Ireland,
8 Castlecourt Centre, Castleknock Road, Castleknock, Dublin 15, D15 XTP3,
Republic of Ireland (email: info@hbgi.ie)

1 3 5 7 9 10 8 6 4 2

A CIP catalogue record for this book is
available from the British Library.

ISBN (Hardback) 978 1 399 61660 7
ISBN (Export Trade Paperback) 978 1 399 61661 4
ISBN (eBook) 978 1 399 61663 8
ISBN (Audio) 978 1 399 61664 5

Typeset by Input Data Services Ltd, Bridgwater, Somerset

Printed in Great Britain by Clays Ltd, Elcograph S.p.A

MIX
Paper | Supporting
responsible forestry
FSC
www.fsc.org   FSC® C104740

www.gollancz.co.uk

For everyone still learning how to forgive yourself.

Or maybe you're just here for the teeth. That's cool, too.

Author's Note

This novel is intended for adult audiences. It includes multiple scenes of explicit sex between consenting adults, including bite play (without drawing blood).

The non-human, immortal race in this world are obligate carnivores, with humans as their primary food source, including on-page description of a deceased human being eaten. Graphic violence includes bite wounds, burn wounds, and beheading.

The main character discusses past experiences with a neglectful parent who abused alcohol, and the past death of that parent. There are discussions of past experiences of near drowning, as well as on-page alcohol consumption and character death.

The Beast from the Forest

They told her not to be afraid. That it wouldn't hurt.

Who'd believe that propaganda bullshit? *Of course* it was going to hurt. She hid her protests, bitter like ice behind every forced smile.

She left home on a sleek metal train, a long day of rattling tracks and crystal glasses clinking on tables, ensconced in a plush booth like some fake aristocrat. Beyond the windows, night sky swirled with bright green auroras – the souls of the dead, gone to the Void.

This time of year, no sun bloomed on the horizon. Frozen valleys passed as pallettes of black forest and moonlit snow. Then, twinkling lights in the distance. The mountains parted, revealing pitched roofs and glowing windows, the capital city of Thomaskweld swathing the valley like a gilded growth.

She was never alone.

Attendants with saccharine smiles sat with her on the train, led her through the glittering city and its maze of marble hallways. They fetched whatever food she asked for: pastries from Thomaskweld's riverside bakeries, warm candied nuts, juices of guava and pomegranate imported from the Summer Plane. She'd always wondered what pomegranates tasted like, dreamed of what delight might be found in buttery bedsheets and down pillows.

All bribes, for her docile behavior. The theatrics were blatant. Unnecessary. She came of her own will, was too far from home to turn back now.

On her final morning, they fetched her for a bath, combed her hair and scrubbed her skin to glowing. Lavish, wasn't it? Almost *kind*, with one chilling omission: no soaps or salts scented the water. When the attendants dressed her in a soft gray robe, they offered no perfume. The preparations left her immaculate. Clean.

Appetizing. As befitted a proper sacrifice, an offering to slate the hunger of an immortal.

The time came too soon. In fur-lined slippers that didn't quite fit, she trailed two attendants in gray robes more ornate than hers, their sleeves embroidered with swirls of Void-black. One carried an energy lantern, its silver glow lighting the snowbanks as they left the road, an unmarked path into the trees.

Mortals built the city. Older creatures lived in the forest.

Fresh powder crunched beneath her feet. The towering shiverpines offered a familiar vanilla scent, a sigh of needles heavy with ice, reminders of a home far away. Her thoughts drifted to memories of playing hide-and-seek in the forest with her younger sister – to their tear-stained parting at the train station, the pleas for her not to go.

Someone had to. Their village sent the call. She answered, so no one else would.

They reached a clearing. The stately granite pillars looked misplaced, framing a patio with no roof. Pine boughs arced over the shrine like ribs of a cathedral, and from each column, energy lanterns glowed in dusk blue. A silver mat awaited her, flanked by two sitting pillows.

The forest went silent. What she would have given for a single hooting night bird, the chuff of a squirrel – and she hated squirrels. She swallowed hard and told herself:

Don't be afraid.

Across the pavilion, a shadow shifted. Silent, the figure stepped into the light.

Bough-stalkers, her father had whispered on long nights, a name carried by only the oldest folktales. 'My Lord,' a more reverent greeting as the attendants bowed their heads.

Daeyari, the creatures called themselves.

At a glance, he could have been a young man: bone pale skin and guarded features, ink-dark hair shaved close at the sides, a lean frame in a midnight jacket and dark breeches. The rest of him was anything but human. Sable antlers crowned his head. Crimson irises latched onto her, framed by sclera black as night. Black as the Void his immortal race dragged themselves back from millennia ago, refusing to succumb to the shackles of death. Never aging.

Still hungry.

The attendants departed in silence. What came next wasn't their business.

Cowards.

She fought a shudder as the daeyari studied her, head tilted like a panther eyeing prey, a disorientating flick as a long, slender *tail* swayed at his ankles. Not human. Not of this Plane.

'You come willingly?' His voice was flat as ice, old as the trees.

'I come willingly, Lord Antal.' Trembling or not, these words couldn't be minced. 'My home is in need of daeyari aid, and I volunteer as payment. It's my honor to serve the pact.'

An *honor*. She'd practiced that word the most on the train, until she could say it without a flinch.

Satisfied, the beast gestured to a pillow, his hand tipped not in nails, but black claws. *Don't be afraid.* She sat, back straight, legs folded beneath her.

He approached on bare feet, clawed toes whispering over stone. His midnight jacket shifted in the light, patches of iridescence patterned as aurora swirls. She'd never seen one of them in person. An old instinct tightened her belly, a shudder at some ancestral memory of red eyes stalking her people through dark forests. But that was a long time ago, legends of man-eaters carved on stone ruins and folktales told to frighten children. Over the centuries, their two races had come to a more civil understanding: coexistence, in exchange for sacrifice.

The daeyari sat cross-legged on the pillow opposite her, immaculately still aside from that tail curled around him, flicking at the tip. He picked up a ceramic teapot. The politest predator she'd ever met, posture perfect as he poured, prim claws strumming the sides of the cup.

'You're young,' he said.

'I'm old enough. Thirty-one last year.' Old enough to decide for herself. Old enough to taste the life she could have had.

The words came out a sliver too curt, for addressing her esteemed Lord Daeyari. The beast's smoldering red eyes narrowed. Another flick of his tail.

He handed her the cup.

She clutched it, warm ceramic heating her hands, spice drifting in the steam. Twilight sorrel. Her mother kept an ointment made from the herb, a numbing salve for skinned knees or mishaps with hunting knives. Never something to taste. She forced a drink, shuddering as a floral heat hit her tongue. Light at first, like starlight on snow. It built into the velvet depth of midnight, a cloying warmth that numbed her mouth and slithered down her throat.

'I come from the town of Sunip.' She'd practiced the words a hundred times, yet they stumbled as her tongue grew leaden. 'On the border of your territory. My family smiths energy weapons, but we've run low on conductive ore. Two weeks ago, the daeyari from your neighboring territory claimed one of our mines is on her land, demanded payment for its use. Please, Lord Antal. It was a simple mistake. We can't afford payment to two daeyari.'

He let her speak without interruption, without expression. Only the twitch of his tail.

'I'll settle this dispute on your behalf,' he said once she'd finished. 'Your town will have my protection. And your smiths will have the ore they need for their craft.'

A sickly relief bowed her shoulders. Her home would be cared for, her little sister heartbroken but safe. As her eyes drooped, numbness spread to her fingertips, turning the cup clumsily as she attempted to set it down.

The daeyari stopped her with a single claw tapped to the ceramic.

'All of it,' he ordered. Not harsh. Just firm.

She downed the remaining tea then forfeited the empty cup.

Haze wrapped her thoughts, smothering smooth and warm as a hearth. She drifted, weightless. Pleasant. She didn't notice the daeyari move until he crouched beside her, claws gentle against her cheek. A pressure on her shoulder.

'Does this hurt?' When he leaned close, she caught the glint of long canines. A smell like pine and ozone as she slumped against his chest.

Run, her baser instinct pleaded. *Don't let this creature touch you.*

'Does . . . what . . .'

He'd pulled back her robe to reveal a bare shoulder, a

5

scalpel-sharp claw carved across her collarbone. Blood welled from the cut, stark against flushed skin. Yet no pain.

Void be damned. They hadn't lied, after all. When words failed, she shook her head.

'Good.'

He tilted her gaze away from the wound. Merciful – as much as a carnivore could be.

Run, but the voice was fading. *Flee into the forest*, as his claws brushed her throat. The smell of pine reminded her of home. She saw slanted sun through needles, heard the crackle of evening bonfires on the crags.

Lost in fog, she barely felt when his teeth ripped her open.

He never asked her name.

Maybe it was easier that way.

Part One

The beast came from the forest, and mortals fled.
Claws made to carve and sharp teeth to devour.
The predator taught prey to fear the dark.
And feasted through nights that forced us to cower.

The beast came from the forest, and mortals fought.
Claws cut too swift and sharp teeth aged too long.
The predator taught prey our flesh was soft.
And tore down the weapons we thought made us strong.

The beast came from the forest, and mortals bowed.
Claws held out soft and sharp teeth for an oath.
The predator taught prey to speak its name.
And offered a deal that would profit us both.

— Children's rhyme, Winter Plane, *The Beast from the Forest*

I

A beginner's guide to extra-dimensional bomb smuggling

Fionamara Kolbeck saw her first door between worlds at eight years old.

The never-melting ice of the Winter Plane had grown thick that year, a slick patch as she'd played along the river rocks near her home. One slip, and the water had snatched her like icy claws, dragging her beneath the current, flooding her lungs as she'd screamed for help.

Then, black. An endless Void that had sought to swallow her.

She'd jolted back to consciousness coughing water on the riverbank, black hair plastered to pale cheeks, shivering hard enough to chatter her teeth. Her father had knelt over her, rubbing her chest raw as worry creased his cold-hardened face.

Behind him, a strange distortion had warped the air, like nothing she'd ever seen before. Some kind of translucent Curtain. Those who'd been touched by the Void and returned to life saw easier through the fabric separating worlds, people claimed.

At age ten, Fi learned to step through her first Curtain.

At fourteen, she'd flee to neighboring Planes of reality to escape house chores.

By twenty-three, she'd discovered the lucrative business of cross-Plane smuggling.

Now, hot off thirty-two and with precious few shits left to show for it, Fi nursed a splitting headache while leaning her shoulder into a tree trunk, the spongy paper bark gleaming cheerful white with an intensity she was entirely too hungover to appreciate.

A crisp breeze sent the forest swirling. Leaves cascaded like spilled paint, a head-throbbing blend of gold and scarlet glaring in afternoon sunlight. The trees of the Autumn Plane lived in eternal fall, an endless cycle of growing and shedding and postcard-perfect vistas that drew the snobbiest tourists and entrepreneurs.

Plus Fi, who was neither of these.

She sought refuge in her binoculars, puckering plum-painted lips while surveying two men in the clearing below. They, too, appeared unenthralled by the wish-you-were-here scenery. No whimsical leaf gazing, all fidgeting boots. The pair hunched in wool coats and low-brimmed hats, stationed like wraiths alongside, by comparison, an amusingly quaint wooden cart. A donkey idled in the harness, fluffy ears twitching at flies. Atop the cart, wooden crates brimmed with apples, yet not an orchard for miles.

Amateurs.

'Half an hour early to a rendezvous.' Fi lowered her binoculars and glowered at the too-bright sunlight. 'Either clueless or desperate. What do you think, Aisinay?'

Behind her, a Void horse sniffed the underbrush, searching for needlemice to snack on. Dappled shade fell upon silver scales from snout to hooves, a finned tail brushing crimson leaves. At Fi's voice, the beast perked webbed ears. Her eyes stayed fixed on the loam, milky blind and framed in black sclera.

The horse huffed, scattering leaves beneath her nose.

'Probably clueless,' Fi agreed. She returned to her binoculars, inspecting the gleam of a golden wristwatch. 'But clueless with money? I can live with that.'

Fi had never arrived late to a client meet-up in her life. Neither had she ever met a client on time. People behaved more genuinely when they thought no one was watching, and these men were hurried. Brazen.

Aisinay snorted. What the Void horse lacked in sight, she made up for with a keen sense for energy sources, and she'd been restless since they arrived. Could be a pack of trade wardens prowling nearby. Better settle business quickly. Fi latched a metal cart to her horse – careful of the fins spining her neck, in place of a mane – then grabbed the lead and headed for the clearing.

Now came the matter of entrances. This, Fi learned early in her career, could make or break a deal.

Crunched leaves alerted the men to her approach. The younger, Fi's age, kept close to his cart with downcast eyes that screamed 'assistant'. The one with the wristwatch pushed middle-age, sixty by her guess. He straightened at Fi's arrival, steel-eyed with the intensity of a man trying too hard to look intimidating. She met them with a crooked grin, arms wide.

'Fear not, gentlemen. I have arrived!'

What an arrival it was. Fi wore a bodysuit of dark gray silviamesh with purple accent lines, tailored tight to her curves, the hexagonal fabric light as silk and tough as steel. Sinfully expensive, paid for by a lucrative job five years back, moving a rare collection of sundrop tulips off the Spring Plane. Her mascara: knife-sharp against smoky eyeshadow. Her weapons: on bold display, the metal hilt of an energy sword at her belt, five glowing silver energy capsules affixed to her gloves. But most eye-catching of all: her hair, Void-black roots shifting to pastel rainbow, curls cut to her collarbone.

At least one of these details solicited a raised brow from the elder man. He masked it with a toothy smile. 'A beautiful day on the Autumn Plane.'

'Always is,' Fi returned. Consistent to the point of dullness.

Aisinay snorted and yanked her bridle. Odd. The Void horse made excellent character judgements, but beyond this man's sour attitude, he wore no visible weapons or energy sources. Just a gaudy green vest and suit jacket with gilded pinstripes and . . . a hint of silviamesh peeking out his collar? Maybe not *completely* clueless.

'Fionamara Kolbeck? Your reputation precedes you. Impressive, for someone so'— his watery gaze slid over her, appraising in a way that made her fist clench —'*young*.' He extended a hand. 'I'm Cardigan.'

Fi snorted. '*Cardigan?* Your mother name you after her favorite knitwear?'

He retracted his hand, a scowl curling thin lips. 'Perhaps we should get to business.'

Rolling over so easy? Not just impatient, then. If dear, sweet *Cardigan* had no rebuttal to her insult, he must be desperate as well. In need of discretion, since their meeting was set up in someone else's name – his sheepish assistant, she assumed. Not local, either. Seasonspeak served as a common language across all four Season-Locked Planes, but he didn't have the crisp enunciation of an Autumn dialect, nor the heavier syllables of her Winter accent. Something lighter, more frivolous with vowels . . . Spring, most likely.

All things considered, Fi smelled an opportunity for a price markup. She reached into her cart and pulled out her most intimidating weapon: a clipboard.

'All right, boys.' She brandished a pen like a threat. 'Where are we headed? I transport to all four Season-Locked Planes, and all pockets of existence in between. Plus, half-price special for anything you want tossed into the infinite Void between realities – that one's popular with the politicians.' She winked.

'The cargo's going to Thomaskweld,' Cardigan answered. 'Winter Plane.'

Fi whistled. 'A territory capital? I can recommend a good drop-off on the outskirts—'

'The delivery point is inside the city.'

Her pen halted. Each territory on the Winter Plane ran a little differently, and Fi had operated out of the one in question for a decade – obviously why Cardigan sought her out. The frigid wilds were plenty dangerous, but capital cities housed trade wardens, regional police, the elected mortal governor. And worse. Something with claws.

'Moving anything inside the city will cost extra,' Fi said.

'Done.' Cardigan offered a slip of paper. 'They're expecting you in two days.'

Fi frowned at the address, a hotel on the city's east side. A too-nice part of town. She resumed scribbling on her clipboard, though no actual words. Only an idiot left a paper trail, but she enjoyed watching people crane their necks trying to spy her notes. Cardigan barely recovered from his ostrich stance when Fi continued.

'Are you transporting any perishable, spillable, corrosive, explosive, or in other way hazardous materials?'

The men glanced at each other a heartbeat too long.

'No,' Cardigan replied.

Brow arched, Fi stepped to the cart and knocked her knuckles against the lower layer of boxes. In contrast to the decoy apple crates up top, these were sealed, a rattle of glass inside. 'What's in the boxes?'

Cardigan puckered. 'We expected discretion.'

13

'Discretion is a given, Cardigan. I need to know proper handling.'

'It's wine. An excellent vintage, from the Autumn Plane.'

Fi drew another swirl on her clipboard, slitted eyes locked with her stubborn client. The bulk of her business came from merchants and private collectors skirting import taxes between Planes, but unless these crates packed an exquisite alcohol collection, Cardigan would be lucky to make profit after her fees. Not her problem.

'Your payment?' At the end of the day, that was all that mattered.

Cardigan pulled a metal case from his pocket. When it clicked open, Fi's eyes widened at the velvet interior, ten metal cards set in individual slots.

The Season-Locked Planes ran on energy chips – currency for daily exchange, the backbone of every industry. Fi kept a stash of energy chips at home to power her furnace. She kept the smaller glass capsules on her gloves for aid in combat. Factories in big cities like Thomaskweld churned out the common varieties.

But *these*. Glass strips along the edges glowed not with silver human magic, but crimson. Immortal energy. Gifts from the race of daeyari who ruled the government of every territory. Compared to mortal energy chips, daeyari-made were a hundred times stronger, more valuable. This box could power a village for a month.

'Where did you get these?' Fi asked, unease knotting her stomach.

Cardigan chuckled. 'Oh, you know. A daeyari passes them off to a governor. Governor slips one to a mistress. And off they go into the world.' He closed the box with a snap. 'Other half is yours on delivery.'

Fi weighed the prize, jaw tight as she tallied outstanding debts, a new harness for Aisinay, maybe a second set of silvia-mesh.

'Load it up,' she said.

Cardigan's assistant snapped into motion, hauling apple crates from the top row to get at the contraband underneath. Fi tugged Aisinay's bridle, moving her cart closer for transfer. The Void horse pawed the soil, but a stroke along her scaled neck quietened her.

Fi stepped aside to let the assistant work. Unfortunately, Cardigan joined her. While she stood stoic, hands folded behind her back, he fidgeted with his suit cuffs.

'This delivery,' Cardigan said, 'requires the utmost discretion.'

'I have nearly a decade of experience moving cargo between Planes of reality,' Fi recited – because business cards *also* left a paper trail. 'I'm well familiar with navigating among all four Season-Locked Planes, and the Winter Plane especially. Your wine is in good hands.'

'You plan to take the Bridge from Autumn to Winter?'

Fi stood a little stiffer, guard raised. 'Seeing as a Bridge is the only way to pass from one Plane to another? Yeah. That's the plan.'

'What about the customs checkpoint?'

'I won't be using any public transit routes.'

'You know another way across?'

She held back an eye roll at the poorly veiled prodding. It never worked. 'A Void smuggler never shares her routes.'

Most traders and tourists crossed the Bridge from one Plane to another using well-established entrances, bustling transit hubs between worlds – complete with guards and customs officers. More *discreet* business called for discreet paths, lesser-known doorways from one reality to the next. The more hidden routes a smuggler discovered, the greater advantage over competitors and law enforcement.

And Voidwalkers like Fi, able to *see* the doorways that normal humans couldn't? The greatest advantage of all.

Cardigan's assistant lifted the first sealed crate. A box full of wine ought to be heavy, yet he didn't strain as he shifted the load, producing another clink of glass. Fi scowled.

'And what about the daeyari?' Cardigan prodded.

A chill hit Fi, an old instinct buried in her bones – in the bones of every human raised across these Planes, alert for the predators who stalked their forests.

Her reply came taut. 'The daeyari who rules in Thomaskweld is one of the most lenient of his species on the Winter Plane. I assume that's why you're shipping there.' Didn't make the possibility of crossing paths with one of the creatures any more palatable.

'Have you ever met one?'

The chill sharpened, ice through her gut. 'Once.' Once was more than enough.

'How do you deal with them?'

'Void smugglers don't *deal* with carnivorous immortals, Cardigan. We avoid them.'

The ice on her tongue should have shut him up, but Cardigan laughed. 'Not *all* of you avoid them. Last year, I saw a sentence go out in the territory next door. Execution, for stealing from a governor. Dragged him to the daeyari screaming. Drew a crowd and everything!'

'Charming,' Fi gritted.

Her fist clenched, knuckles tight against silviamesh gloves. She imagined herself serene. Composed. A glassy mountain lake who *wasn't* tempted to clock her client in the jaw.

Another crate moved onto her cart. Aisinay flattened her ears, blind eyes tilted to the load.

'I hope you'll manage better,' Cardigan said. 'I'm told you're familiar with Antal Territory, enough to ensure—'

Fi left him mid-sentence. She pushed past the assistant and smacked her palm to a crate.

Heat swelled at her fingers. Every living creature had energy, a force to keep organs pumping and cells working. To Shape that energy was a matter of redirecting, leaching out of living tissue and concentrating into physical form. Fi drew a current from her forearm, fed by a breakfast of toast and too much sweetened coffee.

Cold prickled down her arm as she pulled the energy from her muscles. Hot, as a silver glow condensed in her hand. She pushed, sending a small pulse of her magic into the wood.

Something inside the crate shuddered, static thick enough to taste.

Fi recoiled. 'Are these *energy capsules*?' Bigger than the glass vessels affixed to her gloves, judging by the current. A type of energy storage like Cardigan's box of chips, but made for quicker access. Made more *volatile*.

The assistant looked to the ground. Cardigan's lips thinned. 'Our goods are our business.'

The nerve. The sheer audacity. 'Did you not register my question about potentially explosive materials?'

Cardigan. As Fi rolled over the name, it poked a fuzzy memory, some connection to the energy production sector . . .

'What does it matter?' he demanded.

'It matters if you're stacking a fucking *bomb* on my cart.'

He waved a dismissive hand. 'Your payment is more than generous.'

A younger Fi would have backed down. Alone and freshly

run away from home, pockets empty and her father's shouts haunting her heels, the allure of twenty daeyari energy chips would have silenced her sharpest protests. The allure of twenty daeyari energy chips was *still* pretty motivating. Only now, Fi would have them on her terms.

She squared up with Cardigan. He stood taller than her respectable five-foot-seven, but Fi didn't blink, her irreverent tone and barbed exterior drawn up like a cloak of armor.

'Listen, Cardigan. I'll deliver this cargo. Because it's my job, and I'm Void-damned *good* at my job, or you wouldn't be here. But for that to happen, you're going to tell me what's in those crates, and how dangerous—'

She tensed at the snap of a branch. Aisinay's ears perked.

Fi moved without thinking. Thinking was a delay, an invitation to take an energy bolt through the neck. The moment she heard the click of a crossbow, she shoved her clients behind the carts. A burnt taste laced the air. Two bolts of pure silver energy whizzed past to strike a tree, flaring out with a *snap*. Bootsteps crunched the leaves.

'Trade wardens!' a man called out in an Autum accent: crisp, and curt, and hand-crafted to ruin Fi's day. 'Come out with your hands up!'

Fi banged her head against the cart, exhaling an emphatic, '*Fuuuck . . .*'

'*Trade wardens?*' Cardigan hissed. 'Were you followed?'

'Was *I* followed?' Fi pointed to the decoy apple crates. 'While you're out for a pleasant stroll with your apples, *fifty miles from the closest market?*'

'Can you get rid of them?'

Fi squinted through a slat in the cart, counting four figures. She pressed a hand to her temples, the throb of a hangover set aside, but not forgotten.

Twenty energy chips. Anything less wouldn't be worth this.

'Sure. This is . . .' An existential sigh. '*Suboptimal.* But I've handled worse—'

A rustle of loam was her only warning. Without so much as a 'thanks, goodbye,' Cardigan grabbed his assistant and fled into the forest. Fi gawked after them. That useless coward. *That husk of moldy pine needles.* She hissed several more curses as two wardens broke away in pursuit, leaving two to deal with her.

'Fionamara Kolbeck!' one called. 'You're wanted on charges of tax evasion, illegal territorial entry, illegal possession of hazardous substances—'

She banged her head against the cart again, harder. Fuck Fi in the Void, of course they recognized her. One of the perils of rainbow hair. And her glowing personality. Not to mention her all-around iconic approach to the profession of—

'—blackmailing, trespassing, and harassment of livestock. Surrender now!'

She peered out from cover. Two men entered the clearing, uniformed in scarlet jackets with a double row of gold buttons – colors of this territory's governor. One wore the badge of the regional police, but the one with the trade warden bars on his chest . . . Fi vaguely recalled that wiry mustache tilted in equal displeasure a year ago, when she'd passed a shipment of Summer Plane cinnamon trees under his nose. What a quaint reunion.

Both men raised crossbows, metal constructs with bolts of silver energy Shaped onto the tracks. Standing next to several crates of volatile capsules was the last place Fi wanted to be if those bolts went off. She stepped out of cover with hands raised.

But not before popping an energy capsule off her glove and into her palm.

'Afternoon boys,' she greeted with a smile. 'How's the bounty looking these days?'

The warden twitched his moustache, finger itching for his trigger. 'Five chips.'

'*Five?*' Fi scoffed. 'Territory next door is offering eight. Get your shit together.'

She clenched her hand, crushing the glass capsule in her palm.

Fi had started charging her own capsules at age twenty-five, after a bootleg one exploded and nearly took her eyebrows off. She spent too much time sculpting those eyebrows. Basic Shaping drew energy from her own muscles, but mortal reserves only lasted so long before needing rest and food to replenish. Pre-charged capsules created an external energy bank to draw from. A handy power boost, when jobs turned sour.

That, and Fi adored the shock on the warden's face when the glass cracked in her hand, releasing a pulse of silver energy.

She seized the magic before it could dissipate, fingers curled to Shape the external deluge. As she clenched a fist, the energy condensed, flashing a shield in time to catch two crossbow bolts fired at her thigh and shoulder. The air hissed where magic hit magic. Fi's shield extinguished with a snap.

Her attackers pressed palms to their crossbows, a delay as they Shaped energy into new bolts.

Fi yanked the sword hilt from her belt. She popped another capsule off her glove and cracked it into the base of the hilt. As energy pulsed into the conductive metal, Fi Shaped it to form a silver blade, crackling ozone at the edges.

The warden fired first. Fi dodged. The graze of his bolt stung her shoulder, but her silviamesh diffused most of the energy. She caught his thigh with her blade, a slice that sent him howling to his knees. The second man hadn't fired yet. Afraid to hit his superior?

His mistake. Fi swung her sword, striking the crossbow

where an energy capsule was embedded into the stock. His eyes widened as glass cracked, but no time to react before—

BOOM.

An explosion shook the clearing, rattling leaves from maple trees. Even with another shield in place, Fi careened backward from the impact. Three energy capsules exhausted on a single meetup. What a waste. She caught her footing in the loamy soil, ears ringing. The trade warden slumped in the dirt, clutching his bloody leg. The second man sprawled face down. Unmoving.

He might have been dead. Fi avoided that outcome when she could, but survival came first. Especially when the alternative meant getting dragged to a daeyari. Her retirement plans included a cabin in the woods and a century-old bottle of whiskey, not being eaten alive.

Shouts sounded from the forest, a slurry of voices and splintering branches. Fi had precious seconds to appraise her escape route, the vanished Cardigan, the crates of *bombs* he'd loaded onto Aisinay's cart. Abandoning the load would be easy, and though she grimaced to think of sacrificing a lucrative payout, she could stomach lost funds if it meant saving her neck.

The damage a forfeited job would do to her reputation, however? Unacceptable.

Only the worst cowards let fear get the best of them.

Fi closed the metal compartment of her cart with a latch. More shrapnel, if the load exploded, but at least nothing would tumble out. When she vaulted onto Aisinay's bare back, the Void horse snorted and stomped her hooves. Fi lay a hand on the beast's neck, accompanied by a gentle pulse of energy. Reassurance that she was there. Eyes for both of them.

Aisinay charged forward, the cart rumbling behind. Fi guided her not with reins, but soft hands on either side of her neck, flicks of energy to urge the blind horse left or right as they dodged between trees. Impossible to gauge the number of voices swarming the forest, but she wouldn't stay long enough to find out.

She'd chosen this meeting spot for a reason.

They skidded into a ravine. Deep mud dragged the cart wheels, exposed tree roots lashing Fi's shoulders like grasping hands. At the end of the ditch: salvation. A distortion rippled the air, the translucent folds of a Curtain, barely visible amidst slanted Autumn sunlight.

At Fi's urging, Aisinay charged straight in.

2

Just a girl, her horse, and the endless Void

The Curtain had no weight – less like cloth, more like a tear. A thin spot in the fabric of the Autumn Plane. Normal humans couldn't see the doorways sprinkled throughout their worlds, would only note a chill in the air as they passed.

Ever since giving death a solid 'not today, thanks' on that riverbank as a kid, Fi saw Curtains clear as the hand in front of her.

She reached for the translucent shroud, clinging to the back of her Void horse, cart slowed by the mud. Cold rippled goose-bumps down her arms. Fi pushed back. She drew energy out of forearm muscles, Shaped it into a pulse of glowing silver at her fingertips. Like slicing a hand through thick mist. The veil consumed her, crimson leaves and birch trunks fading to black as she left the Autum Plane.

They emerged onto tundra. Dense forest snapped into peat and lichen-crusted stone, firm ground beneath hooves, day turned to night. Moonlight swathed the open expanse, though no moon appeared in the sky. Not a single star.

This wasn't Autumn. Not any Plane, but rather a Bridge, a narrow path connecting worlds like a log felled across a river.

And that starless sky overhead, that maw of black emptiness:

a view straight into the Void, the endless liminal space that stretched between realities.

Fi scanned the hillocks, alert for pursuers. Only Voidwalkers, brushed by death, could *see* Curtains, but other humans could step through one if they knew its location.

Beneath her, Aisinay's nostrils flared at the change in the air, the scent of ozone and eternity from the Void. This was her native land. Millennia ago, horses from some Plane had wandered onto a Bridge, adapting to the barren landscape. The blind beast lurched to a full gallop, guided by currents of energy even Fi couldn't sense, hooves flying over tundra.

Fi breathed deep of the starless sky. The frigid rock underfoot that cracked with the dust of infinity. She may have been born upon a Plane, but she understood the lift in Aisinay's strides. Her greatest freedom had always come from fleeing into nothingness. A second home, ever since that river tried – and failed – to claim her.

Fi steered Aisinay past glassy tundra pools, over heather with ghostly silver leaves, to the base of a ridge. She slipped off the horse's bare back, crouching as she climbed to higher ground. A breeze brushed the Void-and-rainbow curls of her hair, air crisp like after a lightning strike.

Nothing moved upon the tundra. No shouts of pursuing trade wardens.

Fi grinned. Amateurs, thinking they could haul her in for five measly energy chips.

In the valley below, train tracks glinted in phantom moonlight. Trans-Plane trains crossed all the major Bridges, the lifeblood of commerce between the four Season-Locked worlds, but Fi steered clear of the major thoroughfares. After ensuring her crate and cargo remained intact, she swung onto Aisinay's scaled back, urging the horse forward at a more leisurely pace.

Over the next ridge, the ground fell away into black.

While Planes spanned wide enough to encompass great cities, vast territories, Bridges were significantly smaller, mere slivers of reality within the Void. At the border, rock came to a jagged halt, only empty black beyond. Since Fi was a little girl, she could never resist peering over the edge of existence, wondering what it would feel like to just . . . jump in.

Certain death, of course. Bridges offered paths to walk through the Void separating Planes, but no one ever came back after stepping into the abyss itself.

Except for the daeyari.

Legend said the beasts were flesh and blood once. All living creatures passed their energy to the Void when they died. But unlike all other living creatures, the daeyari had refused death, somehow clawing their energy back onto the material Planes, returning as immortal.

Uninterested in a horrific demise on this – and all – occasions, Fi guided Aisinay along the ridgeline, a safe distance from the plummet into doom. Bridges had more than one exit Curtain to the Planes they linked. She'd spent her life poking through hundreds of Curtains, testing where they led, cataloguing useful connections. Some were innocuous: a rural clearing on the Autumn Plane, useful for covert meetings. Her cart rumbled over rocky ground, passing several more Curtains that smelled of tree tannin and loamy soil.

Then, a shift to pine and ice.

Fi steered Aisinay through a familiar Curtain, palm raised to part reality one more time.

Towering pine trees greeted them, a night-shrouded forest quiet with snow and a breeze through dark needles. Frigid air curled Fi's breath, a scent of cold and conifers. The sky of the Winter Plane swam with stars, framed by jagged mountains and a green aurora – the lingering energy of dead souls gone to the Void, a hum of almost-voices on the wind.

Home. No matter how far she wandered.

Fi slipped off Aisinay's back, landing with a crunch of snow beneath her boots. She patted the horse's neck. Then, a shout to the sky.

'*Fuck* Cardigan,' she told the looming shiverpines, the weeping firs bent with ice. 'Void-damned asshole.'

Aisinay snorted, her finned tail brushing snow.

'Right?' Fi agreed with matching indignation.

The horse pawed the ground, ears tilted toward the cart. Fi stroked her muzzle.

'Don't worry, sweet girl. We'll get this load off you right away.'

She'd deliver these crates out of *spite* if nothing else. The cargo, she didn't mind – Fi had moved energy capsules before, for clients with the decency to warn her. Withholding information? Alerting trade wardens to a rendezvous? Someone needed to educate Cardigan in black-market etiquette. Preferably with a slap to the face for good measure.

From her cart, Fi retrieved a coat to layer over her silviamesh: sable elk hide with a collar of snowy hare, more strips of decorative white fur sewn up her ribs and arms. She already wore her snow boots, fur-lined with solid traction. With a guiding hand on Aisinay's neck, she led them out of the forest.

The first signs of civilization came as a stomp of hooves. A snort. The forest opened to a clearing where a herd of aurorabeasts grazed for stalks beneath the snow, bison-like creatures with nubbed horns and dense coats, green energy glowing along humped backs. A ranch house sat amidst the conifers, windows dark. Fi kept her distance from the building, picking up a narrow path down the hill.

The village of Nyskya lay ahead, nestled into the valley like gold dust sprinkled over snow. Glowing windows peered from buildings of dark timber and steep-pitched roofs for sloughing ice, densest at the valley floor, fading into black shiverpines along the slopes. One road cut through the heart of the village. The wide copper piping of an energy conduit ran down the center, smaller channels branching into the surrounding buildings to fuel light and heat.

Beyond that necessary infrastructure, there were no imposing energy factories. No train tracks or trolleys or looming government buildings. People here cut timber and smithed steel. Herded aurorabeasts and hunted pelts from the forest. They sold what they could, but the village prided itself on self-sufficiency.

The perfect place for a smuggler. Fi had lived in Nyskya – well, *adjacent* to Nyskya – for seven years, spoiled by privacy and easy access to Curtains. She led Aisinay down a less-trodden path, keen on avoiding attention with a cart full of contraband. Heading straight home would be the smarter option, but after a long afternoon of coward clients and energy expenditures, Fi was ravenous. The last thing she wanted was to cook her own dinner.

They stopped behind the village tavern. Fi spent enough nights behind taverns – either puking her guts out or winning fist fights – to appreciate this one as impeccably clean, the trash bins lined up with bear-proof lids, door painted cheerful red. A copper lantern hung above the entryway, powered by a silver energy capsule. She nudged open the door.

The heat of the kitchen thawed Fi's cheeks. From the hall beyond came the din of the tavern, but her attention narrowed on dishes clattering upon metal counters. The clack of a knife. The *smell* of roasting fish and cream sauce and Void knew what else. Fi wanted it.

She crept past conduit-powered stoves and wire shelves, wielding the focus of a thieving raccoon. A wisp of a woman stood across the room, chopping onions. While her back was turned, Fi inspected a soup pot, melting at the aroma of salmon and dill. She filled a mason jar, screwed on the lid, then wrapped the hot glass in a kitchen rag. In exchange, she plucked a small energy chip from her pocket and left it on the counter, more than enough for the meal.

On her way out, Fi snatched a couple of spiced ginger cookies off a cooling rack. A strip of elk jerky from a cannister.

Back outside, the cold met her like a jealous lover. Fi hunched into her coat and the warmth of her spoils. The soup and cookies she stashed in her cart. The jerky she held out to Aisinay, who devoured the treat in a snap of fangs.

They both tensed at the crunch of footsteps in the alley. Aisinay's ears perked.

Fi reached instinctively for the hilt of her energy sword.

'Lurking behind taverns again?' called out in a heavy Winter accent.

A familiar voice. A *judgmental* voice. Fi's groan turned to a puff of steam.

Her accuser met her with arms crossed, chest broad from the thickness of his flannel-lined coat more than muscle underneath. Ice crusted his dark beard, a dust of snow on hair pulled into a messy bun. A ruddy cast to pale cheeks suggested he'd been walking in the cold. Always keeping an eye on things: his aurorabeasts outside town, the people inside it.

Always able to sniff Fi out like a foxhound, despite her best skulking.

She pulled her coat into a mock curtsy. 'Good evening, *esteemed* mayor.'

His brow quirked. 'Are you avoiding me?'

'Not successfully, it would appear.'

Fi crouched, feigning interest on the wheels of her cart. Thankfully, nothing looked loose, despite the hurried retreat. When footsteps closed at her side, she hid an eye roll behind the veil of her hair. She was *tired*, she just wanted to go *home*, she—

'Come on, Fi-Fi. Why the sour mood?'

'*Don't* call me that.'

'Or you'll do what?'

Swift as a frost asp, Fi struck at the snow beneath her boots, packed a snowball, and hurled it at his face. He staggered, sputtering ice. Served him right. For anyone but her brother, that snowball would've had a rock in it.

Boden Kolbeck, mayor of Nyskya, glared at the smuggler crouched before him.

Then he dove for a snowbank.

The war was brief. Boden's snowball glanced off Fi's silvia-mesh. She struck one more to his chest and a third to the back of his head. When he kicked a drift of powder, she shouted and shielded her face, an opening for a tackle. Two rolls across the ground, and Fi had him in a headlock. Boden might be three years older, but he exercised by strolling his village, not swinging energy swords. Fi had him beat in both grit and underhandedness.

He tapped her arm in surrender. Fi released him, and they collapsed against her cart, breaths billowing mist in the cold night air.

Boden punched her shoulder. Fi hit back harder, making him wince.

They broke into laughter together.

'Ice-hearted, Fi. I'll have bruises tomorrow!' As Boden rubbed his shoulder, Aisinay nibbled his coat. An excellent judge of character. Their father had been a metallurgist, a craftsman of conduits and machinery parts, but Fi and Boden both preferred live beasts. He patted the horse's muzzle. 'How was the Autumn Plane?'

Fi puckered her lips. 'I never said where I was going.'

He reached into the Void-and-rainbow swirls of her hair, plucking out a crimson leaf like a magic trick. Fi gasped.

'Ugh. *Leaves.*' She flurried her hands through her hair, dislodging several more hitchhikers.

'By all the Shattered Planes,' Boden said. 'I thought I wouldn't see you for a week, after what you did to that bottle of whiskey last night.'

'Birthdays are meant to be celebrated, Bodie.'

His nose scrunched. 'Why do *you* get to call me Bodie, but I can't call you Fi-Fi?'

'Little sister rules. And mayor rules. You have to act professional. I don't.'

He tilted his head, eyes dark as hers, warm in the tavern light. 'What's in the cart?'

Fi debated how to put it delicately.

'I think it's a bomb.'

'*What?*'

Boden lurched to his feet. As if an extra meter would do him any good. Snickering, Fi grabbed a crowbar from her cart and slipped it beneath a crate lid, easing it open with a *pop.*

The inside glowed silver. A low, staticky hum. Energy capsules sat in cardboard cups like volatile eggs – glass spheres with swirling magic inside, several times larger than the capsules on Fi's gloves. Not uncommon for powering lights or larger weapons, but dangerous to pile so many in one box.

Boden peered into the crate with brows raised. 'Where to?'

'Thomaskweld.'

'*Thomaskweld?* Who pays to smuggle energy into one of the biggest energy producing cities on the Winter Plane?'

'See Bodie, this is why you're a mayor, and I'm but a lowly purveyor of illicit goods. You care about these things.' She closed the crate with a definitive *thump*. 'I don't.'

'Don't sell yourself short, Fi-Fi. You also rob taverns.' He cast a dry look at the soup and cookies in her cart.

'I paid for it!' she returned, indignant. 'Speaking of which. How much do I owe you in back taxes?'

'You think I keep a tally off the top of my head?'

'I *know* you keep a tally off the top of your head.'

On principle, Fi would sooner throw herself into the bottomless pit of the Void than pay taxes of the income, import, or any variety. Boden was the exception. She'd fled their childhood home first. He'd left three years later, when their father died. They both wound up in Nyskya, away from the dust of that old house and the cooling ashes of their father's funeral pyre, seeking a place to breathe. Not a bad trade, trusting the mayor to let Fi come and go, in exchange for a cut of her profits.

She tossed him the box with Cardigan's down payment. 'Will this cover it?'

Boden flipped the case open. His pale face went *paler.* 'The *shit.*'

'Right?'

'Are these daeyari energy chips?'

'*Right?*'

The chips would be an extravagance for Fi – more useful for Boden. Energy to power the village, to keep houses warm through the endless winter. Larger cities had central power factories, fleets of human workers to Shape energy into the conduits. Nyskya ran on a smaller workforce, supplemented with chips charged elsewhere.

Most settlements turned to their ruling daeyari for such aide. That had been the pact between mortals and immortals for centuries, when the beasts came down from their trees and offered to stop hunting humans like wild game. Peace and partnership – in exchange for willing sacrifices to keep them fed.

Where Fi and Boden grew up, Verne Territory, the call for sacrifice went out every few years, whenever the town needed new parts for their energy conduits or better commissions for metallurgy. Sometimes, volunteers came forward. Sometimes, meetings stretched long into the night to decide who'd have to go, their father returning silent and hollow-eyed.

She and Boden fled to Antal Territory seeking escape, a less vicious daeyari with an uncommon policy: the village didn't need to send a sacrifice, so long as they didn't ask for aide. That meant repairing their own conduits. Tracking down their own energy chips. Sourcing their own food and medicine. A rare cause worth supporting.

Boden closed the box. Spoke softly. 'Thank you, Fi. This will help.'

'Of course.' She looked away from his sincerity, more comfortable with bristles. 'Keep the people from freezing. Wouldn't look good for your re-election.'

Fi owed him more than this. *Much* more than whatever numbers he kept in his ledger.

Void knew, she was a pain in the ass little sister, flighty as a Curtain, prone to cussing too much and parading bombs across his doorstep. Here was one meager attempt to repay him for everything she'd put him through ten years ago. For giving her safe harbor in a Plane full of claws. For being the only family she had left.

'This was your payment?' Boden said. 'These chips are worth more than the capsules.'

'People pay more when they need something specific.'

Did the job smell off? Of course. Fi kept her margins tight through calculated risk, profit weighed against consequence. Twenty daeyari energy chips were worth *a lot* of consequence.

Boden, who inherited enough worry for both of them, scowled, but didn't press. He never asked for names, details. Safer for both of them.

'Anything else you need? Other than pilfered soup.'

Fi gripped Aisinay's lead. 'Drop off is in two days. I'll lay low until then. As usual, if anyone asks about me . . .'

Boden pressed a hand to his heart, his tone a tad *too* dramatic. 'Fionamara? I haven't seen that woman in months. Selfish thing never visits. Never thinks about family.'

Fi left him with a kiss on the cheek. A punch on the shoulder.

She and her horse and a cart of energy capsules left the village. Her home lay an hour's hike up a snowy canyon, but Fi never took the long way. Once they cleared the houses, she stepped through another Curtain, off the Winter Plane.

The space beyond lay quiet. Snow-dusted. A meadow of silver grass and leafless poplar trees, ground crumbling into the Void within sight in any direction.

Far smaller than a Plane. Smaller, even, than the Bridge that brought her from Autumn. Shards were the tiniest, most *numerous* scraps of reality scattered through the Void.

Prevailing theory claimed a single world existed once, an age that far preceded flimsy human memory. Then, that reality shattered like a dropped mirror. Planes were the largest fragments, hundreds of separate worlds split from the whole, now scattered throughout the Void. Bridges were smaller slivers, connecting one Plane to another.

Shards were dust around the edges, tinier pockets of reality that connected to no more than one Plane. On the surface, this might make Shards seem like nothing more than extra-dimensional holes to hide in – which Fi had done *plenty* of as a kid, avoiding chores or her father's chastisement.

As she got older, Fi discovered the true advantage of Shards lay in how they distorted distance, compared to the neighboring Plane. She walked Aisinay past one Curtain that would return her to the Winter Plane across the valley, at her favorite copse for hunting hare. Another Curtain that, in two days, would take her a hundred miles away to Thomaskweld.

Where the ruling daeyari lived.

Fi huffed the Void-empty air. It was just a city. Just a job. She'd successfully avoided those beasts for a decade.

At last, she reached the Curtain to take her home. She stepped back onto the Winter Plane, onto a forested ridge two miles above Nyskya – traversed in a matter of minutes.

A short walk through sighing shiverpines brought her to a clearing, a cottage with shingled roof and dark windows. Fi unhitched the cart. Finally free of the load, Aisinay cantered into the trees, off to forage dinner in the nearby river. Fi crossed her porch, kicked the snow off her boots, then stepped inside, eager for a hot bath full of pomegranate bubbles, a warm bed piled high with furs.

She'd dream of ten more energy chips waiting for her in Thomaskweld.

Not of claws lurking in the trees beyond her windows.

3

It's unfair to look that sexy

The city of Thomaskweld, capital of Antal Territory, didn't dust the slopes of its valley.

It consumed.

Where once a mighty river reigned amidst the pines, the city tamed the banks with concrete carriageways and train stations of vaulted glass, high-rises plated in decorative copper, trolleys clacking down tracks with silver energy capsules humming at their rears. Factories rose like cathedrals of sheet metal. The Summer Plane grew produce of every variety. Spring Plane flowers were unmatched, and the Autumn Plane boasted a mean maple syrup.

The Winter Plane generated energy. Workers in the power factories Shaped their magic into capsules and chips, energy to keep the city humming, to trade for what the Plane couldn't grow or mine.

Fi led Aisinay along the river parkway, cobblestones clacking beneath hooves and cart. Pruned fir trees lined the center of the road. Along the sidewalks, copper energy conduits fed streetlamps of wrought iron and silver light. Shop windows framed in geometric metal designs displayed the latest Shaping-powered coffee kettles, books in foiled dustjackets, mannequins in embroidered fleeces with colorful scarves. Fi's tailored black

coat with fur collar looked tame by comparison, though her
Void-and-rainbow hair drew glances from several passing ped-
estrians.

Other curious eyes followed her Void horse. An unusual
animal, in a city of trolleys and caribou-drawn carriages.

Fi wasn't concerned, even considering recent drama with
Autumn trade wardens. Law enforcement rarely crossed territories, much less Planes. Daeyari were conscientious carnivores,
one ruler per territory to space out resources, keeping competitors off their hunting grounds.

A kindness, they called it. *Protection* for their human subjects,
a *boon* to only have to feed one predator.

Fortunately, daeyari never walked their streets alongside
lowly mortals. Let the bastard roost in his capitol building; Fi
had a deal to settle.

Cardigan's address led her to a riverside hotel – a busier one
than she'd have liked, but who was bothering to ask her opinion? A young man in a navy bellhop uniform hurried out the
glass door to meet her. When he reached for Aisinay's bridle,
Fi's grip tightened.

'Afternoon, miss. I can take your—'

'No, thank you.'

'We have stables in the back for—'

'No. Thank you.'

Fi slipped a small energy chip into his hand to shoo him off,
then appraised the metal ribs of the building, panels of stained-
glass auroras glowing with interior light. Short days, this time
of year. Late afternoon, yet the sun set hours ago.

A woman stepped outside. Her wool dress fell to her calves,
powder blue with fur cuffs, a contrast to dark hair and brown
skin. She smiled with a demure air, a crafted calm to her strides,
yet keen eyes snapped to Fi's cart.

'Pleasant afternoon,' she greeted.

'Are you sure this is public enough?' Fi returned dryly. 'I could add a sign on my cart: *illicit deal occurring here, everyone please look?*'

The woman tutted. 'Why don't you come inside and warm up with a drink?'

Fi ran down her mental list of reasons why *not* to cuss out a client in public. She fully planned to enjoy the city's recreations – a strong drink, a riverside bar thrumming with music and dancing, some man or woman to push her against a wall and kiss her senseless. On her own time. *After* getting rid of the explosives harnessed to her horse.

The woman headed inside. Fi, an immaculate professional, resolved to keep this brief. After a firm chat with the bellhop to not let horse or cart out of sight, she followed.

Marble tile squeaked beneath her boots as they crossed the lobby. Energy conduits formed geometric patterns across the ceiling, more decorative than those on the street, inlaid with glass channels to display silver magic flowing into the chandeliers. The lounge was dimmer, tile replaced by plush carpet, windows swathed in cream curtains as thick as Fi's coat.

That morning, she'd debated the appropriateness of silviamesh for civilized company, but the protective fabric hiding beneath her outerwear offered reassurance as this job turned stranger.

In a secluded corner of the lounge, Fi's guide gestured to an armchair. The deep upholstery attempted to swallow her, a moment of flailing, but she recovered by plopping her boots upon a low table. Across from her sat another stranger, a white man with mussed hair and gaunt cheeks. Too much stress or not enough calories. Either was perilous in an eternal winter.

A plate of pastries waited on the table: layered chocolate cakes topped with raspberries and powdered sugar, ingredients imported from warmer Planes. A clever bribe. Glasses clinked as the woman poured three shots of amber liquor, wafting a scent of anise and orange.

'I'm Milana. This is Erik.'

Fi downed her drink in one gulp then flipped the glass upside down, a *thunk* against the table. The liquor left a lovely burn in her stomach. 'I mean this in the kindest way possible when I say: I don't care what your names are. I'm here with the cargo.'

Milana took a modest sip. 'We appreciate the work, Miss Kolbeck.'

'I've found that payment is an excellent way to communicate gratitude.'

'And you'll have it. Though, we have one more request, if you'll entertain us.'

There it was. Fi traced a nail around the edge of her glass. First Cardigan's shady cargo descriptions, now this?

'That wasn't the agreement,' Fi said.

The man, Erik, leaned forward. 'You didn't think we'd offer so many energy chips for a simple delivery? We had to be certain you were up to the task. A test of—'

Milana set a hand on his arm. At least *she* noticed Fi's ice-crusted glare.

'We apologize for the duplicity,' Milana said. 'Nothing to reflect a poor opinion of your services. We've been told you have a formidable constitution. That you don't back down from challenging contracts.'

Fi made a sour face. She *had* worked very hard to fabricate that reputation, hadn't she? A different person from the flimsy girl who'd run away from home ten years ago.

Wasn't loving the trajectory of this conversation, though.

This woman didn't speak like a black-market reseller. Milana spoke like a politician – far more concerning. And Fi had to be cautious with clients who paid this well.

'What's the rest of the job?' Fi asked.

'We need you to move the capsules into the capitol building.'

In the following silence, Fi could have heard a mosquito cough.

Or was that ringing sound in her own ears?

She wouldn't bat her mascara-lined lashes at evading back-country police. Slinking past border checkpoints. Emptying estates for scheming mistresses. Success relied on avoiding routes of highest risk. The capitol building rolled every conceivable risk into a single glass-coated cage.

'You're joking.' Fi looked between them. '*Please* tell me you're joking.'

'You'll be finished by this time tomorrow,' Milana said. As if *that* was the issue.

'The governor is in the capitol building.' Along with his retinue of security. More trade wardens than Fi could hurl an energy chip at. Rooms full of people faithful to the territory's law and order, to say nothing of the greatest danger. 'And the Void-damned *daeyari*.'

'The Lord Daeyari is currently gone from the city,' Milana said. 'Inspecting his eastern holdings. And the governor will be busy with meetings tomorrow.'

This was a joke. A test. Cruel retribution for Fi not paying taxes – but merciless Void, *everyone* hated taxes. 'What business could you possibly have in the capitol building?'

'We're looking to acquire a ceramic art piece of consider-able value from the governor's personal collection. The energy capsules you've transported will be our route into the safe.'

'You need that many capsules for a *safe*?'

'A precaution. You get the capsules into the building, then get us out.'

Fi blew out a breath, attacking a rainbow curl that had escaped onto her cheek. 'Ah. See. Here, we have another issue. I transport items. I don't infiltrate.'

'We'll infiltrate. All you have to do is move us.'

'A Void smuggler never reveals her routes.' Neither was she thrilled at the idea of becoming a glorified getaway driver.

'There are no existing Curtains within the capitol grounds,' Erik chimed in. 'Security policy during construction.'

Fi's brow lifted, but before she could argue—

'We need you to cut a new Curtain,' Milana said.

Fi fell silent as permafrost.

Most Curtains existed naturally, remnants of whatever cataclysm shattered the Planes. The ability to cut new Curtains was a difficult, *dangerous* skill. One of Fi's greatest secrets to success, used only in dire need.

'And what makes you think I can do that?' she asked, her tone a warning low.

'Don't be modest,' purred a new voice beside her. 'Your reputation precedes you.'

Fi spun fast enough to pop a few vertebrae. Her boots thunked off the table, fingers clawing instinctively for the sword hilt beneath her coat – only to freeze, at the appearance of a phantom in the dim lounge light.

The newcomer circled their table. She had even paler skin than Fi. Her Void-black hair was shaved on one side, cut straight to her jaw on the other.

Atop her head: two short antlers, black with dual points.

For a moment, Fi's entire stupid heart forgot how to beat.

A vavriter.

What in the merciless Void was a vavriter doing here?

They must have been brave, the early mortals who fucked daeyari, inviting predators into their beds. Perhaps there was allure in the danger. The restraint. Since becoming immortal, daeyari could no longer make children with humans, but in the lost ages when the beasts had been similar flesh and blood, their pairings produced vavriter. Millenia later, the hybrids' descendants still walked the Planes, now a species of their own.

In appearance, they were ghostly reflections of their daeyari sires. Shorter antlers. No tail nor claws, no black sclera, but this woman's ruby irises latched onto Fi with skin-peeling sharpness. A wildcat eyeing prey.

Fi tensed. Breathless. Uncertain who would strike first. Vavriter were as rare on the Season-Locked Planes as sun in Winter, far too close to an immortal carnivore for most humans' comfort, and *this one* was . . .

'Oh, pardon me,' Milana greeted. 'I didn't realize you'd be joining us?'

'How could I miss meeting our esteemed partner?' The vavriter flashed Fi a bright grin – fangless, but still unsettling. 'Astrid. Pleased to meet you.'

Fi's shock snapped to confusion. She watched the woman recline in a chair beside Milana, arms languid upon the rests, her maroon blouse cut in a deep V that revealed an edge of pale breast. Confident. Taunting.

Astrid spoke to her fellow conspirators, but her ruby eyes never left Fi. 'Rough around the edges, this one. But I assure you, she's up to the task.'

Milana hummed. 'She seems reluctant.'

Fi had yet to remember how to breathe. She was supposed to know the rules of these games, false bravado from always having a card up her sleeve – but the vavriter's grin struck her like a knife to the ribs. A wildcat, wandered in through the lobby.

'Then offer better terms.'

Astrid set a metal box on the table, slender fingers skating the edge. 'Consider this a show of good faith.'

Fi didn't need to open the box to know what it contained. She cracked the lid open just to stop the room from spinning.

Inside, ten more daeyari energy chips glinted in velvet.

'She's not agreed to help yet!' Erik protested.

'She will,' Astrid said with perfect confidence.

This was wrong. Something was *wrong* with this trio trying to sneak into the capitol – two wary-tongued humans, a *vavriter* who shouldn't be here. Fi should argue, should push for a higher price. She was talented at arguing.

Just not now, with this chill through her chest. She couldn't escape the snare of Astrid's red eyes, her pantherine posture, an adrenaline-sharp memory of dark trees and . . .

Fi swallowed. Her throat, sandpaper. 'Will you be helping us, vavriter?'

'I'm afraid I'm needed elsewhere. Though I trust in your abilities.'

Fi clenched the box until her knuckles whitened. Ten more energy chips was *significant.*

More urgently, she needed to end this conversation. Get back on solid footing.

'Just in and out?' she asked.

'Under an hour,' Milana assured.

'If it takes more than an hour, I'm leaving. With or without you.'

Milana and Erik exchanged a wary look.

'Agreed,' Astrid said for them.

Fi swallowed approximately a hundred questions splitting her tongue. A hundred curses, bottled into a glare. Astrid reciprocated, fingers light on the arms of her chair, face like granite.

Then, subtle enough for only Fi to see: a smirk that raked a chill down her neck.

After settling Aisinay into a Shard outside the city, Fi retreated to the hotel room her hosts insisted on paying for. She sprawled onto a down comforter, watching the glint of green aurora against window glass.

She wasn't sure when to expect a knock on her door.

But the knock did come.

When Fi answered, Astrid stood in the hall. The vavriter reclined against gold and teal wallpaper, armed with a smirk and sinfully tight pants, that silken shirt cut assaulting low down her pale chest. Her hair and antlers were black as Void. Her eyes, glinting like faceted rubies in the sconce lights.

'I hoped we might discuss your job,' Astrid said. 'If the esteemed smuggler can spare a moment for me?'

She spoke so light. So easy. Fi opened her mouth to say something very rude. And very *loud*. Guaranteed to upset the neighbors.

Instead, she barely mustered a whisper.

'It's been ten years, Astrid.'

The smirk faltered, if only for a heartbeat. 'Time flies, doesn't it?'

Fi stared, as if this haunting visitor might disappear the moment she blinked. A familiar figment of her imagination. Astrid stared back.

'Are you going to invite me in?' Astrid said, low like a taunt.

Slamming the door in her face would be considered rude. Damn manners to the pit of the Void, Fi wasn't ready for this – far too sober, for starters.

She huffed and beckoned Astrid inside.

While Fi sat stiffly on the edge of the bed, the vavriter paced the room. That curtain of black hair veiled half her face, slender brows tilted to appraise the flowery wall moldings. A ghost. A Void-damned ghost, strutting in front of her.

'You look . . . well,' Fi managed, just to break the silence.

Astrid stopped pacing. Ruby-red eyes stared at Fi a moment too long. Too hard.

'Do I?' Astrid said lowly.

Her smirk snapped back, dagger sharp.

'Of course, I look *fabulous*.' Astrid spread her arms, posture unnervingly easy. 'You don't look so awful yourself. For a Void smuggler.'

'You've been keeping tabs on me?'

'You thought I wouldn't?'

Fi's knuckles clenched. 'Then what was that act downstairs?'

'Being careful.' Astrid spoke as if this were a disappointing question. How was she so damn *calm*? 'I assumed you wouldn't want people knowing your personal life.'

She leaned against a dresser, sure and willowy. She'd always been willowy. And wild, Fi's father had called her. A forest beast, as likely to snap as to purr.

Astrid's family had moved to their childhood town to oversee the energy factory. Vavriter were uncommon visitors on the Season-Locked Planes, almost only as administrative hands for daeyari, their human neighbors inclined to keep cautious distance from anything with antlers. Fi's father warned her to do the same – but she'd been old enough by then; any word from that selfish old man sent her sprinting in the other direction, even straight into fire.

Their friendship began as dares to race each other across icy riverbanks. Next, competitions for who could snatch a hair from a heath boar, a game that ended with nine stitches in Fi's arm. Then Fi discovered how to step through Curtains. Astrid was

44

the first person she'd dragged with her, holding hands as they'd stared into the Void.

Astrid's face had changed since then. The hardness seemed foreign, yet fitting for the svelte animal she'd become, the way she'd sculpted muscle and poise onto what once were spindly young limbs.

Fi wasn't sure if she was glad to see her.

'Why are you here?' Here in Thomaskweld. Here in Fi's room. *Anything* to loosen these thorns choking her since Astrid snapped back into her life in a hotel lobby.

Astrid's grin hardened. 'Making sure you don't get cold feet.'

The cut sank deep, the work of a familiar blade. Fi hadn't seen Astrid since she ran away from home.

Not since Astrid pledged herself to Verne, the daeyari who ruled their home territory. To become an Arbiter was an honor without equal, the personal hand of an immortal, a position above even the territory's governor. And the boon to their families? For as long as an Arbiter served, a daeyari ordered no sacrifices from their town. With vavriter lifespans ranging well over two hundred years, Astrid had gifted a blessing to their entire community.

The weight of it hung over her like a death shroud. Moonlight caught silver lines on her arms, scars she hadn't worn ten years ago.

'Arbiter life is treating you well?' Fi said, dry.

Astrid shrugged. 'Well enough.'

That explained where the daeyari energy chips came from, though Astrid's involvement in this heist raised more questions. Why she'd enlist Fi raised even more.

'This isn't your daeyari's territory,' Fi said. 'So why are you here?'

'Errands.'

'Stealing a vase?'

'A classic, I'm told.'

'In another daeyari's capital?'

'Which is why my presence is best kept discreet.' Astrid spoke with the edge of a razor, but this tipped her mouth to a smirk. 'So many questions, Fi. I thought you didn't care about politics?' Her voice lowered. 'So content with your carts and contraband.'

Fi scoffed. 'Seems I've been roped into some politics. By one particular person.'

'You're upset I have faith in your abilities? Whatever your faults, you *are* good at what you do.'

What was this? A dance? A sparring match? Ten years. How had so much changed in *ten years*? Once, Fi could weigh the slant of Astrid's smirk and spot any lie, any scheme, any jest that would leave them giggling like idiots.

'Of course . . .' Astrid traced a finger along the dresser. 'If you're interested in doing *more*, you only have to ask. It's never too late.'

The proposition soured Fi's stomach. 'I won't work for a daeyari.'

Especially not a daeyari like Verne. Fi and Boden fled to Antal Territory to escape the sight of screaming criminals dragged before the hungry beast who ruled them. Of cold families *begging* for aid with sacrifices they couldn't afford.

Was that the source of this new hardness in Astrid's eyes? The vavriter's fingers ceased caressing the dresser and clamped the edge, no claws like her ancestors. Equally fierce.

'Sometimes, Fi,' she said, too quiet. 'You do what you have to. The daeyari are the closest things to gods these Shattered Planes will ever see. They offer power to people like us.'

'They *eat* people like us.' People like Fi, at least. Daeyari could eat vavriter, but seemed to prefer not to, some deference for fellow antlers.

'Stubborn as ever.' Astrid scowled. 'I suppose we're finished, then.'

She rose off the dresser like a cat uncoiling. Fi frowned at the curt dismissal, anger sticking to her ribs as Astrid moved toward the door.

Then, a sharper surge of panic.

The shot of adrenaline pushed Fi to her feet, some slurry of frustration, and guilt, and . . . not yet. She couldn't watch Astrid walk away again.

'Wait.'

Astrid paused.

When she turned, the light from the window cut sharp across her cheeks. Stark down the pale skin of her chest. Silver moonlight and aurora, tangling in dark hair and dark antlers.

'Why are we doing this?' Fi pleaded. 'It's been *years*, Astrid. It's . . . good to see you.'

Every line of her face was a memory, the clamp of her jaw as stubborn as she'd always been. So unyielding.

So beautiful.

'Is it?' Astrid said.

'Of course.' By the endless Void, there were too many things Fi wanted to say. Needed to say. Nowhere to start. 'I wasn't sure you'd come. I didn't know . . . if you'd want to see me again.'

It felt like an eternity, the time Astrid weighed that statement.

'I had to see you,' Astrid said, ice flat. 'I had to know if anything has changed.'

'Has it?'

They'd both changed. Fi had to believe that. She wasn't the frightened, flimsy girl who'd run away from home a decade ago.

47

She'd been hardened by work, honed on Shards, steadied into someone who could finally face an old friend.

So why *the fuck* did her legs still threaten to give out when Astrid stepped closer? Why did her heart try to crack through her chest as Astrid raised a hand to Fi's temple, brushing aside a rainbow curl with those long, cool fingers?

'The hair is new,' Astrid murmured.

That quickly, they were standing too close. As close as they used to be.

Fi moved to kiss her like an old instinct, a muscle trained and worn and never forgotten. Astrid stiffened, every line of her as hard as the glares she'd been shooting since the lobby. Then, she softened. Astrid cupped Fi's cheeks and returned a bruising kiss, ending with a bite to the lip that made Fi gasp. She tasted different, smelled different, the homemade honey lip balm and pine resin of their childhood replaced by satin lipstick and a tang of metal.

Fi's heart hammered harder. This was the worst idea she'd ever had. She needed it like air in her lungs. She kissed Astrid fiercer, clawed her fingers into Astrid's silken shirt, pulling her toward the bed.

Astrid pulled away.

The motion hit sharp as a recoil. She held Fi at arm's length – eyes harder than before, mouth clamped and unreadable.

'An enticing invitation,' Astrid said. 'But I have other work to do.'

That was what had changed.

The words stung with finality. A distance Fi didn't know how to cross. For one horrifying moment, she wondered if they were finally going to talk about what happened between them.

'I . . . understand,' Fi said instead. Immediately, she knew it was wrong, watched Astrid's eyes darken to scuffed ruby.

'Good luck tomorrow,' Astrid said.

The hitch in her voice was nearly undetectable, as she released Fi. Back to that unruffled posture, as she stepped into the hall.

When the door closed, Fi slid the deadbolt into place with a chest-splitting *slank*.

Ten years had been long enough to assume Astrid hadn't forgiven her. To mull the possibility of reunion on nights when Fi found herself staring at the dark rafters of her cottage, haunted by the things she'd said that day. By the things she hadn't.

But she was different now. She told herself she was stronger than ten years ago, even as she curled into an unfamiliar bed, huddled beneath a blanket thick with laundry starch. Deep in her gut, survival instinct nagged Fi to cut her losses and run, flee this city and whatever strange business she'd been contracted for.

But she knew with equal certainty: she had to stay. Fi had to see things through this time.

She owed Astrid that much.

4

Casual cross-reality breaking-and-entering

Fi practiced her morning serenity by ordering the largest, frothiest, most caramel-drenched coffee she could find amongst Thomaskweld's cafes.

She devoured a staggering quantity of pancakes topped with cream and Summer strawberry compote, a warm core to guard against the frigid winds down the valley, replenished energy reserves for whatever bullshit awaited her today.

She bought a heap of the freshest icefish in the river market, presenting them to Aisinay while telling her how she was such a good horse, she was in the fact the *best* Void horse in all the Shattered Planes for tolerating these rude people and their crates of energy capsules. Aisinay munched her meal with finned tail swishing, successfully bribed.

At last, Fi hooked up her cart, groaned to the sky for precisely five seconds, then headed out to meet Milana.

Even near noon, the sun barely crested the encircling mountains, casting Thomaskweld in lavender. The central parkway bustled despite the gloom, bright with shopfronts and capsule-powered heaters on cafe patios, a hum of voices warring against the clatter of passing trolleys.

Quieter, as Fi neared the capitol complex. A wide avenue and a wall of red stone separated the main city from several blocks of gardens and government offices, gates of tall wrought iron to regulate public entry. Beyond the barrier rose the city's most ornate buildings: the plated copper and glass of the trade warden headquarters, silver arches of the treasury, a dome of aurora green and blue atop the courthouse.

A crowd gathered at the main entry gate.

Fi tensed instinctively at any public gathering, rare as they were. Doubly so when angry murmurs perked her ears. Even her small provincial school taught every student the dangers of organizing. Teachers with tight smiles explaining it was best to never cause a fuss. Any concerns should be submitted to the governor's office, or to the daeyari's personal attendants. They were here to help, after all, to keep the territory safe. Even the midnight-clad guards met the crowd at the gate without weapons.

Everyone knew which creature enforced the rules.

Fi led Aisinay past the crowd, not close enough to be construed as part of them, enough to eavesdrop . . .

'When will the governor speak with us?' someone asked.

'The district still has no power,' called another. 'Tonight will be even colder!'

'My daughter has the silver sickness. Another cold snap will put her in the hospital!'

'Your complaints have been received,' a guard said with pacifying hand movements. 'They'll be shared with the governor. In the meantime—'

As Fi passed out of earshot, she pursed plum-painted lips, appraising the copper energy conduits humming down the avenue – daeyari technology, one of the immortals' more generous gifts, as part of the pact. Now, every human city depended on them. Neglecting basic infrastructure didn't bode well for the territory's human governor, come next election year.

The ruling daeyari bore equal responsibility. Larger cities fed most of the territory's sacrifices: everything from wealthy houses trying to curry favor, to a desperate laborer trying to lift their family's fortune. For some people, those lives lost were a drop in the Void compared to Thomaskweld's dense population, a negligible price to pay for reliable infrastructure and protection from other daeyari.

Narcissistic assholes had probably never had to sacrifice a family member. Or been dragged in as an offering themselves.

Aisinay huffed as she walked, lowering finned ears and the spines down her neck.

'Agreed,' Fi muttered back. 'Something's *weird* in this city. But we'll be back home in Nyskya by tonight, then you can spend a whole week eating trout and spooking Bodie in the middle of the night.'

Between the capitol complex and the river, Fi reached a public park full of old cedar trees, snow crusting red trunks and drooping boughs. She'd arrived, as usual, a half hour early – and was admittedly a little impressed to find Milana already waiting for her.

Cold stabbed Fi's gut, seeing what the woman was wearing.

A momentary slip. Fi had no control over how her heart jolted at the sight of the silver robes with fur-lined collar. A swell of nausea at swirls of Void-black embroidered up the sleeves. The attire of a daeyari attendant.

Equally instinctive, she snapped her stupor behind a wall of bristles, not a single crack in her arched brow and dry tone as she appraised the bold disguise.

'What the fuck are you wearing?'

'Good morning!' Milana greeted brightly. 'Timely, I see.'

'If it means we can get this over with—'

'Yes, thank you for your help with our *newest renovation*

project,' Milana chirped over her. 'Right this way with the supplies, if you please.'

Fi's brow arched higher as she followed Milana down a stone path beneath the cedars.

The park was the quietest part of the city. Grouse clucked in the underbrush, accompanying a distant rush from the river. They passed a young man in a coat and work pants, sweeping the walkway clean of needles. A woman in a shawl of metal beads knelt off the path with head bowed, muttering a prayer for a loved one's departed energy to pass safely through the endless black of the Void, to find rest in the Afterplane.

Milana wore her silver-robed attendant disguise *too* well, earning nods from each passerby, not a single suspicious glance straying to Fi and her cart. All this for an art heist?

Not Fi's business. She moved cargo. Her clients decided what to do with it.

At the center of the grove, their path skirted a stone amphitheater.

Fi's people believed in gods, once: Great Beasts who raised the mountains when they fought, carved valleys out of stone. As technology grew vaster, the world grew smaller. Souls were nothing more than energy, gone to the Void in death. Buildings of metal and stone tamed the riverbanks. Explorers found no gods lurking in the forests.

There were only daeyari.

The garden's amphitheater was less a shrine, more a reminder. Energy conduits cobwebbed stone pillars, silver lamplight illuminating the reason Fi kept every visit to Thomaskweld brief: a bronze statue of the reigning Lord Daeyari, Antal.

Metal made harsh lines of his lean frame and raised chin. A slender tail, five feet long at least, arced around his ankles. Astrid's antlers would never surpass a few inches – vavriter, the daeyari word for hybrids, meant 'half antler', she'd told Fi once – but a daeyari's grew with age. Antal's were sharp tipped, sleek to his head as befitted a predator. They arced backward like a circlet, three points each side, the farthest tips just beginning to curve up into the crown worn by older members of his species.

At least, two and a half centuries counted as young by daeyari standards. Territory rulers changed rarely, this one a mere fifty years in power. Maybe inexperience was the reason for Antal's laxness compared to other territories, leaving his human governor to rule without interference.

Or maybe this daeyari just didn't give a shit. So long as food came delivered, why bother with bureaucracy?

In the shadow of the amphitheater, they reached the deepest section of the grove, hardly a trickle of sunlight through needles.

'It's here, yes?' Milana whispered.

She glanced over the empty path, the wide cedar trunks, clearly unable to see it. Fi could: the translucent glint of a Curtain wavering in the shadows. Mildly annoying that she'd never found this one herself, but she supposed that was the price of avoiding this part of the city. She stepped off the path and ran her bare fingers through the cold, weightless ripple on the air.

'There are no existing Curtains inside the capitol complex,' Milana said. 'But this is the closest Shard we know of.'

Fi offered a hand. 'Have you done this before?'

Milana grimaced. 'Not my favorite . . .'

They grasped hands, a stab of cold as Fi pulled them both through the Curtain.

A Shard lay on the other side, a field of frosted shale, crumbling into nothing at the edges. Void sky hung over petrified trees with gossamer leaves – like nothing on the Planes, adapted to survive on the meager light that somehow seeped into this sunless reality. Overhead, the aurora floated purple-red instead of green, humming whispers that were almost words.

Fi's shoulders eased, a breath of familiar ozone-laced air enough to settle nerves.

Beside her, Milana shivered. Most humans were uncomfortable, staring into the emptiness of the Void.

Not that there was *nothing* out there. The four Season-Locked Planes were unusual, linked directly by Bridges, operating more like islands than separate slips of reality. But there were other Planes across the Void – hundreds more, not connected by Bridges, but accessible by navigating the smaller Shards in between, a maze of stepping stones to other civilizations.

Maybe that was why Fi always got that odd prick on her neck when she looked into the Void – as if something, somewhere, was staring back.

Behind her, loose stones clacked. Aisinay stepped through the Curtain on her own, cart in tow, finned ears perked as she inhaled an appreciative huff of Void air.

'Can you see a way through to the capitol?' Milana asked.

Fi was about to find out.

Seeing Curtains came innately to a Voidwalker. Slicing new ones was, energetically speaking, not much more difficult. The danger came in ensuring something lay on the other side.

Planes and Shards were distinct physical spaces, but they weren't necessarily *in* different spaces. Planes lay over each other like stacked parchment, separated by layers of Void, scraps of smaller tissue paper – Shards – scattering the space in between. Fi could move from a Shard to a Plane. From one Shard to another Shard. But cutting a Curtain anywhere one piece of reality *didn't* overlap another? Ended with a step into the deadly maw of the Void itself.

She let her gaze soften. Reality had thinner walls than most people would be comfortable to realize. Where Shards *did* overlap a Plane, boundaries could blur. As Fi's eyes slipped out of focus, transparent images drifted into her vision, phantom outlines of the Winter Plane. A cedar tree. The stone path. She took a step. There lay the city parkway lined in streetlamps. A wall of red stone. Another step.

She Shaped energy out of her forearm, a current of silver thin as a blade at her fingertips.

Then she plunged her hand through the air.

Reality rippled, somehow frigid and scorching simultaneously, a squirm beneath her fingernails. Fi pushed, dragging the distortion wider, until the translucent folds of a new Curtain floated in front of her.

Moment of truth. Or certain death. Fi sucked in a breath and stepped through.

Solid ground met her on the other side. She stumbled in the dim light, colliding with a shelf of . . . filing boxes? A storage room. Fi dug an energy capsule from her coat pocket for light as she navigated to a window. She tipped onto her toes to peer outside.

A plaza stretched before her. Across it, the stone columns and aurora dome of the courthouse, a red perimeter wall at its back – placing her in the basement of the capitol building.

Astrid was right. Fi *was* damn good at what she did.

She stepped back to the Shard where Milana waited. 'We're good to go.'

They carried the crates through the Curtain into the storage room, leaving the cart within the Shard and Aisinay unhitched to browse the meadow for Shard voles. Milana handed Fi a bag.

'You're not very faithful to the daeyari, are you?' Milana asked.

Fi withheld a snort. 'Not particularly.'

'You are today. Put these on.'

Fi opened the bag – another jolt at seeing the silver attendant robes. She scowled, the cloth like slime beneath her fingers. Style varied across territories, but she could picture these too easily on the attendants in Verne Territory, where she grew up.

Too similar to the ones who came to her town a decade ago.

A disguise was a disguise. Fi's stomach squirmed as she removed her coat and donned the wretched robe. Into the pockets she stuffed her sword hilt, a couple of energy capsules, a polished carnelian transport stone, small comforts against suffocating fabric.

Milana beckoned her to follow. 'No sense lurking in a storage room. You can wait for us in the reflection hall. Find a place to sit by the candles, no one will bother you.'

Fi huffed and tied back her rainbow hair, hiding it beneath her raised hood.

Outside the storage room, dark tile set into patterns of conifers and mountain peaks squeaked beneath her boots. Copper energy conduits framed the ceiling, feeding lamps of blown glass in metal casings that spiked like stars. Milana led them through the maze of marble halls with startling ease. *Someone did her research.*

Fi's heart hammered harder with each step.

This was a distressing observation. She'd cut a Curtain into a capitol building, was poised to pull off her most lucrative job to date, all reasonable cause for nerves.

But that wasn't the problem.

It was the robes. The corridors of polished stone. Milana leading her with hardly a backward glance. Sharp little pieces, each tugging at cold-clawed memories.

The weight of hands on her arms.

The lulling voices.

Don't be afraid.

Fi bristled, chin up, metal barbs to reinforce her spine. Milana had assured her the Lord Daeyari was out of the city today. Nothing to worry about.

'We'll fetch you once the work is finished,' Milana said.

She paused on the threshold to a large, circular chamber. On the floor, gray and white marble shaped a mosaic of trees, scattered with pillows for long spells of sitting. Overhead, the ceiling vaulted into a dome of Void black. High walls accentuated the emptiness. The pin-drop quiet. Scents of wax and pine oil mixed with the sulfur of matches, tiers of mahogany shelves lined with candles. Hundreds of them.

One for every sacrifice consumed by the daeyari. The grim memorial stood for anyone who wished to visit, though the sparse offerings of flowers and trinkets suggested few people opted to pay their respects here, of all places. Most families probably spread the ashes closer to home, energy back to the Void and body back to the dust of the Plane – or whatever remained of the body, once the daeyari was done with it.

In other words: one of the least fun places in the entire Plane. At least no one would bother Fi here.

'Under an hour, as promised,' Milana whispered. 'Then back through the Curtain—'

Scuffed footsteps broke the silence.

Milana's accomplice, Erik, hurried across the room. He, too, wore silver attendant robes with Void-embroidered sleeves.

The ashen look on his face had Fi reaching into a pocket for her sword hilt.

'We have a problem,' he hissed. 'A *big* problem!'

Milana raised a calming hand. 'Slow down. What's happened?'

'Look.'

Across the reflection hall, two glass-paned doors stood open, letting in a creep of cold. Outside lay a courtyard, shade from the building preserving a coat of frost upon stone banisters and pots of winter-blooming azaleas.

And there upon the white-dusted steps . . .

Stood a fucking daeyari.

5

What. The fuck. Is that?

Across millennia, humans had endless names for the predators that hunted them. Boughstalkers. Nightmares. *The beast from the forest*, in that old rhyme Fi used to hum when she was a kid.

Then the monsters came down from their trees, offering peace – for a price.

They taught humans to call them by their proper name – daeyari.

His back faced them, antlered silhouette like a slip of shadow in the low light of the courtyard, unmoving aside from the sway of a long, slender tail.

Fi could have screamed. Could have filled that room with curses. She bit her tongue just short of drawing blood, terrified the beast would smell it. Milana promised he wouldn't be here. But even distance meant less to an immortal, not bound by the same flesh and blood, able to flit across their territories even faster than Fi with her Shards.

It had been so long since she'd seen a daeyari in person.

'*What is he doing here?*' Panic quivered Milana's whisper.

'He was gone this morning!' Erik returned. 'No warning he'd be returning early.'

'Get rid of him.'

'What do you think I've been trying to do?'

The daeyari turned, a single eye snapping onto the humans cowering behind him. His irises glowed crimson like midnight coals, the energy inside him seeping out, rimmed by sclera the same depthless black as the Void he'd crawled out of.

Before Fi could bolt, Milana grabbed her wrist, nails digging into flesh.

'Don't run,' Milana hissed. 'You *never run* from a daeyari.'

Never run from any predator.

Fi willed her legs to hold as the daeyari approached.

There was savage elegance to the creature: lacquer black antlers carved with delicate designs and capped with beaten silver. A midnight jacket of no mortal fashion, high-collared and cut low past his clavicle, far too thin for the cold. Subtle panels of iridescence formed a silhouetted tree line along the hem, an aurora above. Vesper fabric. From the Twilit Plane, the first home of the daeyari, before they spread their claws to the Season-Locked Planes and dozens more beyond. His dark breeches ended at the calf, his ankle raised . . . higher than mortals. The way a cat walked on its toes, made for predatory silence.

He moved on svelte strides, lithe with muscle, hands and bare feet tipped in claws.

Yet for every otherworldly feature, just as many looked uncannily like a young man. A light blush colored his lips, mouth set in a perturbed line. Blue-black hair swept back, longer strands over his crown, a shaved fade at the sides, antlers marking the line of separation. There was a softness to his pale cheeks that bronze couldn't capture, a stern jaw that cut fiercer in person. All lures to lull unwitting hares.

'Thank you for fetching me, Erik.' Milana's voice came out level. She nudged Fi. 'I was taking her to light candles. Would you mind?'

While Erik pulled Fi away, Milana folded her hands and bowed to the monster.

'Welcome, Lord Antal.'

The daeyari paused before her. His expression was granite smooth, skin-peeling eyes framed by slender brows. His tail swayed at his ankles.

'Milana.'

He spoke her name like a breeze through pines, low and steady with a ring of swallowed centuries. None of that sent the shock down Fi's spine. Not the velvet of the daeyari's voice, but the familiarity.

He knew her.

Erik guided Fi to the shelves of memorial candles and handed her a lighting stick. She took it in tight fingers but didn't dip into a flame, glaring into his terror-wide eyes, weighing the clamp of his mouth. Milana *did* wear those silver robes too well.

Fuck Fi and hurl her dense ass into the Void.

Milana and Erik were attendants here. Attendants to the *daeyari*.

'We weren't expecting you,' Milana said behind them.

'No,' the daeyari returned. 'My apologies for the impromptu visit.'

'Forgive me for not meeting you sooner. We could have planned for your arrival—'

Milana froze as the daeyari's head tilted. Subtler, a flare of nostrils and a soft inhale.

'Milana . . .' He frowned, one chip through the marble facade. 'What's upset you?'

He could *smell* her unease? Or maybe the beasts could sense their prey's panicked heartbeats. Fi's hammered against her sternum. Erik slapped her fingers to urge her attention away from eavesdropping, back to the facade of lighting candles. She dipped her stick into a flame and held it, trembling, to a cold wick.

Ten years, and still a coward. No better than a frantic hare.

'A busy day. That's all.' Milana stepped back, masking the motion with another bow. 'Please, how may I assist you, my Lord Daeyari?'

The daeyari studied her with an odd pinch to his brow. A tighter flick of his tail.

Milana's shoulders eased when he stepped past her, striding to a window overlooking the capitol plaza. Twilight bathed the beast as the short-lived Winter sun skirted low over rooftops. The contrast of light accentuated his slim silhouette, lean shoulders tapering to a narrow waist, calves cut of sharp muscle. A hunter, built to chase prey through the forest.

'There are complaints in the city,' he said.

'We've heard,' Milana replied, hesitant.

'What do you know of them?'

'A heating failure in the southern district.'

The daeyari turned, scowling. 'Those energy conduits were replaced last year.'

'You needn't worry, Lord Antal. Your governor is handling the matter.'

'Is he here?'

'Of course. I'll take you to him?'

Milana swept a hand to the hall. She played the act with confidence, words betraying only a subtle waver as she attempted to hurry the daeyari along. His eyes narrowed all the same, a smoldering red that chilled Fi to the marrow. And when that gaze flicked onto her and Erik . . .

She turned to the candles with more gusto than she'd shown her past few lovers.

64

Behind her, clawed footsteps padded stone. Crossing the room.

Then fainter, disappearing down the hall.

Once the room fell silent, Fi and Erik stood side-by-side, breaths shallow, lighting sticks burnt to ashes in their hands.

'*You lied to me*,' Fi said with all the venom of a frost asp.

'We may have . . . omitted some details,' Erik admitted.

Merciless Void, Fi could shake him for semantics later. 'What are we going to do now?' There were any number of acceptable options: running, fleeing, cutting losses while they still had their throats.

'We wait for Milana,' Erik said.

'. . . *Excuse me?*'

'There's still time to—'

'There is a *daeyari* here!'

'Milana will get rid of him.'

'You're out of your mind if you think—'

'One hour!' In Erik's fingers, the lighting stick splintered. 'That's what you agreed to. There's still time.'

Fi braced her hands on a shelf while he returned to the charade of candle lighting.

How had this gone to shit so fast? The daeyari saw her. He knew Milana and Erik. Even if the beast could be diverted, the capitol brimmed with supporters, people who could take notice of two attendants and their nervous behavior.

Fi wouldn't go down with them. She could get through this. She *had* to get through this. She took this job because she was bold, unshakeable, the best damn smuggler across the Season-Locked Planes. She clutched the confidence like armor, this cloak of bristles she'd woven to keep herself safe.

To prove she was more now than she'd been on the worst day of her life.

She wouldn't be dragged to a daeyari. Never again.

A small eternity passed before Milana returned, footsteps quick against the tile.

'He's gone,' she reported, breathless. 'Out of the city, back to the eastern border, but we're severely behind schedule. We need to move.'

By the Void. Not her, too.

'Milana,' Fi said. 'You'd be better off—'

'We have half an hour still! We'll meet you here once our business is finished.'

They hurried off, leaving Fi alone in the reflection room. Cold drifted in from the courtyard, flickering the candles. She dropped onto a pillow with a snarl, *reflecting* on how little she wanted to be here.

Fi could run. She could very easily run right now and call this business finished, professional impropriety be damned to the deepest pit of the Void. This wasn't an art heist. That much she'd bet her last rainbow-stranded hair on.

Then why did Milana and Erik need so many energy capsules—

A muffled *BOOM* shuddered the building.

Fi nearly jolted off her pillow. The impact rumbled stone and left the candle shelves rattling. On the high walls, windows groaned, glass cast purple in the growing dusk.

She held still as a startled rabbit in the aftermath.

An explosion. That was an *explosion*, from the neighboring wing of the capitol. Milana and Erik said they'd planned to break into a safe in the governor's office, but . . .

A scent of stone dust itched Fi's nose. Footsteps and frantic voices passed by the hall.

Slowly, she rose to her feet.

In ten years of Void smuggling, Fi had her fair share of jobs gone wrong. How to describe that feeling, the moment before disaster hit? That hot prickle down her arms. The churn of adrenaline in her gut. Like the instinct of an animal caught before a storm, when the wind began to rustle, too late to run for shelter.

That explosion didn't come from the governor's office. It was too *big* for a safe, to have shaken the windows where Fi stood. Her ears perked at a sound like crumbling mortar.

Milana and Erik. Those lichen-mouthed liars. This wasn't about a safe, it was—

A second explosion threw Fi off her feet.

She hit the floor on knees and elbows, curling into a ball as dust and snow billowed in from the courtyard, a cacophony of percussion and stone drowning out everything around her.

Her ears rang as the dust settled.

Moaning, Fi uncurled, hair a snarl of Void and rainbow, face . . . *stinging*. Shards of glass coated the floor, the windows shattered. Her silviamesh saved her from the deluge, but shrapnel ripped the sleeves of her robe and left a cut down her jaw. Overhead, the ceiling groaned.

Then a crack.

'Oh, f—'

Fi lurched to her feet. Her vision spun as she stumbled across the room. Ears still ringing as stone scraped above her. She dove into the hallway seconds before a chunk of ceiling broke loose, crashing to the floor in a spray of rubble and snuffed candles.

More cracks split the walls.

She didn't have time to think. Barely time to catch her breath on the dust-choked air.

With a hearty middle finger to Milana and Erik and *everything about this*, she hurtled into the halls of the capitol, intent on getting the fuck out of here.

The building was chaos. A flood of well-dressed administrators and secretaries surged out of offices and into hallways. Guards in midnight uniforms hurried people toward exits, their shouted directions scarcely audible above the din. Distracted by their own urgency, none bothered Fi with a second glance.

This was no minor explosion. No petty theft. It was a focused attack, and Fi didn't know *why*. Buildings weren't supposed to explode in territories ruled by daeyari, the hard hands of the immortals enough to deter even the bitterest whiffs of insurrection.

Fi pushed counter to the crowd, retracing her path back to the Curtain she'd cut. Milana's route had been labyrinthine, avoiding points of heavier traffic, but Fi could memorize spatial layouts in her sleep. Otherwise, she'd have lost herself in the Void years ago.

She ran into the final hallway, in sight of the storage room she'd entered through. No sign of Milana or Erik. They'd told her to meet them in the reflection hall, but if they had any sense, they'd either find their own exit from the crumbling building, or get to the Curtain.

Maybe Fi would be charitable and wait an extra minute for them. More than they deserved – and only for the chance to snarl at them herself. If she spotted a hint of this roof coming down, she'd book it through that Curtain with or without—

A third explosion went off. Directly above her.

The force shattered windows, throwing Fi against a wall. By the time her head stopped spinning, rubble blocked her path to the Curtain. A heinous *crack* sounded as a fissure spread across the ceiling.

Fi clawed into her pockets and yanked out her transport stone.

The polished carnelian was cool in her palm, the spiral shape of a fossilized shell: a Shard ammonite. Little extra-Planar organisms capable of dematerialization. As the ceiling groaned, Fi cracked the stone in two, a seam pre-cut down the middle. The halves pulled to each other like magnets, eager to rejoin. She hurled one half out a broken window.

The second half, she clutched for dear life. As the ceiling gave way, Fi closed her eyes, palm sizzling as she Shaped energy into the stone.

Hot static shuddered over her skin, stabbing through muscle, through bone. Fi clenched her teeth against the liquifying sensation. A lurch sent her off her feet.

Then she was stumbling. Outside.

Fi careened off balance, skinning her hands as she caught herself on the flagstone of the plaza, hunched over where the thrown half of her transport stone had clattered to a halt. She shook, stomach reeling, skin like a swarm of ants. Human bodies weren't made for dematerialization, but she could survive a jump or two before any organs started melting.

Stone thundered behind her. Fi rolled to face the capitol building, eyes wide as the entire west wing collapsed in a plume of dust. She drew an arm across her face, shielding her eyes as the pulse hit. Mortar struck her arms. The air turned thick as chalk.

Then, an eerie quiet as stone began to settle.

Fi blinked at her surroundings, trying to make sense of silhouettes in the dust, voices shouting across the plaza. How much of the capitol went down?

How many *people* were in there?

She couldn't afford to think about any of that. Shock and adrenaline warred in Fi's muscles, enough to get her out of here. When she tried to stand, every joint protested. She pulled a current of energy out of trembling abdominal muscles, hissing as she Shaped molten silver over scraped hands and chin. Not a pretty fix, but enough to cauterize the bleeding and kickstart her natural healing. She shed the heavy attendant cloak, eager to breathe again, though the dust in the air sent her coughing.

Those shouts in the plaza were guards, guiding evacuees to the exit gates. Either Fi had to slip out with the crowd, or cut another Curtain. The cold in her muscles, a sign of magic depletion, made the second option less attractive. Neither did she trust her ability to relax and spot a proper connection point while the world crumbled around her. She limped toward the nearest voices, ears still ringing from splintering rock. Shifting rubble rumbled in the gloom.

Then, the deep notes of a growl.

Fi froze. The sound was heart-stopping. Otherworldly. Clearly, some type of shock-induced hallucination.

It sounded again, a growl like no human or animal she'd ever heard, low enough to rumble her ribs. She spun in a circle, scanning the dust-shrouded air. She'd already dragged herself out of a collapsing building, what else could possibly . . .

Atop the wall, something moved.

Something hideously large.

Fi's mouth fell fully open as a pantherine creature slunk across the red battlements, twenty feet long at least, white skin like a ghost behind the haze. A long tail swayed behind it. The head tapered like a horse, but too skeletal, skin pulled tight against bones and jaws filled with jagged teeth. Black antlers curved into a gnarled crown.

The guards atop the wall screamed when they spotted it.

The beast fell upon them in a flurry of teeth, batting away crossbow bolts like gnats.

Fi couldn't move. Couldn't tear her eyes away. Her father had spun countless folktales of forest beasts, exaggerated stories where monsters grew more hideous with each retelling. She'd *seen* Summer Plane prairie eagles rip men off their horses, packs of Void hyenas prowling Curtains in search of prey.

She'd never seen a creature like this.

When corpses riddled the wall, the beast's blood-spattered gaze fell on the plaza. On Fi.

It leapt, too fast for a creature that size, taut sinew propelling clawed limbs with feral force. Fi didn't have a single rational thought in her head as she scrambled for her sword. Nothing more than a shout and raw survival instinct as she cracked an energy capsule into the hilt. The mouth, the eyes, the neck – no matter the size, every animal had vulnerabilities.

When her swing glanced off thick hide, the beast swatted with one giant paw.

A flail through the air, then her back struck stone with enough force to drive the breath from her lungs, a crack to the back of her skull.

Skulls weren't supposed to make sounds like that.

Fi slumped against a wall, stars blooming over blurred vision. Too hard to keep her head up. Too hard to even lift her sword as the beast approached with viscera-stained teeth. It regarded Fi with pupil-less red irises, hollow and hungry, the sclera pitch black. A Void-touched creature.

Before it could strike, its attention latched onto other prey.

A group appeared across the plaza, crossbow-armed guards encircling a core of politicians. One of them stood out: a midnight suit with shiny buttons, silver sash across his chest. The territory governor.

The beast moved like no dumb animal. It left Fi and lunged for the group, dodging the first volley of crossbow bolts when the guards spotted it, too close by the time they reloaded. The governor reeled in terror as the beast leapt over his retinue.

A scream, as claws sank into his chest.

Fi tried to move. She really, truly did.

Her head throbbed as she watched an impossible creature rip the governor of Antal Territory into pieces. Vision blackened at the edges as the beast fell upon the remaining retinue.

When a hand settled on her shoulder, she slumped deeper against the wall.

By the black pit of the Void, Fi should have charged double for this.

Then, she didn't remember anything more.

6

Are you lying to me?

Fi hadn't had this nightmare in a long time.

She shivered, rubbing her arms against the cold. She asked the attendants for a thicker coat, but they told her not to worry. It was time to leave. One took her arm and led her away from her home. She looked back one last time.

Her father watched her go, his expression hard. Eyes hollow.

Fi lifted back to consciousness as hands hooked beneath her arms, hauling her into a sitting position. Her head throbbed like a vicious hangover. Vaguely, she recalled hitting a wall, stone striking her skull. She shivered. No coat. Snow at her feet.

Someone pressed a hot mug to her lips. She drank, too eager. The tea scalded her tongue and sank like fire down her throat.

Even awake, the nightmare teetered at the edge of her thoughts.

She was twenty-two. She'd agreed to this years ago, long enough that she should have been prepared. Enough to follow willingly. She'd be given a tea, the attendants told her. When she drank, it would take all her worry away. It would take all the pain away.

Fi's throat clenched when the numbing sensation registered, a cloying creep down the back of her throat. Twilight sorel. For daeyari sacrifices. She spat what remained in her mouth, but

73

another pair of hands held her still. Someone forced the cup to her lips.

'We're sorry.' Milana's voice, thin with fear. 'It wasn't supposed to happen like this. Please. We're so sorry.'

Fi tried to curse, but her tongue was leaden. Too much tea swallowed already, and as her limbs weakened, Erik pulled her head back for Milana to open her mouth. The rest of the drink slid down like honeyed poison.

The attendants dressed her in silver robes and led her through a stone hall. When she hesitated, when her pace began to lag, they gripped her arms and urged her forward with saccharine smiles. Outside. Into the forest.

Milana and Erik hauled Fi to her feet, a limp weight between them as the twilight sorel sank into every muscle. Groggy, she registered the shadows of conifers. Night. The forest outside Thomaskweld. Her captors dragged her through the snow, arguing in hushed tones.

'This is madness,' Erik said.

'He requested a sacrifice,' Milana cut back. 'You want to refuse him *now*, of all times? She's our best option. Our *only* option on such short notice.'

Fi's heart tried to flutter, but even that was muted.

'Don't be afraid,' the attendants told her. 'It won't hurt.'

She didn't believe them. The cold already bit her cheeks. How could teeth be kinder?

The cold cut Fi now, sharp through the thin fabric of a long-sleeved shirt she didn't recognize. More silver of a daeyari attendant, without the extravagant furs. She tried to curl her fingers, but they refused more than a twitch.

'We should be long gone,' Erik said. 'Cut our losses.'

'That would look even more suspicious! We hold out a little longer. It's almost finished.'

'*Is it?* We thought we knew the plan. Then that . . . creature appeared. What *was* that?'

'It doesn't matter.'

The trees parted. A stone structure rose in the clearing, pillars lined by silver lanterns.

At the sight of Verne's shrine, Fi's courage fled. She wasn't ready. She'd been a fool to agree to this. She dug her heels into the frozen ground, but the attendants gripped her harder.

'Don't be afraid,' they said. Stern this time.

Fi rallied every muscle to fight, to bite and scratch her abductors, but the tea left her limp. Where was her cloak of bravado when she needed it? That cage of barbs she'd crafted to hide this brittle heart? Useless. Fionamara Kolbeck, bane of a dozen territories, barely able to focus on the skim of stone beneath her boots. Milana and Erik carried her onto a patio with a silver mat and satin pillows. Pine boughs arced overhead like a vaulted ceiling.

The attendants urged her on, reminding her of her pledge. They told her what a boon this would serve for her town. Didn't she want to honor her family? But Fi fought back. She'd heard of hares throwing themselves against trees as they fled, rupturing their own hearts in panic. Hers didn't feel far off from splitting.

'I changed my mind!' she shouted. 'I don't want to go!'

They laid Fi upon the mat. Milana worked gently, for a cold-hearted bitch, arranging Fi into a comfortable position, clearing the hair from her face.

'It won't hurt,' she whispered.

Fi didn't believe her.

She should have left that cart of energy capsules on the Autumn Plane. Should have thrown those chips back in Milana's face. Should have run the moment their plan started to sour. So many opportunities, each doomed by her own stubbornness.

A shadow shifted across the pavilion. Fi watched in mute horror as darkness coalesced into antlers. The flick of a tail.

The daeyari, Antal, stepped into the light.

A sleek creature, fluid as the dark, more at home here in night-shrouded forest than in the halls of the capitol. He dressed in similar finery: silver caps to his antlers, high-waisted trousers cut slim to narrow hips, embroidery of conifer needles up the sleeves of a dark jacket. A cruel play at civility. As if he weren't a beast come to devour her. His ethereal stillness remained, skin pale as bone and claws sharp at his sides.

How long had she been unconscious?

Long enough for him to learn what happened to his city. To demand a sacrifice. Fi wanted to run, but she couldn't. She tried to shout, but she couldn't.

'A swift response,' the daeyari said lowly. A soft blush brushed his mouth, yet behind the facade came a glint of sharp canines. Crimson eyes slid over Fi, framed in pitch black sclera, but she couldn't even manage a shudder.

Milana bowed. 'Of course, Lord Antal. We're eager to accommodate your request.'

His scowl creased deeper, flashing a fang. 'She's drunk the tea already?'

'At her insistence. To ease her nerves. This day has been harrowing for us all.'

Liar. Fi fought to form the word, but it stalled over frigid lips. Cold seeped from the stone below. She lay defenseless as a rabbit on a chopping block, screaming inside.

A decade ago, Fi hadn't been ready to die. She still wasn't ready.

The daeyari loomed over her. She'd never been so close to one, glowing red eyes fierce enough to scorch. Silver lamplight glinted against the lacquer black of his antlers, the blue-black of his hair. He smelled like pine and ozone. Like the snap of ice that left livestock dead in the field come morning.

'And her request?' he asked.

'A willing sacrifice from among your flock,' Milana said. 'She requests your aid in restoring the city.'

Fi could have laughed. Could have screamed. Milana played a devious hand, from the silver tunic she'd dressed Fi in, to the fact the daeyari had *seen* her with the other attendants at the capitol.

'Very well,' he said.

The attendants bowed and turned to leave. Fi itched to shout every curse she knew.

The daeyari knelt beside her.

With every shred of stubborn will she possessed, Fi fought to shift her head. To lift a single hand against this shadow-honed beast poised to devour her. Nothing.

He rolled back his sleeves, motions crisp, baring forearms lean with muscle. Strong fingers made for carving. Would he slit her neck open? Use energy to stop her heart?

Air sank leaden in Fi's lungs. She'd have settled for a gasp. A pathetic whimper. *Nothing.*

The daeyari traced claws down her throat with horrifying gentleness, the brush of his knuckles cool as a Spring breeze. A mask of composure, but up close, hunger hollowed his cheeks – parted lips and eager fangs.

Fi wished he could feel her heart racing, but even that was stubbornly still. Despite her fiercest effort to fight, to scream, her mouth barely twitched.

The daeyari paused, eyes narrowed.

He leaned closer, head tilted to the whisper of her breath.

A frail hope sparked in Fi's chest. Never mind that their faces were too close. Never mind the chill of his breath against her cheek. Even a rabbit deserved the dignity of a final shriek. She fought every useless muscle in her throat to work. To move. To do *something*. That leaden air in her chest, impossibly heavy as she forced it out all at once.

Her breath escaped as little more than a rasp.

Two scarce syllables, the best she could manage.

'*Kill . . . them . . .*'

The daeyari's eyes sharpened like blades. Like teeth poised to snap.

The moment dragged forever. Fi met his gaze, forcing herself to stare into those unblinking eyes framed in Void-black, pleading that he'd understand. He *had* to understand. His race couldn't have become what they were without being intelligent.

But would he care?

'Milana,' he called out, smooth as fresh snow. 'Stay a moment.'

The words jolted Fi like lightning. She couldn't see Milana's reaction, but she heard the delicious halt of boots against the patio.

That small victory didn't buoy her long. If she couldn't speak, this was still their story to spin. Her terror returned as the daeyari slid his hand beneath her shirt, cool palm settling atop her heart. Fi braced for pain. For the icy snap of death.

A spear of foreign energy sank into her chest.

The current burned hot and cold at the same time, ozone coating her mouth as the pulse careened through her ribs. It sliced through muscle and viscera, flooding every extremity, burning fiercer and fiercer until she shrieked.

Fi tensed at the realization.

She could *shriek* again.

The daeyari's magic washed through her like cleansing fire, burning away the twilight sorel. Fi gasped when he removed his hand. Her muscles trembled even with the current gone, weak as if rousing from too deep a sleep, but when she rolled onto her side and sucked in a breath . . .

'You back-stabbing clump of stale Void lichen!' she shouted at Milana.

The woman went ashen. Beside her, Erik betrayed a gasp.

'How fucking dare you!' Fi spat. Cussing tasted beautiful. She'd never take it for granted again. 'You think you can get rid of me that easy? Think again, you frost-hearted . . .'

Dizziness struck her. Fi caught herself before toppling sideways. Though she could move, could speak, her limbs dragged, relics of tea in her system.

The daeyari rose with menacing grace, clawed feet whisper-quiet as he circled the patio. He looked down at Fi with ember-hard eyes. His voice came out harder.

'This sacrifice doesn't seem so willing, Milana.'

To her credit, Milana held her ground. *Never run from a daeyari*, she'd told Fi. They were about to test if that was wise counsel.

'Of course.' Milana said. 'The truth is . . .'

'The truth is,' Fi interrupted, 'you're a scheming—'

'This woman is responsible for the explosion at the capitol!' Milana pointed at Fi, who could only gape in response. 'My apologies for deceiving you, Lord Antal. We wished to give her this final dignity. To focus on rebuilding.'

'Bullshit!' Fi shouted. 'You hired me to do it!'

Milana clapped a hand to her chest, aghast. 'How dare you make such an accusation. We are faithful servants to the daey-ari!'

'Faithful servants who paid me to smuggle a *bomb* into the capitol building.'

'You claim to bring me a criminal.' The daeyari's tone snapped both mortals to silence. He stood between them, eyes locked on Milana, taut as a panther stalking prey. Even his tail fell motionless. 'Where is her sentence?'

Milana twisted her hands. 'There . . . hasn't been one. We wished to act swiftly. Please, this is a difficult time for—'

She didn't get to finish.

Static laced Fi's tongue as the daeyari vanished.

A blink later, he reappeared in front of Milana. Innate teleportation ranked among the more impressive and terrifying of immortal tricks, and though Fi had heard of the ability, she startled to see the swiftness of it firsthand. Before Milana could bolt, the daeyari snared her head in both hands. He could have skewered her, could have gone for her exposed throat. Instead, red energy bloomed beneath his fingers, sinking into her temples.

Milana didn't move. Hardly breathed. A glassy expression filled her eyes.

'Are you lying to me?' the daeyari asked.

His attendant spoke as if in a trance. Even then, the answer quivered.

'Yes.'

The daeyari tensed, subtle, but compared to his previous stoicism, he might as well have recoiled. '*Who* told you to lie to me?'

Before she could answer, Erik slipped a hand into his robes. He hadn't said a word since Fi regained her tongue, had drifted so wraithlike at the edge of the patio that she could have forgotten he was there.

The daeyari didn't.

Static pricked Fi's tongue again. Erik stabbed a silver energy dagger at the daeyari's heart – slicing air, when the creature vanished again.

Overhead, a bough creaked.

Fi looked up, and there was the moment of terror from every

folktale, every children's rhyme: a daeyari crouched upon a branch, tail swaying, red eyes a smolder in the dark as he glared upon the witless humans who'd come to his shrine – upon the fool who'd fight a creature centuries old, its teeth sharpened on sinew and bone.

There weren't many folktales about fighting daeyari. None where the human won.

'Erik . . .' Milana breathed in horror.

The daeyari leapt, hitting the ground with effortless poise. Erik swiped with his dagger, but the immortal struck faster. For as long as humans remembered, they could draw on the energy in their bodies, but their early forms were raw. Crude. Then daeyari, as part of their deal, taught mortals more refined Shaping, energy conduits and more stable external forms. He Shaped an elegant shield of red energy along his forearm, deflecting Erik's blade. His claws curled fiercer than before, sheaths of crimson sharpening the points.

He grabbed Erik by the throat, severing arteries with a single slash. The human fell in a spray of blood, gurgling as he clutched the rent flesh of his neck.

Fi watched the body fall limp. Watched blood pool across the stones.

She couldn't get to her feet fast enough. The vertical motion punched her with dizziness, limbs heavy, but this would be her only chance. Milana said not to run, but Fi wasn't the one who'd betrayed an immortal. The daeyari faced away from her, blood slick on his fingers, focus elsewhere. Void spare her from that focus a moment longer.

He grabbed Milana. She shrieked as claws pierced her robe, digging into her shoulders. Though guilt pitted Fi's stomach, she needed the noise, masking her footsteps as she stumbled off the patio and into the forest.

'Please!' Milana's voice cracked. 'I've been a loyal servant!'

'Then you should know *better*,' the daeyari snarled back. 'Tell me the truth.'

Fi didn't look back. Her steps didn't falter, even as the screeches began, a spine-numbing echo through silent trees. On the other hand, hard to muster sympathy for a woman who'd betrayed her and blew up a capitol building full of innocent people. Any hesitation, and Fi would be the next one screaming.

The odds stacked against her. No weapons. No energy capsules. Her legs were putty as she fled the shrine down frozen slopes. Her head spun with lingering tendrils of twilight sorel.

A Curtain. Fi only needed one Curtain. She harbored no hope of outrunning a daeyari, much less in his home terrain, much *much* less considering the blatant trail her boots dragged through the snow. She could only hope the creature's preoccupation with Milana bought her enough time to escape. Through tea-rattled thoughts, she wracked her memory for Curtains on the outskirts of Thomaskweld.

A green aurora swirled overhead. The energy of lost souls, those too restless to find the afterlife, left to drift in the Void. Tonight, Fi heard them calling in the dull pop of each wave, a warning of what end awaited if the daeyari caught her.

Ten years since Verne's shrine, and still, all she could do was run.

Fi skidded down a ravine draped in snow-heavy firs. Caught her boot on a fallen trunk. Cursed the Void and the daeyari and everything in between as she scraped her hands stumbling through a patch of thorny bracken. At the base of the slope, a creek cut through the forest, babbling pools crusted with ice.

Upon the bank, a Curtain shifted beneath starlight. Fi sobbed at the sight and sprinted toward it. She pulled energy from feeble arm muscles, only needing a tiny current to slice the Curtain open.

Nothing came. Only numbness, stubborn in her bones.

'Fuck me. This is *not the time!*'

Fi swiped her hand through the Curtain. The ethereal chill washed her skin, but reality didn't part. Her internal energy faltered, blocked by twilight sorel like detritus in a stream. She gritted her teeth and dug deep, *deep* into the muscles of her chest, her abdomen, grasping for any flare of heat. There was no time. Every second of delay meant teeth closer to her neck.

At last, she Shaped a feeble current of silver at her fingers. Little better than when she was a child, flailing her arms through Curtains for weeks before she finally learned to touch them. A small pulse was enough. Fi split the Curtain and staggered through.

A Shard lay on the other side, a dust of snow upon rocky ground, a mirrored crimson aurora twisting across the black of the Void. Fi limped toward the nearest exit Curtain she could see, eager to be far away, drugs and energy exhaustion pulling her toward the ground.

Static prickled her tongue.

The daeyari struck her back.

Fi hit the ground. Stone scraped her arms as she twisted to Shape a shield, but when that failed, she resorted to kicking. A woefully ineffective strategy. Gone was any gentleness the immortal had shown at his shrine. His weight pinned her down like a lame hare. Claws raked her skull as he pressed her head against the ground, cheek crunching gravel.

A stupid plan, in retrospect. The Void was more this creature's home than any forest. He hunched over her, resolute from claws to tail as Fi shook with ragged breaths beneath him. He smelled of blood. A red smear marred his cheek, and when he extended a long black tongue to lick it clean, some frantic part of Fi threatened to laugh. A strange relief, knowing he probably wasn't hungry anymore.

Or maybe it was the cruel irony of dying by daeyari teeth after all this time. After all the lives she'd ruined through her cowardice.

He glanced at the starless sky. The black of the Void had never seemed so depthless as it did now, contrasted against his eyes.

'You can see Curtains,' he said. 'How convenient.'

At the moment, that hardly seemed the case.

Fi gasped as a current of energy pushed into her temple. Not sharp. A dull creep of heat flooded her skull, clouding already muddied thoughts, the same as he'd done to Milana.

'What part did you play in this?' The daeyari's question brushed her ear, cold as ice.

'I smuggled a bomb into the Capitol.'

The words escaped without Fi's permission. Panic followed, a distant flutter in her chest as she drifted beneath the daeyari's magic. She couldn't think straight. Couldn't lie.

'Why?' he pressed.

'They . . . hired me . . .' Her words fell to mumbles. The lull of his touch, the remnants of twilight sorel combined to make her eyes heavy. Sleep sounded blissful. A quiet nap beneath the Void . . .

'*Speak*, human.'

'I think . . . I might have a concussion,' Fi slurred.

The daeyari gave an aggravated huff.

His energy severed. Clarity snapped back like a slap to the face, the bite of cold on Fi's arms and stones digging into her cheek. The daeyari pressed harder against her head, urging her with claws rather than magic.

Claws were pretty damn convincing.

'I've heard Milana's side,' he said. 'Now, I'll have yours.'

Fi was supposed to be good at this: haggling, standing her ground, wearing that confounding cape of confidence. All use-less now, when she couldn't piece together a single reasonable argument to stop this daeyari from splitting her open.

'I didn't know their plan,' she said. The truth, but a flimsy excuse.

'You smuggled a bomb for them.'

'They told me they were stealing a vase!' Fi wasn't normally one to beg. This seemed a fine time to try – not that it did Milana any good. 'Please. I never meant to cross you. You've caught the ones who did.'

Fi's heart thundered hard enough to chisel the stone beneath her. She assumed the daeyari sensed it, that his long silence was intended to strain the muscle to its breaking point. He leaned closer, knee digging into her back, breath raising the hairs on her neck.

'Our business isn't finished, mortal. I honored your request. You owe me payment.'

The demand settled over Fi like a noose of thorns.

She'd asked the daeyari to kill Milana and Erik. He'd ripped them to pieces. For centuries since the pact, their races had agreed upon the price for such an exchange.

'You already have plenty to eat!' She hoped. She *begged*.

'There are other ways to pay a debt.'

No. Fi would rather he flay her. She'd rather—

Another surge of energy hit her temple. Before Fi could cry out, her thoughts blurred, a swift tumble back into uncon-sciousness.

7

Being this obnoxious is a talent, actually

Fi jerked awake in a cold sweat, heart hammering. The world was all dark outlines, groggy thoughts as sleep kept its claws in her.

Void alive, she'd had an awful nightmare.

Her head flickered with memories of falling buildings. Paralyzed limbs. Forest shrines and shadows shifting in the trees, the kind of bone-deep dread that kept a hold long after waking. Fi squinted her eyes shut and burrowed into the furs of her bed, eager to escape into more sleep.

But this bed . . . felt strange.

It *smelled* strange, sharp like ozone.

Still groggy, Fi poked at the pelt draped over her. At home, she'd assembled a blanket of snowshoe hare from her traps, plus a skin of aurorabeast fur she'd bartered off Boden for a cask of Autumn Plane hard cider. The blanket wrapping her now consisted of silver fox. Beneath her, soft mink lined the mattress. Not her bed. Then where . . .

Adrenaline dragged her fully awake, pieces clicking together, breath shallowing in slow-dawning horror. Fi's flight through the forest was no nightmare.

And she was in a daeyari's bed.

An *angry* daeyari, last she recalled.

She clamped her mouth shut on a curse, not wanting to reveal she'd woken. No sign of the beast – for now. Just an empty room where she lay swaddled in blankets. Void save her from whatever twisted power play this was.

After checking to make sure all her limbs were intact, Fi scanned for escape routes. The bed sat upon a rock slab. The entire room appeared chiseled out of stone. Stone floor. Stone walls with recessed shelves, stuffed with books and odd pieces of scrap metal.

Dim light drifted through a doorway.

Fi lowered a foot to the floor. Warmth bloomed beneath her, a spark of red around her boot that made her recoil. When no calamity followed, she tried again. Crimson energy glowed around her foot, emitting heat. She kept a furnace at home, powered by an energy capsule that required daily charging. She'd never seen such thread-thin conduits glinting against stone, heat diffusing through the ground.

Wasteful. Of course, an immortal could afford as much.

Fi's head throbbed when she stood, still sore where she'd struck the wall, less foggy after some rest. She crept toward the door, red splaying beneath each footfall.

This place, wherever it was, must have an exit. A front door, a window to dive out of. She'd run home and hide in her cottage for a month. Move to a new territory, if she had to. Anything to get away from scheming attendants and vengeful immortals. Speaking of which . . . Fi paused, listening. A rumble sounded down the hall.

Wind. She could hear the wind. That meant an exit.

The next room was larger, brighter, also cut out of stone. No exit doors. Or windows – *technically*. Fi's heart sank at the sight of the far wall, completely open to the wind. No rail guarded the edge. Cautious, she stepped closer.

Under better circumstances, the view would have been magnificent. Beyond the ledge, the world fell away, this chamber carved into the highest cliff overlooking Thomaskweld. The valley lay beneath a lavender sky – dusk, not morning, to her horror. The river snaked silver through dark conifers and the lights of the city, energy conduits like golden fractures from the factories.

But the *cold*. Upon the ledge, the floor heating faded, and cold bit into Fi like teeth, wind lashing her Void-and-rainbow hair. She still wore a borrowed tunic of thin gray cotton. No coat.

This wasn't a window she could leap out of. One glance at the dizzying fall sent her empty stomach flipping.

Ok, different plan. Fi spotted no Curtains on the cliffside, but a full night's sleep had replenished some magic. She unfocused her gaze and Shaped energy out of a tired bicep, into her fingertips, intent on cutting her escape—

'Don't try it,' warned a voice behind her.

Fi spun, arms raised like a shield.

What good would that do against claws?

The daeyari loomed at the back of the room like a shadow slipped off the wall. She hadn't spotted him a moment ago, hadn't heard him enter. Even now, he could have been a figment of the dark, betrayed only by the crimson glow of his eyes and the swaying tail. The old stories couldn't capture that deathly stillness. That twist in Fi's stomach like the instincts of a prey animal, urging her to *run*.

Maybe that was what he waited for. Fleeing quarry must make for better entertainment.

'Wherever you can step on Plane or Shard, so can I.' He glanced to the open wall, the slice of wind and purple dusk. 'Don't linger in the wind. Your people don't do well in cold.'

The beast spoke low and measured, his seasonspeak heavy with a Winter accent, though too sharp on several syllables. When he touched the wall, two metal lanterns embedded in stone lit the room in soft twilight blue.

The daeyari approached Fi with prowling strides.

Closer.

Too close.

She flinched as he passed, his long tail brushing her calf. A crass intimidation tactic. Fi scowled fierce enough to curdle icicles, baffled as to why he hadn't butchered her yet.

The wind *was* cold. Giving her host a wide berth, Fi retreated across a rug depicting a moonlit forest in black and silver, into a sheltered sitting area. Blue floor cushions circled a low table. A cabinet sat against the wall, topped by the shine of a . . . gramophone? Far be it from Fi to wonder what a monster did in his free time.

The daeyari stepped to the 'window', perched light upon the lip of rock, like a hawk in his eyrie. He was dressed simpler than before: no silver tips to his antlers, no embroidered jacket, just trousers and a dark shirt with sleeves rolled to the elbow despite the cold. Wind tousled the longer hair between his antlers into shards of blue-black.

'What's your name?' he asked without looking at her.

Oh no. Fi didn't like *this* one bit. She searched the room for any exits she'd missed. As far as she could see, she was blocked by rock on three sides and a daeyari on the fourth.

When she didn't answer, he turned on her with a skin-peeling glare.

'Is *this* what you want to fight me on, human?'

Fi didn't want to fight. She wanted to be a hundred miles away, never having to think of daeyari again. As that option didn't currently sit on the table . . .

'Fionamara.'

His mouth quirked, as if tasting the name. 'Do you know what they did, *Fionamara*?'

Another pressuring tactic. She'd already told him what she knew. 'They blew up the capitol building.' She considered. '*Your* capitol building.'

'Not just in Thomaskweld.' He lowered to a growl. 'Runeyska. Calvariz. Sunip. Every major city in my territory. Offices destroyed, administrators killed, energy conduits severed.'

No. Fi hadn't known any of that.

When she was young, her father put her and Boden to sleep with old folktales. In the stories, daeyari were phantom beasts waiting to snatch mortals from the shadows, deviously difficult to fight. Skin like steel. Fast as a blink. Impossible to kill by mortal means, and any human foolish enough to try typically ended up skinned alive.

As Fi grew, school taught more practical lessons: the boons of energy conduits and cross-Plane trade, facilitated by working *with* the predators, rather than against them. Centuries without warfare, their immortal overseers settling disputes amongst themselves before tensions escalated.

And quieter: histories of once-a-century rebellions by restless territories, crushed swiftly by their ruling Lord Daeyari, a feast for the creature they sought to unseat.

But aside from those rare, heavy-handed reminders of authority, most daeyari kept distant from their subjects. So long as they were fed, so long as their edicts were followed, they left their human governments to run the territories. If this creature spoke the truth, he'd just lost most of the people loyal to him.

Not many ways to misinterpret that.

'Who would try to overthrow a daeyari?' Fi asked.

'That,' he said, 'is what you're going to help me determine.'

'You want me to *help* you?'

Fi's retort came too fast – too *sharp*, speaking to a carnivorous beast. But brazen was the only shield she knew when her heart beat this fast, her cloak of bristles keeping her upright whenever her gut screamed to run and hide like a useless rabbit.

The carnivorous beast in question narrowed his eyes, two smoldering motes of red framed in Void black. His rolled sleeves displayed the lean lines of his forearms, the black claws at his fingertips.

'Are you arguing with me, Fionamara?'

'I . . .' Fi swallowed, a lump like stone in her throat. What *use* was she to him? That felt like a question guaranteed to get her neck ripped open.

'You owe me a debt,' the daeyari said, low as the wind rumbling the cliffs. 'And I have need of mortal help.'

'Get your Arbiter, then.' Anyone but Fi.

'I have none.'

'Surely, you have *someone* better than—'

'There *is* no one else,' he snarled, baring a glint of fang. 'Everyone I had has either betrayed me, or is dead beneath the rubble of the building *you* blew up. So you'll have to do.'

Fi's scowl deepened. No, she *didn't* want any part of this, but no need to be rude—

'Void and Veshri know, I could *hope* for better than . . . *this*.' He swept a clawed hand over her haggard hunch in the corner of his living room – *more* rude. 'But you know what happened in the capitol. You say you weren't part of my attendants' scheme. Help me determine who *was*, if you're so adamant to prove your innocence.'

The bite in his words gave Fi pause. For years, she'd assumed this daeyari's leniency came from apathy. Incompetence, even.

To see him now, overlooking his city with an uncompromising

tilt to his chin? Claws coiled like black sickles at his sides? Speaking of anarchy with a flint of rage on his tongue? For the first time, she got a clearer picture of Antal, the *Lord Daeyari* who'd owned this territory for longer than she'd been alive.

And someone was trying to take that from him.

Someone who'd dragged Fi into this mess. Politics – those larger things she'd spent ten years fleeing. She cursed Milana and Erik, players in some unknown scheme. For the first time since everything went to shit, she thought of Astrid, strutting into her life after all these years, assuring her partners that Fi was perfect for the job.

Had she known this would happen?

Or had Astrid been duped the same, only for Fi to abandon her to another disaster?

To find out, Fi had to survive this daeyari first.

Her stomach growled. She hadn't eaten since before the explosion, and combined with the potent adrenaline circulating her bloodstream, dizziness was catching up to her. So long as the daeyari claimed he wanted to use her rather than eat her . . .

'Do I get breakfast?' she asked, testing the waters. After all, he hadn't let her freeze – or cut her open when she'd raised her voice at him.

The beast blinked.

His frown came slow. Head tilted, as if he couldn't have heard her right.

'Breakfast?' he asked.

'*Breakfast*.' Repeat it, and maybe he'd stop gawking. 'I'm no expert in daeyari nutrition, but I assume you don't devour corpses for three meals a day, or humans would be extinct.'

His tail flicked. 'Your point?'

'That I'—Fi struck her chest with an emphasizing *thump*

—'require three meals a day. So if you don't want me to pass out, I need breakfast.'

His tail swished rougher, wider. Not anger. Not hunger.

Annoyed? Void be damned. If Fi could pull off her finest skill on a daeyari, she wasn't out of her element yet.

He huffed, a disgruntled mutter of, *'Breakfast.* Of course. Yz'vum en zhem jivvi . . .'

Fi didn't speak daeyari. She'd never known a human who did, the immortals miserly about sharing their language, but tone enough told her that wasn't a flattering—

Static sparked Fi's tongue when he vanished.

She blinked at his absence.

Not for an instant . . . had she expected that ploy to actually work.

Fi moved swiftly, no telling how much time she had. She Shaped energy to her fingertips then dulled her gaze to see beyond the Winter Plane, searching for a place to cut a Curtain. A Bridge. A Shard. She'd take anything to get her out of here, but she spotted nothing beyond stone and mood lighting. With a growl, she paced the room in search of a different vantage point.

Static pricked her tongue again.

Fi gasped when the daeyari reappeared, directly in front of her. Chests nearly touching. Ozone filled her nose as thick as when she'd laid in his bed, the waft of cold off his skin enough to drag gooseflesh down her arms.

He was nearly the same height as her. Maybe an inch or two taller, thanks to the odd rise of his ankles – a couple more, if she counted the antlers – yet he loomed like a cliff of ice. It took all her constitution not to flinch away, not to back into the wall like some cornered animal.

Surely, that was what he wanted. Fi swallowed hard and held her ground.

The daeyari appraised her through dark lashes, a sharp look to the energy spooled silver at her fingers. He bared a long canine. 'I told you not to try that.'

'Well. To be fair.' Fi licked her lips. 'You're faster than I thought you'd be.'

When he huffed, the exhale brushed Fi's cheek. She braced for teeth.

Instead, he offered a lump of paper.

Wary, Fi took it. Blessed heat sank into her hands. She unwrapped the package to find a baked roll the size of her fist, oozing glaze and cinnamon. For such a small gesture, this topped the morning's list of baffling developments. Had the dreaded Lord Daeyari stolen a pastry for her? Or demanded it of a terror-stricken baker in Thomaskweld?

'Thanks.' Fi allowed herself to back away a step, itching with his proximity. 'You *are* good, right? I don't need to worry about becoming a mid-morning snack?'

He showed his teeth again. 'You talk more than I expected.'

Another confidence boost. Fi clung to the daeyari's con-foundment like shelter from a gale. Confusion made him less of a wraith, more a creature who could be bartered with.

'Is that right?' Fi shot back. 'You have a lot of experience talking to humans you aren't about to eat?'

'Plenty,' he said. No inflection. Nothing on his face.

Cryptic prick.

He paced back to his perch, gifting Fi space to breathe. And to devour the sugary roll like a starved racoon. She guessed she looked little better: borrowed clothes, hair windblown, eye liner no doubt smudged to ruin.

As food cleared her thoughts, she combed through the ludicrous events of the past two days, trying to make sense of anything. She'd brought the cart to Thomaskweld. Met Astrid.

Got fucked over by Milana and Erik. Then came the explosion, followed by . . .

By the endless black Void. It almost slipped her mind.

'It was more than the explosion,' she said.

The daeyari tilted one crimson eye toward her.

'Afterward,' Fi said. 'When everyone was evacuating, there was a . . . *creature*. A huge panther with white skin. Antlers. It ripped the governor apart.'

A subtle tension snapped over the Lord Daeyari. His veiled expressions left her unsteady, unsure how to gauge where to push or retreat. Fi keyed to what small signs he relinquished: his tail frozen, eyes unblinking.

'Milana said the same,' he replied. 'There are many beasts across the Shattered Planes.'

'I've never seen something like this. It had black sclera. Some kind of Void beast.'

His tail made a sharp flick.

'We focus on one thing at a time.' He spoke with finality. A warning edge not to press. Fi still would have.

If he hadn't startled her, by holding out his hand.

'If you've finished your *breakfast*,' he said.

She backed away. 'What's that for?'

'I need to touch you to teleport.'

'We're going *now*?'

'There's no time to delay.'

Fi could name a hundred reasons to delay: her father told her not to go anywhere with strangers, resting after breakfast was important to good digestion, she still didn't have a Void-damned *coat*. All seemed flimsy against the daeyari's gem-cut glare.

'Your aid, to pay your debt,' the beast repeated. 'Unless you'd prefer the *traditional* payment?'

Fi weighed the threat of being eaten alive against the danger of following an immortal. One of those, she stood a better chance of escaping. She took the daeyari's hand with a wince.

His palm was cool. Surprisingly soft. His fingers tightened, grasping her firmly, but careful not to plunge claws into flesh. When the sharp tips brushed her thumb, she shuddered.

'Hold your breath,' he said.

'Why—'

The world lurched.

Or maybe Fi was the one who fell, tumbling through black. Energy surged over her, cold slicing from every direction. When she tried to gasp, she found no air.

The journey halted as abruptly as it began. The daeyari's grip kept her upright as she staggered, gasping to refill her lungs with frigid air. The lingering prickle on her skin reminded Fi of her transport stone, though not nearly as intense, no nausea. Not a full dematerialization? The immortal stood unfazed. However daeyari teleportation worked, they'd gained the ability after returning from the Void, their grayscale skin no longer the same as mortal flesh, not as vulnerable to damage or energy currents. Convenient for him.

With air back in her lungs, Fi scowled over her surroundings. She stood upon rose quartz tile, dusted in snow. Black-trunked ginkgo lined the walkway, their leaves metallic copper, one of the few non-coniferous trees bred by horticulturists to survive the Winter Plane. Ahead, a stone chateau perched upon a cliff, tall windows and dark minarets narrowing to fanged points tipped in starlight.

A chill of recognition nearly buckled Fi's knees.

Her heart stilled at the sight of this garden, this view onto a valley of conifers. Every bristle gone the moment she spied that moonlit lake in the distance, smooth as glass. She couldn't breathe. Couldn't stop her hands from trembling. Fi hadn't seen this place in ten years.

But there was no mistaking it.

This was Verne Territory.

8

A friendly chat about insurrection

Any schemes abandoned her.

Rational thought? What was that?

Fi was a hare. She was a dumb, defenseless animal, kicking in panic, bolting for the closest hole to hide in.

The daeyari caught her wrist. Her struggle earned a look of warning, the beast restraining her with the ease of a panther pinning a rabbit.

'What are you doing?' he hissed.

They weren't alone. His teleport brought them to a plaza, surrounded by humans who froze like startled prey at the appearance of an immortal in their midst, wide eyes watching him – and Fi – as if a twitch might invite doom. Fi didn't care about them. She flailed against his grip, heedless of claws.

'No! Not here!' Fi saw her father's glassy eyes when the attendants took her. Heard Boden rioting in the background. She'd escaped Verne once. She'd run like a coward, and broken everything she had, and she *couldn't* be back here again.

The daeyari eyed the watching crowd, tail flicking. 'Keep your voice down. And stop this futile flailing.'

'This is Verne Territory!'

'Of course. If we're to discover who seeks to unseat me, we begin with my most cunning neighbor.'

'You can't.'

'You'll find I easily *can*—'

'Not her! You can't take me to *her!*'

Fi's squirming dragged claws against her arm until red welts appeared. A veil of rainbow hair fell across her face as she sagged, breathing hard, curses pooling on chapped lips. She shouldn't be here. She didn't deserve to be dragged back to this wretched place, implicated in schemes she had no hand in. Fear meshed with fury as Fi gathered every bent bristle, clutching them like armor.

She snapped her head up at the daeyari, resolved to fight whatever immortal fire flared in his eyes.

The softness in them sliced her speechless.

His gaze withered her like too light a breeze before a storm, that moment the wind gathered and sighed before unleashing fury. Those otherworldly eyes, those piercing shades of crimson and black shouldn't have been able to look at her this way, as if he hadn't spent two centuries devouring bones. As if Fi's terror meant anything more than the thrill of flailing prey.

'You know Verne?' he asked. Entirely too quiet.

His sincerity struck her off balance. What did he know? What did he *care?*

'I grew up here,' she said. 'I left. To get away from *her.*'

Fi hated the way he looked at her – too long, too slow, too sharp against the barbs she was fighting for her life to keep up. His grip tightened, drawing her closer. His scent of ice and ozone sent her taut.

'You claim you didn't know my attendants' scheme,' he said in a confiding low. 'Make no mistake, Fionamara, that's the only reason you're still alive.'

Fi's mouth curled a sneer, fingers flexing within the cage of his grasp.

'But regardless of your intentions,' he said, lower still, 'you *did* play a role in this. And you'll help me resolve it. That's the debt I ask of you.' His grip softened. 'For now, we walk on the same side. Stand with me, and Verne won't harm you.'

When the daeyari released her, Fi didn't bolt.

Fury gave her firmer ground to stand on. She was *not* responsible for this. She was lied to. Manipulated. Nearly fed to a daeyari. Yet as her fight or flight response leveled, she ground her teeth on an unsavory truth: he could probably force her to come, if he wanted to.

'Do you promise I'll be safe?' Fi demanded.

She could have blinked and missed it: that twitch of a frown on his mouth. A heartbeat, where this lethal beast looked less . . .

He snapped back to granite, cold and unflinching as she expected from an immortal. 'What does my promise mean to you, Fionamara?'

The daeyari didn't wait for her reply, off on lithe strides toward Verne's chateau.

This, to Fi's chagrin, left her with a choice. She weighed how fast she could sprint for the nearest Curtain, how fast the *teleporting immortal* would catch up to her, how much of a fuss she could make while he dragged her behind him . . .

Or, she could make a gamble that this daeyari – that *Antal* might be her strongest shield at the moment. At least until she figured out what was going on.

Fi hissed her displeasure as she trotted to catch up, arms crossed against her too-thin tunic, a shiver digging deeper with each step.

Ten years.

Yet this wretched place brought back a weight she could never shed: she was meant to be Verne's.

She'd been chosen young. Too young to understand. Her father sat her down beside their wide stone hearth, brought a mug of her favorite hot chocolate with peppermint. He asked about the Curtains Fi claimed to see. A rare skill, he'd told her. A gift after surviving that icy river. When Fi came of age, Verne would want her. Voidwalkers were prized by the daeyari.

All sacrifices came ready to sate their immortal's hunger. But those with exceptional potential? More valuable alive. A daeyari could choose to make an Arbiter. As Fi grew, the people of her town were certain she'd be spared, that they would reap the benefits of an Arbiter chosen among them: no more sacrifices for a lifetime, new energy conduits for their ailing infrastructure, better metallurgy contracts.

Fi's confidence waned as the day approached. She'd have to drink the twilight sorel, the attendants told her, *then* declare her request to become an Arbiter. Put herself at the daeyari's mercy. Her nights passed sleepless, imagining what would happen if Verne didn't choose her. If she'd make a better meal than a pet. When the time came, when she saw the hollow look in her father's eyes as the attendants led his daughter away, the last of her courage crumbled like ash.

Now, Fi returned. Still not of her own will.

A stone arch led into the courtyard. She'd never been inside, only viewed the chateau from Verne's shrine in the forest below. Fi's new daeyari – not *her* daeyari, just the one who happened to bring her here, *Antal* – led the way like a streak of vengeance, no pause for the humans who skittered out of his way like lemmings.

There wasn't a guard in sight. After a decade as a smuggler, Fi had a sixth sense for trade wardens, city patrols, bounty hunters. She was so conditioned to skirting attention, the absence of watchful eyes in the courtyard made her itch.

What use did a daeyari have for guards? What human could threaten such a beast, the fiercest mortal swords no match for immortal claws?

No, the humans scattering from Antal's path wore simple coats, work trousers, the occasional pin of an artisan – petitioners, Fi realized with a twist in her stomach. Verne kept a tighter leash on her territory than most daeyari. All edicts were enacted by her governor, yet she still made her subjects climb up here to grovel in the cold and make requests.

Not that Verne entertained such pleas in person. A steward in silver robes paled at Antal's approach, hurrying inside without a word. Fi wasn't sure if she ought to be horrified or relieved to walk beside this beast, while her more level-minded kin had the sense to run.

'Hey, real quick?' Fi hissed.

The daeyari returned a curt – and unappreciated – sigh. 'Yes?'

'Am I meant to shiver quietly at your heels? Or do you have a plan?'

'Milana claimed she was conscripted. Offered reward for her subterfuge, by an Arbiter of Verne.'

He might as well have slapped her. The cold in Fi's bones turned from sharp to numbing, a slow bloom up her spine.

'. . . What?'

'An underhanded tactic.' Antal's tail flicked. 'I must know if the Arbiter acted alone, or at Verne's request.'

No, no, no. He was wrong. Milana lied, or he'd misunderstood. Astrid wouldn't do this. Astrid wouldn't do this to *Fi*, wouldn't lure her in with smiles and reminiscence only to toss her into an exploding building. Sure, Astrid might have been working with Milana and Erik . . .

And sure, they hadn't parted on . . . the best of terms . . .

Another shiver went through her, that memory of the dark forest. Hands on her arms. But that was *ten years* ago.

'Can you be stealthy, smuggler?'

Fi squinted. 'Not really the purview of a *smuggler*, but—'

'While I entertain Verne, you'll speak to her Arbiter. Determine who's behind this.'

'*That's* your plan? That's an awful plan!'

He bared a fang. 'What's wrong with—'

The chateau's double doors opened, timber groaning on cold-strained hinges. Fi froze, arms clutched over her chest, a deeper cold carving her sternum.

Astrid stood upon the threshold.

Astrid – who looked perfectly fine, compared to Fi's feral hunch. A perfect, toothy grin as she bent for a bow.

'Welcome, Lord Antal,' she greeted warmly.

Astrid had wrung Fi's heart a thousand times before this. At seven, their first big fight, Fi accidentally broke Astrid's training crossbow, earning the silent treatment for a week before they made up over cinnamon cookies. At fourteen, Fi confessed a crush on a boy at school. It took her dense brain a month to figure out why Astrid was pouting. At eighteen, they lay alone in Fi's room, limbs tangled, Astrid's skin warm as hearthfire.

Now, Astrid guarded the entry to Verne's chateau, dressed in tight leather trousers and a sable elk coat, dark hair swept across her antlers. Her ruby eyes snapped onto Fi.

A pause. One breathless moment.

But not a word of acknowledgement.

Fi had her fill of granite looks from the daeyari who'd stolen her. Receiving the same blank glare from her oldest friend cut to the bone.

A misunderstanding. It *must* be.

Astrid addressed Antal. 'A pleasure to have you back. You wish an audience with my Lord Daeyari?'

'Please,' he commanded.

The vavriter beckoned them inside, Antal following with svelte strides, Fi stalking his heels like a grimacing poltergeist. Maybe speaking to Verne's Arbiter wasn't an awful plan, after all. Maybe Fi was, in fact, *eager* to hear Astrid explain how this was all a tasteless misunderstanding – and why Fi shouldn't shout her off a cliff.

Just nowhere near Verne.

They entered a large foyer, ceiling vaulted over rafters carved with beasts and flora, energy conduits feeding red light into eyes and petals. Half-moon windows lined the wall, filled with views of the snowy forest far below the cliffs. A long fire pit lent welcome heat, but no crackle of flame. Petrified black wood glowed with veins of red energy.

Astrid gestured them to wait at a sitting area, a low table and cushions arranged on the floor, overlooking a patio with more sweeping views of the valley. Neither Fi nor Antal sat. The moment Astrid vanished down a hall, the daeyari snapped her a withering glare.

'You know Verne's Arbiter?' he demanded.

Good on him for spotting that tension. Any creature with eyes would have been hard-pressed not to.

'That's why this is a *dumb plan*.' Fi itched at the memory of Astrid's easy smirks in Thomaskweld, that purr when she'd assured Milana that Fi was perfect for the job.

No. She wouldn't.

'You failed to mention this connection,' Antal said.

'*You* didn't tell me the plan! Instead, you zapped us here and expected me to play along. Now, if you want me to talk to Astrid, get us alone, without—'

Fi tensed at the sound of footsteps. Astrid's boot-heavy strides, accompanied by something softer: bare feet on stone, a click of claws. Void no. *Anyone* but—

'Welcome!' The voice rang clear as crystal, edges sharp enough to slice Fi's skin.

For the first time in ten years, her nightmare appeared before her in the flesh.

If Antal was a shadow, Verne was a sable-fletched arrow. Her dress clasped in a halter of silver studded by carnelian, black fabric cut lean to her figure, skirt heavy with embroidered silver and quartz that sparkled like a fall of stars. High slits up her thighs showed slashes of ash gray skin. Daeyari were slender built, scant in curves but sharp in angles of lethal muscle. Claws like obsidian. Raven hair barretted in silver, braided in three plaits between her antlers, sides loose to cascade over her shoulders.

Those scarlet eyes and black sclera had haunted Fi for a decade. They'd burned a hole through her marrow, a soul-deep wound to carry to the end of her days. Now, as Verne's gaze slid onto her once more, reunited with the hare who'd escaped so long ago . . .

Her attention flitted past. Disinterested. Unrecognizing.

A small, strangled sound escaped Fi's throat.

Verne met Antal with a fangless grin, arms extended with palms up. An unfamiliar gesture. Antal laid his arms atop hers, claws upturned. She matched his height, though her antlers branched longer: six points per side against his three, curving back then up, the black lengths coated in carvings and dangling silver bells at the tips.

They stood too close. Two predators, playing at etiquette in the form of forced proximity.

'Maelvasi je yzir kezros,' Verne said warmly. 'It's been too long, Antal.'

Her voice was sweet as rotted plums. Fi sickened at the sound of it.

How could Verne not recognize her, after Fi was dragged, screaming, to her shrine?

Or was it worse to consider Verne simply didn't care? A lioness regarding a gnat. Fi startled at the sting of it, how insignificant she might be to this immortal who'd upended her life.

'Please, sit.' Verne gestured Antal to a floor cushion. Her lighter scarlet gaze flicked back to Fi, still no recognition, but an uncomfortable pause. 'I didn't realize you'd taken an Arbiter. Astrid, would you be so kind?'

Astrid beckoned Fi aside with a magnanimous sweep of her arm, still aloof, as if humoring an unfamiliar guest. Her ruby eyes flashed hard like a wildcat.

When Fi glanced to Antal, he nudged his chin at Astrid, then returned his attention to her mistress. Hardly a pep talk.

So Fi gave herself one. *Get your shit together.* The beasts were distracted. *Verne* was distracted, and Fi needed information. She hid her racing heart behind a steel spine, no quiver as she forced her chin up.

At Astrid's gesture, Fi settled stiffly on a sofa against the wall, far enough not to intrude upon their esteemed daeyari lords. Verne settled on a floor cushion. Fi watched the beast like a wary rabbit, but wasn't deemed worthy of another glance.

'I'd offer a drink,' Verne said, light. 'But you know how hard it is to get anything good on these Planes. And what mortals pass as *liquor.*'

Antal sat across from her, cross-legged, tail wrapped around him. He wore a mask of impressive indifference, though he sat with the tension of a creature profoundly uncomfortable. Fine. Let him deal with Verne.

Astrid fell upon the sofa beside Fi, arm draped across the backrest, not looking at her.

'Astrid,' Fi whispered. 'What the fuck is going on?'

'I thought you wanted nothing to do with daeyari,' Astrid returned dryly. 'Now you show up with one? You're full of surprises, Fi. I suppose you always have been.'

Fi scowled her indignation, and a flash of guilt she couldn't afford to let surface. Not now. Antal wanted her to learn if Verne's Arbiter was involved in the Thomaskweld attack, but first, Fi needed her own answers.

'I'm not here for *him*,' Fi said. 'I just need to know—'

'Thank you for your time,' Antal said across the room. 'My apologies for visiting unannounced.'

'Unannounced?' Verne said mildly. 'Nonsense. I assume you're here because I had your governor killed?'

9

We're apparently both very bad at this

The room snapped cold as a Winter stormfront.

Fi sat up straight, a moment of . . . no, she couldn't have heard that right. Antal went as still as his metal sculpture in Thomaskweld, tail frozen in a low curl.

Merciless Void. Fi *had* heard that right.

'I expected you here yesterday,' Verne continued, tail swaying like a contented cat. 'Did it take you this long to figure it out? Or were you being polite?'

Were daeyari negotiations so different from what Fi was used to? Some immortal tactics she couldn't wrap her head around? But no. Antal looked equally stunned. So much for whittling that secret out of Verne's Arbiter.

Astrid lounged against the sofa, chillingly calm.

Unsurprised.

'It was you.' Antal dragged the word over his fangs. 'You sent your Arbiter into my territory? Attacked my capital?'

'Why deny something you're proud of?' Verne batted a hand, fingers flashing black claws. 'I wanted to be thorough – the parts of your government that mattered, at least. The governor. The mayors of the major cities. A handful of head guards and attendants. The rest will cooperate, if they're smart.' When she shrugged, bells chimed from her antlers. 'Though, honestly, I prefer a clean slate. Can always replace anyone who doesn't fall in line.'

Fi didn't recall how to breathe. She stared at Astrid, torn between seizing her friend by the throat or begging her to explain what was happening.

'You knew?' Fi hissed.

At last, Astrid glanced at her, brow raised. Her reply was an innocent, insulting, 'Hm?'

'You knew what was going to happen?' Fi's whisper felt vastly insufficient for this much ire. 'And you didn't *tell me*?'

'I offered. You're the one who didn't want to get involved in "bigger thing".'

'So you sent me into a building about to explode? I could have died!'

Astrid strummed her fingers on the backrest. Shrugged. 'I suppose you could have.'

'But why?' Antal snapped at Verne. His tail swatted his pillow. 'You'd break the peace between us? After five decades?'

Verne clicked her tongue. 'So young, Antal. Do you recall your predecessor's age, when he vacated the territory?'

'What does that matter?'

'Over a thousand. Retired to travel the far Planes, seeking Veshri's path.' Verne touched the highest tip of an antler, reverent. 'May he find wisdom, following the First Voidwalker.'

Fi had no idea what that meant – these daeyari gestures, as foreign as the pit of the Void, leaving her on crumbled footing. Though not as unsettling as Astrid. What did she mean, *I suppose you could have . . .*

'Your point?' Antal pressed.

'That overseeing a territory is an arduous task,' Verne said. 'And I know you never wanted this position to begin with.' She spread her arms, bells clinking from her antlers and dress glistening starlight, a magnanimous tone that stuck to her fangs. 'Consider this a gift. No more obligations. Agree to abdicate, and I'll take care of your territory for you.'

Fuck literally everything about that.

Permafrost cracked Fi's ribs. Antal losing ground was one thing, but she'd never considered Verne replacing him.

'That's all you have to say?' Fi shot at Astrid. And for the wretched life of her, she tried to make it bite, *tried* to hold her head up like she was made of bristles, ignoring the glass lodged in her ribs. 'I could have died? *So what?*'

'I assumed you'd be fine,' Astrid returned. 'You've always been good at running away.'

'And you didn't care what happened to me?'

'Did you care, when you left *me?*'

Fi flinched, fingernails digging into the sofa. When they'd spoken in Thomaskweld, when Astrid greeted her with a smile instead of cussing her off the Plane . . . when she sank into that kiss for even an instant . . . Fi could have believed things were fine again. Somehow, the past was in the past.

What a stupid thought. How could things ever be fine, after what Fi did?

'No,' Antal said.

Fi and Astrid snapped their glares to the pair of predators across the room.

'Antal,' Verne said, still in that lulling lilt. 'Let's be civil about this.'

Antal stood, drawing himself up to fiercer height, a snarl baring all his sharp teeth.

'No,' he said. 'I refuse to abdicate.'

Verne clicked her tongue again. 'Keep your voice down. It's unbecoming—'

'And *oyzen yzru*, if you think you'll convince me otherwise!'

At last, Verne frowned. Those pale lips tilted, and it honed every plane of her face, drawing scarlet irises into fiercer focus.

'I assumed you'd be better at this by now,' she said icily.

When Verne stood, the fabric of her dress shimmered like starlight, posture taut on the balls of her feet.

'I assumed you'd be better *from the start*.' She paced around the table, pressing unnervingly close to Antal. 'A visitor from the esteemed home Plane, an esteemed Old House?' Her words sharpened, not as honey-sweet. 'Your father must place great faith in you.'

Antal tensed, a slip in composure as raw as an open wound.

'Or he wanted to get rid of you,' Verne said, scalpel sharp. 'But let's not mince words, Antal. You never wanted to come to the Winter Plane. You've never been any good at running a territory. Haven't you languished here long enough?'

She circled him with unnerving calm, tail brushing his arm. Now, they certainly stood too close. A contest of proximity and raised hackles. Antal pressed closer, meeting her challenge.

As tensions rose, Astrid shifted to a less lax position on the sofa, keeping Verne in one eye and Fi in the other. Fi, surrounded by entirely too many red glares for any sensible person's liking, inched away.

'Astrid. We can talk about this.'

'Can we? Seems like you've been fine without talking. For ten years.'

Fi's bristles slipped like quicksilver through her fingers. A different kind of panic stabbed her stomach. Not fear, but guilt, screaming at her to flee – like she always did.

'I didn't know . . .'

'Where to find me?' Astrid gestured to the giant-ass castle. 'Fair. It's easy to miss.'

'Ok, well,' Fi snapped. 'You didn't find me either!'

'So that was my responsibility, too? I have to do everything for you?'

Of course not. Fi wasn't saying any of this right. But two daeyari were snarling a few feet away, and this room was alarmingly short on exits, and she didn't have a *weapon*—

'I've kept my territory in line for five decades.' Antal's teeth flashed wicked canines.

'Have you?' Verne's tone rose with his. 'Your mortals do whatever they please. Antal the Lax. Antal the *Generous*. The whispers are maddening.'

'You'd breach our peace on grounds of rumors?'

'Antal, dear.' Verne stepped the closest yet, snarling faces nearly touching. She hovered claws over his antlers, tracing the carvings – lingering on one section left blank. 'I have my choice of rumors about *you*.'

He swatted her arm away. 'That's no business of yours.'

They took up distance, pacing. Fi had seen wolves fight over territory, sensed the bristle of teeth about to snap. But she'd never seen immortals fight. She'd never *heard* of daeyari fighting each other, had zero desire to see what it looked like. Or who'd emerge victorious.

'Well,' Astrid said. 'Doesn't look like this is going to end nicely.'

She stood like a cat uncoiling. Slow and lithe, ruby eyes sharp with hunter's focus.

Fi lurched to grab her hand.

Call it an instinct. A weakness. Fi didn't know the right things to say, but—

'We can leave.' Fi's grip tightened, clammy against Astrid's slender fingers, callus against callus. 'While the daeyari are distracted. We can run away. We can figure this out.' One mistake didn't have to ruin them forever.

Astrid went steel stiff. Eyes wide. Her mouth parted on a shallow inhale, hand flexing within Fi's fingers. Then . . .

'What in the endless black Void makes you think I'd leave with *you*?'

The words struck past every bristle, straight to Fi's heart.

'I will not abdicate,' Antal spat at Verne in unison. 'So unless you plan to take this to the Daey Celva—'

'Why would I *ever* run away with you?' Astrid ripped her hand out of Fi's. 'After what you did?'

Her shout snared the daeyari's attention.

A toss up, for which spiked Fi's pulse worse: Astrid eviscerating her heart? Or two immortals pausing their argument to stare at her? Antal's crimson eyes darted between Fi and Astrid, a subtle furrow on his brow.

While he looked away, Verne vanished, leaving static on Fi's tongue.

Fi could pretend she was brave – while Verne was in sight. So long as she had an active total of the *creatures who could eat her* in the room at any given time. She scoured every window, every red-glowing rafter, searching for the missing beast.

So did Antal. And *there* was the predator she expected him to be: eyes scorching bright, chin raised to scent the air. His ire settled on Astrid.

'Where has your daeyari gone, vavriter?'

Despite a daeyari snarling at her, despite being outnumbered, Astrid was cast of steel. Even in their worst fights, that glare had never been so hard. It warned Fi not to run again. Not to even try.

For the daeyari, Astrid bent at the waist, a mocking bow. 'I assume she's raising the terms, Lord Antal.'

A growl rumbled the room.

Not from Antal. Somewhere outside.

When static hit Fi's tongue, Antal's attention snapped sideways. A latch. A creak. Verne pushed open the tall double-doors from the patio. Cold entered with her, the wind off the cliffs snaring what raven hair wasn't bound in braids, bells a harrowing chime upon her antlers. She stood ice-still upon her threshold.

'I'd have preferred to settle this amicably,' Verne said, her tone anything but.

Another growl joined the groaning wind. The sound shuddered through Fi, a memory of crumbling walls and dust-choked lungs. Of blood spilled over stone.

'If you refuse to abdicate,' Verne announced. 'Then by the edicts of the Daey Celva, I deem you unfit. I *claim* your territory.' Her voice lowered, slicing over teeth. 'And if you won't step down of your own volition, I will make you do it.'

Outside, claws scraped the walls of the chateau.

Fi remembered that sound. Remembered what came after.

Antal looked equally horrified. He scented the air, shuddering as he backed away from Verne.

A monstrous form dropped to the patio, landing with a screech of claws on tile.

The creature gathered itself in a hunch of tail and sickly pale skin, more a Beast than any other in the room, as much a nightmare as it had been in Thomaskweld. Just as *wrong*, the way its pantherine limbs bent at sharp angles. Twilight glinted off gnarled antlers, pooled shadows in the skeletal lines of its horse head. Another growl rumbled its throat, pupil-less red irises latching to prey, saliva thick on its teeth.

Fi froze, not daring to run. Not daring to take her gaze off the creature she'd half hoped was a nightmare.

'Veshri vavrae,' Antal breathed. 'Verne. What have you done?'

That was his best response to a fucking antlered-horse-panther dropping out of the sky?

Fi braced for the Beast to lunge. Energy leached from her arm and warmed her fingertips, hopefully enough for a shield. The creature came at the door in a single lurch, lean muscle shifting beneath its hide.

Then it bowed its head, heeling like a dog beside Verne. When the Beast tilted a blank red eye at her, she stroked a hand down its skeletal snout.

Fi made a sound she'd never recalled uttering in all her mortal life, some squeak between shock and outrage.

But Antal – his reaction was visceral. A hiss through fangs and breath visibly shallow.

'Have you ever seen one in person?' Verne cooed, hand resting upon the abomination's muzzle. 'Or did your travel years not take you far enough from the Twilit Plane? They're not uncommon, out in the fiercer parts of the Planeverse.'

'Where it's *supposed* to be.' Was that a crack in Antal's voice?

Graciously, Fi granted him this one. She'd seen this abomination rip humans to pieces, yet, somehow, Verne had it on a leash?

'Daeyari are meant to wander, as Veshri did,' Verne said. 'Yet those of you from the Twilit Plane? Too rooted. Now you venture here, a child whose antlers have barely curled, one mere Plane cluster away from home. And you think you know enough to rule a territory?'

'It doesn't belong here. Much less as a pet.'

'A pet?' Verne sneered. 'Of course not. They can be feral, yet still intelligent. Amenable, even, given proper incentive.' Her palm shifted calmly to the Beast's shoulder.

Not just calm. Verne was in control, leading every step of this duel. Fi realized too late: this wasn't a negotiation.

This was an ultimatum. And Fi was caught between two immortals.

She had no sword. No energy capsules. Not even a damn coat. Panic soured her stomach – the instincts of a hare caught in a den of carnivores. She backed toward the door.

Only to find Astrid blocking her path. While the daeyari seemed to have forgotten about the lowly mortals in their midst, Verne's Arbiter paced the foyer. Fi had known those ruby eyes for half her life, had seen a hundred emotions spark across them.

Never hatred. Not until now. Fi tried to keep her spine straight, tried to bristle back.

Except she knew, in her hollow core: she deserved every speck of Astrid's ire.

'This is long overdue' Verne levelled at Antal. 'My humans flee to you, children playing to the more spineless parent. But we know what mortals do when not dealt a strict hand. Petty things, too quick to forget what soft flesh they're made of.'

Antal flexed his claws, glaring at her, at the Beast to her side. 'Then guide your territory as you see fit. I won't —'

'Did you see how easily they turned against you?' Verne snapped. 'Even your loyal attendants, uncaring for how kind you'd been, crawling to my hand for a meager promise of power. Their lives are short. They only value immediate gains. And you've proven unfit to keep yours in line.'

Even Fi reeled at that one. She'd never had *kind* thoughts about the Lord Daeyari of Antal Territory. And she sure as shit shuddered at the thought of Verne seizing control.

But for the life of her, she didn't understand why he wasn't backing down.

Maybe she couldn't understand what a hunting field meant to a predator.

The Beast at Verne's side traced a long black tongue over its teeth. She pressed a hand to its hide to hold it steady.

'I'll only ask once more, Antal. Abdicate.'

'Never,' he spat. 'I won't let you take—'

Fi had an abomination to watch. She'd taken her eyes off Astrid.

Energy crackled as Astrid closed in. Her vavriter magic manifested as mauve light at her fingertips, Shaped along a metal cord with barbed ends. When she hurled it at Antal, the cord wrapped around his waist and locked in place. An immortal, bound. Foolhardy in most circumstances. Antal bared his teeth, but when he dug his claws beneath the binding, energy jolted up his arms, making him recoil.

When Verne lifted her hand, her Beast lunged. Antal should have teleported away.

He didn't.

He snarled at another surge of energy from the cord, down his legs, rooting him to the floor. The Beast snapped for his skull. Antal dodged, hitting the ground in a flail of limbs and tail. He sank his claws beneath the bindings again, jaw clenched against the singe of energy as he fought to free himself.

Fi was dumbfounded.

That was it? This fearsome Lord Daeyari she'd avoided for years, who'd promised to protect *her* from Verne . . . and he was already on the floor?

Fuck. Maybe Fi should help. She didn't want to help. He was a daeyari, he shouldn't need a human to—

A pulse of energy struck her back.

Fi hit the floor gasping, a hot prickle of energy thorning her skin as she contemplated cold tile beneath her fingers, a crack in one corner.

Astrid stood over her. The world narrowed until only the two of them existed.

'Astrid?' Fi spoke the name breathless. Pleading.

Fi didn't understand. She couldn't make sense of Astrid staring down at her with such spite. Where was the woman who'd woven camelias into Fi's hair while the aurora danced overhead? Those lips that had lit her skin on fire? Those nimble hands that made Fi sing as they'd laid together with nothing between them?

But those moments no longer defined her and Astrid. For the past ten years, only one had.

'What's wrong, Fi?' Astrid said. 'Trying to run away again?' The memory surfaced like a haul of rotten flotsam, drowning Fi with the numbing taste of twilight sorel. The clutch of hands on her arms. A frigid forest shrine.

'*I changed my mind!*' she'd shouted then.

'I was afraid!' Fi shouted now.

'*You* were afraid? How did you think I felt?'

With a cry of rage, Astrid raised a cross-guarded hilt. She cracked a glass capsule into the base; not her mauve energy, but daeyari scarlet. A gift from her mistress. One of the boons of being an Arbiter. As the Shaped broadsword swung down, Fi scraped energy from her forearm to form a silver shield.

Enough to save herself from losing an arm. Not enough to last. Her meager mortal energy cracked like glass against the daeyari-honed sword, sizzling Fi's fingertips.

'Why would you side with Verne?' Fi shouted.

'You never gave me a choice!'

Astrid's sword crackled scarlet, slicing Fi's shoulder. Fi hissed through the sting of burnt flesh, Shaping energy along her arm as armor, but Astrid's next swing feinted low. She'd always outshot Fi with a crossbow. Her blade skills had improved to match.

One deflection against that daeyari energy sword, and Fi's armor fizzled like a puddle on the Summer Plane. She had no backup energy capsules, only cold muscles of dwindling reserves, not half the rage of Astrid's glower.

Her Astrid, with Fi's blood flecking her hands.

And Void, didn't Fi deserve this?

A roar shook the room.

Antal skidded across the tile, sheaths of crimson magic coating claw tips to fiercer points. The cord still bound his waist. He snarled as a swipe from the Beast raked his chest, spattering Void-black blood across the floor.

A whip of bright scarlet energy caught Antal by the ankle.

'Oyzen!' he shouted as he hit the ground, claws raking stone.

Verne coiled the whip around her arm, her placid facade slipping into a sadistic grin. Fi had thought Antal looked elegant with his Shaping, but Verne's currents were immaculate, energy singing at her claws. She'd thought the immortals would be better matched, but . . .

Antal lunged for Verne's belly. After trading red-laced blows like a pair of spitting cats, Verne lashed another whip around his arm, yanking him off balance. Her Beast sprang, pinning Antal to the ground.

Oh no, he was *bad* at this.

Fi was bad at this, unarmed and unable to look at Astrid without shattering.

They needed to run. Some things never changed.

At Astrid's next swing, Fi dove and snatched a glowing scarlet energy capsule from her belt.

This is your fault, screamed in Fi's head as Astrid brought her hilt down, cracking Fi's elbow with numbing force.

Still a coward, as Fi retreated with her prize. Even through glass, the daeyari magic sank into her palm like a heartbeat from the Void. Pulsing. Foreign. A mere taste threatened to sear her. She didn't dare tap in without knowing how to wield it properly.

Instead, she hurled it at the Beast.

The glass capsule shattered on impact, erupting in a burst of energy. The Beast yowled as shards of red seared its hide, turning its sleek gait into a retreat of writhing paws. Fi had hoped to see more damage, yet the impossible creature seemed more startled than anything.

Good enough as a distraction. Antal shot a startled look between her and the Beast she'd diverted.

Then he dug at his bindings. Teeth gritted, he sawed with energy-sharpened claws, sparks of ozone singeing the air. Until, at last, the cord snapped.

That bastard was her best way out of here. And she very much wanted to be out of here. Fi ran like she always did, ran like she had from Verne's shrine ten years ago.

She tackled Antal, arms locked around his waist.

'What are you doing?' he snarled.

'Stop gawking and get us out of here!'

Across the room, the Beast shook sparks of energy from its flesh. Astrid shifted her grip on her sword, ready to charge, then stiffened, when Verne raised a hand to stop her.

The daeyari coiled her whip around slender fingers. Still calm. Still in control.

'Leave, Antal,' Verne said. 'And don't come back.'

But the last sight etched onto Fi's heart was Astrid, her

knuckles white around a sword hilt. Astrid, her ruby gaze trying to scorch Fi alive.

Astrid, standing at Verne's side – where Fi was supposed to have been.

And Fi, still a coward, left her again. This time in a lurch of black.

10

Don't make this more awkward than it has to be

They emerged from the teleport in a flail of limbs and snow.

Fi collapsed to the frozen ground, breathless and disorientated by whatever cold black sorcery immortals used to blink from one spot to another, vaguely aware of Antal sprawled nearby. Her arm throbbed where Astrid's sword had struck.

The forest lay silent. Fi's ears rang at the calm, the absence of snarls and crackling energy. For a long moment, she held still. Listened past whispering shiverpine needles for any signs of Verne. That Beast. Astrid.

Nothing followed them. A clean escape had never felt so hollow.

Fi curled into a ball in the snow. As adrenaline ebbed and the cold sank in, her breaths stayed shallow.

Astrid.

She'd left Astrid behind again.

Fi had spent ten years trying to forget that day. That harrowing walk to Verne's forest shrine. That panic that stopped her from thinking straight. That moment when her cowardice betrayed not only her.

'*I changed my mind!*' she'd shouted. '*I don't want to go. Take someone else!*'

She hadn't *wanted* Verne's attendants to take Astrid in her place.

But they did.

Astrid wasn't a Voidwalker, but vavriter were equally prized as Arbiters by their immortal kin. And the best crossbow shot in town? Astrid was fiercer. Braver. Longer lived than a human. Far more likely to survive the encounter. She'd marched to Verne's shrine with all the courage Fi lacked. And she wasn't eaten. Verne had accepted her as Arbiter, earning Astrid the gratitude of their town. The power of a daeyari at her back.

But Fi couldn't have known that would be the outcome. Not for sure.

The guilt had eaten her raw, until all she could do was run.

She ran away before she could tell Astrid she was sorry.

Fi had always meant to go back, once she was less broken. Then a year passed. Then two. Then five. Until no amount of 'sorry' would ever be good enough.

Ten years later, Fi didn't want to be that flimsy girl who ran away. She *wanted* to be fierce. She *wanted* to be unflinching. A decade as a Void smuggler had made her very good at pretending. A defense mechanism, masquerading as courage.

And Fi wasn't safe yet.

Beside her, Antal shifted in the snow.

She forced herself to sit upright. Pulled on her bristles, bottling every insecurity where they'd fermented for ten years, burning a hole in her stomach. Fi couldn't afford a slip of weakness with a predator nearby. She couldn't wallow in this cold. Void be damned, how much longer would she have to limp by without proper clothing?

Fi mustered a silver energy current to warm her hands, rubbing them for good measure, idle motions to keep her fingers busy until they stopped trembling. Conifers loomed overhead, night sky beyond, a flicker of green aurora through dark needles. No landmarks. This could be any forest on the Winter Plane.

Fi's pulse picked up again. This could be *any* forest on the Winter Plane. No telling where Antal had brought them, whether she could find a Curtain home before freezing in a ravine. Beside her, the daeyari rose into a crouch, eyes like late-night embers as he surveyed their surroundings.

He tensed, subtle.

'Don't you dare!' Fi shouted.

She tackled him before he could teleport. He snarled as they hit the ground, a writhe of muscle and lashing tail. In what might prove to be Fi's stupidest decision to date, she held on.

'Let go of me!' Antal said.

'No! You can't leave me here!'

Fi locked her legs around his waist. After failing to find handholds on shoulders or arms, she grabbed the base of his antlers. He rolled like a crocodile thrashing snow, knocking the wind from Fi's chest, but she flattened against him and held on for dear life.

Antal came to rest on his back, panting.

Fi lay atop him, breaths equally hard.

A strange smell wrinkled her nose. As Fi gathered her senses, she startled at the claw marks shredding Antal's shirt, his Void-black blood drenching the fabric – she'd never seen daeyari bleed, but that explained their grayscale complexion, no rosy hue like humans. Her cheek pressed a surprisingly warm chest. She *felt* energy simmering beneath his immortal skin, as restless as his heaving sternum.

Around them, the silence of the forest returned.

'You promised I'd be safe,' Fi said.

Antal lay silent a long moment, gaze molten on the mortal hands clutching his antlers. His chest rose and fell at an indignant tempo beneath her, tail swishing the snow.

'I misjudged,' he said.

'No *shit*. What just happened?'

'It would seem I've been deposed.'

An infuriatingly mild way to put it. Verne had orchestrated the Thomaskweld attack to overthrow him? Had a Beast at her command strong enough to fight a daeyari? In all Fi's years of benefitting from this lax territory lord, she'd never considered how his immortal neighbors viewed his policies.

And Astrid helped make this happen. That parting look was seared onto Fi's retinas, the kind of gut-twisting vision to keep her up at night. She should have seen it coming. She'd run away, abandoned Astrid with Verne.

Was it any surprise to find her friend had turned equally vicious?

Now, here was Fi, stuck in the middle of Void-knew-where with a daeyari.

She shifted her grip on his antlers. The lacquer black was slick beneath her fingers, roughened by carvings.

'You're supposed to *protect* this territory from other daeyari,' Fi accused. Whether lax or strict, all daeyari territories demanded the same human sacrifices for their services. 'So what are you going to—'

She yelped as Antal tried to buck her off. Fi barely held on as he flipped her sideways, rocks and snow digging into her shoulders. She *held on*, even as the livid daeyari pinned her back against the ground, her legs locked around his hips, hands achingly tight on his antlers.

'*Release me*,' he hissed through clamped teeth.

Pine and ozone filled Fi's lungs as the daeyari mantled over her, a cage of lean muscle, iron-taut forearms bracing her head and black claws splayed against the ground. Fangs bared above her throat. Any one of those weapons could dislodge her, if he used them.

But he didn't.

'Take me home,' Fi countered. Never squander a chance to negotiate a better price. She had no idea if the same bartering tricks worked with immortals, but they were all she knew.

Antal's eyes flared with fury. 'You have the *gall* to ask another favor of me?'

Gall seemed a misleading word. Fi had been a coward since she'd abandoned Astrid, ran away from home, let her father wither in their old house without ever returning to say goodbye. But she could act tough for difficult clients.

'You can't leave me here in the middle of nowhere,' she said. 'Take me home.'

'You've no place giving *me* orders.'

'Take me home. Then we never have to see each other again.'

'I could flay you alive!'

'Do it, then!'

They both fell silent. Antal stared at her, eyes wide with depthless black, back to his unnatural stillness. Dacyari were supposed to be sly. Vicious. Shadows who could rip a mortal throat out before their prey had time to gasp. Antal *could* kill her in a single snap of teeth.

But Fi had helped him escape Verne. He had no one else on his side.

A *bluff*? This, she could work with.

'That's what I thought.' Fi fought the quiver in her voice, trying to bluff past her own racing heart. 'Take me home.'

Antal gritted his canines. 'Release me. And I'll consider it.'

'Home first.'

His head tilted to contemplate her hands locked around his antlers. Next, the compromising position of her legs around his waist. 'You can't be serious.'

'Try me.'

Each word came with greater confidence. Fi didn't let herself think of this as a game between prey and predator. A contest of stubbornness, she stood better chance at.

Antal let out half a growl, half a beleaguered mutter of, '*Veshri's fucking teeth* . . .'

He stood.

A cumbersome prospect, with Fi wrapped around his front like a burr. She stiffened when he braced an arm around her back – startled at how easily he lifted her. His only sway came from her grip on his antlers, tipping his head to an awkward angle. As a show of good faith, she tucked her hands around the back of his neck.

Fi repressed a shudder, pressed so close to a flesh-eating beast.

Antal's exhale brushed her cheek, eyes smoldering crimson beneath dark lashes. She tried not to think of the fangs behind his scowl. Her stomach squirmed at the heat off his chest, the firm wrap of his arm around her waist, steadying her against him.

A predator, made to hunt hares like her. Only civil to get what he wanted.

'I need directions,' he said.

Fi mulled the words, alert for another diversion. 'What do you mean?'

'I can't just *appear* wherever I wish. I can only teleport to places I've been before, or where I can see.'

There came a small reassurance amidst this trainwreck: the knowledge that daeyari had *some* limits to their abilities.

'Two miles northeast of Nyskya,' she said. 'On the ridgeline. There's a cabin in a clearing below the summit.'

He nodded. She held her breath.

The world snapped black then back again, leaving Fi colder and dizzier with each teleport. Mortal flesh wasn't made for this kind of transit, but her misery eased at a welcome sight: a familiar snowy ridge, the village of Nyskya glowing like gold dust on the valley below. Fi tipped her chin to a clearing in the firs.

'Down there,' she said.

One more time. The quick jumps passed easier, yet Fi's stomach rioted as they lurched to a halt. They emerged in a clearing, quiet in the moonlight.

At the sight of her cottage, she toppled off Antal, eager for the crunch of familiar snow beneath her boots, the shelter of familiar conifers. Three days away from home, yet Fi might as well have stress-aged a decade.

Within the dark trunks, a shadow shifted, horse-shaped.

Fi made a pathetic, high-pitched sound.

She ran to Aisinay as the horse trotted forward, finned ears perked and a snort in greeting. Fi hugged her scaled neck. Aisinay nibbled her shoulder.

'You beautiful girl! I'm so sorry I left you.' Fortunate, that Fi had left Aisinay safe on a Shard while the building exploded. And that Void horses were as good at navigating Curtains as Fi was. When she didn't return, Aisinay must have wandered home for a more comfortable wait.

The horse snorted, ears flat as she pulled away and pranced back into the trees.

Reluctantly, Fi faced the source of her agitation.

Antal stood like a wraith, clothes and antlers pitch-dark in the meager moonlight. His red eyes held Fi like a hand around her throat.

'Thank you,' she said, backing toward her cottage. 'This has been the opposite of fun in every way. I say we call it even.'

A growl rumbled his chest as he stepped toward her. Sleek movements. Arms tensing as he flexed his claws. 'Our business isn't finished.'

Fi was on her porch. Hand on the door. 'Well, that's strange. Because I think our business is *absolutely* finished.'

'Fionamara—'

She dove inside and slammed the door on his face.

Fuck. What good would that do, against a teleporting immortal?

Back braced against the wall, Fi surveyed the dark interior of the cottage, cataloging weapons. A couple of energy capsules sat on her bedside table. Some knives in the kitchen. Nothing suited for heavy combat, much less against a daeyari.

She'd have to improvise. Fi snatched an energy capsule then waited for Antal to appear.

Nothing happened.

No red eyes by her bathtub. No footsteps on her porch. Fi glanced out a window, but spied no sight of her unwanted visitor.

Nothing happened, as she backed away from the door.

Nothing, as she circled her dining table, within reach of a kitchen knife.

A moan of wind against her shingles made Fi jump clear off the floor, slumping against her counter and hand pressed to her racing heart as she hissed an emphatic, 'Shit, shit, *shit* . . .'

This was going to be a long night, wasn't it?

II

As long as you're still here

When Fi eventually collapsed into bed, she never expected to fall asleep. Alarming, how several consecutive brushes with death could exhaust a person. She woke in the morning to panic, jolting upright amidst her nest of rabbit and aurorabeast fur, scanning her home for red eyes.

A single room formed the interior, wooden panel walls and exposed rafters, no bother for divisions. Fi lived alone, and she had a strict policy of keeping intimate dalliances to hotel rooms or secluded bar corners, preserving the anonymity of her safe house.

Now, she'd broken that rule for a daeyari, of all things.

Yet she found no intruder lurking on her sofa, nor the dining table with legs of gnarled ironwood. Nothing amiss upon her slate kitchen counter, the cabinets closed, pots of herbs tidy beneath a growing light that had lost its charge in her absence. Her cedar bathtub sat empty. A screen stood beside it, pine panels carved into trees against a paper sky. Fi crept across the room, bare feet padding cold wood and fur rugs, wary as she peered behind the barrier.

Nothing.

She touched a metal plate on the wall. Energy leached from her forearm into a copper conduit, turning on the glass light panels beneath the rafters.

Still nothing.

Fi hissed as her shoulder throbbed.

She wrestled out of the crimson sweater she'd donned the night before, revealing a tattoo sleeve on her right arm, a matching swath down her left hip, flowers of several dozen varieties. The gash from Astrid's sword clipped petals of a honeysuckle on her arm. Cauterized, thanks to the energy blade. Still angry red with inflammation. Her torso ached from collarbone to core, muscles fatigued from too much energy draw. An empty stomach didn't help.

Fi Shaped energy from her healthier left bicep, accepting a muscle cramp as payment to feed the current into her injury, fuel to speed her body's natural healing. With steady supplement, the slash could heal in a week.

Astrid did this to her. That wound would take longer to heal.

What other lows had the Arbiter sunk to in the decade they'd been separated? Leading sacrifices to Verne's shrine? Silencing dissent to her Lord Daeyari's rule? Astrid might be descended from daeyari, but she grew up alongside humans, ought to empathize with her fellow hares rather than sharpening the teeth of a lion.

If Fi had become an Arbiter, would she have done any better?

She had more immediate danger to settle, embers of fight or flight rekindling in her belly. Fi smeared numbing twilight sorel ointment onto her arm, fighting nausea at the familiar spiced scent. She donned her sweater and a wool coat. Stashed an energy capsule in a pocket. Mourned her sword, lost somewhere in Thomaskweld.

Warily, Fi peeked out her door, floorboards squeaking beneath slippers.

Fresh snow lay upon the clearing, pillowy upon the boughs of the firs and the shingles of her cottage. The purple dawn, normally calming, threatened beasts lurking in shadows. Fi appraised the distant trill of a lark, the *slick* then *thump* of snow sliding off a burdened limb. Nothing amiss. Void have mercy, maybe her rotten luck finally ran its course, and that wretched daeyari left during the night. Wrapped in her coat, she stepped onto her porch.

Contrary to the horrific folktales Fi's father told to keep his rebellious child inside the house at night, she found no red eyes among the trees waiting to devour her.

Only a suspicious mound of snow in her yard. Two black antlers poking out.

She shrieked as the shape stirred, a small avalanche uncovering pale skin and dark clothes. The daeyari had been coiled like a cat, blanketed by snowfall. He surveyed the clearing with slow blinks, eyes the smolder of old coals.

'*The fuck*,' Fi said. 'Did you *sleep* out here?'

His slitted gaze snapped onto her. 'Where else?'

A shake of antlers freed the final bits of snow, frozen crystals catching on his hair and tumbling down bare forearms. He appeared unphased.

'But *why?*' Fi groaned, as much to the pitiless Planeverse as to him. He'd dragged her to a rival immortal, had their asses handed to them, barely escaped Verne's nightmare creature with their lives. What more could he want?

Antal rose with feline grace, all svelte limbs and silent footfalls as he stalked the yard. Onto her porch. Fi backed away, but the hunter yielded no space, pushing until her back struck the wall and ozone teased her nose.

'I told you, Fionamara.' He spoke with the rumble of a storm. Flat ice in moonlight. 'Our business isn't finished. You still owe me a debt.'

Fi held excruciatingly still, wary of bolting like a startled rabbit and *very* distracted by fangs lurking behind parted lips. His clean jaw tilted without compromise. He loomed over her like a midwinter chill, the most ageless thing she'd ever faced, the depthless Void framing his eyes and hands curled with claws that could rip her throat out.

'So . . .' she breathed, 'you let me slam a door in your face?'

He huffed, but while Fi's breath fogged against the morning chill, his left nothing. 'Would you prefer I be *less* gracious?'

She appraised the warning snap of his tail. Despite their harrowing escape the night before, his wounds had healed, pale skin showing through ripped cloth and crusted black blood. That blood had no copper tang. He smelled of . . . emptiness. A night sky in winter.

Cowering hadn't gotten Fi anywhere. And for all this daeyari's honed exterior, he seemed a *little* less imposing after watching Verne drag him across the floor.

In their standoff, Antal and Verne had bristled against each other, a contest of power as two daeyari pressed their personal space. Just as Antal pressed Fi's now. In any Plane, any culture, no strategy gifted a greater edge than speaking the local dialect.

So Fi forced her chin up. She pushed *closer*, the space between them dwindling to inches, his ice and ozone scent heady on every inhale.

The daeyari yielded no ground, only a furrow across his brow.

'Graciously,' she said, 'you look like shit.'

He growled so deep, Fi assumed the next five seconds would involve her heart ripped from her chest. Claws, teeth – either tool would suit the task.

Instead, he turned away, tail nearly lashing her face as he stepped off the porch.

Fi spent a moment remembering how to breathe. Another, hissing several curses at the Void and the fickle immortals it spawned. Once her thoughts achieved a semblance of collection, she lurched forward, eyeing the daeyari as he crossed the clearing toward the river.

Aisinay waded in the current, silver scales shimmering as she snapped at trout for breakfast. The Void horse perked her ears, greeting the immortal with an intrigued snort. Useless guard horse hadn't even warned Fi about their lingering visitor. Antal acknowledged the animal with a wary glance.

Fi's mouth dropped open when he stepped, unflinching, into the water.

Wider still, as he gripped his tattered shirt, yanking it off his shoulders with a wince, fabric unsticking from skin.

The Season-Locked Planes had endless stories of these creatures: how they once stalked humans from shadowed treetops, how easily energy-laced claws sliced mortal arteries. Nothing that made daeyari seem so . . . *tangible* as the sight before her: his scowling mouth, the flush of cold on his cheeks. He undressed to the waist, his shoulders and back all stark lines of lethal muscle, arms taut, a lean form built to pursue and carve. High-waisted trousers framed narrow hips. A belt of fabric buttoned over the root of his tail, long and swaying in the current.

Antal plunged beneath the water then rose with a sigh, nimble fingers sweeping over the shaved sides of his head, combing between antlers to dislodge blood from his longer hair.

Against all better judgment, Fi drifted closer, arms folded in her coat, gaping like a toad.

'Isn't that . . . *cold?*' she asked. In this Plane's perpetual winter, a single toe in that creek would leave her screaming.

The daeyari cut her a look dry enough to crack bone. Scalding as boiled oil.

'Yes,' he said. 'It is.'

He dragged his shirt through the water then held it up, scowling at the ruined fabric. Clearly, immortal flesh was woven as differently as the stories said, to not succumb to hypothermia. But clearly, he still *noticed* the cold, if his grumbling was any indicator.

Fi bit her Void-damned tongue. She couldn't. She *shouldn't*.

'Come inside,' she blurted.

The daeyari cast her a barbed look. 'What?'

'Come inside. I have a bath. As long as you're still here . . . you might as well use it.'

His tail flicked like a panther appraising a trap – or calculating how fast his prey could flee. Fi hoped for the former as the daeyari climbed out of the creek, frigid water dripping down his bare torso, ice-drenched trousers molded to his thighs.

This was a stupid idea. A reckless idea. Fi's thoughts blared chastisement as the daeyari trailed her, wary, back to her cottage. She held the door open as he stalked across the porch.

He paused on the threshold, scowling at every detail from floor to rafters – at Fi, keeping her distance, as she would for any feral animal that stumbled through her door. He padded inside on the balls of his feet, that inhuman rise to his ankle, soundless as a cat.

Maybe she could still salvage this. Maybe a show of hospitality would urge the beast on his way – since ignoring him hadn't worked. Fi touched the heater beside the tub, Shaping energy out of the capsule in her pocket instead of tired muscle, warming the water cistern until it came out of the tap steaming. She guessed the pomegranate bubble bath on the shelf would push her luck.

Fi sidled to her kitchen, facing away to offer privacy. A stagnant moment passed before she heard the whisper of fabric hitting the floor. The lap of water in the tub.

A sigh of appeasement.

A stupid idea. What choice did Fi have? She steadied her elbows against the counter. Eyed the knife hilts in the kitchen block. *No.* That would be even stupider.

'You shouldn't turn your back on a daeyari,' came a low voice behind her.

What a fucking prick.

Fi faced him, leant against the counter, pushing every inch of space between them. They'd confronted Verne together out of convenience. That didn't mean she could trust this lethal creature.

'You'd rather look someone in the eye while peeling their skin off?' she returned, honey-sharp.

Antal reclined in the tub, arms draping the edges, claws strumming cedar.

'You have some sharp teeth of your own,' he muttered.

Hard to say, whether his tone was insult or compliment.

He returned to untangling his hair, easier amidst swaths of steam. For a creature of ice and emptiness, he sank into the heat with surprising relish. Fi would have preferred he stay rigid. The way his shoulders unknotted, the stream of his fingers through water-slick hair felt too intimate for the space they'd been forced to share.

She busied herself with the herbs on her counter, touching the charging panel to light the growing lamp, enough energy to last the day. Her furnace had greater demands. She popped the energy capsule into a slot. A clamping pin completed the circuit, sending a warming current through metal coils.

As she worked, Fi kept the daeyari in sight.

His eyes glowed calmer now, irises dimmed to old-coal crimson. His ears pulled to a slight taper. The carvings on his antlers stood out in lighter blues and greens than the surface

black, depictions of flowers and auroras and strange sigils divided into three bands. Beyond those anomalies? The rest of him
looked chillingly like a normal man, from the lean slope of his
shoulders to the soft curves of his cheeks.

Fi resisted the urge to peek at what *other* ways he resembled a
man. Obviously, daeyari had cocks. They did when they'd been
flesh and blood, or else there'd be no vavriter. They did still, after
returning from the Void in their immortal forms. Her father
avoided telling *those* kinds of stories, though even as Fi grew,
tales of tangled mortals and immortals circulated as rumors at
best. She had to wonder how many survived the teeth.

'Why didn't you barge in here last night?' Fi asked when she
could bear the quiet no longer. She made sure to sound stern.
No hint of the dread she'd stomached on his behalf.

'Had I done so, would you have treated me this amicably?'
Antal picked at his claws. 'Cast me as a beast all you wish. I've
walked the Planes for two and a half centuries, enough to guess
when patience will be more effective than pressure.'

Fi didn't like that. Not one bit.

'And,' Antal said, lower, 'I wanted to make sure Verne didn't
find you here.'

Fi liked that even *less*. Making her sound more indebted to
him, as if he cared whether she was ripped to pieces in the
night. 'What more do you want from me?'

'I want to know what part you played in this.'

'I *told* you. Milana hired me. I didn't know the plan.'

'So you claimed, Fionamara.' Her name lashed off his tongue.
'Yet you come from Verne's territory. You know her Arbiter.'

'I *knew* her Arbiter.' Fi slouched against her counter, shoulder
aching. 'Thomaskweld was the first time I spoke to Astrid in
ten years. I agreed to help her for old times' sake.' A grimace.
'And apparently, she *used me* for old times' sake.'

'That's not very helpful.' If Antal noticed the angst in her confession, his flat tone said nothing of it.

'Look. I'm sorry for whatever part I played in this. Truly, I am. But I move contraband. Wine for rich snobs, energy capsules for rural settlements. Not *blowing up buildings*. Or do immortals not believe in coincidences?'

Antal huffed. 'Only the rotten kind.'

He sank into the water until his nose rested above the surface, antlers hooked against the tub to keep afloat. The fiercest predator across a hundred Planes. A hunter made to stalk from trees and chase down human prey . . . *sulking* in her bathtub?

Fi decided a sulking daeyari as preferable to an *angry* daeyari, though both seemed perilous.

When Fi and her brother were little, one of their father's bedtime tales told of a great hunter tracking pinecats through a forest thick as the Void. As the man rested by his fire one night, his keen gaze spotted red eyes in the trees. Instead of reaching for his crossbow, the hunter called out, 'The night is cold. Join me by my fire.' Intrigued by such bold prey, the daeyari approached. Sat across from him. They talked deep into the night, trading stories of their most impressive quarry.

Then, the daeyari ate him.

Fi heard variations on the ending. Some storytellers spun more optimistic conclusions, the daeyari impressed by a fellow hunter and his hospitality, enough to part amicably. Her father preferred the original ending. *Don't expect a beast to change its nature*, the moral went.

The question remained: would Fi be rewarded for playing along? Or was she the witless prey, foolish to think she could earn civility from a predator?

'That Beast.' Fi spoke low. Testing. 'The one Verne summoned. That's what I saw in Thomaskweld.'

Antal slitted one eye open. Not to look at her. He studied the steam floating off the bath.

'What was it?' Fi asked.

'Why do you ask.' His reply came so flat, it was hardly a question.

'Why do I *ask*? It nearly killed me in Thomaskweld. It nearly killed *both of us* at Verne's chateau. You took one look at it and shit yourself.'

Antal growled. 'I did nothing of the sort.'

'What was it?'

He bared his teeth at the rafters.

'Holy shit.' Fi straightened. 'Is this . . . a *secret*?'

'I didn't say that.'

'Damn me to the endless Void. It *is* a secret?'

'You enjoy hearing yourself talk far too much.'

'You useless immortal. *Tell me.*'

'That Beast is . . .' He gritted his teeth. 'A daeyari.'

Fi blinked.

Sometimes, people lied to her about where their cargo came from. Sometimes, they told her stupid things, like the latest trick their pet anteater could perform. Or unbelievable things, like how to walk through the Void. All to say: few statements had ever tripped Fi up as much as whatever nonsense Antal just spouted.

'I'm sorry,' she said. 'I don't think I understand.'

He slunk into the water with a world-weary sigh, as if all of this – all of *her* – was terribly inconvenient. 'Daeyari don't die of age. That's our gift of immortality. But we can be slain, and there in lies our curse. When a daeyari falls, their energy doesn't pass to the Afterplane. It lingers within the Void, eventually rematerializing upon the Planes.'

Fi blinked again. Hard. 'Literally. You're telling me that Beast is *literally* a daeyari?'

'Yes.'

'Daeyari *reincarnate?*' Each word brewed more hysterical. 'As *that?*'

'The greater the number of rematerializations, the cruder the form that returns.'

'*Cruder forms?* That creature with a fucking horse skull and scrambling on four paws used to be . . .' Fi gestured over Antal's decidedly – and she couldn't believe she was thinking this – less monstrous appearance.

'A different form of daeyari. Derived. But they never come back . . . right. With each return, more sense slips away. Until only hunger remains.' His words seethed distaste. Claws gouged the soft wood of her tub.

Fi's own nails dug into her arm. Daeyari could become even graver beasts. Daeyari could *die* in the first place, though she'd never heard such a feat in any of her father's folktales. What could kill a daeyari? *Another* daeyari, maybe? No weapon of mortal make.

'If that's true,' she said, 'why have I never seen one? Never *heard* of one?'

'That Beast shouldn't be here. They're kept far away from the Twilit Plane.'

The daeyari's Plane of origin, the closest world beyond Fi's Season-Locked cluster. If she were doomed to transform into a feral Beast upon death, she wouldn't be keen on the creatures lurking close to home, either. Endless Planes and Shards lay beyond the world she knew, yet she'd never dipped into that terrifying unknown.

Even less reason to, if other Planes lurked with reincarnated immortals.

'So what are you going to do?' Fi asked. Demanded, more like. This seemed a suitably dire scenario for demands.

Antal slouched, gloomy as a wet cat. 'I don't know.'

'What do you mean you *don't know*. What's your plan to get rid of Verne and take your territory back?'

'I don't know.'

'She tried to kill you!'

He scoffed. 'Killing me wasn't Verne's intention. Daeyari don't plot each other's demise lightly. She made her point that I'm outmatched, enough to assure herself I won't return.'

'And you're going to accept that? You don't have some grand scheme to march in and take her head?'

'Even if I *could* kill her, I'd rather not have another derived beast after me in a century when she rematerializes.'

Fi had to admit, that was a shitty caveat to revenge: the most lethal race in the Shattered Planes, locked into nonlethal bickering for fear of horrid transformation.

'So what about allies?' Surely, this immortal, this creature who'd walked the Planes for centuries, must know someone who could help. 'You don't have an Arbiter?'

'Correct,' Antal muttered.

'What about attendants? Other than Milana and Erik?'

'All dead or missing. I checked.'

Fucking *ouch*. Bitch or not, Verne had been thorough.

The territories had no armies. Local guards kept the peace, but the daeyari settled larger conflicts. That was *supposed* to be an advantage of their rule. Not so helpful, when daeyari were the ones fighting.

'You and Verne kept mentioning the . . . Daey . . . Celva?'

Antal sank deeper into the water. 'Our administrative body, on the Twilit Plane.'

'So could they—?'

'No. Verne declared me unfit. And I retreated. By daeyari law, her claim to the territory is valid.'

'But Verne *also* said you're from an'—Fi made air quotes—
'*esteemed Old House*. Does that mean someone you could ask
for—'

A single look from Antal silenced her. No words. No twitch
of his tail draped over the tub. Two slicing red irises warned
her not to speak another word.

So daeyari could be as touchy as humans when it came to
family.

Not that Fi had any idea what a daeyari *family* looked like.
A pair of proud parents watching their toddler teethe on bones?
She didn't know what the daeyari Plane looked like. Didn't
know they could die. Didn't know they returned as monstros-
ities.

Fi knew nothing of these creatures, except that they were
meant to be feared.

And she wanted nothing to do with this one.

'What about your mortal government?' she said. 'Verne can't
replace them with people loyal to her overnight.'

Antal unwound from his withering glare. 'Depends how long
she's been planning. She's been distant since I took power.'

'Fifty years?' Fi gaped. 'You think Verne's been planning this
for *fifty years?*'

'A short time,' he muttered. 'Relatively.'

Thomaskweld would be no help. With half the capitol
collapsed, the governor dead, the bureaucracy would be in
shambles. And whoever remained? Every government was
bound to obey the daeyari in charge. No human in their right
mind would back an ousted immortal – she elected to disregard,
for the moment, what that said about *her*.

Fi buried her face in her hands. She needed breakfast. Or a
drink. 'Verne *did* hand your ass to you. I thought daeyari were
supposed to be powerful Shapers?'

Antal straightened, water shifting with the indignant swish of his tail. 'My apologies. Daeyari don't *pop* into existence with flawless knowledge of Shaping.'

'I'm just saying, it would help.'

'I'm still a better Shaper than you.'

'I've got an energy sword to argue that.'

'Do you?' Antal swept a clawed hand around her home. 'Where is it?'

Fi pushed off the counter, bristling to full height, haggard with unruly curls of Void-and-rainbow hair because *someone* was using her bath before she'd had a chance. Her sword, taken from her in Thomaskweld by his traitorous attendants. A snarling retort sizzled her tongue.

She stopped herself, realizing how much her guard had slipped.

Of course a daeyari would know how to lull his prey, how to disarm Fi by lounging in her tub with water slicking the smooth plane of his chest.

She shut her mouth and weighed her miserable options.

'I need to go to town.' Fi pulled a fur-lined hat over her hair, heaved on her snow boots. 'Enjoy my amenities, *Lord Daeyari*. Someone needs to warn the common folk that a man-eating tyrant and her pet man-eating Beast have claimed this territory.'

She braced for rebuttal, but Antal fell still again. Guarded again. Back to that statue of marble skin and obsidian claws.

'It would be best if you didn't tell anyone I was here,' he said. 'For both of us.'

'I'm not an idiot. I don't want Verne tearing this place apart looking for you.' Fi yanked the door open. A gust of cold hit her cheeks. 'Don't fight with Aisinay while I'm gone.'

Antal's eyes narrowed. 'What does that mean?'

'My horse.'

A deeper furrow. 'You named your Void horse . . . *Icy Neigh?*'

'A brilliant pun, I know.'

Fi left with confident strides, an act crafted to convince this daeyari she was unflustered. Unafraid. Unintimidated by the visitor in her home and whatever fallout lay ahead.

All of it, lies. Beneath false bravado, Fi's stomach knotted as if she walked the edge of the Void, one misstep from tumbling into oblivion.

And she had no idea which direction would tip her in.

They drew their sword against the daeyari, who came not from this world, matching the beast's claws blow for blow. Until at last, they plunged their blade into the daeyari's heart.

But the immortal didn't fall. It laughed.

'What need have I for a heart?' it said. 'Not the way you mortals do.'

Then the daeyari ripped the human's heart from their chest. Ripped their foolish name from any who'd remember it.

So let this be a lesson, a fate to avoid.
Futile to fight the beasts born of the Void.

— Excerpt from a folktale, Autumn Plane, *The Folly of the Nameless Warrior*

12

What have you done?

For the last seven years, Nyskya had been Fi's refuge.

Whether work had her fleeing trade wardens on the Autumn Plane, stowed away on a Summer train past cerulean seasides, drenched in a warm Spring rain while contraband bottles clacked in her cart, she could always retreat here to the cold and quiet. She'd hide away in her cottage, enjoying hot bubble baths and the music of her gramophone, pestering Boden until her next job.

Out here, problems like capitol explosions and daeyari coups could seem blissfully distant, buffered by miles of forest and snow. Distant, but not inescapable. All these years, Antal *could* have come to Nyskya to press the settlement beneath a firmer claw. Nothing stood in Verne's way of doing so.

And it was all Fi's fault.

She could weave excuses about lying clients, a friend's betrayal manipulating her into business she should have no part in. But Fi put the bomb in that building. She'd let her guilt over Astrid make her complacent. Who knew how many bodies lay under the rubble of the capitol? What fate awaited Nyskya, under Verne's rule?

Maybe Boden would know what to do – if he could forgive Fi for screwing up again.

She stepped off the Plane through the Curtain near her cottage, crossed the distorted distance of a Shard, out another Curtain that placed her at the outskirts of the village. The streets were drowsy in the early hour, muffled by fresh powder. With hair tucked into her hat and face obscured by the white fur collar of her coat, Fi slunk past buildings, over boot tracks and sled trails heading into the forest, coming at last to the ranch south of town. A herd of aurorabeasts browsed the pasture, hooves rooting for forage beneath the snow, green energy glowing along their backs.

Daeyari had brought the animals to the Season-Locked Planes, bred as a high-energy food source to sustain the immortals if their preferred prey ever ran scarce. Humans found other uses for the beasts: meat and milk and fur, valuable in endless Winter.

But mostly, Boden enjoyed their company. Fi found Nyskya's mayor amongst his herd, tromping through snow to haul hay into feeding troughs.

He stilled when he spotted her, ice crusting his beard, exhale billowing into steam.

Boden broke into a run.

Fi cracked at the sight. Aurorabeasts snorted as he passed, his strides laboring against the crust of old snow on the field, closing the distance to grab her in a rib-crushing hug. There were normal, sibling hugs. Then there were Boden's worry hugs, that sixth sense he had whenever Fi acted too recklessly. Normally, she'd tease him for the sentiment.

This time, Fi hugged back, distressed to find herself no less desperate for the anchor. His coat smelled of aurorabeasts. His messy hair, of the old wood musk and hearth ash from their family home. The only one left who did.

'*Fi*,' he breathed, heavy with relief.

'*Bodie*,' she returned, muffled by the shoulder he'd smushed her face into.

He held her at arm's length, worry creasing his thick brows. Shadows framing his eyes. 'We've gotten telegrams from Thomaskweld. People say the capitol building collapsed. Some kind of *explosion*. And when you didn't come back . . . are you all right?'

Curse him for piecing this together before a word left her mouth. Curse him for caring so damn much. Which would be worse: watching Verne cut Boden down as an example against rebellious magistrates? Or Fi abandoning him again so she wouldn't have to witness the aftermath? Either would shatter her.

'I could use breakfast.' She forced a smile. 'Kashvi's tavern?'

No hiding the strain in her voice, or her uncharacteristic lack of proper eyeliner. Boden chewed his lip but didn't push. For now.

Still, Fi endured an onslaught of worried glances as they retrieved a crate of aurorabeast milk from his home, then set off into the village. They had the paths to themselves, flanked by houses with steep roofs and dark windows, wreaths of purple peatberry brightening several doors.

Boden's bottles clinked as they walked. Across town, a pack of sled dogs barked.

Then a *fitz*. A *clang*.

The tavern sat at Nyskya's center, the general store on one side of the common square, general socializing on the other. Though opening time wouldn't come for another couple of hours, light glowed within metal-paned windows.

A woman stood in the yard. She wore a red wool coat lined in gray fur, a single dangling earring with a pendant of glowing silver glass, her skin a warm brown more common on sunny

Planes. Her build was sturdy as a wolverine. She planted her boots and aimed a crossbow. Fired.

A silver energy bolt flashed across the yard, clanging into a metal target.

Spotting visitors, she rested her crossbow on one broad shoulder. A sleek copper piece, powered by a silver energy capsule in the stock, heat from the mechanisms snagging as steam in her short black bob. Her family moved from Summer to Winter two generations ago, seeking prospects as weaponsmiths. She stayed because she liked the calm of long nights. Fi could relate.

'Well, well.' She tilted a brow. 'If it isn't Nyskya's two biggest miscreants.'

Boden nodded. 'Morning, Kashvi.'

'Mayor,' she returned, respectful with a tease of familiarity. For Fi, only the tease. 'What's got you looking like frizzed shit?'

Fi debated tackling her to the snow. Boden intervened with a hand on her shoulder.

'We're hoping for breakfast,' he said. 'If it's not too early.'

Kashvi flexed stiff fingers against her crossbow, dark eyes narrowed to prospecting slits. 'What's it worth to you?'

Boden held up the milk bottles.

She grinned. 'I suppose that will do.'

They stepped inside to a swell of warmth, a dark tavern room. Dim light fought through windows fogged with condensation, framed in energy conduits to fight the infringing cold. Brighter light slanted out of the hall, glinting off copper tabletops and stools, timber floor and walls accented in brushed tin, a steel bar counter decorated with aurora stained glass. Kashvi reached for a wall panel, conduits connecting to orb lamps in the rafters.

Her arm went rigid.

The lights flickered on then off again as she hunched, hand clenched, breaths shallowing to gasps. Fi and Boden shared a sympathetic glance but said nothing. When he stepped forward to turn on the light for her, Kashvi swatted his hand and took the crate of milk.

'Shit in the Void,' she rasped around strained vocal cords. 'I used to shoot targets all morning. Now, I can barely Shape three bolts without a flare up. Oh, stop with the pitiful looks before I throw your asses back in the snow. You know it will pass.'

When she waved them to a table, an argent sheen glinted on her hand, an internal inflammation, veining her skin like quicksilver.

As part of the pact centuries ago, humans had learned more complex energy Shaping from daeyari. But mortals were made of different flesh, more easily damaged when pulling stronger currents. Fi's overuse manifested as fatigued muscles, a cold stomach, usually fixed by food and sleep. She'd only pushed too far a couple of times, hard lessons learned through energy burns, plus a nerve in her pinky that prickled at random times.

Humans with silver sickness suffered steeper penalties. A disease of the immune system. No cure. Heightened sensitivity to energy made the body attack itself, the corrosion worst while Shaping, affecting muscles in the arms. Legs. Lungs.

Kashvi was fortunate, the spasms had never struck her heart.

As with most daeyari gifts, boon came with burden.

Kashvi passed it off with several slow, steadying breaths to relax her diaphragm. A cautious stretch of stiff fingers. Then, 'Iliha! We have visitors.'

While she toted milk and crossbow into the hall, Fi and Boden settled at a table. A record player sat dark in the corner, glass case and steel frame brushed by overhead lights. A flock of automaton birds perched on copper rails above the bar, lively with clacking beaks during open hours, currently dormant amidst shelves of liquor bottles.

Too quiet. Enough to hear each groan of wind over the roof.

What Fi wouldn't give for a break in the silence, a reprieve from Boden's dissecting stare. She couldn't fault him for it. They'd both honed perception from a young age: the crimped edge of their mother's mouth, less and less subtle leading up to the day she left. The hunch in their father's work-worn back that preceded him reaching for a liquor bottle.

The overhead lights flickered. This time, no fault of Kashvi's. Fi was used to fluctuating power, having to charge everything in her cottage, but Nyskya's conduit grid ought to be more stable. Boden's curse spurred her concern.

'What happened to those daeyari energy chips?' she said. 'They should last *months*.'

'They will. Just some conduits acting up. We've been working on repairs.'

Boden didn't speak with the confidence Fi wanted to hear. Nyskya needed power. They *needed* self-sufficiency. If they had to turn to Thomaskweld for replacement parts now, with a new daeyari seizing control . . . Fi fidgeted with her coat sleeves.

Boden tracked every move. 'Fi. What's wrong? You seem—'

Voices rose from the kitchen. Steps erupted down the hall. A wisp of a woman stormed into the room, eyes like seafoam, pale skinned with a bun of straw-blonde hair. She swept aside the ties of her apron, hitched her sleeves then cracked a wooden spoon across Fi's arm.

'You've got some nerve, Fionamara Kolbeck! Waltzing in here after stealing my soup!'

Fi hissed, hands raised in defense. 'Calm your tits, Iliha. I left an energy capsule!'

'Can't even bother saying hello. Here and gone like a thief!'

'I was on a job!'

Kashvi followed with two breakfast plates. 'Careful, Fi. Never spite the woman who makes the food.' She leaned down to Iliha's slighter stature, pressing a kiss to her wife's scowling cheek. 'Don't fret yourself, dove. I'll handle the vagabonds.'

Fi had been called worse. Her nose wrinkled at a stale smell – coming from *her*. First, she'd break the news, then she could worry about reclaiming her bathtub from a daeyari.

Iliha stalked across the room, muttering like an irate shrew as she brought on the rest of the lights, turned up the furnace, snapped the automaton birds to life. They fluttered awake with a click of gears, heads swiveling with copper crests.

Kashvi dropped into a chair, boots propped on the table. 'Wondered when you'd pop up, Fi. Boden says you were in Thomaskweld?'

Fi nodded. Her ceramic plate held a flaky pastry, oozing cream cheese and honey glaze, almonds sliced on top. Despite feeling ravenous, she struggled to keep a bite down.

If Boden was the administrative head of Nyskya, Kashvi was its heart, curating every drunken rivalry and sliver of gossip that passed through her doors. Best to tell them both the foul news in one go.

'You should've seen this man.' Kashvi jerked a thumb at Boden. 'Moping in here every morning, wondering when you'd be back.'

'For good reason.' Boden poked his pastry. 'Everything we've heard from Thomaskweld is piecemeal. And Fi's usually good about—'

'But you know what I said?' Kashvi grinned. 'That Fi? She's like a cockroach. Always crawls her way out of things.'

From the bar, Iliha muttered agreement. Kashvi smirked at her contribution, absently tapping a finger to her single earring, a dangling glass capsule glowing silver – a match to the pendant Iliha wore around her neck, both their energy combined as part of the marriage pact. A dandelion wisp wedded to a lioness, both with ferocious temperaments.

'Thanks, Kashvi.' Fi flicked a pastry flake off her finger. 'You must be the only person on all four Season-Locked Planes who uses cockroach as a *compliment.*'

'Well?' Kashvi said. 'What's the news?'

Iliha circled the table with mugs. Kashvi accepted her tea with a brush of Iliha's thumb, then a huff when Iliha nudged her boots off the table. Boden took his coffee with a nod. Fi's coffee was frothed to the rim, tan with cream and sugar. She clutched the ceramic. Breathed.

Maybe they'd understand. Maybe she could fix this.

'It *was* a bomb, Bodie,' Fi said in a hush. 'All those energy capsules. The clients asked me to move them into the capitol building, then . . .'

Overhead, energy lights hummed. A flock of automaton birds ratcheted and clicked. But the people: silent. Iliha cast wide eyes from the bar. Boden paused with crumbs in his beard.

The table creaked as Kashvi crashed forward on her elbows. 'Fuck me in the Void. That was *you?*'

You.

The accusation sliced deep. *You* did this. *You're* to blame, like always.

'Not just me,' Fi argued.

'You were there for the explosion?' Boden's pastry lay forgotten. His brow, worry-creased tenfold. 'Are you all right?'

'I—'

'What happened?' Kashvi demanded.

'Give her a moment,' Boden countered.

'A *moment*, Boden?' Kashvi slammed a hand to the table. 'Your sister blew up the capitol building in a daeyari's city. Who would *do* that?'

'They were working for Verne.'

Another silence. Iliha crossed the room like a wraith, settling a hand on the back of Kashvi's chair. Three pairs of eyes locked on Fi.

'Verne?' Kashvi hissed. 'The *daeyari*, Verne?'

'The governor's dead.' Fi forced words through a sandpaper throat. 'And Antal . . . removed. Verne plans to claim this territory for herself.'

More silence. Fi had to keep talking, had to rid herself of every wretched detail before they ate her insides. 'I don't know how much you've heard, whether Verne has announced her intentions yet. I wanted to warn you—'

Kashvi's chair legs scraped as she stood. 'Warn us *what*? That you might have doomed us all?' She ran a hand through her hair, dark strands damp with melted ice. 'Void have mercy, Fi. What have you done?'

'Kashvi,' Boden chided. 'There's no need—'

'Smuggling capsules into a government building?' Kashvi continued. 'What did you *think* they were for? A birthday party?'

'I didn't know!' Fi clawed her hands against the table. Kashvi was right. Every damn word was right, and Fi hadn't thought this through, and she couldn't roll over like a coward again. She was supposed to be better now. 'I did what they hired me for. To earn a shit ton of energy chips for *this* village.'

'Energy chips? What good will those do us, when a daeyari comes . . .'

Kashvi hunched into a rasping breath, silver-veined hands bracing the table.

Iliha was at her side in an instant, urging Kashvi back into her seat, gentle hands nudging the tea mug closer. Kashvi brushed a tender hand down Iliha's arm then breathed in the steam.

Boden stared at his hands. At Fi.

His incessant worry, she could stomach. *This* struck every fear she'd had about telling him – that hard look that told Fi *he* was the older sibling. *He* was the responsible one holding their lives together. And she was the batty, reality-skipping sister who'd unleashed a man-eating monster upon their home.

'I'm glad you aren't hurt,' Boden said. 'Are you *sure*, Fi? About Verne being behind this?'

'I *saw* her, Bodie.' Fi's voice came out too small. 'Barely got away alive.'

'This is absolute *shit*,' Kashvi groaned.

Boden slumped in his chair. 'I'll . . . try to get more information. Reach out to contacts in Thomaskweld. For now, we should be cautious. Iliha? Could you send a telegram to Yvette and their metalworkers, suggest they delay any trips they might have planned to the capital?'

Iliha appraised her wife. Only after a nod from Kashvi and another press of the mug into her hands did Iliha glide away into the hall.

A temporary solution. Nyskya could avoid sourcing supplies from Thomaskweld, for now. They shouldn't have to. They *should* be able to ask their capital city for aide, without fear of repercussions.

'What are we going to do?' Fi asked. Something to fix this. Anything to not have ruined another home.

'Nyskya will ride it out,' Boden said. 'We're remote enough, we can let politics run their course in Thomaskweld. No need to panic until we see where the pieces land.'

'I came here to get away from daeyari,' Kashvi rasped. 'We

all did. That man-eating monster in charge of this territory was bad enough. Now we have to survive a new one?'

Fi frowned at the description of Antal. She shouldn't have. Just . . . strange, to reconcile 'man-eating monster' with the gloomy cat slumped in her bathtub.

'What else do you want us to do?' Boden asked. 'Write a petition?'

'I've got a crossbow,' Kashvi said. 'If one of those bastards tries to come here.'

'We aren't fighting a daeyari, Kashvi. I'm not sure we even *can*.'

'Energy bolt through the skull would be a good start.'

Fi pictured Verne coiling a whip of red energy, a Beast at her side. She pictured Antal, how easily he'd dispatched his traitorous attendants, how swiftly he'd healed wounds that would have leveled a human.

'I don't think that's a good idea,' Fi said.

Kashvi scoffed. 'And you're a fountain of good ideas today? When did you get back? Did anyone follow you?'

Fi bit her lip. Void help her if they knew she'd invited a daeyari to her cottage.

'Give her a rest,' Boden said.

'*We'll* be lucky to get any rest!' Kashvi snapped. 'We should be prepared for—'

She hunched into another rasping breath.

This spasm didn't let up.

Fi and Boden waited several seconds before Kashvi gave in. She marched to the front door, letting in a spike of cold as she stepped outside for fresh air.

Only Fi and Boden remained.

Funny, how it always came to that.

'I didn't mean it,' Fi said. 'I swear on the endless Void, Bodie,

I didn't know this would happen.' Kashvi's derision, Fi could bear. She *needed* Boden to understand.

He rubbed a hand over his brow. 'Don't let Kashvi get to you. You know she's . . . had a rough past with daeyari.'

'So have we.'

He sighed. 'So have we.'

Fi played with the crumbs on her plate. As kids, Boden had been the one who kept a straight face when she skinned her knees on river rocks, calmly cleaning the scrapes while she wallowed and sniffed. He'd nearly punched a boy from school who'd tried to kiss Fi without asking – *nearly*, but only because Fi punched the boy first.

But Boden was also the one she'd catch caring for sparrows who'd gotten their wings caught in rat traps. Who'd hardly spoken for a month after their mother left.

'We left to get away from Verne,' she said. 'If she comes here . . . what do we do?'

'We wait. See what happens.'

'We can't wait for everything, Bodie.'

'Sometimes, it's the best we can do. Maybe things won't be as bad as you think.'

Fi ground her teeth. 'Easy for you to say. You didn't almost get eaten by her.'

'She wouldn't have.'

'You don't know that. You *didn't* know that. I remember you yelling, Bodie. Trying to stop them from taking me. Unlike . . .'

Unlike their father. Fi's memories flashed with night-shrouded forest, attendants leading her away from home. The hollow look in her father's eyes – yet he'd let them take her anyway. His own daughter.

'He didn't *want* them to take you.' Boden turned defensive. For *who*?

'Of course he wanted them to take me. *He* proposed it. *He* wanted the prestige of an Arbiter daughter.' Always telling her how daeyari prized Voidwalkers – a prize for him to hand over. Fi was his ticket to respect, recognition, even while he wasted his days barely sober enough to hold down a job, barely bringing home enough energy capsules to keep their furnace running.

'He believed you'd be ok,' Boden said, 'that Verne would spare you.'

'He didn't know.'

'And then you left. So call it even.'

Fi's nails raked the copper tabletop, finding every dent and scrape of old beer mugs. She reached for her coat of barbs, her bristles and bravado. All desperate defenses to hide the fragile creature she kept inside. That terrified girl who ran from home ten years ago, her father shouting behind her that she'd be back – she'd *better* come back, if she cared about her family.

'You weren't there with him in the end.' Boden kept his voice low, eyes on his breakfast. 'He asked about you, when his mind started going. Every Void-damned day, he asked about you. *Where's my little girl? Doesn't she want her bedtime story?*'

Fi's nails pressed close to cracking. 'I couldn't stay in that place.'

'I know. You don't have to . . .' Another sigh. 'Forget it. That doesn't matter now.'

Of course it mattered.

Fi hadn't just left Astrid to Verne ten years ago. Hadn't just left their father to die.

She'd left Boden. Left her only brother to care for their ailing father alone, to build his funeral pyre when he passed. They'd found their way back together after that – Boden had found her flitting across Planes like kelp ripped from its roots, had convinced her to settle in Nyskya. For seven years, she'd helped him build a home here. Seven years, hoping to redeem herself with the only family she had left.

Only to drop this latest burden on him.

He looked so tired. His eyes, shadowed by worry for his reckless sister. His shoulders, weighed by the news she'd brought. She hadn't even told him all of it.

'I saw Astrid,' Fi said. 'In Thomaskweld.'

Boden straightened. Not the ghost-stricken pale Fi had suffered upon reuniting with her oldest phantom, but still surprised. Still cautious.

'Astrid?' he said.

'She's helping Verne. Astrid is the reason I—'

The door slammed open. Kashvi stormed inside, a billow of cold at her back.

'Kashvi?' Boden stood in alarm. 'What are you—'

Fi snarled as Kashvi grabbed her arm.

'You!' Kashvi pointed at Boden. 'Stay. You'—she pulled Fi out of her chair—'with me.'

Subtle as a charging aurorabeast. But Kashvi's voice didn't hit that warning low without reason. Fi followed into a hall that smelled of timber and yeast, iced air warring against the heat of Iliha's cooking. Kashvi shoved her into the kitchen. After catching herself against a wire cooling rack full of scones, Fi swiveled with a scowl, but her assailant had already vanished. She peered down a narrow sightline into the common room as Kashvi took Fi's chair at the table, hunched over the plate of breakfast crumbs.

The tavern door opened.

13

What's a little death threat between friends

Fi would have been perfectly pleased to see a rabid moose barge inside. Perhaps a scurry of vengeful squirrels. Anything, – *anyone* – but this ghost she'd evaded for a decade, now set to haunt the rest of her days.

Astrid surveyed the tavern with snow dusting her sable elk coat, frost glistening the low rise of her antlers. Something colder crystallized her ruby eyes.

Fi ducked out of sight in the kitchen, pressed against the cabinets like the small, craven creature she was. She heard chair legs scrape. Boden's inhale.

'Astrid?' he exclaimed. A talent. He crafted the breathless hush of seeing a long-lost friend, no hint of her name on his tongue moments before.

'Boden,' Astrid returned. Flat as a stripped screw. They'd never been close. Fi, drawn to Astrid like a hand to a flame, Boden hovering nearby lest she burn herself.

'Void take me, it's been . . . seven years? Kashvi! This is Astrid. An old friend.'

'You may have mentioned her a time or two,' Kashvi replied dryly.

'Not enough, then.' Boden laughed. 'Come in, Astrid. It's good to see—'

'Where's Fi?' Astrid said.

No pleasantries. No preamble. Just Fi's past come to hunt her down.

'Fi?' Boden said. 'We haven't spoken in all this time, and *that's* who you want to talk about?'

'We can skip the dancing, Boden. You've always been too good at it, and I don't have the time. I know Fi passes through here. Where is she?'

Fi flinched at soft footsteps. Iliha leaned over a counter, energy crossbow ready at her shoulder. She shot Fi a questioning look. Four on one? They could overpower Astrid.

And send a beacon to Verne. Fi couldn't risk bringing the daeyari's attention to Nyskya.

In the other room, Boden sighed. 'Fi's . . . hard to pin down. She shows up now and then, when she needs something. Haven't heard from her in months.'

'You're talking about that useless sister of yours?' Kashvi scoffed. 'Good riddance.'

In the silence, Fi pictured Astrid's razor cheekbones. That stubborn clamp of her mouth.

'Dreadful, that woman,' Boden said. 'Surely, we can do better. How are you, Astrid? Kashvi and I were just finishing breakfast, but could we get you something?'

'I'm not here for *breakfast*.' Astrid hissed. 'Not for your nostalgia, either.' Boots creaked floorboards, pacing like a wildcat. 'I bear a message on behalf of my Lord Daeyari, Verne. Antal has abdicated.'

A pause. A fitting crack in Boden's voice, act or not. 'Abdicated?'

'Verne has claimed her right to this territory. She expects a sacrifice from Nyskya by the end of the year. As a show of good will.'

Fi's heart dropped clear through her stomach. Ice in all her bones. She'd come here worried that she'd bring ruin to Nyskya.

But even she hadn't expected it this swiftly.

'A *sacrifice?*' Boden said. 'Nyskya hasn't sent a sacrifice in years.'

'You're overdue, then.'

'We ask for no daeyari aid.'

'You're part of this territory. Verne's territory. She'll have you behave as such.'

'Astrid. Can't we talk about this? As friends? The people here ask so little—'

'*Friends?*' Astrid boomed. 'Since when, Boden? Since we were *children?* Since you abandoned our town as a lost cause, like your sister did?'

'Astrid—'

'You've spent seven years hiding in the woods, letting others pay their price to the daeyari. Send your sacrifice. Or tell me where Fi is, and I'll consider putting in a good word.'

Footsteps moved to the door. Fi barely heard them above the flail of her heart.

'Astrid, please,' Boden said. 'There must be another way—'

'There's no *other way* with daeyari.' Then, lower. More vicious. 'You don't know what I've had to do. *I* stayed behind. *I* kept our town safe.'

Boden might have kept arguing.

Then the power went out.

A momentary darkness. The lights flickered back on in swift order, conduits humming, but the damage was done. Nyskya was in no position to negotiate.

A long silence stretched.

Then, so quiet that Fi barely overheard, 'It's not worth

fighting them, Boden. Send your sacrifice. Get the help you need. Don't make this harder than it needs to be.'

The door slammed shut.

Fi shriveled into a ball on the floor, head in her hands. Just a job. Just a few energy chips. Just a debt to an old friend she thought she could repay too easily.

Iliha slipped out the back door, knuckles white on her cross-bow stock. Fi didn't move for several minutes. When at last Boden appeared in the kitchen doorway, she crumbled at one look from those shadow-hung eyes.

Her barbs, useless against someone who'd seen her as a sniveling girl with scraped knees, who knew that was all she would ever be.

'I'm sorry, Bodie,' Fi whispered.

'You're part of Nyskya. No one's taking you.' He ran a hand through his hair, fingers tangling on frost-worn knots. 'Can you get home without being seen?'

Fi nodded. A jaunt through a Curtain, and she'd be fine.

'Kashvi will make sure Astrid leaves,' Boden said. 'Lay low for a few days. I'll send along any news.'

Lay low. Don't get in the way. Don't make this worse than you already have. Every moment she sat here made Fi feel smaller.

Boden continued, 'Anything else I should put an ear out for?'

Fi raked through the chaos of the last few days, searching for threads to grasp.

'Cardigan.'

Boden's brow lifted.

'He gave me the energy capsules,' Fi said. 'Then ran like a coward's ass when we got jumped by trade wardens. Not sure if he'd know Verne's plans.' But that was all she had.

Boden hummed. 'Cardigan . . . swear I've heard that name. Somewhere in the energy conduit market? I'll track him down.'

Another weight on his shoulders.

Fi snuck out the back door. Her heart raced all the way to the Curtain, but Nyskya's streets stayed sleepy. She saw no one.

Astrid was hunting her. So long as Fi fled, Nyskya wouldn't know peace.

She reached her cottage on heavy footfalls, kicked her boots clean on the porch. Fi paused at the door to collect herself. Astrid wasn't the only one who'd followed her here.

But inside, her home was empty.

Lights glowed from the rafters, the furnace pumping heat from its energy capsule. The tub had been drained. Water droplets spattered the floor, but beyond that, nothing out of place. Only a scent of ozone on the air.

Good riddance. If Fi never saw that useless daeyari again, it would be too soon.

She poured herself a scalding bath and sank into pomegranate-scented bubbles, willing them to swallow her. Smother her. She soaked until her fingers shriveled and the lather dwindled to tepid skim.

For hundreds of years, all of the Winter Plane had been carved into daeyari territories.

All of Summer, Spring, and Autumn.

And beyond these Season-Locked Planes, dozens more. Hundreds more. Worlds Fi had never seen, but she knew they looked the same, more carnivorous immortals to appease. From their origin on the Twilit Plane, the daeyari had spread their hunting grounds throughout the Planeverse. How far would Fi have to run, to truly escape?

She didn't want to run. Not this time. Nyskya was her home,

Boden's home, and she wouldn't let Verne take it from them.
Resolution burned into the marrow of her sternum.

Fi would fix this.

She just . . . didn't know how.

14

When life brings you an immortal carnivore

Fi idled for a week. She spent every molasses-creeping second working on a plan.

Normally, she could burn a month after a job with nothing but bubble baths and chocolate pastries. Ice fishing with Aisinay. A weekend on the Summer Plane enjoying live music on a humid canal patio, dancing until the world reduced to starlight and the perfect clarinet solo.

Instead, she cocooned on her sofa and guzzled coffee while snow clogged her windows, waiting for automaton birds to flutter up every couple of days. All Boden's messages read the same: *Nothing new. Stay put.*

Fi read between the lines. He wanted her out of the way while he fixed her mess.

How could she fix this, short of *fighting a daeyari*? An immortal creature too swift and strong for any mere human to vanquish? Fi might as well throw herself onto a pike and deny Astrid the satisfaction.

Further annoyance came when her gramophone developed a stutter. The internal conduits had to be rewired, but after several static shocks and a trainload of curses, she got her music playing with only occasional static. She put on a record from her last Summer Plane sojourn: a seaside city of colorful porticos and bands on every other street corner, air muggy as soup and the best damn crayfish she'd ever eaten. The bass line beat like a second heart. And there came that horn, nimble as a breeze.

Fi couldn't *fight* a daeyari. Could Verne be distracted? Coerced? Tricked to fall into a very deep hole? No, that wouldn't work, only because daeyari teleportation was bullshit.

Her foot tapped to the music as she spread a pile of empty glass capsules onto her table.

In the oldest stories of the Season-Locked Planes, mortals Shaped using only their internal energy. Then daeyari taught them more demanding forms of Shaping, energy conduits and external tools. Over time, humans developed tougher skin, though flesh could still burn from pulling too strong a current. Their muscles built stronger reserves, but charging energy capsules provided useful external storage. Plus, she could charge them in her downtime while she was well fed and rested, fuel for her furnace or future emergencies.

Not a hole to trap a daeyari. Some other binding, then? Astrid had trapped Antal with that energy cord . . . only for him to break loose minutes later.

Fi pressed her thumbs to the capsule. The current had to come slow, otherwise the glass would shatter. Astrid had taught her that. They'd holed up in her room one night, Astrid grinning like a wildcat with a bag of empty capsules she'd swiped from her father at the energy plant. They'd had no idea what they were doing, blew Astrid's bed in half and got grounded for a month.

Fi's fingers ached as she pinched the copper electrodes, cold shivering down her forearms as she Shaped silver energy out of muscle and into the orb.

Traps were probably a dead end. What if Fi poisoned Verne's water? Did carnivorous Void immortals *drink* water?

A knock pounded her door. Fi swore as energy seared her fingertips, nearly cracking the capsule.

The knock sounded again. Intentionally few people knew where Fi lived. Only one of them would bother hiking all the way up here to harass her. *Fucking Bodie.* After shaking her hands out, she marched across the room, starved for company but equally set on giving her useless brother a piece of her mind for stringing her along all week.

'About time.' Fi yanked the door open. 'Can't even bother to warn me when . . .'

It wasn't Boden who greeted her.

It was a daeyari. One specific daeyari she'd begged the Void to never see again, perched on her porch with a mild frown and tail flicking.

Fi sprang into defense. She shifted onto the balls of fuzzy-socked feet, brandishing a half-charged energy capsule ready to hurl.

'What do *you* want?' she said. 'You won't eat me that easily, fiend!'

Antal – former Lord Dacyari of this territory, immortal spawn of the Void between realities – swept a dry look over her flannel pajamas. The drift of music from inside. Last, and least impressed of all, the energy capsule leveled at his head.

'That seems unnecessary,' he said.

'Does it? Then why in the endless black Void are you—'

Fi grunted as he tossed a bag to her chest.

'These belong to you, I assume?'

Why was he here. *Why* was he *here*? Naïve, to hope she'd endured the last of him, that her sour-milk luck would allow her to focus on a singular crisis at one time. Fi dug into the bag, keeping the daeyari in one eye as—

Her fingers closed around something cool. Metal. Fi yanked

out the hilt of an energy sword. *Her* energy sword, side nicked from a crossbow bolt in a sagebrush town on the Spring Plane. She dug deeper, a thrill at the sight of her energy capsules, her transport stone, and . . . bless the Void, her silviamesh. She nuzzled the light, scaled fabric to her cheek.

'Milana had them in her quarters,' Antal said.

Fi tore her attention away from his gifts. 'You've been in Thomaskweld?'

'As much as I dare. Verne's derived daeyari prowls the cliffs, though she tolerated me long enough to retrieve my clothes. So kind of her.'

He sneered at his dark blue shirt, sleeves rolled to the elbows. He had, obnoxiously, neglected to fasten the top three buttons. Why did a daeyari need to waltz around with half his chest showing? His hair tousled blue-black between his antlers. High-waisted trousers clung snug to his thighs. Without the formalwear, the embroidered cuffs or iridescent fabric, he looked unsettlingly like a man out for a stroll in Thomaskweld.

Where he belonged.

How could Fi sleep, knowing a daeyari might appear in her home at any time? What if he decided to pop in for a midnight snack?

Though . . . he didn't *have* to return her things.

'What's the catch, daeyari?'

Antal's nostrils flared, a muttered, 'Veshri grant me patience.' Then, louder, 'You don't know much about immortals.'

Accurate. The nebulousness of this creature, combined with the sheer weight of her recent fuck-ups, did, in fact, make Fi want to curl into a ball. *He* didn't need to know that.

'And?'

'Small favors, spread across a long life, aren't to be overlooked.

Any sensible daeyari knows that.' He stepped off her porch. 'Consider your debt repaid.'

'Repaid?'

'I asked you to help uncover this plot. We did so. Our business is finished.'

'But what about . . . wait, wait, *wait!*'

For a moment, Fi had something akin to an out-of-body experience, observing in horror as she once again moved toward a daeyari of her own volition, hand raised, as if swiping at air could stop him from teleporting away. A daeyari like Verne would have flayed her on the spot.

But *this* daeyari paused, slitted red eyes and black sclera cast over a shoulder.

Maybe she ought to be more afraid of him. The squirm of adrenaline in her stomach certainly thought so. And yet as she pictured this lethal beast moping in her bathtub, recalled his fluster when she'd stood her ground before, her demands came easier.

'Verne's taken Thomaskweld?' Fi asked. Boden's messages said as much, but hearing the news in person stung. 'What are you going to do?'

'Strange. It seems as if you've asked me that exact question, several times already.'

Smartass. 'You've had a week to think about it.'

He fell quiet.

'Surely, you plan to do *something*,' Fi said. 'I came to this territory to get away from Verne. You aren't great, but at least you're better than her.'

Antal muttered something else, foreign syllables Fi couldn't translate.

'I'll speak with Tyvo,' he said.

The name rolled off his black tongue like split ice. Verne,

Antal's neighbor to the east, was a tyrant. Tyvo, his neighbor to the north, was . . . a predator, straight out of the folktales. Reclusive. Unyielding.

'How will that help?' Fi asked.

'Daeyari territories are strict agreements. Verne has over-stepped hers. My other neighbor might be agreeable to keeping her in line.'

This was the best idea Fi had heard all week. Better than Boden's waiting game. Better than Kashvi itching to point her crossbow at a daeyari skull. Better than any of her half-baked plans. Let the immortals settle their feud, get Antal back in power, Verne gone. Then things could return to normal. Best case, Antal resumed his policy of ignoring Nyskya.

He might be more likely to do so if Fi helped.

She didn't want to. By the endless Void, she'd rather shut her eyes and hope for someone better than her to sort this mess. But it was *her* mess.

'Do you want help?' she asked.

The daeyari's head tilted. He surveyed her from tip to toe, the baffled part of his mouth slowly sinking to a frown.

'From *you*?' he said.

'Yes, from me. I'm more useful with an energy sword.'

'Your debt is repaid.'

'I heard you. And I'm offering to help.'

'I thought you were eager to be rid of me?'

'I'm eager to get you back where you belong.' She pointed over the trees in, vaguely, the direction of Thomaskweld. 'But the last time I saw you confront another daeyari? Things didn't go well. So do you want backup, or not?'

Antal stared at her so long, it felt like an intimidation tactic. His facial expressions came and went like river ice, jaw tight and focus fierce enough to send a chill down her neck. The tail, though. It swayed behind him, shifting from sharp arcs into something smoother. Contemplative. Fi played the only card she had: chin up, no hint of surrender.

The act came easier with strangers, those who didn't know her well enough to spot the lie.

'If you wish,' he conceded.

Fi's heart skipped with triumph. And a sliver of terror. 'When?'

'Now. I suppose.'

'*Now?*' She considered her flannel pajamas, the tangled hair she'd forgotten to brush that morning. 'Wait here. Don't leave without me.'

His eyes were arrows through her ribs. Not for the first time, Fi struggled to interpret his scowl as seething annoyance . . . or bafflement.

'And risk your ire, Fionamara?' he said, flat. 'I would never.'

If Fi were feeling bold, she might admit some satisfaction in flustering this daeyari. A life raft, when otherwise she'd be drowning.

She ducked inside. If she had to confront another immortal, she'd do it armed this time. Her silviamesh bodysuit slipped on like a second skin, slate gray fabric with purple lining to accent her curves. She donned her boots, a wool coat, transport stone in her pocket. And her sword. Fi kissed the hilt then clipped it to her belt.

A kind gesture, returning these to her. Fi had to be cautious thinking such things. The daeyari had fangs, even if they weren't eager for her throat at the moment.

Testament to her frazzled state, she nearly left the house like this. On further thought, she swung by her mirror to apply a quick eyeshadow and dark lipstick. Wrapped her Void-and-rainbow hair around energy-heated fingers to refresh the curls.

When she stepped outside, cold pressed her silviamesh-coated calves.

Aisinay had wandered from the trees to inspect their visitor. Antal held glacially still as the Void horse smelled him, tail low by his ankles. Aisinay nibbled his collar.

Traitor.

Antal broke his narrowed gaze from the horse, turning an even narrower look over Fi, slowing a moment too long over the curves hugged by her bodysuit. A crack in his stone facade.

'Did you . . . curl your hair?' he accused.

'Thanks for noticing. Never underestimate the importance of looking fierce. Not that *you* have to worry, born with claws at the ready.'

Something tight crossed his face, before snapping back to impassive.

He offered a clawed hand. Fi recoiled.

'Do we *have* to teleport?' she complained. 'I'm a Voidwalker, we can use Curtains.'

Antal huffed. 'You're not a Voidwalker. A silly mortal name. Your version is more a . . . Shardwalker.'

Fi tipped an indignant brow. 'I walk on Shards. Through the Void. That's literally Voidwalking.'

'You walk on Shards. That's *literally* Shardwalking. You don't walk through the Void.'

'No one can walk *through* the Void.'

'Veshri can.'

Fi's brow migrated higher.

'Veshri,' Antal said. 'The first immortal daeyari. The First Voidwalker, who wove a new body out of—'

'So Voidwalking is, what, the daeyari term for teleporting?'

Antal huffed harder. 'Teleporting and Voidwalking aren't the same.'

176

Some really annoying immortal semantics was all Fi heard. His hand stayed extended.

If Fi helped this daeyari reclaim his territory, how was she any different than Astrid serving Verne? This option, at least, would hurt fewer people. That had to count for something.

Fi grabbed his palm, cool against her hand, that restrained brush of claws as he held her tight.

Then the world lurched into black.

15

Too close again

The cold hit her first.

Nyskya endured standard cold, biting to cheeks and numbing to fingers, kept at bay by a thick coat. The cold here came sharper. Ravenous. It sliced Fi's layers and crystallized in her lungs. She hunched to keep her core warm.

Antal breathed deep of the frigid air, sleeves still rolled to expose his lean forearms. He set off walking through calf-deep snow.

Fi followed. She followed a daeyari, to meet another daeyari, and that was the most ridiculous string of words her brain had ever assembled.

Get Tyvo's help. Get Antal back in Thomaskweld. She could manage that, for Nyskya.

Black shiverpines loomed overhead, no sound but the crunch of ice beneath Fi's boots and Antal's upsettingly bare feet. Through needles, she spotted a waxing moon, some dagger-crisp stars in the dusk.

'Where are we?' Fi asked.

'Tyvo Territory.'

Void stop her from slapping him. 'Why did you bring us to the middle of nowhere?'

'Daeyari prefer solitude.' Antal picked his way over a fallen trunk, agile as a panther. 'Most don't live in their cities. Tyvo keeps his residence here, in the forest.'

'Sure,' Fi said through chattering teeth. 'Couldn't you teleport us *to* his residence?'

'It's not polite to appear in someone's home without invitation, Fionamara. Among daeyari, walking is a show of respect.'

'How far?'

'A half mile should be more than gracious.'

Fi wrinkled her nose, half in annoyance, half to keep the blood flowing. She Shaped warm energy out of her abdomen, into aching extremities.

One of her father's bedtime stories, *The Selfish Herder*, spoke of a human lost in the woods with his aurorabeasts. When a daeyari found him, the man pleaded for his life, promising a meal of an aurorabeast *and* his neighbor should he escape the forest alive. The daeyari agreed. Guided him out of the trees. But when the man's worried neighbor appeared to welcome him home, the daeyari dragged the herdsman into the forest screaming, leaving the neighbor with not only his life, but a bolstered aurorabeast herd.

Admittedly, the story didn't exactly match Fi's situation. She struggled to recall *any* cautionary tale pertinent to her predicament, beyond the recurring moral of, 'never trust a daeyari'. And for the record, she didn't. She kept her guard up so high it itched her nose.

'Why haven't you eaten me yet?' Fi asked.

Antal's tail flicked. 'Why are you so fixated on that?'

'It's a *reasonable* thing to fixate on. No one wants to be eaten.'

'Devouring mortals is far from my only priority.'

'Then why'd you demand a sacrifice after the capitol explosion?'

Antal cut her a sharp look. Fi couldn't back down, couldn't reveal an inch of vulnerable flesh to this beast.

'Milana and Erik were chatting about it,' she said. 'While dragging me to my doom.'

'Hmm . . .' He turned up a snow-drifted slope with infuriating ease. Fi huffed to keep up. 'Daeyari are strongest when well fed. I anticipated trouble. I needed the best edge I could.'

'So you would have been *more* useless against Verne, if you hadn't eaten?'

Antal clamped his teeth. Sighed. 'I *am* sorry. Milana shouldn't have brought you against your will.'

Fi gave a bitter laugh.

She shouldn't have. This daeyari had fangs, even if he'd yet to use them. But she had to stand her ground. It felt *good* to stand her ground against one of these wretched immortals she'd feared for a lifetime. This one betrayed a sliver of restraint, and she latched on like a leech.

'Thanks,' Fi said. 'Do you apologize to all your meals?'

'That's unfair. To both of us.'

'*Both of us?*' Fi tripped on a submerged root. Righted herself. Glowered. 'Please. Tell me all about how feasting on humans is inconvenient for you.'

'Daeyari are carnivorous. We only take what we need to sustain ourselves. You wouldn't fault a wolf for hunting a deer.'

Fi went rigid. She shouldn't fight with him, shouldn't sow more conflict with the man-eater who knew where she lived, but—

'But . . .' Antal said slowly. 'The wolf has no choice. The deer doesn't laugh, doesn't write music. This has long been a dilemma for some daeyari, or the peace between our races wouldn't exist. Vavriter wouldn't exist.'

'*Peace.*' Fi scoffed. 'The pact gave your sheep a nicer looking pen, was all.'

His tone sharpened. 'I *need* to eat—'

'So eat something else!' Fi shouted before common sense stopped her. But Void, she was so damn *tired* of these creatures and the prey-animal coil in her stomach. 'Aurorabeasts were bred to feed daeyari. Better than culling humans.'

'What a *brilliant* idea. Why have I never thought of that?' Antal rolled his eyes, the gesture entirely too mortal. Another fissure in his ice-carved exterior.

'What's wrong with it, smartass?'

'Daeyari must consume flesh infused with energy. Only humans offer sufficient quantities of both. Aurorabeasts can supplement our diet, not sustain us indefinitely.'

'So I should feel *bad* for you? There's no better option than dragging humans to your shrine?'

'They come willingly.'

'No one dies willingly, Antal. They come because someone has to. Because their villages and families need protection you only sell for blood.'

Fi's blood, almost. Nyskya's blood, if she couldn't fix this.

His teeth clenched, a flash of canines and sharp premolars. 'This was the system given to me. Daeyari society has lasted this long thanks to tactful division of resources.'

'Resources? Is that all we are to you?'

'*No. You aren't.*'

He stopped in front of her. Fi's breath billowed steam. In this wretched cold, even Antal's exhale blushed into fog. Static pricked her tongue, energy simmering beneath his skin, too close.

Always too close.

'Would you rather I treat you like a beast, Fionamara?' His

words skated a growl, low enough to rumble her arteries. 'I could flay your skin instead of trading words. Enjoy the crack of your marrow. Would that be more *amenable* to your conception of me?'

Fi didn't want to be this close to him, that swell of ozone in her nose. The heat of his Void-rimmed eyes. She held her ground.

'How am I supposed to know your plans, daeyari? Maybe you want to keep me around, a convenient meal for later.'

Antal scoffed. 'I could find less nagging dinner options.'

'You'd be so lucky.'

Fi couldn't say where the courage came to shove him. Like two drunks arguing in a tavern alley. She'd survived brawls with only the occasional concussion or fractured finger.

This time she never made contact.

Too fast, Antal caught her wrists.

He pinned her arms between them, pulling her chest flush to his.

Fi's fluster snapped to a cold sweat. Antal held her against him, faces level and far too close, not an inch to breathe without sharing the ice-and-ozone air. Fangs, one lunge away from her throat. That was how all her father's stories ended.

What was she thinking, yelling at a daeyari? Once again, Fi braced for teeth.

Once again, his claws gripped alarmingly soft, even as he restrained her.

'Why are you here?' Antal asked. And that cut deeper than fangs.

'Your attendants dragged me into this.'

Fi tried to pull away, but he locked her arms against his chest, alarmingly strong despite his lean frame. A shock of heat in the cold, too close to escape the flint of his glare. There came that flutter in her stomach, that rabbit's urge to run even when she knew it was the stupidest option.

'I gave you an out,' Antal said. 'If you find me so unpalatable.'

'How unpalatable I find you has nothing to do with it.'

'Then why are you here?'

'Because this is my fault!'

Bravado wasn't Fi's only weapon. Those little surprises, the things the daeyari didn't expect her to say seemed equally effective at breaking his guard. His grip slackened. Not enough for Fi to escape when she yanked against his claws. She pressed her assault.

'Is that what you want me to say, daeyari?' she spat into the scant space between them. 'It's. My. Fucking. Fault. *I* got a stupid, mushy heart for Astrid. *I* transported that bomb. *I* was as useless as you against Verne. I can't have that weight on my shoulders. I can't . . .' Fi swallowed all she couldn't say out loud, memories of cold shrines and her father's haunted eyes she couldn't speak in front of *him*. 'I won't let Verne tear my life apart a second time.'

Fi braced for his taunt. The clash of her words against his teeth.

Antal's silence left her reeling. His grip loosened to a whisper of claws, crimson eyes piercing too deep. Why was he looking at her like that? Why didn't he *say* something?

'Why are *you* here?' she snarled.

Antal kept her pinned for one long, too-quiet breath.

'Because this is my fault.'

He released her.

Fi staggered away, his words rattling her balance. His sincerity, a splinter in her skin. *His* fault? Why would a daeyari say something like that? Another snare. Another game.

'I could be back on the Twilit Plane by now,' Antal said,

low. As if the forest might overhear. 'Not trudging through snow with an ungrateful human, risking my neck to fix this. Verne's counting on me slinking away with my tail between my legs. But I don't want to leave my people to her, either. You deserve . . . better.'

Fi didn't know what to say.

Antal resumed his disgruntled walk while she stood in the snow, arms crossed into the cuffs of her coat, shivering.

Daeyari weren't supposed to be like this.

They were supposed to be cold. Monsters in stories told to make children behave. Vicious, ravenous creatures, like Verne's hollow-eyed Beast.

What was Antal, if not the monster she'd expected?

Easy for him to *say* he didn't relish playing the wolf. He took sacrifices, but no younger than thirty, old enough to understand the choice. That said nothing of whether their choice was coerced. He'd left Nyskya untouched. He'd spared Fi.

He still ate people.

Because he needed to eat. No different than Fi gutting rabbits.

The same, but not the same. No other option, but there were *always* other options.

Fi found no clear answer.

She jogged to catch up with him, afraid to linger in another daeyari's forest. The slope leveled out, a ridgeline of trees catching the wind like black sails. In the canopy, boughs moaned. On the ground, a separate world, still and snow-locked.

When they fell into step, Antal didn't look at her. He trudged forward, agile strides unhindered by the deep snow, though Fi noted his pace slowed to let her keep up. As much as this daeyari shifted the ground beneath her feet, she recognized confidence and cooperation as currency. He'd shown her both.

A truce, then. A common enemy. That was her best option on the table.

'What's your problem with Verne, anyway?' Fi asked, because she never did learn to keep her mouth shut. 'Why'd she do all this? Kill your governor, kick you out.'

Antal seemed to weigh the levity of her question, this offer of an olive branch. His concession came as a dry glance, a scathingly arched brow.

'Other than her being a spiteful hag?' he said.

One thing they could agree on. 'Sure. But why do *you* think she's a spiteful hag?'

'Verne claims to champion *tradition*, but she only cares for herself. Thinks she's entitled to more territory. More humans to tremble at her feet. And so confident in her cleverness.' Antal bared his teeth in distaste. 'When I first arrived on the Winter Plane, set out to meet my neighbors, Verne didn't wait five minutes before trying to seduce me.'

Fi inhaled too fast, choking on her own saliva.

As she coughed herself straight, any conundrums over mortal death or immortal hunger toppled to a backburner. *This* had her full attention.

'Hold on. *Hold on.* You're talking about . . . *fucking* Verne?'

'Immortality has no use for prudishness,' he chided. 'Daeyari aren't self-conscious about carnal pleasures.'

'Neither are humans. The surprised face'—Fi gestured to her eyebrows—'is for Verne specifically. You two weren't . . . together?'

'Of course not. There's intimacy for passion. Then intimacy for negotiations.'

'Negotiations?'

'A way of weighing potential adversaries. Daeyari don't fall easily onto our backs. We fight, to see who will end up on top. Verne tried to subdue me, so sure of herself.'

Fi contemplated the terrifying image of two daeyari wrapped in sheets, claws bared. 'And you let her?'

'You think so little of me, Fionamara. I pinned her down until she *begged*.'

The roughness of Antal's words rumbled something in Fi.

An unexpected flutter filled her stomach, not that sour of adrenaline, but something . . . warmer. Confusing. Curious? Never in her life had she considered the politics of daeyari tumbling. Fi enjoyed some quality biting as much as the next girl, but *that*?

It might not be *so* bad, with caution. Antal and Verne had emerged unscathed.

'So, you used to be stronger than her?' Fi said.

If Antal ground his teeth this much on a regular basis, she was surprised he still had fangs. 'That was without magic. Just the two of us. Verne knows her strengths, enough to put me at disadvantage when . . .'

He stopped. Sniffed the air.

'What's wrong?' Fi snapped alert.

'Tyvo's noticed us.'

'What?' She scanned the trees, but spotted nothing. 'How do you know?'

'I smell his energy.'

'You *what*?'

Antal frowned. 'Why do you say that like it's an odd thing?'

'I'm not a daeyari. I can't *smell* energy.'

'Keep your voice down.' Another clench of teeth. 'And stay behind me.'

Didn't have to tell Fi twice.

The conifers parted on a clearing of untouched snow, silver in moonlight, wind lifting ice crystals into flurries. Beyond the ridge, lights glowed in the distance, a far-off city.

Fi rarely set foot in Tyvo territory, her fees twenty percent higher in any jurisdiction without a judicial system. Tyvo's approach to governance was simpler, more iron-clawed than most daeyari. He chose a governor. The governor did as Tyvo ordered. Fi didn't want to touch that dynamic with a hundred-yard pole.

She spotted the eyes first.

All her life, she'd avoided immortals. Now, here was the third in a matter of days, perched amidst the high branches of the shiverpines.

The daeyari reclined against the trunk, tail wrapped around the bough beneath him. His eyes glowed orange-red like an old hearth. His skin, deathly white. Onyx stone crusted a high-collared black shirt, aglint like eyes in the dark.

Daeyari didn't age like mortals. Despite Antal's two and a half centuries, he was . . . fine, Fi would admit he was *handsome*. Handsome in that ethereal way, a man carved from Void and ice and a dissonantly soft curve to his mouth.

Tyvo had a harsher face, sharper brow and leaner cheekbones, hair shaved at the sides and a slate-gray herringbone plait between black antlers. And those *antlers*. Tyvo's rack arced back over his head before curving up in a barbed crown, eight tips each side against Antal's three, the points razor sharp.

Antal stepped forward, a brush of Fi's arm urging her to stay back. Gladly. She didn't want to be anywhere near that creature.

He entered the fray as a different person entirely, no trace of the taunts or whispered words he'd let slip on their walk, as ice-chiseled as his kin. Above, Tyvo's mouth curled a grin.

'Antal,' he called down. 'Ka Voz grel ef yzru.'

The daeyari language had syllables sharp like teeth, rhythm smooth as an aurora.

'Void smile upon you as well, Tyvo,' Antal returned in seasonspeak – for Fi's benefit, she realized with no small fluster. 'Thank you for seeing me.'

He held out his arms, palms up, the way Verne had greeted him.

Tyvo didn't move. He appraised his guest with the cocked head of a raptor, tail swaying.

The start of a deal always set the stage. Fi sensed that shift in the air, silence dragging too long. Tyvo's response was, she gathered, not polite.

Even more so, when he snapped out of sight, reappearing inches in front of his visitor. Antal flinched.

'A visit from a neighbor?' Tyvo said, voice deep, teeth glinting. 'Anytime.'

He didn't lay his hands palm up, as Antal had done for Verne. He *gripped* Antal beneath the forearms. From a distance, Fi thought she saw claws too tight on flesh. They held the posture, a play of power in purposeful proximity.

'To what do I owe this unusual pleasure?' Tyvo backed away on prowling strides, his build fuller than the younger daeyari. His shirt shifted inlaid onyx and iridescent vesper fabric. Antal's humble attire seemed drab by comparison.

'Unusual?' Antal returned with his guarded countenance.

'To see you away from your cave. You've visited, what . . . twice in five decades? Once to introduce yourself. Once to complain about borders.'

'I know you prefer your solitude.'

'And yet here you are.' Tyvo's grin showed a single fang. 'A shame. If you'd have visited more often, I'd have gladly brought you hunting.'

Fi didn't want to know what that meant. Antal's tail betrayed a flick at the tip.

'My apologies,' he said. 'I'll . . . keep that in mind.'

'Apologies, apologies. Ah, but you have that serious look about you.' Tyvo's tail was a demur sway at his calves, posture taut like a hawk. 'What brings you?'

'I come to discuss our shared neighbor. Verne.'

Tyvo's tail never broke pace. 'Yes?'

'She's moved upon my territory. Claimed it as her own.'

'And?'

In the silence, Fi listened to the moan of shiverpines in the wind. The scratch of snow abrading snow. The thrum of her heart against her ribs.

'*And,*' Antal said, 'I come seeking your counsel on how we should address this.'

Tyvo's head tilted, claws tapping his chin.

'Ah, I see,' he lamented, the grim tone at odds with his grin. 'There seems to be a misunderstanding. Did you come here thinking I'd help you?'

16

Not as tough as you look

Fi retracted her earlier statement.

Seeking help from a neighbor daeyari wasn't the best idea she'd heard all week. It was, in swiftly unfolding certainty, an atrocious idea. She shivered against the wind, trying to keep both immortals in sight despite eyeballs freezing in their sockets.

'You knew about Verne?' Antal's icy facade didn't break. His tail coiled a sharp arc.

'Did I know about Verne's recent claim to Thomaskweld?' Tyvo's grin flashed fangs. His eyes, molten orange. 'I "enjoy my solitude" as you say, yclz dacyari. But I'd be a fool not to listen for important news.'

He spoke so slow. Unrushed. Unintimidated by Antal's glare. His black antlers glinted in the moonlight, carvings divided into sections, one band per century, Fi guessed from Antal's decorations. Tyvo's antlers bore eight bands. Not just the oldest creature she'd ever met, but one of the oldest *things* she'd ever met, on par with the granite monuments of a capital city, his voice like lichen-caked grout.

'You knew,' Antal said. 'Yet you've done nothing to intervene?'

'Antal. You're playing this game several steps behind. Verne opened negotiations months ago. Asked for my cooperation.'

'And you gave it?'

'She made a compelling case.'

'To *displace* me?' Antal's tail flicked fiercer.

'Why not? One fewer neighbor, Verne in my debt. An easy trade.'

They squared off, two predators perched on the balls of clawed feet. Eyes bright.

Tyvo laughed.

'Oyzen yzri. You have your father's scowl down *perfectly*.' Tyvo circled a claw at Antal's chiseled face. 'Even that scrunch between your eyes. Marvelous. There's just one problem, yelz daeyari.'

He moved before Antal could flinch, a firm grasp of his opponent's antler.

'You haven't got *these* to back it up,' Tyvo said.

He skirted Antal's swat, snatching the tip of his thrashing tail.

'And this?' Tyvo scoffed. 'Gives you away.'

Fi hung at the edge of the clearing, cursing herself for allying with the only daeyari on the Plane who apparently had no friends. Antal didn't snap at the insult, tension confined to ramrod posture and that flicking tail. Certainly, he must feel *something* at this betrayal.

Which made Fi wonder why he was so good at hiding it.

'Go home, Antal,' Tyvo said, and Fi's entire concept of 'condescending' shifted as she heard it off a centuries-old tongue. 'He'll be glad to have you back. A few decades taking air on another Plane?' Another fang-sharp grin. 'Maybe he can finally make something useful out of you.'

At last, Antal's stone face fissured. He pressed closer to Tyvo with a snarl.

'And who will Verne make her next case to, when she comes over *your* border?'

'You think so?' Tyvo chuckled like crunching bone. 'Verne chooses her fights carefully, prefers stepping on things smaller than her. I suppose that's what made you an attractive mark.'

'And while you plotted treachery, did Verne share the rest of her scheme? She brought a derived daeyari to do her bidding.'

Tyvo's grin faltered.

'She commands the creature,' Antal furthered. 'Like a pet on a leash.'

Tyvo considered the news with narrowed eyes, a flicked tail. 'Can she control it?'

'What does that matter? It's improper.'

'Improper? Verne is the *definition* of proper. So she's indulged one . . . transgression. The rest of this, she's played by every etiquette. Even letting you live.' Tyvo's voice dropped to a growl. '*I* wouldn't have.'

Antal backed toward Fi.

She agreed: time to call this a failed plan and get out before the very crusty daeyari got very fed up with their intrusion. Her gloved fingers brushed the hilt of her energy sword, warm from body heat beneath her coat.

Tyvo's molten eyes snapped to her.

Static pricked Fi's tongue. Too fast to react as the daeyari appeared beside her, one icy hand locked around her wrist, blocking her from grabbing her sword. A claw tipped her chin. She froze as the point pinned soft flesh, curses boiling her tongue.

'But who's this?' Tyvo purred.

Nope. Fuck him and everything about—

'She's with me,' Antal said. Hard.

'Obviously,' Tyvo returned. 'I'm surprised, Antal. Bringing a gift? Perhaps you aren't as clueless as I took you for.' He twisted Fi's arm, exposing skin. 'Some fine muscle on her.'

Fi was an idiot to come here. She fought to keep her breath steady, even as Tyvo's proximity trickled cold down her vertebrae. A hot stab of adrenaline at his horrific proposition. She'd volunteered for this reckless venture, but would that stop Antal from using her for his benefit? Just another daeyari, trading human lives like currency.

'She isn't food,' Antal said. Harder.

'No?'

Tyvo's nostrils flared at the scent of her. *He* smelled of forest musk, old bones moldering in loam. And ice. Always ice and emptiness.

Fi yanked her arm like a flailing hare. He didn't budge. Fast and strong, how absurdly unfair. Energy prickled her fingertips, but what good would it do against an immortal? Daeyari were too swift for a human to fight. To invulnerable.

'She's not willing.' Antal pressed closer.

'Isn't she?' Tyvo pinned Fi with ravenous eyes. 'What do you say about that?'

She spit in his face.

Tyvo's lips curled a snarl. 'Spirited. No matter. No one notices if a few slip through the cracks, do they?'

A black tongue traced his teeth, too long, summoning bile in Fi's throat. Antal's presence prickled her skin, a lurch in her stomach urging her to stay on guard. Tyvo was a different beast. The hunger in his eyes shocked her system like an aurorabeast prod.

'*Release her.*' Antal flexed his claws.

Why would he care?

'How about a deal?' Tyvo offered. 'Leave her. And I'll let *you* walk away.'

Fi swallowed, claws tugging the tender skin of her neck. An easy trade. What could Antal gain by standing up for her, when he'd be better off—

Static struck her tongue. A flash of claws.

Fi fell against snow as Antal tackled Tyvo. The daeyari snarled. Rolled. Another snap fizzled her tongue as they blinked apart, facing off. Tyvo discarded civility like a cloak out of fashion, eyes the lethal gleam of a predator defending his territory.

Antal reached for Fi.

Why? He could be gone already. He could leave her and never look back.

Before they grasped hands, Tyvo lunged. He dragged Antal to the ground in a flurry of snow and thrashing tails. Daeyari dressed in finery. They connived like humans and spoke in civil measure. They fought like wildcats, a blur of snarling and scratching, red energy rippling at clawtips. Tyvo held the upper hand in size.

But Antal wasn't useless.

Without the disadvantage of Verne's magic or an outnumbered fight, he slashed claws across Tyvo's chest, rending fabric and spattering black blood across the snow. He coiled around his larger opponent, tail snaring Tyvo's arm, legs braced to leverage every cord of lithe muscle, pinning the rival daeyari to the ground. Maybe he *had* triumphed over Verne once.

Tyvo threw his head forward, driving antlers into Antal's face.

The wicked points skewered Antal's cheek and ripped upward, gouging one eye in a mess of blood and punctured sclera. Antal recoiled. Tyvo grabbed the younger daeyari by the antlers and held him down.

His teeth sank into Antal's throat.

Antal let out the heinous snarl of a skewered cat. A racoon in the throes of death. Tyvo's fangs ripped into Antal's neck, red energy crackling along rent sinew. As Fi pushed to her feet,

Antal dug claws into Tyvo's ribs. As she fumbled for balance, Antal kicked snow, tail flailing.

Tyvo bit *deeper.* Red energy snapped the air, sizzling against cold as Antal clawed. Then slowed. Then slumped, hands falling weak against the cage of Tyvo's arms.

Realization sliced sharp in Fi's chest. This wasn't like Verne's intimidation game.

Tyvo intended to kill him.

Not if she had any-fucking-thing to say about it.

Fi ripped the hilt from her belt. Cracked an energy capsule into the pommel. The blade Shaped silver, tongues of energy rippling off the edge. Lethal against mortal flesh, but immortal? Her school teachers didn't cover fighting immortals. They never covered *regular* fighting. Fi ran drills for heating tea kettles or Shaping kitchen knives ad nauseam, but she taught herself swordplay on trade wardens and black marketeers and even a few things with teeth.

Never anything with black eternity in its eyes.

But Antal – Plane's worst negotiator – was on the ground again, and she couldn't leave him.

Fi didn't shout. The snap of energy must have given her away, or the crunch of snow beneath her boots. Tyvo looked up, black blood slicking his chin.

She swung.

A moment of resistance. A spark on her tongue. By the end of the arc, Fi's sword cleaved empty air. Tyvo reappeared several feet away.

A single antler fell to the snow.

Fi and Tyvo stared at it together. He raised a slow hand, claws clacking against the severed base. The casualty rested upon the ground, black lacquer glinting, snow clumped in carvings of stars and prey fleeing through trees.

'You . . .' Tyvo began as a hiss. 'You *fleck of dust.*' Rose to a rupture. 'By Veshri's teeth and sharpened antlers, *I'll crack your marrow while you still breathe!*'

Fi had wondered how Verne's twisted Beast could be a daeyari. Yet here stood Tyvo with that same devouring blaze in his eyes, that feral swish of tail. She looked to Antal, bloody and unmoving in the snow. Too far to reach.

Static spiked her tongue.

Fi swung at nothing. Everything. She'd volunteered to come as backup, not a solo act, shouting through a wide arc of her energy sword as the daeyari reappeared. She only saw claws. Teeth. So Void-damned fast. He came at her like a winter gale, slashing for the soft flesh of her stomach.

She angled her sword to parry. Claws shrieked off silver.

Tyvo swiped for her neck. She raised to deflect.

He came for her ribs. Fi brought her sword down like a shield.

What the fuck was happening?

Fi swayed on unsteady steps, fingers strangling the hilt, yet she kept moving. Backing up. Parrying energy-coated claws. She ought to be flayed to pieces by now. She ought to be on the ground with her ribs cracked open and a daeyari ripping her heart out, like every human who'd dared raise a weapon to an immortal in the stories.

A claw glanced off her sword. The sickle tip carved across her lips. Blood red – *not* Fi's preferred lipstick shade.

In her flinch, Tyvo grabbed her sword. The son-of-a-bitch *grabbed* the blade in his bare hands, a shriek of red and silver as he shielded his palms with energy. A shiver ran up Fi's arm. Her energy blade flickered against the rival current, and fighting immortal energy . . .

Her sword shattered with a *crack.*

Claws struck Fi's abdomen. She hunched, gasping as her wool coat shredded, but her silviamesh held. At first. A deeper press of claws, of destructive daeyari energy, and the armor-like fabric popped its threads. Fi staggered back in time, taking several gouges across her skin rather than losing her bowels.

All she had left were energy capsules. Fi cracked one to detonate and Shaped another into a shield. Tyvo retreated from the blast with a snarl, his seared skin repairing itself before her eyes in a flash of red.

'Fionamara.'

Her name came to her as a rasp.

The syllables mixed with gravel, filtered over broken glass. Across the clearing, Antal dragged himself to his knees, dripping blood. Reaching for her.

Reaching.

For *her*.

Fi ripped her carnelian transport stone from her pocket and cracked the fossil into its two halves. One half, she hurled toward Antal. A pulse of energy activated the second half in her palm, a heartbeat before Tyvo's claws came for her. She lurched. Not nearly as smooth as a daeyari teleport.

Out the other side of the jump, she staggered, skin hot and prickling from dematerialization. She scooped her thrown transport stone from the snow, retrieved the severed antler – or else *no one* would believe this – then grabbed Antal's hand.

A snarl closed behind her. Then the black of a teleport.

Black like the Void, she realized. Too cold and empty to be anything else.

Antal had called her not a true Voidwalker.

He would know, wouldn't he?

17

That's not supposed to be visible

Fi collapsed onto her back in the snow.

As she gasped, no claws closed around her throat.

She lay still, skin a swarm of ants after transport stones and teleportation in swift succession, treetops swirling in her vision. Tatters of silviamesh fluttered on her stomach. Beneath that were stinging claw marks, skin exposed to cold. A familiar cold. Not that biting, piercing kind from Tyvo Territory.

At the sight of her cottage, she half laughed, half groaned. Another narrow escape.

A wet cough jolted her back to reality.

Antal hunched on his knees, cradling his neck. What *remained* of it. Fi's stomach lurched as black blood slicked his fingers, gaping from a hole of stripped flesh, muscle, and a glimpse of honest-to-Void *spine*. Like Tyvo had tried to take Antal's head off with his bare teeth. He should be *dead*.

'Antal?' Fi hurried to his side, ozone sharp on the air, the smell of that copper-less blood.

He could have run. He could have left her behind and suffered none of this.

Before she could touch him, Antal snatched her wrist. A lashing motion, swift as a frost asp. The daeyari held her at arm's length, fangs bared in a growl, his uninjured eye sharp like a cornered animal.

Almost as if everyone he knew had recently betrayed him.

Fi could do the same, leave him bleeding in the snow.

'Let me help,' she asked. Ordered. She couldn't tell, her voice hoarse and lip split.

Antal searched her with some tangled expression. Was it confusion? Worry?

Fear? From a daeyari?

He collapsed against her.

Fi wrapped an arm beneath his shoulders. 'Inside?'

His nod was weak.

They limped to her porch, Fi wincing at the slashes across her stomach, Antal leaning most of his weight against her. In the brief moments they'd been this close, he'd sometimes seemed cold, sometimes warm. Now, he *burned*. Energy hummed through his skin, warring to keep him upright, prickling static everywhere she touched.

Daeyari could bleed. They could die. Antal might still be dying.

But he'd *saved* her.

She dragged him to the bathtub. They collapsed together, his back propped against the cedar, black blood spattering floorboards. He reached a trembling hand to his throat.

Fi watched in equal horror and fascination as tendrils of red energy laced Antal's neck, thickening, then firming into muscle and sinew. Building flesh out of nothing – or whatever odd flesh immortals were made of.

Too soon, the energy faded. The wound looked less revolting, but far from healed.

'*Oyzen yzri,*' he rasped, voice a smidge more decipherable.

Not in imminent danger of collapsing, at least. Fi groaned

to her feet and pressed a current to the water heater. Opened the spigot.

Antal could have let Tyvo eat her. She already owed him her life, spared upon his altar. But sparing a life wasn't the same as saving one, risking himself the way he did.

Keeping her barbs up proved too exhausting. For a moment, Fi let slip her defensive bristle, kneeling with weary shoulders and weary knees at Antal's side, fumbling to peel off the bloody remnants of his shirt. He winced as she unstuck ruined fabric from ruined skin, his torso gouged with claw marks that only looked less severe when compared to the mess of his throat.

'Do daeyari . . . feel pain?' Fi asked.

'*Fuck!*' Antal spat as she pulled a strip of shirt off his shoulder. 'Oyzen yzri, kasek aza—'

'All right, sorry! I'll try not to . . .' She freed his other shoulder with less cursing, hands brushing his bare chest. Down his heaving ribs. Down the taut muscles of his abdomen.

Fi halted at his trousers. Her fingers hooked the fabric, settling warm against his waist.

Uncertain.

She shouldn't be. Medical care was more pressing than propriety, but her bravado faltered for a creature with claws.

'So modest.'

Antal's voice scraped like gravel. His cheek was flayed where Tyvo's antler had struck, his eye a socket of Void.

'I can assure you,' Fi said. 'I'm not.' Only well-warranted caution around daeyari. Their brush with death, responsible for the heat flushing her cheeks.

'Why am I not surprised?'

'Do you want me to take your pants off or not, daeyari?'

When Fi let her guard down, the back-and-forth came easier. No barbs. Fewer teeth.

She tensed when Antal touched her shoulder, not claws, but knuckles pressing her coat, the weapons on his fingers curled away. Fi's blood-spattered thoughts puzzled a moment before registering the non-threatening intent of the gesture. A nudge urged her away. His remaining iris dimmed nearly black, drained of energy.

Fi gave him space to finish undressing.

With rustling fabric behind her, she inspected her slashed stomach. Not too deep, thanks to . . . Fi didn't want to *think* of her shredded silviamesh. A loss to mourn later. She splayed fingers over flesh and pulled energy from the muscles of her core, teeth gritted as she cauterized. A finer current she Shaped from trembling biceps, weaving silver-light stitches to sew the gashes closed. She finished with numbing twilight sorel ointment and a slim energy chip held against the wound with gauze, fuel to speed the healing.

A splash sounded from the bathtub.

Then, silence.

'Antal?'

She rushed over and plunged her arms into scalding water, grabbing the daeyari's antlers to haul him to the surface. He emerged with a wretched cough, water thrashing as his tail settled.

So much for modesty. Fi averted her gaze as Antal sank against the tub, a scowl her only protest at having to prevent an immortal from *drowning* himself, of all things. Her eyes did wander, though not to anything scandalous. She couldn't look away from the cavern of his throat.

'You healed before,' Fi said, only a little frantic. 'Why aren't you healing now?'

Antal spoke between gasps. 'Needs . . . too much energy . . . will . . . take time.'

'Are you sure? I've never heard a story about a daeyari injured like this.'

'Why the fuck would we let mortals tell stories about how to hurt us?'

Fi stared at him. She stared at this creature she used to understand in such vicious simplicity, opening before her like a splay of viscera. Valuable, to know her enemies could bleed, could die.

But what was she supposed to do with the knowledge of how his voice cracked when he felt pain?

Of how he'd reached for *her* before saving himself?

Antal pressed a palm to his ruined eye socket, trembling, breaths hissed, a creature in exquisite agony. Red energy sizzled at his touch, the smell wretched with ozone and burnt flesh. Every inch of him tensed. Shuddered. With a labored exhale, he hunched over the bathwater, hand slumping away from his face.

Revealing a reconstructed eye, where a gaping hole had been. Talk about a wicked party trick – suffering aside. No human flesh could regenerate like this.

He squinted, blinking as black blood caked his lashes.

Someone should clean him up. As Antal had to focus on literally putting himself together . . . Fi grabbed a puffy face towel, dipped it in water, then raised it to his gore-spattered shoulder.

Antal snatched her wrist a second time, pinning her arm against the tub. His growl spiked that instinctive fear in her belly.

Then, Fi was *so very* over it.

'Will you calm your cranky teeth? I'm trying to help!'

Antal bared his fangs. Fi didn't budge. She had no time for this nonsense while he bled all over her house with a third of his Void-damned throat missing.

She set to work, Antal's claws still threatening on her arm, but not stopping her. She'd met house cats less dramatic. Fi did *try* to be gentle as she dabbed the cloth around the rent sinew of his neck, not enjoying his wince.

Softer, she wiped blood off the tapered edge of his ear. A careful brush over his cheek, along the tense line of his jaw. He had hair *only* atop his head. Not a speck of stubble, more smooth planes across his chest. Fi dared not pry any lower, though damn if she wasn't curious.

'If you'd died,' she said, 'would you turn into one of those beasts?'

A red current ran up Antal's neck, closing a section of flesh. He swallowed, the motion labored. 'Not for decades. Centuries. Some take longer to return than others.'

'But they always come back . . . different?'

'It varies. Some derived daeyari return immediately as beasts. Some hold themselves together better, only a few features lost. But each iteration becomes more animalistic. Verne's Beast has probably been through multiple rematerializations. A fate worse than death.'

Yet he'd risked his life by staying here in opposition to Verne. By confronting Tyvo.

By saving Fi.

He blinked again, his repaired eye half open against a crust of blood.

'Hold still,' Fi said. 'Let me . . .'

She cupped Antal's chin and raised the cloth to his face. When he refrained from biting any fingers off, Fi mustered her courage, leaning closer for a feather-soft wipe of the daeyari's eye. Wary, at first. She didn't know what to expect of immortal healing, whether the wound would be tender, but beneath the grime, his features seemed fully repaired.

His skin wasn't steel, like the folktales said. Not stone or ice. Beneath the press of Fi's fingers, this man-eating beast was alarmingly . . . soft, his eyelids pale, cheeks flushed with energy instead of blood. The daeyari were mortal, once. Chiseled anew by the Void. Just not as sharp as she'd expected, up close.

Antal's fresh eye snapped open, pinning her with black sclera and a dim red iris.

'Why are you doing this?' he asked, low.

His exhale feathered her wrist. Fi scowled and focused on her work. 'Tyvo would have eaten me. You stopped him.'

'He would have killed me,' Antal returned. 'You stopped him.'

Fi scoffed. 'You were my only way out of there. Of course I had to save you. But *you*. You could have left. Why didn't you?'

A pause. Fi didn't notice she was holding her breath until her chest began to ache.

'Would you have left me?' Antal asked, too quiet.

Yes. No. Fi didn't know anymore. She scrubbed a stubborn crust of blood on his jaw. 'It's the least I could do. After all the trouble I've caused.'

Antal's claws loosened on her arm, gripping with softer finger pads. 'This isn't your fault, Fionamara.'

'But you said—'

'I shouldn't have blamed you. Verne would have acted, with you as accessory or not.'

Fi hated the rawness scraping his throat. She hated how it made her shiver. 'You said this is *your* fault?'

'You heard Verne. She saw an opportunity. Saw me as *weak*. All because . . .'

'Because daeyari are supposed to be vile? Mysterious? Not give a shit about the humans they rule?'

'Yes.'

For a heartbeat, neither of them was fighting.

A denial would have been easier. Fighting him was *easier* than whatever this was, his words too soft around the rasp of breath, neck barely strong enough to hold his head up.

'So what's wrong with *you*?' Fi said.

'Too many things, Fionamara.' His words came weak. Weary. 'I tried. As Veshri watches from the Void, I *tried*. I don't want things to be this way. If I had any other option . . . but I'm sorry. That you had to be part of this.' His lidded gaze slid down her face.

And stalled on her mouth.

He frowned.

When he reached for her, Fi flinched.

Another instinct. She saw claws, and red eyes, and all of her stiffened like a dumb hare before she realized what he'd intended – Antal, reaching for the bloody cut Tyvo's claw left across her lips. To heal? To comfort?

She'd never know. He pulled back in an instant.

Antal straightened in the tub. Fi *watched* his expression snap back into that granite facade, that shield of teeth and tightened jaw. A mask – but once she'd seen the cracks, she couldn't unsee them, that uneven tempo of his breath and the too-tight clamp of claws against the cedar. A slip of vulnerability he shouldn't have shown.

Fi said nothing of it. She didn't know where to begin *thinking* of it, this daeyari half dead in her tub, his words hollowed with guilt an immortal shouldn't possess.

She returned to the simpler task of cleaning blood from Antal's shoulders. He pulled more energy into his neck, repairing flesh, giving her room to work while he gritted his teeth. Easier, this way. So much easier than that fleeting moment his thumb had brushed her wrist.

'You spoke the truth,' he said. 'You *are* more useful, with an energy sword.'

Fi let her cloth stray over still-raw skin. Antal hissed.

'You were unconscious for most of it,' she countered.

'I saw enough. Few humans can hold their ground against a daeyari, much less one as old as Tyvo.'

'Will his antler grow back?'

'Antlers regenerate slower than flesh. It will take time to recover, and never as it was before. He'll be very angry.'

'Good. Fuck him.'

Fi startled when Antal laughed.

Had she heard him laugh before? Scoffs perhaps, humorless and biting things, the sounds of the two of them waging battle without blood. This was new. Despite the rasp in his throat, Antal's laugh came deep, trembling the water of the tub.

'What?' Fi bristled.

'A week ago, you cowered at my feet. Now, you boast for cutting a daeyari's antler off? You couldn't have done Tyvo worse insult. Antlers are a source of great pride.'

'Are they?' Fi eyed his, blank at the tips and that odd patch in the second band, otherwise carved with flowers, auroras, some sigils she didn't recognize. Too delicate, for a carnivore. 'Then you'd better not get on my bad side.'

Perhaps a bolder dare than Fi ought to risk. Even injured, she guessed Antal would be a treacherous enemy. But not invincible. That bolstered her confidence.

Antal's look pierced her to the marrow, a silent promise of teeth in her neck, should she make good on her threat. Yet in the subtle tilt of his brow, she thought she glimpsed a concession of respect. Not used to humans standing their ground?

'Your clothes are a mess,' Fi said. 'I'll find you something to wear.'

She did not, unsurprisingly, have any daeyari-appropriate attire on hand. From her armoire, she retrieved a plush bathrobe, a fleece blanket. She left them beside the tub and gave Antal space, listening for the sound of sloshing water in case she had to rescue him again.

When he emerged, Fi stifled a laugh. She'd never seen a more ridiculous combination: the lethal lines of a daeyari ensconced in a pink robe, a blanket draped over his shoulders like a child caught out after bedtime. Antal's nose wrinkled. He smelled of rose oil and mothballs.

Fi had a taunt ready . . . until Antal collapsed on her sofa. He coiled beneath the blanket like a wounded animal, some pitiful thing trying to make himself small.

On second thought, Fi was too exhausted to needle him. Too exhausted to dwell on how their fuck-up with Tyvo put them back at square one, still no plan for unseating Verne.

Modesty be damned. She drained the tub and poured a fresh bath. Though she pulled the screen up for privacy and surveyed the sofa at every opportunity, she never spotted prying eyes. At last, wrapped in her flannel and tired to the bone, she turned off the lights and dragged herself to bed.

No point worrying over a daeyari lurking across the room, Fi tried to assure herself. Even if she sent him away, he could sneak back once she'd fallen asleep.

In the dark, she spotted a glow of red, a single eye following her. Once she fell still in her bed, it closed, Antal curling deeper into his cocoon.

A tense silence. An unsteady peace.

Yet as Fi drifted toward sleep, it wasn't a fear of claws that made her clutch her blankets.

Antal's eyes haunted her, that look of a frightened beast. That rasp in his voice when he spoke of things he wished he'd done differently. Daeyari weren't supposed to act like this.

Then again, two centuries was a long time to live. Long enough to gather regrets.

And Fi knew too well, how it felt to regret.

18

Bite me

Fi dreamt of a seaside on the Summer Plane. A coconut cocktail chilled her hand, hair tussled by salt as she swayed in a hammock shaded by big, frilly palm trees. The pleasant mood lingered as she woke, a tranquil start to the day.

Reality hit her as a sting of claw marks healing in her stomach.

Oh, and she'd invited a daeyari to a sleepover.

Sunny reveries crumbled to curses, but Fi stifled them with more resignation than fear. If Antal planned to eat her, wouldn't he have done so by now? She'd wake not to a nest of furs, but her fingers turned to daeyari appetizers? Fi pushed herself upright in bed, rabbit fur draping her like a cloak, braced to confront the bullshit of a new day.

Her sofa was empty.

Concerning, considering she'd left a carnivorous immortal there the night before.

Fi scanned the room. Twilight drifted through the curtains, casting counters and furniture in dull shadow. She touched an energy current to the panel beside her bed, bringing on the overhead lights – aside from one obnoxious pane in the corner that flickered whenever the aurora got too strong. Still no sign of her visitor. No discarded blanket on the floor, no 'goodbye, see you never' note on the kitchen counter.

Increasingly concerning. Fi tipped bare feet onto the cold floor. At last, she looked up.

Fi bit back a yelp, though the hand that snapped to her heart looked no less undignified. There in the shadow of her rafters, Antal perched on a beam, still bundled in a bathrobe and blanket, squinting at the panel lights like some feral racoon who'd accidentally stumbled inside.

'What in the merciless Void are you doing up there?' Fi demanded.

Antal's eyes narrowed further. 'I feel more . . . comfortable here.'

'Comfortable from *what*? You're an apex predator!'

The daeyari didn't indulge her a reply. At least he no longer looked on the verge of collapse, his eyes back to a red smolder amidst the burrow of his blanket. *This* was the creature from her father's folktales? Who'd reincarnate as a feral monstrosity? Fi spotted none of Verne's Beast hiding in the terry cloth.

'Glad you're feeling better,' she said. 'Do you have clothes, somewhere?'

'Of course.'

She held his glare until he sighed. Vanished. Parting static lingered on her tongue.

He'd be back. Fi felt it in the pit of her grumbling stomach.

She donned a coat of dark wool and silver ermine fur from her dwindling supply – one coat lost beneath building rubble, one shredded by a daeyari, Void knew what awful fate awaited this one – then headed out to check her hare traps. When her boots creaked the porch, Aisinay trotted from the trees like a scaled phantom, finned tail swaying in greeting. Fi patted her neck.

'Morning, Aisinay. Do I have some shit to catch you up on.'

The Void horse snorted, a billow of mist on cold morning air.

'Thanks for nothing, by the way. Letting that daeyari walk right up here. Just because you're both from the Void, doesn't mean you have to be *pals.*'

After an indignant nudge from Aisinay's muzzle, Fi climbed onto her bare back.

They traversed a couple of Curtains, emerging in a stretch of forest across the mountains from Nyskya. Beyond the canopy, dawn rose in shades of violet. The sun would barely crest the trees this time of year, days growing shorter, until night settled in for several long months. Kashvi's tavern would be busy, packed with warm drinks and traders bartering for furs.

That was, if they still had power by then. And if Verne didn't raze the village to ash for her amusement. Fi carried a pit in her stomach as she moved through the trap line, empathy for every rabbit caught in a noose.

She returned home with two fresh hares for breakfast – and a prickle down her neck, the moment she stepped inside.

Antal perched in the rafters again, dressed in a midnight shirt and trousers, tail dangling. Fi made eye contact and a single command.

'*Down.*' She pointed to the floor. 'I will not have a man-eating creature lurking above my head in my own home.'

Last night, she'd let her barbs drop. They both had. Fi wasn't sure how long that stalemate could last, whether a new morning heralded a return to arms, or a continuation of this strange new peace.

A growl rumbled Antal's chest. He dropped from the rafters, landing with the ease of a cat. Feeling *much* better, then. The useless daeyari had neglected to fasten four Void-damned shirt buttons this time, leaving ample view of pale chest and sharp collarbones, his neck intact. He settled on her sofa, cross-legged, tail curled around him.

Fi inspected her home. The borrowed robe and blanket sat folded by the tub. Her growing lights had kicked on, glowing over pots of basil and sage and turmeric hoarded from warmer Planes. The fussy light panel in the corner . . . had stopped flickering?

'It was obnoxious,' Antal muttered, noting her attention.

During Fi's brief visit to his home, she'd seen those masterful conduits in his floor, the metal scraps on his shelves. Then there were Thomaskweld's energy circuits, some of the most efficient on the Winter Plane. Not the best Shaper, but a knack for technology?

'You ought to fix my gramophone,' Fi said. 'Hasn't played right for a year.'

Maybe if she asked extra nice, he'd tell her how to install that blissful floor heating in her own cottage.

Antal huffed at her request. Yet as Fi set her hares down on the kitchen counter, her peripheral vision tracked a shadow. He circled her gramophone beside the sofa, running a claw along the copper frame. Seemed they both sought distractions this morning. Easier to dwell on small tasks than their failure with Tyvo, their pathetic lack of a plan for confronting Verne. Fi's tongue worried her split lip, tracing tender flesh.

She grabbed a knife hilt from the kitchen block. Shaped a silver energy blade. She skinned the hare with practiced motions, preserving the pelt, separating lean muscle for breakfast. The prospect of skillet-crisped meat stirred her stomach into eager knots.

At the thought, Fi's knuckles tightened on the knife. There was *another* problem added to an already abysmal list. Even if Antal didn't need to eat as often as a human, over a week had passed since the last meal she knew of.

'Hey, Antlers.'

He stiffened. A palpable moment stretched before he faced her, the tilt of his head so dramatically slow, it verged on comedy.

'My name is *Antal*.'

'I like mine better.'

'That doesn't—'

'Do you want breakfast?' Fi held up a hare, the plumper of the two. So kind of her.

Antal's nose wrinkled. 'I can take care of myself.'

'Yeah. That's exactly what I'm concerned about, actually.' She set the hare down then wiped her hands on a rag with authoritative swipes. 'If you're going to hang around here? I need to know you won't pick off any villagers. Or, you know, *me*, while I'm sleeping.'

He huffed. 'You think it would be while you're sleeping?'

Look at him, being *funny*. Fi wasn't amused. 'How long can you last?'

He considered, a tight flick to his tail that left her uneasy. 'I could go a month without food before . . . unpleasant con-sequences. Shorter, if I must make large energy expenditures.'

They both fell grim, reliving their bout with Tyvo, the heinous condition Antal had returned in. Even Fi felt that heightened pang of hunger this morning, her body seeking to replenish the energy she'd spent fighting a daeyari and healing her wounds.

'I can last a little longer,' Antal said. 'Regardless. A meager rabbit won't help.'

'If you say so, Antlers. Let me know if you change your mind.'

Setting aside the past several days of bad to worse to unfathomably atrocious, Fi enjoyed his gritted teeth at the name. Maybe she was playing with fire. But Antal betrayed a crucial hand during yesterday's escape, revealing he cared at least a *little* about keeping her alive. She bored into weakness like a weevil took to rotten wood.

Anything to convince Fi she wasn't doomed already. That inviting this daeyari into her home a second time hadn't tightened a snare on her neck.

'Careful, mortal.' Antal spoke low, serrated. 'I can imagine plenty of uses for your bones.'

'Oh, please. Bone threats? Give it a rest.'

'You think I'm *bluffing?*'

He prowled closer. Fi had noted the daeyari's silent footfalls enough times, she recognized the clack of claws against floorboards as an intimidation tactic. Should she fall quiet at the threat? Slink away like a defenseless hare? Antal was the strongest ally she had, her best chance of saving Nyskya. She couldn't afford to lose his favor.

But he'd only ever suffered her when she stood her ground.

'You know, when I was growing up'—Fi pushed away from the counter, closing the distance between them—'we had a pet cat. Matted gray fur, one milky eye from a fight with a raccoon. Hideous bastard. The meanest temper you've ever seen. Every month, we had to douse that little monster for fleas, and he'd spit and hiss and claw. But the moment you pinned him down? He flopped over like a wet rag. All noise. No action.'

Antal's eyes simmered crimson. Less than a stride between them now, ozone sharp in her nose, but Fi couldn't back down. Those were the rules of this game.

'That's you,' she said. 'You're the cat.'

'You press your luck, Fionamara. *My* claws do more damage than a house cat.'

'I'm not afraid of you.' Not since seeing him caked in blood in her tub. Not since he'd fought Tyvo for her. Why save her life, just to cut her open the next day?

'Then why is your heart beating so fast?'

That one, Fi wasn't ready for. The thunder in her ears should have been her little secret. Could Antal hear it? Smell it? Didn't matter. She'd made too much progress to slip back.

'Involuntary reactions don't count.' She clicked her tongue, a sound to mask the quiver. 'Just because my dumb lizard brain says you *could* eat me, doesn't mean I believe you'd do it.'

'Prove it.'

Another surprise. Fi hesitated. 'Prove what?'

'You claim you aren't afraid of me? Prove it.'

'How the fuck am I supposed to do that?'

The truth was, Fi didn't know how far she could push this beast. She could study every flick of his tail, could read into that crack in his guard when he'd reached for her face the night before, but she didn't *know* if he really was a house cat who'd flop when his bluff got called. Just as likely, she could be near an inflection point, a jab too far that would bring those fangs down upon her. A perilous line to dance around.

No point in dancing, then.

'Bite me,' Fi said.

That round went to her. Antal pulled back, weighing her with a slow blink.

'Excuse me?' He drew the syllables out.

'I'm not afraid of you.' If her heart was thunder before, it deafened now. 'You talk tough, but you haven't hurt me. You *won't* hurt me. Prove me wrong. *Bite me*, asshole.'

'Bite you. That's what you want?'

Antal pressed closer, narrowing the space between them to a foot. An *inch*. Nowhere to hide from those piercing red-and-Void eyes, that flash of fangs as he spoke. If this was how daeyari always argued, a duel of proximity, Fi couldn't back down.

She didn't *want* to back down.

Even as her breaths shallowed, there was a thrill to the stand-off, a creep of heat beneath her skin as she pressed this line with him. This ageless, predatory creature made not of shadow and nightmare as she'd always feared, but flesh and bone, balking at her punches. Each step toward the edge brought her closer to tumbling over. Each nudge, and she wanted to push a little more, to peer unflinching into the Void of his eyes and scream that she *wasn't afraid anymore.*

'Am I not speaking clearly?' Fi met his raise and leaned closer, their faces nearly touching. 'Bite. Me. Or are you nothing more than bristle?'

His tail cut a wide, swift arc.

She must be close to the line. A fraction more. She'd call *one* more bluff, then—

Antal lunged faster than Fi could gasp.

He shoved her by the hips. One firm motion, all momentum halting together at once – Fi's back striking the wall, the air fleeing her lungs.

Antal's teeth, on her throat.

At the stab of fangs, Fi's composure cracked. No time for incredulity, just that disorienting surge of prey instinct screaming at her to run, fight, *live*. She flailed like a snared rabbit, clawing against the daeyari's head, nails scraping the slick root of an antler. Her other hand raked his arm. Cold. Unyielding. Void, he was strong, a snare of lean muscle and claws pinning her waist.

But . . . no pain.

They fell still together.

Fi, tangled in limbs and drowning in ozone, risked an inhale. Another.

She didn't understand. Antal's mouth was hot on her throat,

Void-honed fangs clamping vulnerable skin. But nothing more. No carved flesh, no digging deep for arteries

Just firm enough to pin her in place.

A show of strength, Fi realized with mounting incredulity. A rebuttal she didn't know how to counter. This carnivorous beast with teeth framing her jugular, lines of lethal muscle pressing her against the wall, holding her down like a misbehaving kitten.

Fi couldn't move.

She could scarcely breathe, each shallow inhale tugging fangs against her neck.

Each taunting prick, shifting fear to *insult*. How dare he call her bluff. How dare he shove her against a wall, bare his teeth, then *not* rip her to pieces. Fi's blood boiled, indignant by how this creature surprised her at every turn.

And how much she liked it.

Fi went still as permafrost. Of course she didn't like this. In her ears, blood roared. In her ribs, the pounding of a panicked heart. All perfectly normal reactions to a daeyari's teeth on her throat.

But then, as they settled against each other . . . a shiver, where Antal's mouth pressed her pulse. The brush of his exhale, warmer than expected. That heat beneath her skin, fiercer now, sinking through her chest then down, down to the where claws held her waist. Insufferably *chaste*, these teeth, pressed against her without even a taunt of tongue. Only a cautious press of lips.

Fi's breaths turned shallower, adrift against a starless sky, snared by velvet claws and feather-soft fangs.

Why did she like this?

She couldn't like this.

The middle of an argument with a carnivore: *not* the ideal time for discovering kinks.

Fi wriggled to break Antal's grip, dizzy on ice and ozone as she fisted his shirt collar and its obnoxious buttons, fingers tangling the hair between his antlers. Despite his lean build, this daeyari was a menace, immovable with all his steel-taut weight turned against her – and fuck, if that didn't stoke her useless pulse faster.

Antal forfeited no ground. He bit *harder*, fangs dragging flesh until a soft ache bloomed. A warning or a tease, such a narrow line to tread. When Fi writhed, he dug his hip into hers to hold her still. Pinned her lashing arm against the wall. A firmer hand braced her head, stopping her from ripping her own throat open with her struggle.

The rake of claws through Fi's hair threatened an unbecoming sound on her lips. His growl, low in warning, shuddered down her spine.

At last, she was terrified.

Terrified of how gently he held her. Terrified of the heat pooling low in her belly, absurdly inappropriate in such a compromising position. A whisper of doubt that, maybe, being devoured wouldn't be the horrific end she'd envisioned.

She gasped when Antal's fangs lifted off her, a dull throb in their absence.

Void have mercy, she *liked* it. Fi liked the press of his teeth, the hard lines of him holding her down.

And Antal? What should she make of his low, swaying tail? The way he lingered too close, breath warm on her neck, fingers knotted in her hair. He held her against the wall, still claiming the high ground. In the slow caress of his exhale, Fi heard a speechless taunt.

'*Had enough?*' his slitted eyes said. '*Admit it. Concede.*'

'You see?' she breathed. 'I'm not afraid of you.'

What a gorgeous flicker of incredulity across his face. Fi

could eat it for breakfast. He shifted, still not backing away, untangling his claws from her hair. His thumb traced the arc of an artery down her neck.

'Your heart is racing,' he said again.

Swifter than before. Verging on hyperventilation, in fact, the whole Plane shifting beneath her.

'Is it?' Fi said, light. 'I hadn't noticed.'

'You'd lie about something so petty?'

'A lie? I'm *bluffing*, you melodramatic wall cactus.'

Antal scowled. Whether at her tone or the name, hard to disentangle. 'What difference does it make?'

'All the difference.' Why was he still so *close*? Fi scrambled for her barbs, her only defense against his taunts, against the unyielding heat of him flush against her. 'Being afraid is natural. Survival instinct. I can be afraid, but that won't stop me bluffing out my ass when I need to get something done. It won't stop me looking you in the eye to call you a brooding house cat.' She scoffed. 'Honestly. It's like you've never met a proper smuggler.'

Antal considered her too long. The drift of smoldering eyes across Fi's face sparked another shudder. The flare of his nostrils *should* have terrified her, a predator scenting prey. That trace of his tongue across his teeth, clearly contemplating how she'd taste if he split her open.

'I suppose I haven't,' he said at last.

He stepped away.

Fi fought to keep her chin up, not succumbing to the relief that threatened to slump her against the wall. With distance came breathing room, but not a return to where they'd stood before. This time, neither of them had backed down, a new field to spar upon.

She ran a hand over her neck. Tender skin, but when she examined her fingers . . . not a drop of blood.

'You're an unusually brazen human, Fionamara.'

Antal watched her like a panther searching for a limp. No telling, anymore, what he'd do if he spotted one. Still too close, mere feet away across her kitchen, his scent of ice and ozone sharp enough to taste.

'Some call it stubborn,' she returned.

'Stubborn is a word for it . . .' His words came out too rough. Too long of a pause as his tongue brushed his mouth again, tail an agitated flick. 'Was there a point to this?'

A point. What in the wide black Void was her point in pushing a daeyari? Other than pride, of course. A distraction from perennial helplessness.

Fi could use a distraction now. Anything to escape the thought of teeth on her neck, how upsettingly *good* this monster felt against her. They had a common enemy. Nothing more. She'd be stupid to show a sliver of vulnerable flesh to a creature like this.

'The point is, I won't run from you. And I won't run from Verne.' Fi refused to be that flighty girl who always ran.

'You're a fool,' he replied with insulting swiftness. 'Or you don't fear death. Unsettling. Usually, that's a reliable trait in mortals.'

'Of course I'm afraid to die. Don't pretend *you* aren't. Afraid you'll come back as some . . . rabid chinchilla, or something.' Antal opened his mouth in protest, but Fi spoke over him. 'None of that matters. Verne can't have this territory.'

'I have no allies to muster. And with Tyvo refusing aide—'

'Could we take her down?'

'. . . *We?*'

'The two of us.'

On Fi's kitchen table lay several empty energy capsules. Her silviamesh, shredded by daeyari claws.

And an eight-pointed black antler, severed at the stump. A trophy. A stroke of courage.

Fi grabbed the antler off the table, a reminder that daeyari weren't as untouchable as the stories said. She'd stood her ground against Tyvo. She'd seen Antal ripped to shreds. Terrifying, powerful creatures, but they *could* be fought.

Antal's eyes narrowed on the severed antler of his kin.

He paced around the table, around *her*, letting his long tail drift against her arm as he passed. Fi raised her guard, tasting this alliance with hesitant sips, worried he'd spotted weakness. Had he felt her shudder at his touch? Could he use it against her? He seemed tense as he studied her, eyes sharp and mouth clamped into a firm line.

For the love of the Void, she had to stop staring at his mouth.

'What do you hope to gain from this?' he said slowly. Testing.

A negotiation. Fi stood firmer. 'Verne's a problem for both of us.'

'She's a problem for *me*. Why would you aide me, risk your life to trade one daeyari for another?'

'I want Nyskya to be safe. Promise they'll never have to send a sacrifice, and I'll help you get rid of her.'

'*That's* what you want?' Antal frowned, his guarded exterior cracking beneath a creased brow. 'You're a smuggler. Yet you have no aspirations for fortune? Amnesty?'

Never. Fi didn't turn to Void smuggling for riches or infamy, only because it was the easiest way to keep running. But this, she couldn't outrun. She couldn't do that to Boden again.

'Nyskya is my home. *You* might be able to slink back to your Old House on the Twilit Plane if this doesn't work out, but I don't have anywhere else.'

Antal went so stiff, he didn't appear to be breathing.

His tail dropped near the floor. More than a glare this time, a low growl in his chest warned her of the thin ice she stood on. Fi didn't balk. No wandering gazes to teeth.

'Sure, you're a daeyari, like Verne,' she said. 'But you let the elections run. You let your mortals govern. You've let Nyskya keep to ourselves. If I have to choose someone to replace that bitch, I'll settle for you.'

Fi thought he might bite her again, in earnest this time. Antal's breath hitched, a grating rise of his chest as he skewered her with glowing crimson irises.

But when he finally spoke, it came out too soft.

'You're wrong on one count,' he said. 'I can't go home. But I accept your terms.'

Fi scowled. 'What kind of cryptic-ass answer—'

She tensed as Antal reached past her, plucking an empty energy capsule from the table. The air *cracked*. Fi's vision flashed red as a current bloomed on Antal's fingertips, energy flooding the capsule in seconds, glass glowing with crimson light that writhed like a thing alive.

Fi's eyes widened on the offering.

The taste of ozone fluttered her stomach, not entirely unpleasant.

'If we're to face Verne,' Antal said. 'You'll need this. And enough luck to fill the Void.'

19

No repressed feelings whatsoever

Daeyari energy felt like splinters beneath Fi's nails. Like a pick of lightning through her arteries, charring from the inside out.

She liked it more than she ought to, this touch of power that could destroy her.

At the start of the week, Antal joined her in the clearing by her cottage, a capsule of daeyari energy scorching her palm. Fi could Shape from her own capsules as easy as breathing. Daeyari magic came to her like inhaling ice water. A more powerful current, Antal explained – concentrated, when they became immortal, and their new bodies could withstand the fiercer energy. Fi *did* listen. She picked through every damn word.

Still nearly burned a hand off the first time she tried to grasp the capsule's current.

The danger didn't deter her. Nor the pain of immortal power searing her lesser flesh. To stand any chance against Verne – against Astrid – Fi needed this edge.

Antal left again, surveying Verne's tightening grip on his territory. Still no news from Boden. To maintain sanity, Fi wrestled into her boots and coat, out into the cold to practice.

She gripped a crimson energy capsule, perched on bare fingertips to limit skin contact. The current hummed through her nails. Oddly, she couldn't decide if the energy felt scalding or freezing, or some other sensation she had no word to describe.

A deep breath. Then Fi reached for the energy inside the capsule.

The current exploded into her, surging that otherworldly hot-and-cold down her arm. Fi clamped her teeth as the foreign energy tightened her chest. She held her stance as it carved her stomach, dredging that fight-or-flight panic of a hare, an instinct to hurl the capsule at the ground.

It was terrible and delicious, how the energy tried to consume her. In that moment, Fi wasn't some tiny thing cowering in the forest. Ozone burned her tongue, a taste of eternity plaquing her teeth.

She raised her sword hilt. Energy surged into the conductive metal, writhing as she Shaped it, until a crimson blade formed, too rough on the edges, but keener every day, crackling the cold air. Fi envisioned Verne facing her across the clearing, those mocking eyes regarding her like a gnat. She envisioned Astrid leant against a tree in too-tight pants, lips coiled to a sneer.

Ten years. Fi abandoned Astrid for *ten years*. Understandable, that Astrid would blame her, hate her, betray her. But to side with Verne? To hold a guillotine above Nyskya and Void knew how many other villages desperate to survive this shift in regime?

Energy fed off Fi's ire, sparking crimson down the blade. Maybe *this* was what turned Astrid to that cold creature Fi had seen. This siren's song of power. This sip of eternity. The current burned and froze through the marrow of her bones.

One slip, and . . .

Pain speared Fi's arm. The daeyari energy bucked her control, searing muscles and snapping red tendrils through the air. Her shout rang across the clearing. Her fingers spasmed, dropping the capsule to the snow as she fell onto her ass.

She shuddered as the energy fled her system, leaving her cold.

'Fuck,' Fi said. Then, '*fuck*,' more emphatically. Then a shout for good measure.

She flexed each finger, tendons prickling. In a few places, the sensation didn't fade. There was her problem pinkie, nerves fuzzy since a past overdraw. The energy burns down her thumb and pointer finger were new: charred veins against pale flesh, heaviest at the fingertips, roots feathering her wrist. The biggest downside of human energy Shaping: destructible casting material. Not a problem for daeyari and their 'Void-woven' flesh, as Antal described it.

Across the clearing, Aisinay paused from hunting needlemice under the porch, lifting her head for a snort.

'I don't want to hear it from you,' Fi said.

Astrid wielded daeyari energy just fine. *Astrid* had put Fi on the ground when they fought. Fi didn't need a judgmental Void horse reminding her how much ground she had to make up.

But Aisinay's finned ears didn't perk toward her. The forest went quiet, squabbling jays and squirrels turned to silence, usually a sign of . . . Fi scanned the trees. Not the trunks, she was learning. Her chin tipped up to the dark canopy.

She spotted them faster each time, those red eyes staring down at her.

Antal perched upon the high bough of a shiverpine, still as a phantom, tail balanced against the branch. Not the first time she'd caught a daeyari watching from the woods this week. Her visitor had appeared once upon the shingles, another time within the drapery of a fir.

Fi disliked how her heart sped at the sight of him. She loathed the reason it did so, no longer purely out of fear.

She stood, tidying her coat with as much dignity as one could wipe snow off their ass.

'Listen, Antlers,' she called up. 'I'll *give you* permission to teleport straight to my doorstep, if it will stop you being a dick and lurking in trees.'

He'd taken to ignoring the nickname, perhaps thinking this would dull her amusement, clearly not realizing the challenge would only stoke Fi's determination. He descended the tree in several agile hops, a scrape of claws against bark then a muffled footfall on snow. Could have teleported down easier. Show-off.

'I didn't wish to interrupt,' he greeted.

Within the dusk, he moved like another shadow, red eyes glowing, dark clothes contrasting bone-pale skin. A bough-stalker, straight out of the trees. A hunter, who could rend her to pieces. She held her ground as the beast approached.

He paused at a polite distance, tail a low and docile sway.

How tenuous, this thing growing between them. Fi wouldn't go so far as calling it *trust*. But partnership required concession, didn't it? A mutual lowering of guards so they could focus on their common enemy. Antal had earned that much. A week passed, and he hadn't pushed her against a wall again.

Would he, if she asked him to?

That thought.

That, right the fuck there, was a *problem.*

A new problem. A concerning problem. The bane of Fi's entire week, as a matter of fact. And that was saying something, wasn't it? She'd grown familiar with nightmares of Verne's claws, of Astrid's wretched glare. She didn't know where to begin untangling these ridiculous thoughts of teeth on her throat, simmering eyes beneath dark lashes, how it might feel if he held her down in earnest and—

'How long have you been watching?' Fi demanded.

Antal's brow quirked. Little chips in the mask. 'Careful, Fionamara. Cause too much disturbance, and someone in the village will notice.'

The words chided, but his gaze dropped to her hands. Fi had been fidgeting, thumb tracing the tingling length of an energy burn. Predators always searched for injuries on their prey. That must be the reason for his furrowed brow. Fi would be mad, an absolutely daft little rabbit if she weighed his reaction as anything like *concern*.

She retrieved the dropped energy capsule.

Never mind that they had to work together. Never mind how good his claws had felt in her hair, those enticing lines of his collarbone framed by an open shirt. He was a daeyari. He was a fucking *daeyari*, and he could rip Fi's throat open if he wanted to.

'What's it like out there?' The sooner they got rid of Verne, the sooner things could return to normal: Antal back in Thomaskweld, Fi back to avoiding daeyari for the rest of her life.

Antal spoke low. 'You're sure you wish to know?'

'Why do people ask that? *Of course* I want to know.' Better than waiting for Boden's automaton birds and their frustratingly brief messages.

'Verne is . . . feasting. A year's worth of sacrifices, in two weeks.'

Fi's stomach lurched. Boden's messages hadn't mentioned *that*.

'An aggressive strategy,' Antal said. 'Verne will test the loyalty of her new supplicants, make them vie for her good will. Some offerings, she'll gorge upon herself. The rest, she'll send to the Twilit Plane, gifts to curry favor with the Old Houses.'

And daeyari were strongest when well fed. Verne was keeping herself in prime form. Meanwhile, Antal still hadn't eaten. Fi hoped she was imagining the growing leanness of his cheeks, his eyes glowing dimmer each time she saw him.

'And Astrid?' she asked.

'Verne's Arbiter?' Antal bared a fang. 'She's been traveling throughout the territory, making Verne's demands known.'

Fi couldn't reconcile this version of Astrid. They'd pierced their ears together using sewing needles heated over her bedroom furnace. They'd pilfered alcohol from their parents and snuck onto Shards, drinking and kissing themselves silly beneath the starless Void. Astrid had always been a wild thing, a glint of cunning immortal ancestors in her eyes, but not *this*.

'You were never like this,' Fi told Antal, more accusing than gracious. 'So what's different? Why doesn't Verne give a shit about humans, but you do?'

Antal chided, 'I've probably known more humans than you.'

'And such diversity, no doubt. Sacrifices, come to be eaten? Cowering attendants? Obedient governors?'

'Not all of them.'

His quiet gave Fi pause. She'd braced for attack, some biting speech about how free-range livestock were more complacent. He scowled at the snow, a cold breeze tousling blue-black hair against his antlers.

'I've known many humans. Even as . . .' Antal's mouth made a strange shape, a stutter into a frown. 'A friend. One of the best friends I've ever had.'

Fi gaped wide enough, she could have gathered gnats on a warmer Plane.

He huffed. 'You wound me, Fionamara. I told you, I see your kind as more than food.'

'Sure. But a *friend*?' In the folktales, there were no happily ever afters with daeyari. The human protagonists ended up flayed alive. Hearts ripped from chests. Frozen in the woods.

'He tended aurorabeasts for my family on the Twilit Plane,' Antal said.

'There are humans on the Twilit Plane?'

'Fewer than here. Mostly daeyari and vavriter. But several mortal settlements remain as . . . sustenance, in addition to what the territories provide. Other humans find safety in service to the Old Houses.'

'So where is he now?'

'Now?'

Antal's tone lost all inflection. His posture, stiff as ice.

'That was early in my second century,' he said. 'A long time ago.'

A long time. Humans, no matter how their magic and technology grew, had always found an insurmountable enemy in time.

But that was no satisfying end. Fi was ravenous for more: how did they meet? Why did Antal speak with this human rather than devouring him? This daeyari, so guarded, yet full of surprises, like a shiny box Fi had to pry open.

He'd distracted her again.

Maybe this was his most dangerous weapon: not fangs or claws, but velvet words and that soft part to his mouth, dragging her to the precipice of sympathy. Lulling Fi to lower her guard. A treacherous creature, for more reasons than she'd expected.

She rolled the energy capsule in her palm, the current as alluring as it was dangerous.

The plan. Just stick to the *plan*.

'So how do we kill Verne?' Fi asked.

Antal responded with visible alarm. Annoyingly so.

'Yeah, yeah,' she said. 'Only if we *have* to kill her. Terrible reincarnated Beasts and all.' Antal seemed more distressed by the prospect of a dead Verne than Fi did, but until he offered a better option . . . 'If *necessary*, how do I kill a daeyari?'

She brandished sword hilt in one hand, energy capsule in the other. Antal scowled at both.

'Is the sword crucial for this conversation?' he asked.

'I think it's motivating.'

'I think I'd be more motivated to tell you something like that if you weren't holding—'

The air cracked as Fi tapped the current, fighting red energy into a blade. Not just any energy. *Antal's* energy. *His* magic burned through her, leaving ice and ozone on her tongue.

She couldn't stop herself from wondering: would he taste the same?

With a shout, she charged.

Fi had deduced several things this week. The first: she'd defended herself against Tyvo for a short time, which worked overwhelmingly in her favor.

The second: teleportation was, indeed, utter bullshit.

She swung at Antal, but instead of blocking or parrying or anything reasonable, he vanished. Her sword cleaved empty air. Fi fought the shivering blade back into Shape with a tingle through her fingers.

Static struck her tongue. Antal reappeared beside her.

'You'll never be fast enough if you only react,' he said.

'I hope moss grows on your antlers!'

Fi swung again. He vanished again.

Another prick of static, taunting on her tongue. Antal appeared behind her.

'Pay attention,' he chided. '*Taste* it.'

'What in the endless black Void does *that* mean?'

This continued. Fi's pride waffled with each fruitless swing, each zap of static in her mouth. She tried to gauge trajectory.

Tried to guess where he'd reappear. In her frustration, her sword crackled. She reined the energy like a bucking horse, until a fresh prickle hit her mouth, concentrated at the tip of her tongue.

Antal appeared in front of her.

Fi froze. Blinked. When she didn't swing, his head tilted.

'Do that again,' she ordered.

He vanished. Fi waited, chewing her cheek. She might have imagined it, but . . .

There came the static, sharp on her tongue, slightly stronger on her right side.

Antal appeared to her right.

Fi gasped. Taste it. She had to *taste* the energy?

When he disappeared again, she was ready. Alert to every scrape of tongue against her teeth. The prickle came near her throat, a little left. Fi spun, pointing at Antal as he appeared.

He grinned.

So did Fi.

It crept up on her. She'd thought his scowls were vicious, but his grin was a sharper thing entirely, bright fangs and brighter eyes, slicing past her bristled exterior. She sparred back with a smirk. Maybe she shouldn't trust him. Maybe, the moment she lowered her guard in earnest, he'd go for her jugular.

But fuck, it felt good to hold her own against one of these nightmares she'd spent her life running from.

'You learn quickly, Fionamara.'

'Is that your best, daeyari? Better guard your antlers, or I'll add another to—'

His tail cut a wide, swift arc. Not a common motion in Fi's growing catalogue, but she did recognize it. A week ago. In her cottage. Right before he—

Antal pounced. In the shock of his weight hitting her, Fi's

sword extinguished in a snap of cold. She hit the ground with Antal on top of her. For the second time in too few days, fangs came for her throat.

His mouth snapped shut above her, teeth striking empty air with a dramatized *clack*.

A daeyari middle finger. Antal's insufferable smirk said as much. '*Look, I could eat you if I wanted to*,' danced goading in his gaze.

Fi went rigid. She wished she could blame the teeth. In some part, it was indignation that he'd gotten the best of her again. But indignation, she knew how to fight.

Antal had pinned her arms above her head. Firm thighs caged her hips, his weight holding her down as Fi lay breathless beneath him. All of *her*, exposed, splayed to stillness by ozone and his fang-laced smirk.

She shuddered. Why in the merciless Void did Fi *shudder*?

Antal's smirk vanished. He released her, sitting swiftly upright.

'Apologies. I didn't mean to—'

'Don't apologize to me!' She pushed onto her elbows, trapped beneath him, upsettingly warm as he sat on her hips. 'Verne won't hold back her teeth. Why should you?'

Fi bellowed bravado. She needed it, to hide how breathless he'd made her. A daeyari. He was a *daeyari*, and her stupid brain hadn't figured out how to counter him yet, and that was *all*.

Atop her, Antal blinked. 'You want me . . . to go harder on you?'

To Fi's abject horror, a blush heated her cheeks. 'Well, not when you put it like *that*.'

'How should I put it?'

He mantled over her. Fi tensed as he braced a hand beside

234

her head. A snarl pulled her lips as he closed the space between them.

'You'd prefer I try to rip you open in earnest?' he said. The threat came out different this time. Somehow softer and rougher and far more dangerous.

Fi scoffed. 'I thought we were playing nice.'

'You came at me with a sword.'

'Don't be dramatic, daeyari. You're more useful to me alive. For now.'

'Am I?'

The way he stared at her *felt* like being ripped open.

Then he laughed.

For the second time, Fi startled at that genuine laugh, this intimate thing she didn't know how to parry. The gesture was so insultingly soft, so wretchedly disarming, it *must* be some cunning new tactic. The daeyari's snarls hadn't cowed her, so he resorted to this trickery? She mustered every barb, just to stop herself smiling back.

Instead, Fi stared at his mouth. When he laughed, when his lips curved into that grin again, even fangs didn't seem as vicious. They hadn't been, when they were on her throat.

'You can let me go now.' Fi squirmed beneath him. A mistake. His weight against her hips made her cheeks burn hotter.

'I thought you didn't want me to go easy on you?' Antal sat upright again, pinning her firmer, arms held taunting at his sides. 'Shouldn't I let you thwart me on your own?'

This was, Fi decided, far more insufferable than if he'd just try to eat her and be done with it.

'You're enjoying this,' she accused. 'You prefer your prey cowering? Is that it?'

'Hardly,' he purred. 'I prefer the ones who stand their ground.'

His words rumbled Fi's chest, through the soft of her belly, down into . . .

She couldn't sit still. With a growl of her own, Fi gripped Antal's shirt for an anchor. She pulled herself up. Surprise lit his eyes as she held their faces an inch apart.

'Careful what you ask for, daeyari.'

She grabbed an antler.

Pulling him off balance was easy, with the leverage. Flipping him was harder. Antal's build was lean, but Fi felt every muscle tense against her. She heaved, throwing him to the snow, her thighs pinning his waist just as he'd done to her. Then, *she* perched atop this immortal. *She* held him down by his antlers.

The bastard's smirk made her want to carve him alive.

'So *fierce*,' Antal taunted. 'For someone who smells like pomegranates.'

His grin cut through her, even on the ground – *especially* on the ground, his dark hair mussed by their scuffle.

Absolutely not. Fi could not have this kind of reaction to a daeyari, of all things. He had fangs . . . which scraped surprisingly soft. Claws . . . that had tangled in her hair.

And this wouldn't be the first time she'd fallen for antlers.

Fi snarled and pressed her sword hilt to his chest, an angle that would have skewered his heart had the blade been Shaped.

'I'm afraid that won't do much good,' he said, unflustered.

'Daeyari don't have hearts?' she snapped back.

'We have hearts. Not like yours. Daeyari are energy, at our core. The body is a shell, created so we could walk the Planes again, crafted as a memory of what our mortal bodies looked like. Not all necessary to function. A blade through the heart will slow a daeyari, but won't kill.'

Well, there was one thing the stories got right: that old cautionary tale of the 'nameless warrior' who managed to put a sword through a daeyari's chest, only for the beast to laugh.

Fi spun her sword hilt, jabbing it to the soft hollow of Antal's throat.

He stilled. Fi's stomach warmed at the weight of him between her legs, the subtle shift of his waist as his tail swished the snow. But even more, at how his eyes sharpened. Like she could surprise him, too. His exhale feathered the exposed skin of her wrist.

'That will do it,' he said, soft as a secret between them. 'Taking off the head breaks the body, sends a daeyari's energy back to the Void. *If* you can get a blade through. The capsules will help. Next time, try it without letting your guard down.'

Fi scoffed. 'How have I—'

She wasn't wearing her silviamesh. This came to Fi's attention when claws slipped beneath her coat. Antal's warm palms splayed across her abdomen, cool clawtips poised to disembowel. The sensation should have turned her stomach. She should have recoiled like a startled hare.

She sucked in a sharp breath.

Oh no.

No. No. This wasn't right *at all.*

But Fi had no other explanation for the heat blooming beneath his touch. A slow, treacherous ache sank between her legs, countering every rational survival instinct that screamed at her to pull away.

Instead, she fought an urge to lean in. To surrender.

Maybe something was wrong with her. Maybe her dumb brain got a circuit crossed, confusing terror with lust.

Antal stared up at her. Fi feared she might fully combust as the beast's head tilted, crimson eyes narrowed on her traitorously flushed cheeks.

'Mine would kill faster,' she argued, pressing her hilt against his throat. It took all her willpower to sit tall, chin up.

'Questionable,' he returned. 'You've neglected an important variable.'

A pressure closed on Fi's neck.

This made no sense. She *felt* both his hands beneath her shirt. His legs were pinned beneath her.

But his tail.

Fi snarled as the noose yanked her sideways. Her hands swiped air as she was pulled off him, twisting, falling.

Antal caught her before her head cracked the ground.

Her back thumped ice with his palm cradling her skull, claws slipping through the rainbow snarls of her hair. Always softer than expected. He leaned over her, knee pinning her waist. So close, every breath was ozone. So close, she watched the flare of his nose, his eyes lidded as he breathed her in.

'Careful, Fionamara. You're more useful to me alive, as well.'

Her full name rolled off his tongue, slow like a purr. Warm like embers. Fi fisted her hands into the fabric of his shirt collar, unyielding.

Antal's smile had gone. A heavy pause furrowed his brow, parted his mouth. Void have mercy, Fi *had to* stop staring at that mouth.

'Why do you look at me like that?' he asked.

Shit. 'Like what, daeyari?'

'Like you aren't afraid.'

Fi didn't expect that. She didn't understand how his words came so soft. Such a challenge ought to snap like fangs, not the whisper-quiet thing that passed his lips.

'I already said, I'm not afraid of you.'

'You *were* afraid of me. When we met. But now . . .'

Fi watched every flick of crimson irises, scouring her raw. As if she, too, were a difficult box to pry open, all rusted latches and hidden seams.

Maybe this flutter in her pulse was curiosity. Fi had spent so many years cowering, of course she'd find allure in something forbidden, something dangerous. As tempting as that energy capsule and its kiss of soul-searing power.

But why had Antal fallen so still? Why was his palm still cradling her head above the snow, claws tightening in her hair? Some strategy to disarm her. Or a wicked game to play with his prey. He was more than a box. A puzzle.

Fi wanted to tear him apart and understand what made him tick. She wanted to—

Antal's head snapped up. His nostrils flared, scenting the air. Wordless, he released her, vanishing the moment they no longer touched.

Fi sat alone in the snow, blinking. Heart like thunder in her ears.

She pushed to her feet. A moment passed before she recalled how to *breathe*, another before she gathered the sense to scan the trees. The daeyari was nowhere in sight, but she soon detected what he had: the crack of a branch, a crunch of snow. Heading closer. Who in their right mind would trek all the way up here . . .

'Fi-Fi?' Boden called out.

Fuck.

20

Awkward introductions

Fi didn't have much time.

Hooves tromped through the forest, snapping branches and crunching ice, approaching fast. She scrambled to straighten her curls, bat the snow off her coat, sweeping away all signs she'd been tussling with a daeyari who she'd *definitely not* told Boden about. When had she had the chance?

Ok, maybe she'd had several chances to fess up, but she'd never expected Antal to hang around this long. Still made her the Plane's worst sister. As usual.

Boden burst into the clearing, perched in the saddle of a boreal horse. The beast's black hooves sliced snow, winter-thick coat sable as night, an aurora fade of green and blue striping its legs and bristled mane. Fi had tried convincing her bland older brother to get a Void horse, but her argument received a firm, 'What the fuck would I use it for?' Her rebuttal of 'but it would look *cool*' met with equal dismissal.

Should have talked him into a mechanized snow sled. Anything to give advance notice of an impromptu visit. But no, Boden had a soft spot for hooves and reins and breathing things, so distant from the metal their father had worked.

As Boden dropped from his saddle, Fi adopted a casual stance, brow quirked at his haggard gait and ice-crusted beard.

'Fi! Are you all right?'

'I'm splendid. Why wouldn't I be?'

Boden hunched in his aurorabeast coat, gloved hands bracing his thighs, breaths hard. His hair had probably started the morning in a tidy bun, now devolved to frizz.

Behind him, Aisinay greeted the boreal horse with a snort. The striped beast stomped its hooves, dislodging snow clumped to the fur.

'I heard an *explosion*,' Boden said. 'On my way up here. I hurried as fast as I could.'

Antal was right. Fi held back a curse. 'I don't know what you're talking about.'

'You . . . didn't hear an explosion?'

'I think I'd know if something exploded in my front yard, Bodie.'

'So I was imagining things?'

'Maybe you heard a tree falling? Snow came in thick the other night, too much weight on the . . . *OW!*'

Fi winced when Boden punched her arm.

She punched back, *harder*. 'What's that for?'

'Don't lie to me, Fi. What's going on?'

'I'm killing time! Since *someone* ordered me to wait it out up here.'

Boden deflated. All that mustered authority, crumbling the moment his shoulders sagged. Fi wished they hadn't. It was easier to lie to him when he didn't wear those tired eyes, enough to crack her like sheet ice.

'I'm sorry for leaving you in the lurch, Fi. You know I am.' He ran a hand through his hair. 'I meant to visit sooner, but our energy conduits are acting up again.'

'. . . Oh.'

'Even the newest lines we put in. Been trying to keep everyone warm, but I don't want to send anyone to Thomaskweld for spare parts.'

'Sure.'

'After Astrid's visit, we're already in Verne's sights. Wouldn't want to give her any ideas about us needing help, pushing our sacrifice deadline up.'

'Right.'

'I know things looks bad. But we'll fix things on our own. Like always.'

As he spoke, Fi nodded like a bobblehead doll. She didn't typically allow Boden to monologue this long without some puckered face or snide remark, but her focus drifted over his shoulder, her expression forced blank with thinly-veiled horror.

Antal perched in the bough of a shiverpine, watching with red eyes and tail swaying. Fi's thoughts became a string of expletives. She'd let her guard down again, distracted by a tussle in the snow and a flutter in her stomach. Of course she'd *thought* of telling Boden.

What if he disapproved of her pact with Antal? What if she disappointed him again? What if—

'Fi-Fi?'

Boden spoke in a hush. He stared at her mouth.

Fi went cold at his keen focus, his dark eyes wide in alarm. A week of energy mending had healed the cut across her lips – mostly. The scar felt tight against her teeth. A thin silver line spread past her lipstick, visible upon scrutiny.

Boden was scrutinizing.

'It's nothing,' she said, too quickly.

'What happened?'

'Nothing.'

'Fi.'

'An accident.'

'*Fi.*' Her name cut deep, not the hardness of it, but Boden's pleading undertone.

She itched for an out. Her easiest option would be evasion, getting rid of Boden before he noticed the beast poised in her trees. Lies leapt to her tongue, swift as survival instinct.

But he was her brother.

He was her brother, and he deserved so much better than her, and if this absurd alliance with a daeyari went anywhere, she'd have to tell Boden eventually. Fi loathed the quiver on her lips, that slip of dread she couldn't hide.

'So. Boden. You know how we promised not to keep secrets from each other?'

Serious Fi made Boden look mildly panicked. Understandable.

'Yeah,' he said slowly. 'We did.'

'Are you sure you want to know?' Void have mercy, now *she* was the one asking dumb, stalling questions.

'Of course, Fi. What's wrong?' He gripped her shoulders, gloved hands a calm and reassuring clamp, making Fi feel impossibly small.

In the tree, Antal stiffened.

'Don't freak out,' Fi said. 'I think there's . . . someone you need to meet.'

Boden scowled. '*Someone* I need to—'

A shadow flicked through the corner of her eye.

Boden shouted, tackled to the snow with a snarling daeyari atop him. *Shit.* Fi lurched into the fray, dodging the lashing tail, grabbing antlers before any teeth got involved.

'*Off!*' she ordered. 'You useless beast, that's not what I meant!'

Antal growled like a hawk mantling over prey. Beneath him, Boden sprawled in frozen horror.

At a yank from Fi, Antal released his quarry. Boden scuttled backward through the snow on hands and ass, wide eyes never leaving the daeyari, curses fogging his breath.

'*Fi?*' he demanded. As if he automatically assumed this was her fault. Granted, it was largely her fault, but she didn't appreciate that ice pick of guilt.

Fi stood between them, hands raised to broker peace. She'd done this before, played intermediary between rival black marketeers, at least until one side could pay her. This was no different. She told herself it was *no different*.

'Boden. This is Antal, former Lord Daeyari of this territory.'

'*I'm aware.*' Boden's retort was half hysteria, half chiding older brother.

'Antal,' Fi continued. 'This is Boden. Mayor of Nyskya.'

The daeyari stood stone still, glowering. 'I'm aware.'

'My *brother*,' she clarified, with a strong undertone of *not to be eaten*.

'Brother?' Antal looked slowly between them. Then, a scowl. A dramatic exhale. 'Veshri's teeth. Of course, stubbornness runs in the family . . .'

'Fi,' Boden said. 'What the *fuck* is going on? What is *that thing* doing here? Why are you so calm?'

'No, no.' She waved a hand to silence him. 'This is a conversation for indoors. Let's go.'

By the time Fi pulled her panic-stricken brother to his feet, Antal was gone. Boden spun a circle, scouring the dusk-lit forest, but they were alone with trampled snow and dark pines. Static pricked her tongue. Once. Then again.

'Fi.' Each time he hissed her name, it grew more urgent.

'Shhh . . .' She pressed a hand to the back of his coat and steered him toward her cottage. 'It's a lot. I'm aware. Believe me, I am *so* aware.'

Maybe this was a horrible idea. Fi made her best and worst

decisions under duress, with frustratingly little middle ground. She just had to avoid Boden's eyes. That way, she couldn't see how angry he was.

They kicked snow off their boots and stepped inside. A warm furnace greeted them, soft overhead lights and . . . of course Antal waited in the rafters. He crouched on a beam, tail coiled, watching like a panther.

Boden grabbed Fi's arm, leaning in to whisper, 'I'm not used to seeing one of them so . . . close.'

'*He* is a person,' Fi said at full volume, 'not a circus exhibit.' She tipped her glare up and her voice louder. 'And he can *act* like a person by coming down and sitting properly.'

'*Kasek aza* . . .' Antal grumbled.

Despite having demonstrated his ability to drop from heights on several occasions, he made a dramatic show of snapping out of sight then reappearing upon the sofa, cross-legged and rigid, tail swishing the fabric.

Fi's stomach fluttered, stirred by the assertive tilt of his jaw. Stop it. Focus.

She pulled out a chair from the kitchen table for Boden. Without taking eyes off Antal, he sat, a stiff motion that she'd have preferred to end with him missing his target and tumbling ass to floor. Drama queens, both of them. Not that she could blame Boden for keeping wary around a daeyari, but Antal's bristle was . . .

Guarded. Distrustful. Far more than he had been with her this past week. His last attendants *had* turned on him, she supposed. Betrayal must hurt, even for immortals.

'All right, Fi.' Boden kept his glare on the daeyari. 'I'm all ears.'

'Would you like some coffee first?' Fi asked.

'How long has he been here?'

'*I* could use some coffee.' She pressed a hand to her temple, fighting a headache. 'And liquor.' That probably wouldn't help the headache.

'*Fi.*'

'No coffee then. Fair.' Fi crossed her arms and slouched. She'd have preferred to collapse into a chair, but instead stood awkwardly between Boden and Antal, lest their glaring escalate. 'After the explosion in Thomaskweld, I . . . met Antal.'

Antal huffed. A strong contender for today's 'not helping' award.

'His attendants tried to sacrifice me,' Fi clarified.

Boden nearly fell out of his chair.

'But Antal *didn't* eat me. As you can see.' She gestured to her intact person. 'Now, we're going to get rid of Verne. Together.'

She looked to Antal for backup.

'Yes,' he said, unenthused. 'That is, apparently, what we're doing.'

Void stop her from slapping him, just to see what would happen.

Boden gawked at Fi. At Antal. Back to her. 'So there's a deposed daeyari lurking in the forest above my village? How long has he been here?'

'Off and on . . .' Fi muttered. 'For a couple weeks.'

'*Weeks?* Why didn't you tell me!'

'I didn't know what to tell you!'

'What about my people? Are they in danger?'

'Calm down, Boden, he's not going to eat any villagers.'

'Unless someone's offering,' Antal grumbled with the enthusiasm of a wet cat.

Fi shoved his antlers. Antal snarled.

Boden looked stunned. Not at the fang-flashing immortal, but at *Fi.*

She didn't want to look at him. She didn't want those tired, worry-creased eyes picking her to pieces. She'd rather stare at her boots, watch the droplets of snow melt onto far less judgmental floorboards. But she had to look at him. She had to stand tall like there wasn't the weight of a village on her shoulders, tip her chin up as if she weren't fighting to stop it quivering.

Because the moment she stopped pretending, she'd shatter.

'You want to fight *Verne?*' Boden's voice cracked with disapproval.

Fi's fists clenched, tingling her energy burns. 'We have to do something. We both heard Astrid's demands. We both know Nyskya isn't safe.'

'That's no reason to fight a daeyari. We have to be smart. Patient. If we can wait for—'

Fi grabbed the severed antler from her table and thrust it into Boden's hands. He paled, fingers cradling carved points.

'What is this?' he whispered.

'We visited Tyvo. Trying to find an ally. But we failed.' Fi loomed over Boden, hands on her hips, hair spilling in angry rainbow curls. 'We're on our own, Bodie. No waiting for someone else to fix this.'

He knew that. Everyone on this ever-frigid Plane knew if you got stranded in the snow, you didn't sit down and resign to freeze. You got up, stoked a current, and kept walking.

Boden glared at Antal. 'So you cut your neighbor's antler off? How does *that* help?'

'*I* didn't.' Antal tipped his chin at Fi. 'She did.'

The antler fell slack in Boden's lap. A stillness came over him as he looked up, looked at his little sister with bafflement thinning his lips.

'Fi?' he whispered.

She felt miniscule. No different than when she'd been a little girl with scraped knees and puffed cheeks, holding back tears while Boden patched her back together.

The greater Fi's doubt, the firmer her words. 'I won't wait until Verne comes for us. I won't run away again. We need to do something, and with a *daeyari* willing to help—'

Fi waved at Antal, her star evidence, arrogant shirt buttons and all.

He returned a bland look, tail twitching.

'I agreed to maybe help *one* of you,' he said.

'Stop it, you moody housecat! We don't have time for your aloof bullshit.' Fi had found him charming moments ago. He was still a little charming, lips curled to bare one canine of protest. She faced Boden. 'And we don't have time to wait and second-guess. We all want Verne gone. We stand the best chance if we work together.'

Boden always went silent when he was thinking. His fingers strummed the severed antler, an appraising look that shifted to Antal. What frost had coated him on the journey up the cliffside had melted, glinting dew along his beard and the seams of his coat.

'You have a daeyari,' Boden said slowly.

'Yes,' Fi said. Still an alarming concept.

'You think we can trust him?'

Wait until Boden learned what else Fi had been thinking about this daeyari.

No. Scratch that. Boden would *never* learn that particular indiscretion, or Fi would have to throw herself into the Void.

'So far,' she said.

'And he's agreed to help?'

They both looked to Antal.

249

'To our mutual interest,' the daeyari said begrudgingly. Fi would take it.

Boden rubbed a hand to his temple. 'And you've been up here, planning to go against Verne. Just the two of you?'

'There's only *one* of her,' Fi said.

Boden arced a brow.

'And Astrid,' Fi conceded. And a reincarnated Beast daeyari. She made the executive decision to save that logistical detail for a time when Boden looked less haggard.

'A small force is preferable.' Antal startled Fi with his contribution, muttered though it was. 'We'll be less likely to alert Verne. She won't have time to prepare, or worse, to seek support from the Twilit Plane.'

'What about Tyvo?' Boden pressed.

Antal huffed. 'He might have agreed to Verne's bid. But fighting for her would be an act of aggression. He'll stay out of this, or face repercussions from the Daey Celva.'

Boden fell quiet, weighing the arguments with a slump to his shoulders.

Then, he surprised Fi.

He straightened in his chair, meeting Antal's gaze with the same resolve Fi had tried to master, as if the same instinct told him he couldn't cower if he wanted this creature to take him seriously. This new man of resolve wasn't Fi's worry-prone Bodie. This was Boden Kolbeck, Mayor of Nyskya.

'Five years ago,' Boden told Antal, 'when I became mayor. You visited me.'

Fi went stiff as a corpse. Her brain did that thing where it sort of . . . stopped working a moment, a fizzle between her ears as she reset.

When she and Boden had dragged themselves to Nyskya seven years ago, an evening of hard confessions and harder cider in a corner of Kashvi's tavern, they'd forged a path forward under a pact of honesty. No more lies. No evasions. Since then, Boden told her everything. He told her which aurorabeasts were picky eaters. He told her who in the village paid taxes late. He told her when she was being a reckless idiot, letting deals turn too dicey.

He'd never told her about meeting a daeyari.

Antal's tail swayed as he appraised Nyskya's mayor.

'You offered me coffee,' the daeyari said.

'You told me you don't drink coffee,' Boden returned.

'But humans don't usually offer.'

'You promised me,' Boden said, 'if I didn't request aid from Thomaskweld, I'd never see you again. I'd never have to send a sacrifice.'

'And I kept that promise.' Antal flashed a grimace. 'To the best of my ability.'

Fi couldn't believe this. They'd met before, and Boden never told her?

Of course he hadn't told her. She was rash. Jumpy around daeyari. Not to be trusted with political intricacy. The slight didn't have to sting, if she saw the rationale behind it.

But it did sting a little.

'Do you promise me now.' Boden leaned forward his chair. 'My people will be safe while you stay here?'

Antal weighed the request.

'I swear.' The daeyari dipped his head, tapping a claw to the highest point of his antlers. 'As Veshri watches from the Void.'

Veshri. The first immortal daeyari, Antal had called him, though he spoke the name with the hush Fi's people once used for their old gods. Only, her gods turned out to be make-believe. Was a daeyari deity more likely to be real?

She shuddered at the thought. One of the comforts of the

Void was its emptiness. Fi didn't like the idea of something out there watching her.

Antal's oath stripped some tension from the room. Boden leaned back in his chair, letting out a long breath. 'Ok.' He looked to Fi. 'Confronting Verne. Do you have a plan?'

They kept coming back to that, didn't they?

'Working on it.' Fi flicked a glance at Antal. 'He . . . hasn't eaten in a while. If you can spare an aurorabeast, I'll buy one off you.'

Boden's scowl, Fi expected. He loved those big, dumb creatures. But if the choice came down to an aurorabeast or a villager to keep Antal from going feral?

Boden stared at his boots, fingers combed in contemplation through the frizz of his beard. 'What if . . . I could do you one better?'

Fi had no clue what that meant.

'I've been fishing for information,' Boden explained. 'About Cardigan?'

She groaned at the name. Amidst two weeks of chaos, Cardigan's sour attitude and abandoning her to trade wardens on the Autumn Plane made for smaller concerns. That didn't stop the reminder from ticking her off.

'Cardigan *Rothmauk*?' Antal said.

Fi and Boden shared a startled look.

'Yeah . . .' she said, slow in confusion. 'Cardigan's the asshole who gave me that cart of energy capsules to blow up your capitol building.'

'He did *what*?'

She'd only seen Antal this livid when facing Verne, claws curled, tail lashing. His clenched fangs looked ready to rip a throat out.

'How do *you* know him?' Fi asked.

'Cardigan Rothmauk oversaw the most recent energy conduit renovations in Thomaskweld. Milana recommended him.'

On the morning of the explosion, Fi had passed a crowd at the gate to the capitol complex—citizens of Thomaskweld demanding audience with their governor, complaining of faulty conduits.

Cardigan. That turncoat bastard.

'Cardigan's name pops up for several questionable energy projects,' Boden said, grim. 'Faulty equipment. Crates of energy capsules missing from smaller communities. I'd guess that's where your contraband came from. He's a conman. A thief. Whatever you want to call it.'

Antal perched on the sofa, a picture of rage. His tail coiled a tight circle. His eyes glowed the red of hot steel. If Cardigan had sabotaged the energy conduits in Thomaskweld, that would make Antal's citizens more desperate, more willing to accept a new ruler so long as Verne promised to save them from freezing.

How many died to the cold anyway? How many lost in the capitol explosion?

'If Cardigan's working for Verne,' Fi said, 'he might be able to tell us more about her coup plan. Maybe even her next moves.' If nothing else, she'd relish punching his teeth in. 'But what does that have to do with getting Antal a meal . . .'

The pieces clicked as she spoke. Then, a blink of surprise. Fi was far enough removed from a noble paragon, she felt little qualm tossing a double-crossing traitor to a daeyari. But Boden? He'd condone a plan like that?

'You know the type, Fi.' Boden spoke quietly. 'If we confront Cardigan, I don't imagine he'll cooperate. If it comes to blows and he ends up dead?' He mustered a shrug. 'I don't care what happens to the body.'

Fi was so fucking proud, she could have hugged him.

At last, the gloomy racoon on her sofa perked up. Antal's eyes glowed brighter. A black tongue flicked hungry over his teeth.

Fi had made it ten whole minutes without staring at that mouth. A noble milestone.

'What price do you ask for this?' Antal said.

Boden's brow knit. 'Price?'

'You offer me a meal. I must repay you. This is the pact between our people.'

'This isn't a barter, daeyari. I won't ask you for anything – *fmi mtma fwk.*'

Boden shouted angry gibberish against Fi's hand clapped over his mouth. Apparently, her pride in him was short-lived. Passing up an opportunity for a deal? Not a desperate deal, either, like the rushed words she'd muttered at Antal's shrine. A true favor from an immortal.

Sometimes, she was ashamed they were related.

Especially now, when Nyskya needed every advantage. Fi considered the energy capsules Antal had charged for her, the times she'd caught him poking at her machinery.

'Can you fix energy conduits?' she asked. 'Nyskya has a few acting up.'

Boden fell silent. Fi released him, grimacing at the slobber on her palm. A low blow.

'I can,' Antal said. 'Depending on what materials you have available.'

Better than the town going dark. Fi, the intermediary, looked to her brother. 'Mayor Boden? How do you find these terms?'

Boden nodded, slow with trepidation. But when his village stood to benefit?

'Deal,' he said. 'I'll get you Cardigan. You get my conduits running again.'

21

Just say you forgive me

Fi finally made coffee.

Once the copper kettle sang, she drowned one mug in sugar and cream for herself. Next, a semi-sweet concoction for Boden.

They shared a look of surprise when Antal accepted a cup, bitter and black as the Void.

Boden leaned over the kitchen table, scowling. 'But you told me you don't drink—'

'I don't. Not with mortals.' Antal clacked his claws to the mug and sipped.

Fi cocked a brow at Boden, a wordless, *'Can you believe this shit?'*

But Boden was staring at her hands, the dark fractal of an energy burn down her thumb. He looked to the daeyari, then back at her. But said nothing.

They spent a long time hammering out details, Boden laying out what he'd learned of Cardigan's villa on the Spring Plane. By the time they had a workable strategy, the hour was late, their mugs empty. Fi pushed Boden out the door to get some sleep.

He kept looking between her and Antal, like she'd be devoured the moment he left.

255

'I'll be fine, Bodie. I've survived two weeks without your incessant worrying.'

She got him onto the porch. Antal stayed inside.

When the door shut, a cold quiet wrapped around them. Night air carried the hoot of a distant owl through the trees. In the clearing, Aisinay conversed with Boden's boreal horse in soft snorts, little nuzzles to each other's necks.

Fi didn't know how angry he was for keeping all this from him, for bringing a daeyari to their village without asking. She wasn't sure she wanted to know. Instead, she watched the green aurora drift above the trees, a soft hiss then snap with each wave, whispers of lost souls reaching out from the Void with—

Boden grabbed her coat and pulled her into a rib-crushing hug.

Fi froze in surprise. She forgot how to hug back, arms falling awkward to her sides as Boden wrapped her in an unflinching embrace. He smelled of dust and aurorabeasts. Of safety.

'You should have told me,' he said in a hush.

Fi's throat tightened. At her silence, Boden cupped the back of her head and pulled her tighter against his shoulder.

'You should have told me,' he said, 'so you didn't have to do this alone. Void have mercy, Fi. Are you all right?'

Why did it sound like an apology?

And no, come to think of it, Fi wasn't all right. She wanted to sink into him. She wanted to cry out that she was afraid, and she didn't know what to do, and wouldn't someone please help her fix this.

'You never told me you'd met Antal,' she said in the flattest, safest tone she could.

Boden shifted her to arm's length, hands tight on her shoulders. Then, a sigh. 'I came home after the election, and he was out in the paddock. Watching the aurorabeasts. He couldn't have stayed more than ten minutes. I didn't want to worry you.'

A partial truth, Fi guessed. Boden didn't want her to run away again. Same reason he'd stowed her up here the past two weeks, out of the way.

'I'm not going anywhere,' she said.

'I know, Fi. But—'

'I won't leave you again, Boden. I going to fix this. I'm going to—'

He grabbed her into another hug, smothering her fervor against his coat.

'Stop it,' he whispered. 'Stop it, you stubborn girl. None of that matters anymore.'

Of course it mattered. Fi wriggled in protest. 'I left you.'

'That was a long time ago.'

'You're my brother, and I left you.'

'You're my sister. And you're the only family I have left.'

Boden held her so tight. As if she might vanish the moment he let go. Fi fought through the hitch in her breath, a treacherous prickle in her eyes.

She wanted to believe it was that simple. She wanted to believe it didn't matter how she'd run away, how she'd left Boden to tend their father as alcohol rotted his liver and picked holes through his brain. How Boden had to track her down in a backwoods village on the Winter Plane to set their record straight.

Boden had never given up on her. For that, Fi loved him more than anyone on all the Shattered Planes. She wanted his forgiveness as desperately as she needed air in her lungs.

But he refused to talk about the past.

Anytime Fi approached the subject of reconciliation, Boden deflected, shut down. Like he could stomach moving forward, only by refusing to look behind. Seven years they'd worked together, this gaping wound between them, scabbed but still leaking puss.

Maybe he could still forgive her, if she didn't fuck this up. That sole hope gave her the strength to hug him back, a moment of weakness as she sank against his chest and buried her face in his coat.

'You aren't doing this alone,' Boden told her.

'Of course not. We have a daeyari to help us.' Fi broke from his embrace, snapping back to practiced nonchalance. 'Let's get you home. I can take you through a Curtain.'

She climbed onto Aisinay's back before Boden could protest. The Void horse poked her snout at his coat pockets, a huff when she found no treats. He patted behind her finned ears then headed for his own mount.

Fi guided Boden through the Curtain nearby, across a Shard, out another Curtain by his ranch. He hugged her again when they bid goodnight. Too long. More earnest than she deserved.

She returned alone to her home on the ridge, to her quiet shiverpines and aurora-kissed needles, riding slow to let cold air clear her head. At last, they had a fresh plan. Only time would prove whether it was sounder than all her failures so far.

Ahead, golden light spilled out the windows of her cottage. She wondered if Antal would be gone, slipped away in her absence like a shadow in the night.

She cursed her relief when she cracked the door open, greeted by red eyes.

Antal lounged on her sofa, arms sprawled across the backrest, an empty coffee mug dangling from his claws. His tail swayed a slow arc as he glanced between her and the door, no Boden in sight, something dry and questioning in his look.

Fi sighed.

'He means well,' she said. 'He's a worrier. And a little stubborn. But he cares about Nyskya, and he's good for a promise. He won't rat you out to Verne.'

Antal propped his head on a palm. The slow spread of his smirk put Fi on guard.

'*Fi-Fi?*' he said.

She sucked in a sharp breath.

'I will end you myself,' Fi said in a low, warning tone. 'Then end you *again*, when you come back for me.'

Antal laughed. The sound startled her every time, deep notes reverberating through her rafters. She breathed a little easier, the weight of her talk with Boden slipping to a safer recess of her mind.

'Fi, then?' He spoke the name like a curiosity. Like he was tasting it.

'If you'd like.'

'What would *you* like?'

'I mean it, Antlers. I don't care.' Fi made the words forcibly flat.

Because she did care. More than was good for her.

Growing up, Fi had loathed her full name and its lengthy syllables, had lobbied and threatened against it, until close acquaintances knew her by nickname alone. Older now, that spite had diminished. Fionamara was a name spoken with authority, the respect of satisfied clients or the curses of thwarted foes.

Yet the way *he* said it. Something else entirely. The syllables tumbled off Antal's tongue like a warm Spring breeze. Like a whisper through midnight shadows. Fi wanted him to say it, just so she could dissect the cadence.

She couldn't tell *him* that.

Antal rose. Fi watched him cross the room on those easy

strides, returning his mug to her kitchen. She recognized the movements of a night coming to its close, a visitor making his play to depart.

She couldn't tell him about her name. Instead, she said something more dangerous.

'Do you . . . have a place to sleep?' Fi asked.

Two weeks of him flitting through her life, yet she'd hardly spared a thought for where he disappeared to. Not to his home, so long as Verne banished him from Thomaskweld.

Antal's movements slowed, that guarded posture she'd come to recognize.

'The cold is no trouble to daeyari,' he said.

'Sure. But you'd prefer somewhere warm?' He'd survived the river outside, but still relished sinking into her tub.

'What would you propose?'

What, indeed. Fi steadied herself, careful not to betray too much inflection. A simple offer of cooperation.

'You can stay here,' she said. 'If you'd like.'

Antal kept his guard up, studying her crossed arms and defiant chin. 'I've already accepted your price for my help. You don't need to offer anything further.'

'It's not about . . .' Fi wrinkled her nose. She'd berated Boden for this moments ago, only to find herself slipping the same way. Different. This was *different*. 'It's not a matter of payment. We're partners now, right? You deserve to be comfortable.'

And she didn't want to be alone tonight.

Antal stayed rigid. It was artful, the way he stood like carved ice, the crafted menace of his narrowed eyes. This was his response to kindness?

Was he so unaccustomed to it?

'I don't wish to inconvenience you,' he said.

'It's no inconvenience. Honestly? You're not as terrible as I thought a daeyari would be. So far. And cottage life can get lonely. Having company has been . . . nice.'

Fi stopped herself right there. Not another word, or she'd combust.

She sweltered all the same, when Antal smiled.

Not a smirk. Not any of the goading grins she'd parried during their sparring earlier. It came on slow. As if Antal, too, were testing the feel on his lips.

He smiled like a slip of moonbeam through trees. Like that first sight of stars after stepping back from the Void. A subtle shift, yet one curve of his mouth changed every line of his face, softening chiseled edges into velvet, a carnivore into . . .

A man. Different flesh. Different blood. Heart stilling, all the same.

'Just don't be a dick about it,' Fi deflected, too close to breathless. 'And you can stay.'

The beast regarded her with those too-keen eyes. Then, a bow of his head.

'Your hospitality is much appreciated, Fionamara.'

22

It's not a party until there's blood on the floor

Fi spent one futile night trying to fight Antal out of her rafters.

She delivered impassioned arguments on the merits of her sofa, or the damn floor if nothing else. In the end, their agreement became: rafters at night for sleeping, off-limits during the day when she wanted to enjoy her home without a predator lurking overhead. Compromise was crucial to any partnership.

She supposed this arrangement wasn't so different from having an odd, arboreal guard dog. Antal slept like a panther in a tree, stomach stretched along the rafter, head pillowed in his arms as his tail dangled. Fi caught herself watching him too often, captive to curiosity for this strange housemate who melded with shadows and prowled on whisper-quiet feet.

Graciously, he disappeared when she requested privacy.

This morning, Fi indulged a long bath. She sipped her sugary coffee. Her silviamesh bodysuit, normally a delight to don, summoned a grimace as she examined the shredded stomach and her laughable attempt to mend the tatters with regular thread. The intact parts were still worth wearing. She armed herself with dark lipstick and violet eyeshadow, drew her hair into a Void-and rainbow ponytail.

Then, off to meet Boden.

His ranch lay on the outskirts of Nyskya, a low building at

the edge of the forest, porch crusted with icicles and shingles sheened with overnight snow. When Fi arrived, her brother waited on the steps, bundled in his coat, eyeing the tree line. So did the herd of aurorabeasts in the paddock.

Fi spotted the source of their consternation: Antal, perched near the crown of a fir, an antlered silhouette and red eyes amidst dark needles.

'Is he trying to freak me out?' Boden greeted as Fi joined him on the porch.

She considered Antal's obsession with her rafters. His home in a cave overlooking Thomaskweld. Verne's cliffside chateau, and Tyvo lurking in treetops.

'I think they just like to be up high,' she said.

'They?'

'Daeyari, in general.'

'You're a fucking expert, now?'

Fi punched his arm.

'You don't have to come, Bodie. Antal and I can handle Cardigan. If someone realizes you're helping us, Verne will be on Nyskya in a heartbeat.'

'Good thing I'm *not* helping you,' he returned, in that smug tone that made Fi want to throw a snowball between his eyes. 'My awful sister? Gone too far, scorning our new *Lord Daeyari.*' That one oozed air quotes, though Boden's hands stayed stuffed in his pockets. 'And with Astrid searching for that wretched Fionamara? I'd be foolish *not* to offer a bounty, bringing a spiteful criminal to justice.'

Fi regarded him with lips puckered, indulging none of his stuffy attempts at humor. This was the plan they'd agreed to. If Boden played it right, he'd get himself invited into Cardigan's estate, convince the weasel they were on the same side, sweet-talk some information about Verne. If that failed, Fi and Antal would be waiting to offer more forceful coercion.

Overall, she found the plan unnecessarily obtuse and unreasonably perilous to Boden's well-being. Unfortunately, stubbornness did run in the family.

'Make it a good bounty,' she grumbled. 'My average on the Spring Plane has been increasing for five years. Don't you dare bring that down.'

'Of course.' Boden tapped his chin. 'What's a good offer? One energy chip?'

'Boden.'

'I don't know these things. I'm not a criminal, like my sister.'

'*Boden.*'

Static pricked Fi's tongue.

At Antal's appearance in the yard, the aurorabeasts shied toward the far edge of the paddock. He scented the air, circling on predatory strides, wind tousling the dark hair between his antlers.

Otherworldly. A being from the depths of the Void, returned to walk this mortal Plane. Fi found herself forgetting that too often, lulled by how comfortably he sprawled on her sofa and lured her with toothy smirks.

When he reached Fi and Boden, he held out both hands.

'Ready to leave?' Antal asked.

Ready to greet Cardigan with a not-so-fond reunion. Fi grasped Antal's hand. Boden eyed the other with understandable hesitation.

'Hold your breath,' she warned.

After the first teleport, Fi caught herself on staggered boots. Boden wheezed.

She had a split second to register snow, shiverpines, still the Winter Plane, a Curtain directly in front of them.

'Hold on,' Boden gasped. 'I—'

Antal yanked them through the Curtain.

Out the other side, Boden dropped to his knees, hissing curses at his first daeyari teleport.

'It's like that every time?' he rasped.

Antal cast a tarnished look upon Nyskya's mayor. 'Would you prefer walking to the Spring Plane, Mayor Kolbeck? Gather yourself. Our journey isn't finished.'

'Sure. Just. Shit, give me a second . . .'

Fi patted his back. Not everyone had the constitution for cross-world travel.

Around them, salt flats sprawled around shallow pools, reflecting a starless Void sky and pink aurora. Pale coral colonies branched out of the water, bleached trunks with blue frills, leaching energy from minerals instead of sunlight.

'This place gives me the creeps,' Boden muttered. 'Don't know how you spend so much time on Shards.'

Not just a Shard. Fi recognized this Bridge, the splinter of reality connecting Winter to Spring.

While Boden caught his breath, Fi joined Antal beside a pool. The daeyari stood stunningly still in this quiet landscape, his eyes as depthless black as their native Void, sharp as Fi approached, gauging the space between them more noticeably than he had a week ago.

'At least I wasn't that bad my first time,' Fi huffed, too low for Boden to overhear.

Antal softened swifter than he would have a week ago, too, a smirk lighting his mouth.

'You weren't.' At his rumble of approval, Fi had to look away. She'd sooner throw herself into the Void than let him see her blush again.

266

She scowled at the Bridge instead. 'I thought you'd take us straight to Spring?'

'Daeyari can teleport within a Plane, within a Shard. Not between. I need Curtains to cross, same as you.'

Despite Fi's best play at indifference, curiosity sank its claws into her. 'When you teleport, it feels cold and black, like . . .' She looked up into the Void.

So did Antal. 'Distance doesn't exist in the Void. When daeyari teleport, we step off reality briefly, then back on at our destination.'

'But you said teleportation isn't the same as Voidwalking?'

'It isn't. It's . . .' Antal frowned. Then held an arm horizontal. 'Teleporting is a dip into the Void.' He moved his finger from over his arm, briefly below, back up again, a shallow dive beneath water. 'Then Voidwalking is . . .' He dropped his finger below his arm and sank, sank. 'A full plunge. But if done properly, you can re-emerge anywhere in the Planeverse.'

As Fi stared into the endless black above them, she shuddered. 'Can you do it?'

'I'd rather not,' Antal muttered. 'Teleporting is faster. Safer. Just more limitations.'

Humbling, to see even immortals intimidated by the Void they came from.

Once Boden stopped grumbling, Antal grasped their hands again. Daeyari might not be able to teleport between Planes, but the jumps cut travel time, even after he and Fi wasted several minutes heckling over which exit Curtain would bring them closest to Cardigan's villa.

She'd never had anyone to argue Curtains with. Fi knew no one else who could see them.

*

They emerged to birdsong. Warm air thick with sweetgrass and magnolia. The trees beyond the Curtain weren't the gnarled conifers of the Winter Plane, but slender trunks sprouting blossoms and tender green leaves. Dappled sunlight filtered through the canopy and danced on loamy, unfrozen ground, the new arrivals causing a scurry of sparrows into the underbrush.

Eternal seasons were an oddity unique to the Season-Locked Planes – something about their close proximity. Most other, more distant Planes maintained fully-functional climate routines. The Spring Plane was, of course, more popular than Winter, for those who could afford it. Fi could never get past the allergies.

Antal appeared equally unenthused, grimacing at the bright light. Supposedly, the Twilit Plane received little sun. That explained the grayscale skin of its native predators, evolved for shadows rather than dappled forests.

Cardigan's villa lay ahead, bordered in wild roses and daffodils.

'Ostentatious,' was a word that came to mind. 'Compensating for something' shortly after. Wealthy retreats on the Spring Plane typically were. Compared to Fi's humble cottage, she couldn't fathom how Cardigan would use three sprawling stories of tan marble, accented in clay-tiled porticos and balconies dripping potted blooms. The perimeter wall alone must have depleted a small quarry.

Antal's tree-hopping came in handy. He confirmed the villa's occupants: Cardigan, two guards in the outer grounds, and one slouching man who matched the description of the assistant Fi had met during their ill-fated rendezvous on the Autumn Plane.

At dusk, Boden approached the villa alone.

The guards met him at the gate. As the light faded past a

peach sunset, fireflies flickered on within the trees. Chanting cicadas masked any drift of conversation, but Fi took Boden's confident posture as a good sign. He was ushered in, the gate closing behind him.

Now came Fi's turn to get inside.

Her tongue pricked, static along the top. She looked up. Antal perched above her in a maple – wearing his *second* approving smirk of the day. Fi loathed the swell of pride in her chest.

'Come,' he whispered.

He moved through the trees like liquid night, as swift and silent as the stories claimed. Fi followed, circling the villa on quiet footfalls. Antal brought her to a Curtain, the translucent shimmer barely visible in dusk.

She bit back a gasp when he appeared beside her, bit her tongue as he leaned close enough for his breath to brush her ear.

'Straight through, ten paces,' he whispered. 'Pass one Curtain on your right. Take the second. I'll find you inside.'

His tail swayed, a parting graze against her calf. *A game*, Fi reminded herself for the hundredth time. A dance between predator and prey, even as that flutter filled her stomach. They both tested. They both adapted. He was still the one with claws ready, if she ever stumbled.

Fi pushed through the Curtain, onto a Shard, grateful for the cold to clear her head.

Here lay another forest, more twisting than the Spring Plane, Void above and fog low between silvered trunks. She followed Antal's directions, past the shimmer of one Curtain, through the second.

She emerged in a hall inside Cardigan's villa.

Not only was Fi unaccustomed to a partner who could see Curtains, but she'd never met anyone so good at it. She'd have to find a way to tell Antal how impressed she was, without stoking his ego. Some sort of reverse compliment sandwich: *'Hey, your sleeping habits are insufferable, but you navigate Curtains like a savant. Also, your teeth are unsettling.'*

In contrast, she couldn't scrounge a single compliment for Cardigan's decor.

Fi snuck down a hall of Spring Plane marble polished to a squeak, oil paintings of Summer vistas, curtains of Autumn velvet, fixtures of Winter metal shaped like . . . lizards? Abstract mice? They held orb lights in crooked teeth, emitting dim silver energy.

A murmur of voices led her to a doorway. She paused outside, her view limited to a shaggy rug, bookshelves packed with curios and insultingly few books.

'Your *sister*?' came Cardigan's grating voice, that lilting Spring accent.

Bingo.

'My condolences,' the bastard continued. 'Family can be such a burden.'

'Unfortunately,' Boden agreed. A little too earnest.

'Can you believe that bitch accused *me* of alerting trade wardens to our rendezvous?'

'She's always been thankless.'

'And that hair. Alarmingly unprofessional. Those kinds of people, always looking for attention.'

Fi couldn't groan without giving away her position. She rolled her eyes instead. Her ears perked at the tap of distant boots, guards moving outside the villa. Not a problem. Yet.

'You can understand why I'm eager to be rid of her,' Boden said. 'Would twelve energy chips be enough incentive to track her down?'

That a boy, Boden. Aim high.

A chair creaked. Fi pictured Cardigan leaning back his stocky build, lacing his fingers. 'You think she's worth that much?'

'If it means keeping Verne happy?'

Silence.

'Forgive me,' Boden said. 'I assumed we both had similar motivation, in that regard.'

'Do we?' Cardigan spoke slowly. 'She *is* a dangerous mistress to disappoint. But also a purveyor of attractive rewards. Perhaps if you'd be interested in sharing those rewards . . .'

Fi's pulse skipped higher. Not just at Cardigan taking the bait. She inched down the hall, drawn by a flicker on the air.

A Curtain. Another one inside the house?

It wasn't alone. A courtyard lay at the villa's center. Two more Curtains fluttered in the still air, one near a tiered fountain, the other tangled in a trellis of blooming jasmine. This many in such density couldn't be naturally occurring.

Someone must have cut them.

A hand clamped over Fi's mouth. She was dismayed to *not* feel claws.

Fi spat a muffled curse as her assailant pinned her to his chest. Before she could draw her sword, cold raked her skin. She fell backward.

Pulled through a Curtain.

They emerged on a different Shard to the one she'd entered through. One of the smallest fragments she'd seen, edges crumbling into the Void on all sides, ground a stagnant mix of bog and gravel. Several sheds sat at the center, and combined with the multiple Curtains cut into Cardigan's villa?

Fi was livid *she'd* never thought of such an efficient setup for storing contraband.

Add it to her growing list of reasons to loathe Cardigan. He'd conned her into transporting energy capsules when he already had his own Voidwalker on staff?

'Don't fight,' the man warned in a Spring Plane accent. And stupidly.

Fi elbowed his stomach.

Heat leached from her muscles as she Shaped energy over her arms, enough to zap his hands off her. Fi lurched free then faced her attacker: a slouched and unassuming man, cradling his gut.

The *assistant?*

He lunged. Splayed a hand across the damaged silviamesh of her stomach. A pulse of energy sent Fi staggering like a gut punch.

Cardigan's assistant was a fucking *Voidwalker?* And he'd still hired Fi to walk those energy capsules into a building about to explode?

Fi dug into her pockets. Her opponent grabbed one wrist and twisted, forcing her to drop her transport stone. He kicked it over the Shard edge, lost into the Void. Fi gasped her indignation. Transport stones were *expensive.*

But he'd disarmed the wrong hand. A daeyari energy capsule burned hot and cold in her palm. She pressed it to his side.

The current spiked molten up her arm, but at least she prepared for it, Shaping the chaotic energy away from her flesh and into her assailant. A ripple of crimson hit the man's ribs. He screamed. Released her. They tore apart, his shirt tattered, a horrific energy burn across his chest. Fi's arm throbbed. Better than some of her practice rounds with daeyari energy, but the black blotches along her fingers weren't pleasant to look at.

With a frantic swipe, the assistant dove back through a Curtain. Fi barreled after him.

'*Intruder!*' he bellowed down the hall of Cardigan's villa. 'It's—'

Fi tackled him. As they hit the ground, she clenched a fist.

Though she held no physical hilt, she Shaped silver energy from the heat of her sternum, forming a dagger. The raw magic seared her skin without any buffer. She didn't have to hold it long.

One plunge drove the blade into the man's heart.

Fi didn't hesitate. Not for people complicit in daeyari coups. Not when the threat of more guards remained. Survival came first.

As the man fell limp beneath her, bootsteps thundered outside, two guards emerging from the courtyard. They looked at Fi. The body of their comrade. Both lifted energy crossbows.

The shadows moved faster.

One man disappeared from the doorway in a flash of tail and antlers, his scream melting to a gurgle. The second man had barely swiveled his crossbow before Antal shoved him to the wall, claws rending his throat open in one deep slash.

Horrifying to watch.

But damn was a daeyari useful in a fight.

They were in motion now, too much blood on the floor to turn back. Fi burst into the office to find Cardigan wide-eyed behind his desk. His green pinstripe vest strained its buttons as he reeled, attempting to meld with his leather chair. Across from him, Boden lurched to his feet.

'Fionamara!' he shouted with theatrical surprise. 'What are you doing here?'

'Great delivery, Bodie.' She patted his shoulder. 'Really top notch. But we've progressed solidly into Plan B territory.' In other words: no more pleasant chatting. Time to take what they needed and kill anyone who got in their way. Just . . . happened a little out of order.

Boden shifted from bristle to groan. 'Well fuck, Fi, you didn't give me much time.'

'Things escalated!'

'*You.*' Cardigan slammed his hands to the desk. 'You dare intrude upon my home? Damage my vintage door?'—to Fi's credit, she hadn't meant to hit the door so hard on entry— 'Stain my carpet?'—blood, it was definitely blood on her boots—'Guards! I'll have you—'

Cardigan fell mute. Jaw slack.

Antal appeared in the doorway like a winter chill. Like death from the Void. The daeyari's eyes burned red, fangs bared. This creature who lounged in Fi's rafters, all the fiercer by contrast, a heart-stilling reminder of exactly *what* she'd let into her home.

She and Boden stepped aside.

'Antal,' Cardigan wheezed. 'My Lord Daeyari. So good to see you well. I heard what happened in Thomaskweld. Such unsavory business with—'

Antal vaulted over the desk. Cardigan sent paper and ink-wells scattering like confetti as he flailed to escape, unsuccessful as the daeyari grabbed his collar and slammed his head to the wood.

'What did you do to my energy conduits in Thomaskweld?' Antal demanded.

Red energy bloomed as Antal's fingertips pressed Cardigan's temple, the same magic he'd used on Fi to turn her thoughts to sludge. Cardigan's eyes went glassy, his voice a rasp.

'We installed . . . unstable copper alloy . . . prone to degradation . . .'

'You *sabotaged* them?'

'I . . . we . . . . yes.'

'For Verne?'

'Yes.'

In their planning, they'd humored the possibility where Cardigan turned out to be a witless pawn. With his confession, Fi watched any chance of a merciful resolution melt away. Antal's claws tightened on Cardigan's skull until blood welled beneath the tips.

'*What else?*' Antal said.

Cardigan gasped, a spark of pain warring against watery eyes. 'We sold faulty conduit parts throughout the territory . . . to the Tsuga Cartel . . . the Glacier Crest Market.'

'The Glacier Crest Market?' Boden clamped his hands against the desk, bent level with Cardigan. 'That's where Nyskya gets our materials.'

'How unfortunate,' Cardigan mumbled.

'What happens to the people who rely on those conduits?'

'Let them freeze. They'll turn to Verne's side easier, begging for the help their last Lord Daeyari couldn't provide.'

Fi clenched her fists to stop from shaking, stinging fresh energy burns along her knuckles. When Antal had used that magic on her, she wasn't able to lie. Cardigan *wasn't* lying, didn't give a shit about Thomaskweld or Nyskya or anyone in between.

If Antal didn't kill this piece of bog moss, Fi would.

The daeyari didn't sneer as openly as her or Boden, falling back to deathly stillness. 'What does Verne plan next?'

'I don't know.'

'Where is she keeping her Beast?'

'I don't know. I haven't spoken to her . . . not for weeks. We were supposed to be partners. Why won't she speak to me? Why won't she . . .' Cardigan's words slurred.

Another dead end.

The room fell quiet. Just Cardigan's labored breaths, the tick of a clock on a bookshelf, and lower, a buzzing in Fi's ears. As if she could hear the failing energy conduits all the way from Nyskya, the cold seeping through the windows. Nyskya, which was supposed to be safe from all this. Hidden in the wild, distant from daeyari prying. Not distant enough.

Antal tipped a razored glance to his fellow conspirators. 'Anything else?'

Boden shook his head. Fi did the same.

When Antal released Cardigan, sense returned slowly to his eyes. Then, fear. Unnecessary perhaps: giving him that moment of clarity.

Antal buried black claws in Cardigan's throat, a jagged slice through the jugular. Too swift a death.

Fi winced as Cardigan collapsed to the floor, blood gushing onto his rug. Boden watched with a hollower look. Not for Cardigan, she assumed.

'He sold faulty conduits to Nyskya. That's why we've had outages. That's why . . .'

Fi heard that shake in Boden's voice, blame leveled on himself for not recognizing the danger sooner. They'd been snared in this mess even before Fi took that ill-fated smuggling job.

Antal flicked blood from his claws then sniffed the air. Another whiff led him to a drawer in Cardigan's desk. He pulled out a familiar metal case, flipping it open to reveal a set of daeyari energy chips. One, he pinched between his claws then ran his black tongue along the edge. A grimace.

'At least Verne paid well,' Antal muttered.

Boden paced the room, as if he'd find some answers in the mussed desk or useless bookshelf curios. 'We shouldn't linger. Take your payment, daeyari.' Lower. 'Looks like you have your pick.'

'You as well.' Antal slid the energy chips toward Boden. He wrinkled his nose at Cardigan's corpse, disappearing into the hall instead.

Fi caught herself watching him again. Curious again, in a way every rational survival instinct said she shouldn't be.

'I'll search the office,' Boden said dismally, 'see if there's anything we can use.'

'Aren't you . . . a little curious?' Fi asked.

He looked at her. The door Antal had disappeared through. Back at her, paler than before. 'Not *remotely*.'

Fi always had the tougher stomach. And her hands were shaking too fiercely to sort through bookshelves.

'Do your snooping. I'll keep watch.'

She felt Boden's gawk dig into her back as she left the room.

23

Nothing to waste

The hall was a mess. Fi stepped around blood spatter, around the corpses of two felled guards sprawled across the marble. The Voidwalker assistant was missing. She followed the smear of red dragged across the floor, steeling herself as she approached the courtyard.

A reckless curiosity, even by her standards. But Fi needed to know, didn't she? What kind of beast she'd truly let into her home. What she was risking, if she misstepped.

Cicadas buzzed in the courtyard. Fragrant jasmine drifted from the trellises.

Antal crouched beside the body. Fi's heart stilled at the sight: his lean and Void-hewn form poised over quarry, antlers sleek with moonlight. In the dark, his eyes burned.

Fi shuddered when they snapped onto her.

'Why him?' she asked.

Antal sniffed his prey. 'The strongest Shaper amongst them. The richest energy.' His tail flicked the flagstone. 'You don't want to watch this, Fionamara.'

He might be right. Fi had watched crag panthers take down elk, ravens picking at carrion. She'd skinned game since she was old enough for her father to put a knife in her hand. How different could that be from . . .

A person.

Fi knelt across the corpse from Antal. 'Someone should keep watch. In case Cardigan had any more backup.'

Antal held her with a bone-scraping stare. His irises were faded crimson against black sclera, his crouch wound too tight. Breaths too shallow.

He was shaking.

How long had it been since he'd eaten? Nearly three weeks, since Milana dragged Fi to his shrine. Merciless Void, how was he standing. How had he not ripped Fi open while she slept.

'Eat,' she ordered. Then, softer, 'You need to eat, Antal. He's already dead. Don't let it go to waste.'

The daeyari bared his teeth at her, this beast who'd cut down three corpses today alone, a vicious timbre to his growl. Should Fi be afraid? A fresh throat, too close to a predator and his meal.

Most predators were defensive while they ate. Vulnerable, while they set teeth to flesh. Behind the fangs, Fi recognized that defensive bristle, desperation and hunger fracturing through the facade.

'Let me keep watch,' she repeated. 'So you don't have to worry while you eat.' It had to count for something, that they'd shared a roof, that *neither of them* had ripped the other open while they slept.

Antal settled slowly, sinking onto his heels.

When Fi refused to back down, he grumbled and rolled back his sleeves.

He set to work with the precision of a butcher. First, the man's jacket. A slice of energy-sharpened claws rent fabric like tissue paper, exposing bare arm, probably saturated with energy after such recent Shaping. Antal's fingers were strong, dexterous.

Carving tools. He flayed skin with clean cuts. Separated tissue and tendon. Shaking more, now.

Antal gripped the arm in both hands and sank his teeth into exposed muscle.

A small, wretched groan wracked his chest. When he swallowed, his entire body sagged, an exhale trembling in relief.

Three weeks. He hadn't eaten for *three weeks*, starving himself, because he wouldn't touch Fi. Wouldn't touch anyone in Nyskya.

He ate greedily, teeth slicing easy through flesh, inhaling mouthfuls of muscle with the fervor of an alley cat. Fi held to her watch as promised, knuckles clenched against her knees. She braced herself to be sick. To revolt at the sight of a fellow human reduced to meat.

But the longer she watched, the more *anger* stirred her gut.

For as long as Antal had held his territory, he'd had a reputation for taking fewer sacrifices than most daeyari. That was one reason Fi settled in Nyskya, profiting off lax policy. How often had he deprived himself? Suffering, to try to ease his part in an unjust system?

Once Antal had cleared the larger muscles of the forearm, his breaths came noticeably smoother. His posture, less wretchedly taut. He paused, wary eyes flicking onto Fi, blood painting his mouth in vivid crimson.

'You don't even cook it?' she said, aghast. No magical sautéing, not even a pinch of seasoning?

Antal blinked at her. '*That's* your question?'

'Start with that. We can work up to . . .' She gestured over the grisly scene.

'Cooking would diminish the energy.'

Antal set to the second arm with less urgency. He carved out choicer pieces of forearm, worked through half a bicep, before finally sitting back on his haunches. An ease settled over him that Fi hadn't seen in . . . *ever*. His long, black tongue slicked across his mouth, cleaning every speck of gore. Red energy zapped any lingering flesh from his claws. The rest of him he'd kept immaculate.

'That's . . . it?' Fi asked.

'My needs are meager, Fionamara.' Antal spoke in a low, shadowed tone. 'Only the means are vile.'

She gestured to the mostly intact body. 'But there's so much *left*.'

'On the Twilit Plane, daeyari commonly eat in packs, one body enough to feed several. In the territories, we live more sparsely. One human is far more than enough.'

Watching him eat was unsettling . . . just not as much as she'd expected. It wasn't grotesque. It wasn't cruel. Not nauseating, the way Fi felt after her nightmares of being dragged onto Verne's altar, her stomach split open while she screamed.

But it was *wasteful*. An entire life, for a couple cuts of meat?

'You said daeyari can go up to a month without eating?'

Antal grimaced. 'Eating once a month is possible but . . . unpleasant.'

'What would be more pleasant?'

'Once a week.'

Before Verne took over, Fi had never heard of sacrifices being dragged to Thomaskweld every week. Antal had been moderating himself, but even so—

'Why do you insist on living sacrifices?'

Antal blinked again, slower this time. A warier pinch to his brow. 'What do you mean?'

Evasive. He ought to know better. 'You can eat dead bodies? Same as live ones?'

His tail twitched. 'Fresher is better. Energy deteriorates, but within the first hour or two after death, it's comparable.'

'So why *living* sacrifices? Why not eat corpses? People would be less afraid of you.'

'Daeyari have ruled these territories for millennia. This is the system set in place.'

'But *why*?'

'You're clever, Fionamara. You know why.'

She did. She wanted him to say it. But if he wouldn't—

'Because daeyari want us to be afraid?'

That was why every daeyari-controlled Plane paraded sacrifices to their shrines? Why Fi's people had no stories of how to fight their immortal masters? Not because daeyari were invincible. The prickly bastards just built the narrative that way.

'Live prey tastes better,' Antal said, brittle. 'More exciting, for some. But most important: fear means fewer uprisings. Less bloodshed. A kinder compromise than hunting you outright. That's how the daeyari see it.'

He stood, signaling the conversation was over.

As if Fi would let him get off that easy.

She stood with him, planting herself in his path like concrete. The truth was crushing. It left her feeling small, like she ought to curl up and hide from everything.

Which meant she needed to fight *harder*.

'Is that what Verne would say?' Fi challenged.

Antal's eyes always glowed to some extent. They blazed now, crisper crimson after being fed, scalding beneath his lashes. 'She has. Many times.'

'What do *you* want?'

'Not this. I need food, but I don't want it to cause pain. Grief.' His tail swished low at his ankles. 'It doesn't matter what I want. This is the system I was given.'

He tried to step around her.

Fi cut him off again. A warning growl rumbled his chest. Dramatic ass. They'd been through this show of snarling and snapping enough times to cut through the bullshit.

'What's an Old House?' Fi asked.

A crack hit Antal's facade like shattered porcelain. Deeper than any blow or curse she threw at him, that trembling inhale and eyes narrowed to slits.

'You're from an Old House,' Fi pushed, heedless. 'Do *they* tell you who to eat?'

'The Daey Celva is the governing body of all daeyari.' Antal's words grated like fractured glass. 'We're a solitary people. Civil service is regarded as a role of great sacrifice and honor. The Old Houses are daeyari families who've served on the Daey Celva since its founding.'

Fi offered her most unimpressed eyebrows. 'Your family are politicians?'

'My *father* is a politician.'

'You ran an entire territory, Antal.'

'And I never wanted to come here!'

They stared at each other. Antal hadn't used that slicing tone since their early days.

Had he softened so much to her, that they both looked surprised?

He softened now, clawed feet whispering over flagstone as he retreated a step. 'When the previous daeyari of my territory retired, my father volunteered me. An opportunity to learn independence. Responsibility.' Antal scoffed. 'That's gone *well*, as you can see.'

Of all the unsavory attributes Fi had assumed of Antal, a nepotism hire was never one of them. 'Have you considered telling your father what happened? Asking for help?'

Antal laughed, back to that biting and humorless thing, none

of the warmth he'd let slip before. 'I guarantee you, he's heard
what happened by now. And look at all the help he's sent.' Antal
held his arms wide on the blood-spattered courtyard. 'Either I
return home in disgrace, or I fix this myself. He won't lift a
finger for me. Not if there's a lesson to be learned.'

'Is that why you stayed? To impress your father?'

'I don't give a *fuck* what my father thinks of me. I only want
to do the right thing.' Antal's voice dipped. 'For once.'

Fi's voice didn't dip. 'Then do the right fucking thing!'

'It's not that simple!'

He bared his fangs at her. She bared her blunt teeth right
back, pressing their faces too close, making *him* balk in surprise.
His breath smelled like ozone and the sweet of fresh blood.

'You think it's easier for us?' Fi hissed. '*Kinder* to us?' She
grabbed his shirt, dragging the fabric like claws of her own.
'You think *you* were the first time I escaped a daeyari altar?'

Antal stilled. His tail fell slack at his ankles, all his fight
gone in startling swiftness. The look on his face knocked Fi
breathless, not just shock but . . . horror. Eyes so wide, they
couldn't belong to a predator. Mouth parted, and all Fi could
look at was the flushed curve of his lips.

He looked down. Her fist clenched his shirt, blotched in
fresh energy burns.

'You're hurt,' he whispered.

Deflecting piece of shit.

'Getting better with the capsules,' Fi said. 'Still not perfect.
I'll be—'

Slowly, he lifted his hand. Fi raised every bristle, spine
straight as steel, but when he touched her, his palm settled cool
against her aching knuckles. His claws, so much softer than the
carving tools she'd just witnessed.

They both stilled. Fi, waiting for the strike. Antal, she

realized, giving her the chance to pull away.

When she didn't, he said, 'Daeyari Shaping is poor at healing mortals. But I can . . .'

Crimson energy glowed at his fingertips. It skated Fi's skin, not penetrating but pulling, gathering shards of red energy that lingered in the burn like splinters.

'I'm sorry, Fionamara,' he said lowly. 'I didn't realize what you've been through.'

He released her. Fi inspected her hand with a scowl, poking at tender flesh. The burns didn't vanish. The stinging did, replaced by a milder ache.

So soft, when he wanted to be. Soft, as he lounged in her rafters. Soft, when he spoke her name. Soft, despite every barb she threw at him, even their worst snarls leading them back to this moment of unfathomable quiet.

Fi's anger didn't disappear. She only redirected it. Focused it. He wanted to do the right thing.

'Will you change?' she said. 'If we get your territory back?'

His tail brushed the flagstones. 'I'll try, Fionamara.'

'Swear it.'

'I—'

'Swear it on that wretched god of yours.'

'He's not a—'

'Do it.'

Antal sucked a breath through his teeth. 'I swear I'll do better. On Veshri's teeth and watchful eyes, on the path of the First Void Weaver. May my antlers grow crooked in the next life if I don't.'

The oath turned out funnier than she'd expected. Fi would have to remember that one.

For now, movement caught her eye. Boden poked his head into the courtyard.

'Are you all right?' he called. 'I heard raised voices and . . .' He blanched at the butchered corpse.

Fi met him on commanding strides. 'Mayor Boden of Nyskya! I have a new proposal.'

'Oh no,' Boden muttered. 'Fi, can this wait until—'

'Verne has sabotaged your energy conduits. She demands a sacrifice. We need to stop her.' Fi turned to Antal. 'You can't take down Verne and Astrid and her Beast on your own. The two of us probably won't be enough. You aren't getting help from Tyvo, or your family, or any other daeyari. We need help. *Human* help.'

Boden listened with an expression that said either 'you're onto something brilliant' or 'I cannot fathom why you thought those words were acceptable to come out of your mouth'. She had trouble telling those two faces apart.

He understood, though. 'I can't order Nyskya to fight for him, Fi.'

'Then ask,' she said. 'Give them a choice. It's the only way we'll win this.'

Boden gnawed his lip, not an outright refusal.

It was Antal who looked dubious. He didn't scoff when Fi faced him. Didn't jeer at the naïve plan. His tail fell low enough to brush the floor again.

'Why would they fight for me?' he asked. 'Why risk their lives for a daeyari?'

'Because you're going to promise them something different,' Fi said. 'You're going to do the right thing, Antal.'

Part Three

The woman wandered through the trees,
Lost in the dark and drifts of snow.
Trailing her, she met a beast,
With antlers black and eyes aglow.

'Shelter here,' the creature purred,
And took her hand to lead her home.
'You must be cold,' spoke velvet words,
And danced with her until she warmed.

The beast clothed her in moonspun silk,
And laid a feast to see her fed.
But as she ate of sweets and milk,
Her host touched nothing of the spread.

'Fair beast,' she said, 'you've been so kind,'
'To show my thanks, what shall I do?'
The creature grinned, sharp fangs outlined,
'Tonight,' it said, 'I'll feast on you.'

—Poem from the Winter Plane, *Lost to the Woods*

24

At what cost?

Fi crouched beside Boden in a night-shrouded Winter forest, surveying the dark lines of Nyskya's power center. Not a towering factory like the ones in Thomaskweld. The concrete walls were broken by a line of high windows, glowing silver. The yard sparkled with fresh snow. Above the rustle of shiverpine needles, a hum infused the air, one central copper energy conduit striking out across the ground before splitting into the village. A green aurora snapped overhead, glinting against the metal fixtures.

'I don't see anyone.' Fi squinted into darkness, struggling to see *anything*.

'Should be empty at this hour,' Boden said, 'but better be safe. We could wait for—'

'Are you two finished?' Antal said from his perch on a branch above. 'Or do you want to loiter all night? The place is empty.'

Fi didn't appreciate his dry tone. 'What, as if you can see in the dark or . . .'

Antal's glowing eyes peered down at her, an insufferable tilt to his brow.

'You know,' Boden said slowly, 'that *does* make sense.'

They let Antal and his night vision – apparently – lead the way into the building. They'd paid the daeyari his meal. Now came his end of the bargain: repairing the village's faulty conduits. Sabotaged conduits, according to Cardigan.

Inside, Boden confirmed the admin office was empty before beckoning the others forward. 'Nothing that will draw too much attention. We don't want—'

'Don't worry, Mayor Kolbeck.' Antal strode past him, tone flat. 'The people of my city are no more accustomed to my presence. I'm used to avoiding notice.'

The hall opened into a large room of non-conductive stone, windows catching starlight two stories overhead. A brighter glow came from four towering glass tanks, stores of energy built up during working hours, three filled high with wisping silver, another brimming crimson. The fruits of Fi's first donation of daeyari energy chips.

Plenty of energy. Distribution was the problem.

'We've got conduits acting up all over town,' Boden said. 'But might as well start with the main culprit.'

Antal circled the transformer like a vulture appraising carrion. Copper plates formed the body of the construct, framed in aluminum piping and glass channels to view the energy movement. Conduits of copper alloy fed from the storage tanks into the transformer, then out the building into the village. Antal's claws clacked over a dormant channel. Red energy danced from his fingertips, following a conduit a few feet before sputtering out. He scowled.

'Your equipment is alarmingly outdated,' Antal said.

Boden huffed. 'We've made do with what we can get our hands on.'

'I could have helped. If you'd only asked.'

'At what cost, daeyari?'

They held a brief staring contest. To Fi's surprise, Antal conceded, returning his gaze to the conduits with a tail flick. 'I'll do what I can.'

He pried open an access panel, claws nimble amidst conduit wires, snaps of red energy sparking ozone on the air. A welcome change. The normal smells of metal and lubricant reminded Fi too much of the smithy where their father had worked, the odors that clung to his jacket when he sank into his chair each night.

Metal shrieked as Antal ripped a section of conduit from its fittings. Boden's cry of protest came out equally shrill.

'Careful with that!' Boden said. 'If another channel goes out, we'll have people bunking in the general store.'

Antal studied the mess of metal. 'I can reroute the current past the faulty parts. A temporary fix.'

'You're sure you know what you're doing?'

'These conduits are a *daeyari* invention.'

'It's delicate technology.'

'It's simple technology. Do you have any replacement copper alloy? Ones that didn't come from Cardigan?'

Boden grumbled over to a supply shelf and returned with a box of copper wiring. Apparently, he hadn't noticed Antal's slip of words.

Fi did.

Simple technology. Energy conduits were a gift from the daeyari, one of the biggest bartering chips offered in exchange for sacrifices. But daeyari were liars. They twisted stories and stoked fear. What else had they been keeping from humans?

Antal caught her eye with face guarded, a flick of his tail before returning to work. Fi had to step carefully around this beast. He could be as conniving as every other daeyari, playing on her sympathy to get his territory back.

But Fi wanted to believe he'd do the right thing. What a wretched, dangerous whim.

'How's your new roommate treating you?' Boden joined Fi, voice low beneath the scrape of tinkering metal.

He didn't approve of Antal staying with her. That much dripped from his tone. Fi had been apprehensive herself, inviting a carnivorous creature into her cottage.

'Well.' She poked her stomach. 'I haven't woken up to any missing organs. That's nice.'

Boden glared.

'*Kidding*,' Fi said. 'He's not so bad. Keeps to himself. Doesn't leave dirty dishes in the sink. The teeth are really the only downside.' And those were becoming less of a downside, the more time Fi spent with him. She doubted Boden would relate with her thinking on that one.

Boden sighed. The older he grew, the more exhaustion weighed his shoulders, a foreseeable side effect of too much responsibility. Fi missed lighthearted Bodie, the man who'd declared impromptu snowball fights and snuck chocolates into her room when she got grounded for sneaking out in the middle of the night with Astrid.

'How are you handling all this?' Fi asked.

'My first responsibility is to Nyskya. I won't drag anyone into this against their will.' The reply came premeditated, measured by a couple of nights' consideration since they'd returned from Cardigan's villa.

'Sure,' Fi said. 'But if it means keeping their homes safe? You might find more people willing to stand against Verne than you expect. Kashvi would probably go on a one-woman rampage without much prompting.'

'Kashvi would rather put a crossbow bolt through a daeyari than work with one.'

'Maybe we can change her mind. Could use a sharp-shooter.'

Boden ran a hand through frizzed hair. 'I'll speak with my advisory council. See what they think of all this.'

'Soon, Bodie.'

'I know. I will. But . . . are you sure you want to be a part of that?'

She bristled. 'What do you mean?'

He ran a hand through his hair again. Too obvious a tell. Growing a beard had only given Boden more outlet to betray his unease, fingers scratching the scruff.

'If you don't want to be tangled up in this anymore,' he said. 'I understand. I can take over from here.'

Another downside of older Boden: his ability to shift from sweet to infuriating.

'Why?' Fi demanded. She knew why. She always knew why.

'It's a lot to deal with,' he deflected.

'You think I'm not responsible enough?'

'That's not true at all, Fi.'

'Then *why*?'

Her tone was a dagger, sharp but stealthy, not distracting Antal from his conduit wires.

Boden sharpened to parry her. 'You have history with this shit. With daeyari.'

'We both have history.'

'You have *more* history. I don't want you to feel . . . overwhelmed.'

'I've grown past that.'

'You weren't past it when I found you seven years ago, running away from every Void-damned thing you could glance at. You aren't past it now.'

There it was. Even when Fi saw it coming, even wrapped in every defensive bristle, she winced at the hurt they always danced around, the truth Boden could never just come out and tell her.

She'd run away. She'd left him to deal with their father. He knew what a coward she'd always been, the guilt she'd spent a decade trying to bury.

'I'm fine now.' The lie cut her teeth.

Boden gave her that condescending sigh he ought to have patented at the Thomaskweld trade office. 'That's bullshit, Fi. I saw how spooked you were when you got back from Thomaskweld – I understand *why*, now. But you refused to tell me then.'

'I didn't want you to worry—'

'So you took it all on yourself?' He huffed, exasperated. 'You don't have to act like nothing on the Planes can shake you. You don't have to always pretend like—'

A tiny gasp cut him off.

What an odd sound. Too meek to have come from Boden. Not from Fi, obviously. At the transfer hub, Antal stood silent, eyes wide at . . .

A little girl stood in the doorway, gloved hands tight on the frame, shielded by the wall so only one startled eye and a poof of black hair were visible.

She stared at the daeyari like a nightmare come to life.

'Anisa?' Boden hurried to her.

'Mayor Boden.' The girl shrank, brown cheeks nearly disappearing in the fur ruff of her coat. 'Why's there a monster here? Daddy says monsters aren't allowed in Nyskya.'

What was she doing here? This late, the building should have been empty of workers, much less a child. Antal hadn't moved, his tail swaying an uncertain arc, as if he had no idea what to do with this tiny, defenseless creature staring at him in such terror. Fair. Fi wasn't great with kids, either.

So why wasn't he *gone*? Vanished like a bad nightmare. His eyes snapped higher, staring down the hall at—

'Anisa.' Boden crouched in front of the girl, his tone forced levity. 'It's late. What are you doing here?'

'Daddy forgot some papers. He brought me with him.'

'You came with Savo? Where—'

'Anisa!'

The shout came from the hall. A man followed, wire-built and dark-skinned, spectacles askew against a knitted hat. Savo. The power foreman. Fresh snow dusted his jacket, sprinkling the floor as he grabbed his daughter and pulled her safe behind him.

Savo didn't look at the daeyari like an apparition. His gaze hardened on Antal like a wolf caught prowling a henhouse.

'*Boden?*' Savo demanded. His eyes never left the daeyari.

Boden raised placating hands. 'Everything's fine, Savo.'

'What is that creature doing here, Boden?'

'He's here at my invitation. Fixing our energy conduits.'

'*Fixing* them?' Savo pulled Anisa against his leg. 'At what cost?'

Antal flinched at the repeated line. At how this man shielded his daughter, fingers clutched in the puff of her coat while she peeked around him with doe-like eyes. '*Unfair. To both of us,*' Antal had told Fi some time ago. Savo had every right to distrust this man-eating creature, but Antal had never taken *children* as sacrifices.

'Nyskya is safe,' Boden said. 'I would never risk our people, you know that.'

'At no cost,' Fi added.

Savo gave her a more guarded look than he offered Boden, lines dug deep into his snow-leathered skin. He wore that conflict often for her – gratitude for the energy chips she brought to Nyskya, hesitance over how she acquired them.

'Didn't know you were back in town, Fi. And there's *always* a cost.'

Fi shot Antal a scowl of, *'say something, or I'll file your antlers off while you sleep'*.

'It's as they say.' Antal stepped closer, then thought better of it when Savo stiffened. 'Your hospitality has been payment enough. I'll repair your machinery here, and whatever conduits are faulty in the village.'

Savo's brow creased deeper. As if hearing this creature speak eliminated some fleeting hope of it being a hallucination. How could Antal expect anything else? Daeyari kindness never came without a price.

Fi had always believed that. Until she met him.

She'd always believed immortals had no care for the flitting emotions of prey. But now, a scowl tugged Antal's lips, his tail low at his ankles. He was upset. Guilty, that his own people saw him this way?

Be it empathy. Be it the hustler in her blood always searching for weakness. Fi saw their plan gaining speed. Savo's intrusion was unexpected, but she could work with this.

'You'd bring a daeyari to Nyskya?' Savo said, hushed now. 'Sneak around in the night? That's not like you, Boden. Not like you at all.'

Boden hesitated. 'I didn't want—'

'We had to make sure the daeyari was good to his word,' Fi interjected, before Boden could spin some diplomatic diversion. They couldn't wait, couldn't drown in what-ifs. 'What comes next, the whole village should have a say in. Which is why both of us are calling the advisory council together, to discuss what Antal can offer.'

Fi's look dared Boden to challenge her. She wasn't going anywhere. Not this time.

His displeasure passed as a twitch of the mouth. But he couldn't argue with the corner they'd been backed into. Mayor Boden stood tall to address Savo. 'It's late, my friend, and for that I apologize. But Fi's right. This shouldn't wait. Notify the rest of the council. We'll meet in Kashvi's tavern in an hour.'

25

As long as we're making deals

Savo left quickly, pulling his daughter with him. She tugged at his grip, wide eyes seeking a final look at the monster looming behind.

Antal returned to work with a tight line to his mouth. The sound of claws against metal scraped uncomfortably loud in the empty room. Fi and Boden both stood silent. Both tense as iron. Tonight was about to get more difficult.

After giving Savo the allotted time, they headed into Nyskya.

The late hour left roads empty, windows dark, boots crunching on the skim of fresh snow still fluttering down in lazy puffs. Antal kept out of sight, a shadow on the rooftops, until they reached the yard behind Kashvi's tavern. He dropped to the snow with a whisper-soft impact and tail flicking. Agitation. Fi felt the same.

She'd whittled out a workable relationship with Boden's advisory council. Fi gave them preferential treatment for contraband requests, and, in return, they pretended they'd never heard of her. Thick-skinned people, cold-hardened to practicality. Hopefully, that practicality would see the benefit of Antal's partnership.

Boden faced the daeyari. 'I serve my people. If they decide they don't want you in Nyskya, you'll have to leave.'

'I understand,' Antal returned.

'There's . . . one particular person who might cause trouble—'

The back door of the tavern flew open.

Kashvi stepped out into the snow with black hair wild at her shoulders, red coat half buttoned. She marched past Fi without a glance. Swerved around Boden when he tried to step in her way. Her dark eyes glinted, cold as the crossbow in her hands.

She shoved the barrel against Antal's chest. Straight over his heart.

'Kashvi, wait!' Boden said.

'That won't kill him,' Fi added.

Kashvi snarled like a wolverine and pressed her crossbow harder, metal digging into the fabric of Antal's shirt. This meeting stood a snowball's chance on Summer of going well, but Fi had hoped they'd last a full minute before weapons got involved. She braced for the daeyari's response, their plan doomed the moment blood hit the snow.

But Antal did nothing. Kashvi's assault didn't budge his stone stance.

'This is . . . an ally of yours?' Antal asked, a razored glare his only retaliation.

'I hardly believed it.' Kashvi started in a hiss. 'I *hardly believed it* when Savo came by. What he claimed he'd seen.' Louder, lifting to a roar. 'Boden. What is this beast doing here?'

'He can tell you himself,' Boden said. 'Without weapons.'

Kashvi didn't budge. 'Offering to rip his own claws out, is he?'

'I come to aid,' Antal said.

She laughed like metal scraping stone. 'Oh. That's rich. Daeyari are always so *helpful*, aren't you?'

Antal frowned. 'I've . . . perhaps not always acted in your best interest . . .'

'You ate my *sister*, you fucker!'

VOIDWALKER

Her words cracked like split ice, fracturing the common ground they'd hoped to stand on.

Tense as the stand-off was, neither Fi nor Boden intervened. Not their place to do so. Fi had lived in Nyskya a full year before Kashvi, down half a bottle of whiskey, finally shared why she left home to settle in the middle of nowhere. Why she still practiced with a crossbow, though it aggravated her illness – but again, Fi had hoped they'd have time for gentler introductions.

Antal fell deathly still. Maybe to the others he appeared the same unruffled creature. Maybe Fi was the only one who noticed his low tail, the stiff inhale.

When Antal didn't speak, Kashvi snarled and shifted her crossbow to his throat, barrel raking soft flesh beneath his jaw. This caused more visible upset, a curling of claws at his sides.

'*Kashvi*,' Boden pleaded.

'Do you remember her?' Kashvi demanded. 'From Sunip, a border town. Verne accused us of pushing her boundary, claimed we owed her a sacrifice. So my sister went to *you*.'

Antal hesitated. 'She came willingly?'

'She had no choice! She sacrificed herself to save the rest of us. Do you remember her *name*?'

A longer pause.

'I don't . . . ask their names.'

Kashvi screamed. Antal shoved her arm aside as she loosed the bolt, a snap of silver energy striking a wall. Kashvi Shaped a current to her fingertips to reload.

The projectile dispersed when her arm spasmed. Kashvi warred against rage and failing body as her silver sickness shook her muscles, forcing her to her knees in the snow.

Boden knelt beside her, crossbow pushed aside, supporting Kashvi as she steadied her breath. The tavern door opened again. Iliha stepped out in a hastily-shrugged coat, legs bare and feet stuffed into slippers. Wide blue eyes snapped to the daeyari before she hurried to her wife's side, gentle fingers drawing the hair away from Kashvi's face.

Antal looked on. Ashen.

Stillness seemed to be an innate daeyari trait, yet Fi had never seen this type of stillness fall over him. His eyes lost their glow, a hollow red like scuffed glass. As if he'd never had to face this side of his sacrifices before.

'Kashvi.' Boden held her shoulders.

'He took my sister,' Kashvi rasped.

'I know. And you have every right to be angry. But we need him, to fight Verne.'

'Those fuckers can both fall to pieces in the Void!'

Boden gripped her firmer. 'Kashvi. I need you, too. You want to fight, don't you? Well, we're going to *fight*. We're not sending any sacrifice to Verne.'

At last, Kashvi quieted.

Fi fell in and out of good graces with the woman, but they shared an understanding born of common pain. A daeyari stole Fi's life from her. Kashvi knew similar grief, even if she'd never made that walk to the forest shrine herself. An aching kind of grief, the type that nested in the bones, waiting for a chance to shatter free.

Kashvi shoved Boden off her. When she stood, she spat at Antal's feet.

'For Boden,' she told him. 'Not for you. Walk into my tavern, and you'd better have something good to say, daeyari. I don't guarantee you walking out.'

Kashvi grabbed her crossbow and marched inside, Iliha drifting at her heels like a worried wraith.

Boden slipped Antal a warning look before he followed.

Fi stayed behind.

She had to be careful, reading into Antal's stillness. That shaken look seemed too close to remorse. He had to eat. But he'd spoken of grief, of not wanting to cause pain, enough that he must realize how many lives like Kashvi's he'd shredded into pieces?

'You really don't ask their names?' she whispered.

Antal took a slow breath. 'It's harder to eat someone with a name.'

Why should she believe him? Immortals were clever creatures. His penitence might be nothing more than an act to lure his human partners into sympathy, helping him reclaim his city.

Fi found herself pulled to him all the same. Wary steps, yet she drew close enough to draw a breath of ozone on cold air.

'Antal,' she said. 'This is your chance to be different. To be *better*.'

A strange tension snapped over him, eyes sharp on her in shock. Then, down.

Fi had laid her hand on his arm.

She hardly registered reaching for him, some subconscious gesture of consolation or coercion. Now, she joined Antal in stunned silence, fingers light against pale skin.

Antal held still. As if waiting for her to realize her mistake. To flinch away.

Fi didn't. It was . . . warm beside him, a narrow shelter from the cold. Something calming in his stillness, something raw in the hum of energy beneath his skin, barely detectable against her fingertips. That tang of pine and ozone, lulling with each breath.

Antal didn't pull away, either. She stiffened as he leaned closer.

As he slowly, gently, pressed his forehead to hers.

'You're too kind to me, Fionamara.'

His touch stunned her like a blow, crimson eyes soft beneath low lashes. His voice, not a growl, but a rasp, hesitant as the breath they shared. Since they'd first clashed, proximity meant bristles and claws, never this tender thing hanging whisper-quiet between them.

It locked Fi's lungs. It pulled at her with velvet tethers.

It vanished, before she could grasp it.

Antal stepped away. His absence left Fi in a shock of cold, a swift moment of panic as she straightened her spine and clawed for composure.

As he moved to the tavern door, Antal straightened as well, tail smoothing from its restless sway. When he looked back at her, soft eyes had returned to coals, that slip of vulnerability buried beneath his stone facade.

Indifference didn't suit him. Fi preferred him rougher. Raw.

'Shall we?' he asked.

Which was the act: the stone or the silk? If this was all a cunning trick, Fi might be out of her depth. She steadied her breath and followed him inside.

The floorboards hardly creaked beneath Antal's steps. In the quiet, Fi's ears pricked at murmured voices down the hall.

When Antal stepped into the room, all conversation ceased.

The tavern had closed for the night, lights dimmed except for the glow of the furnace, the dormant glass interior of the music box, a couple of copper fixtures closest to the bar. Boden paced. Kashvi sat on a barstool, crossbow on her knee, Iliha watching from behind the counter while her flock of mechanical birds dozed beside the bottles on the shelves.

A table had been pulled into the light. Steaming mugs sat upon the beaten brass, filling the room with the smell of fresh coffee, accompanied by a platter of cinnamon buns and hardy Winter cranberries, untouched. Savo leaned forward, a much slighter man with the bulk of his jacket draped over his chair, face drawn into a squint.

Beside him sat Mal, owner of Nyskya's general store, his stature like several logs had grown a beard and stuffed themselves into flannel, skin light brown and eyes like tar. One of the most meticulously infuriating barterers Fi had ever met.

Last was Yvette, head of the metal smithy, seated in their chair like a wire rod soldered to the wood. Their silver hair was tied into a long braid, pale cheeks flushed from cold, coat peppered with singe marks and a smell of woodsmoke.

Boden's advisory council eyed Antal with hard eyes, chairs creaking under legs prepared to flee. The mayor stepped forward to address them, his back exposed to the daeyari. An opening vote of confidence. Surprised murmurs flitted around the table.

'Thank you for coming at such a late hour,' Boden said. 'This is an issue that shouldn't wait.'

Kashvi strummed her nails against the stock of her crossbow. 'Because you got caught, you mean?'

Fuck, Kashvi. Fi knew she was upset, and rightly so. But this wasn't helping.

Boden held out a hand, deferring to Savo.

'I had a late check-in at the power plant,' Savo said. 'Found Boden and Fi there. With the daeyari.'

'Doing *what?*' Fi pushed.

Savo considered her with lips pressed. 'Repairing energy conduits, looked like.'

'Really, Fi?' Kashvi said. 'You're on the daeyari's side?' She spoke like this was a betrayal, their common history demanding they hate this beast together.

Kashvi hadn't seen the side of Antal that Fi knew. None of these people had. Yet his demeanor now was hard to parse. He appraised the assembly of humans in silence, sharp eyes flitting from speaker to speaker.

'This is Antal,' Boden said. 'Former Lord Daeyari of this territory. Since Verne's coup, he's come to us seeking shelter. As many of us came to Nyskya seeking shelter.'

'Seeking shelter *from him*,' Kashvi said.

A murmur of agreement passed through the others.

'I come to ask your input,' Boden pressed. 'Whether the daeyari should be allowed to stay.'

Yvette answered first, eyes like polished steel. 'Why would we want him to stay?'

'Our conduits are breaking down,' Boden said. 'Sabotaged, as part of Verne's coup.'

'Sabotaged?' Savo said. 'That's why the transformer keeps losing connection?'

'Ours,' Boden said. 'And others all over the territory. Antal has offered to repair our equipment.'

'At what cost?' Mal demanded through the thick of his beard.

Again, that line. Antal's expression didn't change. The tip of his tail flicked.

'He's offered to help,' Boden deflected. 'And he's made good on that promise so far.'

'Because he wants us to fight Verne for him,' Kashvi said.

Silence.

The attendees looked to each other. To Boden and his stiff nod.

'We have a common enemy,' he said. 'We ought to consider—'

'Which is wild, don't you think?' Kashvi laughed, the caustic hitch of a cough at the end. 'Why fight for a daeyari? We ought to be getting rid of the bastards entirely.'

Yvette scoffed. 'Be reasonable, Kashvi.'

'Why not?' Kashvi tipped forward on her stool. 'Why not fight for our own freedom?'

'Open a space, and another daeyari will move in. Tyvo. Or another neighbor.'

'Then we fight until they stop coming!'

'Verne is our immediate threat,' Boden said, a voice of forced calm.

'And we all know how rebellions against daeyari go,' Mal grumbled. 'Over a century since the Brackenport uprising in Tyvo Territory, and they're still pulling bodies out of that bog.'

While the others argued, Fi leaned a hip against the bar. She bit her tongue against Boden's meek defense, didn't say a damn word against Kashvi's outbursts.

Too busy watching Antal.

Bastard still hadn't said a word.

A politician's son, she connected at last. Two centuries to hone that guarded facade, to decide when speaking benefited him, and when to let the humans run their mouths.

'But those rebellions are a little bit bullshit, aren't they?' Fi spoke to the room, the others falling quiet at her comment, but she looked straight at Antal. 'Because it's calculated. Daeyari keep themselves mysterious, so they'll seem more terrifying. They suppress stories of how to fight them.' Her voice dipped in accusation. 'And you're holding back technology from us, aren't you?'

Antal didn't balk at her attack. She did spot a flicker of surprise, a low twitch of his tail that suggested he'd not expected her to fight against him. But Fi was no fool. She'd not stand at his side if he promised her change but only spoke in half-truths, deflecting rather than—

'The conduits we give you are rudimentary,' he said. 'Inefficient. Daeyari have had better technology for decades.'

Every human in the room flinched at his voice. Then fell very quiet at the implication.

The truth. He was finally telling the truth.

'Why?' Fi didn't care about the startled eyes of the others, the creaks of their chairs. She only spoke to him. 'To keep us afraid of you?'

'Daeyari have metered mortal technology for centuries,' he said. 'Kept territories separate so governments can't become self-sufficient. Buried any knowledge of how to fight back. You'll say it's because we think little of you. Or perhaps we miss the days of hunting you wild through the forests. But the truth is much simpler than that . . .'

Antal hesitated. Drew a stiff breath.

'It's because you learned how to kill us,' he said.

The room hung on his words. Still silent.

'Your species started out defenseless,' Antal said. 'Easy prey. Then you grew stronger at Shaping. You developed metallurgy, weapon making. The first daeyari fell to your hands. This was unacceptable.' He paused. Images of reincarnated beasts flitted through Fi's head, hollow red eyes and feral roars. 'So my kind brokered peace with yours. Humane treatment, in exchange for sacrifice. A raw deal . . . *for you*. The daeyari offer boons, but they'll never allow you to threaten us again.'

Still, silence.

Until Kashvi slammed a fist to the counter.

'You knew this?' she hissed. 'You knew this, you went along with it, and you still expect us to help you?'

'It's a wretched system,' Antal said with a flash of fangs. 'On that, we agree.'

'Then why didn't you change it?'

'I did what I could. I kept my distance, let you rule yourselves. Took barely what food I needed to survive. Daeyari are free to rule our territories as we wish, but the sacrifice system stays the same. If *one* territory allows its humans to lose their fear, we risk your entire species becoming emboldened again.'

'So you won't change,' Yvette accused. 'We help put you back in power, and everything will stay the same?'

Fi braced for his evasion. For him to prove his oaths to her were flitting words.

'No,' Antal said. 'Help me reclaim my seat as territory lord, and I vow to never take a living sacrifice again.'

If the room was quiet before, it fell deafening now.

'Half measures did me no good,' Antal finished. 'Verne saw me as weak for my lenience. My people loathe me for the flesh I've taken. If I'm allowed to return to my post, I'll do so with a system that won't perpetuate fear.'

He wanted to do the right thing – he was *doing* the right thing.

Fuck Fi in the Void, they might really have a chance at this.

'Daeyari must eat,' Mal countered. 'They must eat humans. Or is that also a lie?'

'That one is true,' Antal said with a grimace.

He looked to Fi.

It took her a moment, snared in the glow of those crimson irises, to realize he was waiting for her to speak on his behalf. Asking her, with that brief softening of his gaze, if she would stand with him. Not as combatants.

As partners.

'Corpse donation,' she said. The plan they'd sketched out the night before, Fi sprawled on her couch and Antal dangling in her rafters. 'Most humans get cremated anyway. What do they care, what happens to their body once they're dead and energy gone to the Void? They could volunteer. A victimless exchange, in return for daeyari aid.'

A wave of wide eyes crashed onto Antal.

'You agree to this?' Yvette asked. Their words tinged with intrigue.

A shifting tide.

Antal bowed his head. 'I will accept the dead, if you see fit to offer them.'

'And in return, you still offer energy production? Defense against other daeyari?'

'Wherever it's needed. As much as I'm able.'

'Because he *needs* us!' Kashvi cut in.

'I do,' Antal said without hesitation. 'I need you desperately. I can't remove Verne on my own. But whatever you think, rightly, of my kind, you must know we're good to our deals.' He pressed a hand to his chest. 'I have always been good to my deals.'

This time, Antal looked to Boden.

'He has,' Boden agreed. 'He told me he'd leave Nyskya untouched, and he has.'

'I don't ask you to forgive,' Antal said. 'I don't ask you to like me. I ask us to work together, for our best interest.'

And he claimed he wasn't a politician.

This time, the murmurs through the room rang less of outrage, more uncertainty.

'Verne would be easier to face,' Mal mused, 'with another daeyari's help.'

'So long as he doesn't eat us, first,' Savo countered.

'Are you all mad?' Kashvi snarled. 'You can't be considering this.'

'We need to do what's best for Nyskya,' Boden said.

'By allying with one of the creatures who used to hunt us through the woods?'

'Verne's already coming for us,' Fi shot back. 'This is the best ally we'll get.'

Yvette strummed their nails along the tabletop. A thoughtful lean in their chair. 'So long as we're making deals, I want more daeyari technology for my metalworks. *Better* technology.'

Again, the mood shifted. A spark of opportunity.

Antal considered. Nodded. 'You'll have it. I'm familiar enough with the technology, I can teach what I know.'

'And updated energy conduits?' Savo added.

'Of course,' Antal agreed.

Fi drank in the exchanges with forced calm, heart racing.

'Well hold the fuck on!' Mal said. 'If we're all making demands? I want better stock for my general store. Summer Plane strawberries, *year-round*.'

'That's . . .' Antal paused. Sighed. 'Consider it done.'

This was working. It was actually working.

'How about a better governing council for the territory?' Boden added. Because of course he did. 'Not just a governor. Input from all the settlements.'

'A fine proposal,' Antal said. 'I'd be glad to have your input, Mayor Kolbeck.'

As the deal came together, Fi wondered if the others saw the shape of it like she did, the *immensity* of it. For millennia, deals with daeyari had always looked the same: a sacrifice of flesh, in exchange for aid. This was something new. Two sides working toward a common purpose, not coerced by fear. A pact that might actually benefit them both.

Next came Kashvi. As everyone looked to her, she scowled with renewed vigor.

'I want my dead sister back, fucker. Until you figure out how to pull that off, you can move right along.'

Well, maybe not a benefit to everyone. Still, a start. Antal's jaw feathered, but he didn't argue.

Last, he looked to Fi.

'And you, Fionamara? What would you ask of me, to have your aid?'

Fi straightened. She opened her mouth, but to her dismay, nothing jumped to her tongue. That wasn't right. She ought to be ready to haggle at a moment's notice.

But the way Antal looked at her. That crack of exhaustion and relief pulling his brow. The way she could almost see the shape of 'thank you' in the curve of his lips . . .

'A favor,' she said. 'For me to call on when I wish.'

Antal nodded without hesitation.

A fool. He was a *fool* to trust her that easily, to grant a deal so broad.

And they were partners in this.

'Well,' Yvette said, an enterprising glint in their eye, 'I'd like to hear the daeyari out.'

'How many in Nyskya will fight?' Savo said.

'How many *can* fight?' Mal amended.

'We don't need many.' Fi took the floor. 'We only have three targets. A small force will be enough to clear a path, then . . .' She glanced to her side, locked eyes with crimson irises. 'Antal and I will take care of Verne.'

Antal nodded, though there was a grimness to it. Couldn't fault him for that.

'We don't have many fighters in Nysksa,' Boden said. 'But perhaps they'll be eager to learn. If another daeyari is willing to teach?'

'And weapons?' Mal pressed. 'Where will we get those?'

'We can smith weapons.' Yvette strummed their fingers

again. 'Though we'll need better metal, conductive alloy. Not easy to come by.'

Fi lit with smug anticipation before anyone even said it. A wicked grin, by the time Boden looked to her.

'How fortunate,' he said dryly, 'that we have an accomplished smuggler at our disposal.'

26

A dance with claws

Trust didn't bloom overnight. But in the following days, Nyskya's advisory council grew to regard Antal with less open spite – aside from Kashvi, the stubborn ice toad.

Under Savo's direction, Fi and Antal paid nightly visits to the village's energy conduits. Antal was, Fi had to admit, impressively good with his hands, his improvised engineering enough to get most of the system running again.

With Mal and Boden, they met in the general store after hours, strategizing supplies and shelter for Nyskya's residents who didn't want to fight when the time came.

With Yvette, they toured the metal smithy, taking inventory of what metal they'd need for new crossbows and sword hilts. Yvette brought villagers to meet them in small groups, those willing to fight, and who could be trusted with knowledge of Antal's involvement.

Kashvi, they avoided. Though Fi had to listen to Boden groan daily about the tavern keeper's complaints. Fi started out sympathetic. By midweek, she was thoroughly over Kashvi's stubborn spite. Warranted spite, but the greater enemy they faced required cooperation, even if forgiveness was out of the cards.

Exhausted, Fi dragged herself through meetings with Boden

and his council, grumbling an internal monologue on how this was why she'd always left politics to her brother. Give her a Void sky and an empty horizon. Her latest meeting – discussing vulnerabilities of upcoming metal shipments with Boden and Kashvi – ran late. Antal, for the sake of productive conversation, didn't attend. When at last she trudged back to her cottage, the forest was dark, a green aurora whispering overhead.

The lights were on ahead of her.

Fi, accustomed to dark windows and a quiet sofa to sprawl on after a draining day, still found this homecoming strange. Though not unpleasant.

She entered to find Antal cross-legged on her cushions, tinkering with a disassembled crossbow. He appeared fresh-clothed and freshly-bathed, lingering drops of water glinting on his antlers. Still an upsetting number of buttons undone, baring a wide view of smooth chest, the clean lines of his clavicle.

Fi never seemed to adjust to that first sight of him: the predatory tilt of his head, the glint in his eyes when he looked up to greet her.

'Welcome ba—'

She groaned and collapsed onto the sofa. Handsome immortal visitors or not, Fi had every right to relax in her own home.

'I see.' Antal's smirk teased a fang. He returned to his tinkering, giving Fi time to wrestle out of her coat and kick her boots off. Dressed down to a more comfortable sweater, she sprawled anew.

'How's Yvette treating you?' she asked.

'They only joked about impaling me twice today. An improvement.'

'That's nice.'

Exhausting work, but welcome progress. Fi had less kind

things to say about Boden's tight scheduling, which made her miss lunch. She ought to eat something before—

Fi sniffed, noticing the warm, nutty aroma.

She rose, following the smell to her kitchen. A mug waited on the counter, still hot.

'What's this?'

'Coffee,' Antal said, not looking up from his work.

Fi squinted at the offering. 'Is it poisoned?'

A scoff. 'I have far more direct means of ending you, Fiona-mara.'

'Salted, then?'

'Now, that's just rude.'

Fi sipped the drink, annoyed to find it prepared immaculately, frothed and sugared exactly how she liked. Was it her glower that drew Antal's chuckle? Or simply his game of constantly shifting the ground beneath her?

'Thank you,' she conceded quietly. A sigh through tired lips, tired hands too used to always taking care of herself.

Antal said nothing. His grin was more treacherous than claws. And the way his neck craned over his work, the easy slope of muscled shoulders . . .

Enough of *that*. Fi selected a record and set it on her gramophone. The song opened with a piano solo, filling the cottage with soulful keys. She settled on her sofa. Closed her eyes. The day's tension fled as she tapped her fingers to the rhythm, the joining accompaniment of snare drums and bass stirring beats through her ribs. The brass joined next, quick and deep, lifting the song to a new height.

Then, a low *swish swish* she didn't recognize.

Antal's claws stilled on his work, the metal fixture settling against his knee. His eyes went half closed. Unfocused. His tail swished her sofa, moving in time to the music.

'You shouldn't stare at a daeyari's tail,' Antal said, clipped. 'It's rude.'

Fi stiffened, torn between defensive and embarrassed that he'd caught her looking. 'Sorry! I just thought, your tail seems to change based on what you're feeling, and . . .'

Antal gave her a dry look, his tail coiled defensively around one leg.

'Oh.' Now that Fi thought of it, she wouldn't be keen on someone reading her emotions so openly, either.

'It's a valuable skill,' Antal said, softer. 'Noticing these things. Just do it more subtly.'

'Sure,' she agreed, because he *had* made her a nice cup of coffee. 'You . . . like music?'

Antal's tail uncurled – Fi noticed from the corner of her eye, *not* staring. When the horn solo started, his gaze slipped soft again.

'This is Old River Infirmary,' he said. 'A Spring Plane recording.'

He was spot on, the record picked up at a canal-side music house while Fi unwound after a successful barter of contraband copper. She'd seen that gramophone in his home, but never thought more of it.

'I'm surprised,' she admitted.

'That I know music?'

'That you'd bother with such small things.' Surely, music solos must seem like trivialities to an immortal from the Void beyond Planes.

Fi watched the quirk of his mouth too closely. The scrape of a fang across his lips. He reclined against her sofa, entrancing, the way his toned torso shifted beneath his shirt. Inhumane, how tightly his trousers showed the spread of his thighs.

'Some daeyari lose interest in little things,' he said, 'letting time become a haze. Others seek small moments that make each day different from the last. Each year, each century different from the last.'

Here was that abyss again, a view into something so beyond her. Fi couldn't resist teetering on the edge.

'And you?' she asked.

'Immortality seems wasted, if every day becomes the same.'

A new song started, the roll of a horn into deeper bass. Antal set his metalwork aside. Let his eyes drift languid beneath his lashes. He was so much handsomer with that softness on his brow, that careless part of his mouth.

A flutter brushed Fi's stomach, recalling the press of his forehead against hers in the tavern yard. His breath against her cheek.

'I snuck into the Thomaskweld music hall sometimes.' Antal spoke low, not overpowering the sound. 'Listened to the symphonies, the ensembles. Up in the rafters, where no one could see me.'

Fi scowled over her coffee. 'In the rafters? I know those box seats are hard to get, but, surely, when you rule over an entire city . . .'

'Most people aren't comfortable around daeyari, Fionamara. I'd rather stay out of sight than cause a panic.'

So blunt. So defeated. Fi scowled deeper. 'You don't have to lurk all the time. Go out into your city. Let people get used to you.'

'And how would I do that? I offer a hand, and they flinch at the claws. A smile, and all they see is fangs.'

Fi strummed her nails against her mug. Hadn't she been the same, when they first met? Before he saved her life. Before he pledged to save her home.

'You had a human friend before,' she said. 'He wasn't afraid of you, was he?'

Something sharp flicked over Antal's eyes. A twitch of the tail almost too quick to spot.

'No. He wasn't.'

'And I don't think you're so bad,' Fi said. Dismissive, lest it go to his head.

'You're unusual,' he returned, frustration roughing the words.

'Am I?' she pushed, just to hear him sound like that again. To snack on how it stroked her ego. 'Maybe you're right, Antlers. Maybe you're insufferable, and I'm just starved for company.'

He narrowed his eyes at her. Fi ruffled at the weight of it.

Then, a smirk. A *laugh*. 'Vicious woman. You can't say anything nicely, can you?'

Maybe she could. Maybe it was the fight she enjoyed. She set her coffee aside, leaning back to match his aloof posture. Comparatively, she must look a hot mess in her day-old curls, no bra beneath her sweater.

Antal's gaze scraped over her, a tug in his throat as he swallowed.

That look veered precariously close to hunger: whether for ripped clothes, or ripped flesh. Or some mix of the two? Fi still didn't know exactly what game they were playing, staring at each other like this. Only that she was tired, after plotting rebellion all week.

And there came that treacherous whisper again: *would it be so bad, to be devoured?*

'What would you want to do?' she asked mildly, despite the pulse in her throat. 'If you didn't have to worry about people being afraid?'

Antal's wicked grin heated her cheeks.

'Do you dance, Fionamara?'

She appraised his smug words, the swish of his tail to the music. 'Do *you*?'

'What a strange picture you've formed of my last two hundred years. Do you imagine I spent the entire time cloistered in a cave, emerging only to devour flesh and order governors?'

Well, when he put it that way. But *dancing*?

'What kind of dance?'

Antal stood and perused her records. With delicate claws, he swapped a new one onto the gramophone. The room filled with another Spring Plane recording: an opening blare of horns, joined by bass and drums in an eight-count. A dancing song.

He offered his hand.

Fi had started dancing when she'd left home. Those first couple years on her own, she'd sought sanctuary in dim clubs and distracting music, the touch of a dance partner who could share her soul for a four-minute number then disappear without further demand. She still visited some old haunts when work brought her through the cities, but it was hard to find anyone to twirl her in Nyskya.

She rose with every bristle raised.

It occurred to Fi, this daeyari wasn't a stupid creature. He must have noticed the treacherous flush on her cheeks. The tension, as she lay her hand in his, a whispered touch, claws soft against her fingers.

His other arm wrapped her lower back. Fi knew the stance. And *he* wanted to lead? She settled in like a mare with a reluctant bridle, easing her shoulders, tapping a foot to the music.

The first steps came simple. When Antal pushed, she swayed away. He pulled, and she glided back. He guided her through a spin that would have twirled the skirt of a dress. All Fi wore was a sweater and snow-weathered pants.

'Why are you scowling, Fionamara?' Antal sounded weary.

Or guarded. 'You bare your teeth like a daeyari with a stomachache.'

He deserved every inch of snarled lip, for hiding this from her. 'You really do know how to dance?'

'Does this displease you?'

'Wait here.' She broke from his grasp. 'If you're going to dance properly, then we have to dance *properly.*'

'What do you mean—'

'Turn around!'

Antal grumbled something about Veshri and black eternities as he faced away. Game or not, she had appearances to maintain. Fi opened her closet, engulfed in the scent of cedar, the musk of furs.

She retrieved a dress.

It was a ruthless thing, black and simple. The top wrapped her chest like armor, clasping around her neck and leaving arms bare. The waist cut tight. Below that, a flare of Void fabric, sleek folds weighted to hang when still and fly with motion. She returned to her dance partner with fists on her hips.

'There,' Fi said.

Antal tipped a glance over his shoulder, expression dry with annoyance.

His brow lifted. He stared first at her uncompromising face. Then, another slow slip of eyes downward, less subtle than before. The correct response. This dress made Fi's tits look fantastic.

Gratifying, that a daeyari would notice.

'There?' His voice came rougher than usual.

'It's been weeks since I had a proper dance. With what we're up against, who knows if . . .' She severed the thought. Held out her hand. 'Go ahead.'

Antal clasped her fingers, his cool touch sending a shiver

through her bare arms. He tilted her wrist, inspecting her floral tattoos. Daisies. Dahlias. Lilacs and snowy lily. All of them usually hidden by her coats.

'One per job,' Fi said with a taunting sort of pride. 'Remember that art heist at the Karvez Estate, south end of your territory?'

Antal nodded. Fi pointed to a water lily, an homage to one of the paintings she'd smuggled to a collector on the Summer Plane. 'And this one, a load of conductive ore from Tyvo Territory.' She indicated a pink tundra orchid. 'A stolen dowry from the Autumn Plane.' Next, a lilac, resembling one of the load's sapphire-crusted necklaces.

'A menace,' Antal all but growled. His smirk snared Fi like thorns to soft flesh, pulling her into the waiting crook of his arm. 'Impressive, that we never crossed paths sooner.'

'I made sure we didn't, daeyari.'

A new song started, quick with a clarinet above the bass. They resumed their stance, hands clasped, Fi's arm on his shoulder and his around her back. He smelled like fresh snow and a snap of eternity.

This dance had no memorized routine, only a common language of rhythm, the rest left to improvisation. Antal pushed them into motion on gliding steps, his hand holding Fi's only tight enough to tell his intention. As she relaxed, he pressed his arm at her back, pulling them into a turn. Close enough to share a breath. Then he sent her out again, connected only by fingertips, a twirl that lifted her dress and spun her hair into a flurry of curls.

Though he led, Fi pushed her own reply. When he pulled, she lingered in the motion, flaring her skirt to the rise of a horn in the music. He grinned. His response came seamlessly, shifting to match her, following the rhythm of the new instrument she'd called them to.

And then, they were speaking without words. A push and pull of melody, Antal asking and Fi answering. She spun at arm's length and swung tight at his side, hips brushing, grins like warring blades.

The song ended too soon.

With silence came stillness, the easing of breaths and softening of stances. This was the time to say 'thank you for the dance' then politely step away.

Neither of them did.

The next song came on like thunder through Fi's ribs, a burst of horn and drums, twice the tempo of the previous number. Antal flashed a fanged smile.

Fi smirked back.

He pulled her into the song like plunging into a current. He walked on water, his turns tighter, feet impossibly light despite the breath-stilling pace. Fi swirled through steps she'd never seen before – words she'd never spoken before – yet he led with such surety. She followed, trusting his direction, the pulse of music replacing the heartbeat in her chest.

This type of dance didn't have to be so tight. Fi had kept plenty of partners at arm's length, yet she leaned into Antal like the pull of a star, keeping close to keep their movements quick. Keeping close because she wanted to. The smell of him was like tumbling through a thunderstorm. When she glimpsed his eyes, they gleamed with the heat of an inferno and the depthless black of the Void.

Again, the song ended.

They spun to a standstill, breathless, sweat sheening Fi's skin. Antal's arm wrapped her waist, the rise and fall of his chest such a tangible thing, not the wraith she'd once taken daeyari for.

'You dance better than I expected,' she panted. Always a

surprise, this creature. Always finding new ways to take her breath away, no matter how fiercely she fought to keep her barbs up.

'And you dance as well as I expected,' he murmured. 'Like fire beneath your feet.'

The next song began. They didn't join it, motionless together as the music spun a slow soliloquy of clarinet, a heartbeat drum.

Pull away.

Fi ought to pull away, but she didn't.

Who was this creature, who'd filled her with terror when they met? Who'd just danced her into a stupor? Once, their game had been a contest of who'd back down first. Now, they both refused to balk. His proximity was a weapon, stirring the same thrill in her heart as when she'd first stood her ground against him. The same smolder in her belly as when he'd held her against the wall with his teeth. The same shudder as when he'd pressed his forehead soft to hers.

She thought about kissing him. Would his mouth taste like blood and old flesh? How would his teeth scrape against her lips?

Antal studied her breathless perplexion with the ghost of a smirk, that quiet acuity that came with agelessness. As if he could read every thought in the flicker of her lashes. Or maybe, just in the quickening of her pulse.

'What's wrong, Fionamara?' Her name rumbled off his tongue, velvet and slow. 'You look like you want something.'

She wanted *him*. Wanted to know what he felt like. What he tasted like. She'd wanted him for weeks, and no matter how she fought it, the ache had only fiercened. Enough to make her stupid. Enough to make her reckless.

Enough to shiver through every inch of cruelly thin dress pressed to his side.

'What do I look like when I want something?' she sparred, feigning indifference.

'You're a frustrating creature. Sometimes, you look like you want to rip my throat out.'

She hummed, not in disagreement.

'And sometimes,' he said, lower. 'You look like you want . . . something else. I worry I'm not able to tell the difference.'

Fi ought to feel foolish for leaning into him.

Only, he leaned into her, too. A brush of tail against her bare ankle, a flare of nostrils as he breathed her in, that flutter in her stomach that didn't feel like fear anymore.

'Maybe,' she said.

'*Maybe?* You're usually so assertive.' His voice dipped, a *purr* that rattled every sensible piece of her. 'I do enjoy that about you.'

'Maybe . . . I'm not sure it's something I *should* want.' Her throat, exposed to fangs. Soft skin bared to claws.

'I see. You aren't alone in that.'

Fi's breath caught at the words. At the glint of his eyes as they swept her face, her mouth, the straps of her dress. It was one thing to catalogue his taunts and speculate what they might mean.

Another thing entirely, to hear him say it.

To hear them both say it. This thing they'd danced around, strained to a breaking point, already no space between them as she leaned against his chest.

He reached for her face. Fi didn't flinch.

Antal brushed a swirl of rainbow hair off her cheek and tucked it behind her ear. Fi shivered at the whisper of claws over skin. At the gentleness of it. At how she wasn't sure she *wanted* him to be gentle. Was he still playing with her? A game to delight in her discomfort?

She ran an experimental hand down his chest. Soft fabric. Hard muscle. The rumble in his throat didn't sound like playing.

'Small moments?' she asked, her voice too soft for either of their good.

'Small moments,' he agreed with equal treachery.

'What other small moments do you enjoy?'

When he hummed, Fi felt it in her bones. His gaze raked her like claws. The real things pressed her waist. She wanted them in her hair. Under her dress.

'Some things you'd enjoy as well,' he said.

'Would I?'

'Why else does your breath come short whenever I'm this close to you?'

He leaned closer.

Then froze, when Fi jabbed a finger beneath the soft hollow of his chin.

'That's not what I asked, daeyari.'

She held him there. An immortal captive, commanded with the tip of a single finger. Had he always looked at her so ravenously? Or had she assumed it a different type of hunger? He seemed to like when she fought.

Fi liked when he fought, too. That line pulled taut between them.

'You'd enjoy it,' Antal vowed. Then, bolder, 'I dread how you'd torment me otherwise. Certainly, I'd never hear the end of it.'

Void save her, Fi devoured his taunts. His goading grin and the spark in his eyes. Heat kindled in her belly, sinking with perilous surety where she pressed her thighs together.

She wanted him. And what was stopping her? Survival instinct? He'd shared her home, and never crossed a single line she set down. Caution? Swiftly vanishing, every moment the hard weight of his body pressed flush against her. Daeyari carried no diseases in their immortal forms, couldn't make children with mortals.

And what was wrong with a little curiosity? A night of unwinding, before their next dance with mortal danger?

Antal didn't flinch, when Fi's fingers settled on his jaw.

A semblance of stone, as her thumb traced the smooth line of his chin.

Barely a twitch, as she touched his mouth, following the curve of soft lips.

'You're the frustrating creature,' she whispered, heart racing off a cliff ledge. 'Some parts of you don't seem so terrifying. But then there's . . .' She pressed harder, parting his lips.

Revealing the teeth. Not just the long canines he flashed with each grimace, but sharp molars, the clamp of a carnivore. Fi had seen those teeth carve flesh from bone.

They'd held her down, soft enough to leave no mark.

'You think I can't keep my appetites separate, Fionamara?' He didn't pull away, didn't snap at her challenge. His eyes burned down to her core.

She snared his face in both hands.

'I think you bring out the worst in me.'

Then, just as ferocious, Fi pulled him into a kiss.

27

One time

The kiss was a plunge, one deep breath before diving under ice.

Fi surrendered her mouth to his with a spike of panic. As if this would finally be the moment, the beast's chance to bury claws in her throat while she lowered her guard.

The claws did come – wretchedly soft, tightening around her waist and cupping her neck to pull her deeper into him. He was a spark on her tongue. Electric air in the back of her throat. But as she tasted his mouth, savored the hungry press in his reply, a deeper note bloomed, some crisp cold homecoming she couldn't quite place.

Fi broke away first.

They paused, but neither softened. She weighed the closeness of Antal's teeth as if her life depended on it, only to find his mouth softly parted, lips messy with her lipstick. Claws locked around her waist, holding her flush against his front. Fi pulled herself *closer,* fingers dragging creases against his shirt.

They were breathing hard again. Both of them.

'Well, shit,' she said. 'That's . . . not as bad as I thought it might be.'

So much worse. He was delicious, a taste of ozone and forbidden fangs on her tongue.

Antal's chuckle rumbled through her. 'What did you think

I'd taste like? Old bones and moldering flesh?' His mouth brushed hers, but didn't press. 'Is there more of me you'd like to taste?'

Wicked creature. Fi fought a shaky exhale as he nipped her jaw. What kind of dumb, thrill-seeking rabbit threw herself at the mouth of a panther?

But it *was* a thrill. Entirely too tempting not to savor.

'One time,' she relented, rougher than intended. Just to sate Fi's curiosity. Just to cleanse this distracting want from her blood.

The smolder in Antal's eyes combusted her. 'Is that all?'

'You'd better make the most of it.' Then, with all her mustered resolve. 'One. Time.'

'One time,' he agreed, the solemnity of an oath as his nose nestled against her cheek. 'How shall I leave a lasting impression, Fionamara?'

She kissed him again.

Antal pushed her backward. They crossed the room on warier steps than before. Testing. Claws and fingers locked around each other, watching for one of them to flinch, for a strike at anywhere too soft. The thud of the wall against Fi's back knocked the breath from her lungs. An instinctive jolt of panic when teeth flashed toward her.

A purr, as his mouth met hers, fangs snagging the curve of her lip.

Sweat already kissed Fi's skin from their dance. Antal wound his fingers into the mussed curls of her hair, brushing damp strands off her cheek, claws ghosting her scalp. His tail curled around her calf. Too slow. Too gentle.

'You really aren't afraid of me?' he asked in barely a whisper. Barely a breath.

'Does this feel like I'm afraid of you, daeyari?' Fi hooked her fingers in his trousers and pulled their hips together, relishing his growl against her neck. For all the foreignness of claws and antlers, she found familiarity in the delicious hardness between his legs.

Yet still he held back.

More than that. He pulled away.

'*Tell me*,' he said. If Fi had been thinking clearly, she might have called it distress.

They both fell too still. It was like standing on glass, the way he looked at her, waiting for a reply. Fi's barbs were useless against that moment of quiet, the earnest hitch in his breath.

'I'm not afraid of you,' she said.

Crimson eyes scoured every inch of her face. 'You want this?'

'Fucker. If I have to tell you any more explicitly how to take this dress off me, I'll—'

His kiss shoved her against the wall. Deep enough to summon a moan. A bruising clash of lips and teeth, his knee pressed firm between the waiting gap of her thighs. There went the crumbling remnants of her guard. Fi was falling so fast, she never bothered looking for ground below.

Let him consume her.

Their hands fought together to lift her dress. Cool fabric slipped up the flushed heat of her thighs, pooling in a silken bundle at her waist. Antal's fingers ran the curves of her hips, the hidden garden of floral tattoos along her stomach. A taunting brush beneath her breast. Fi arced into his touch, not withholding an inch of bared skin, even if he was a . . .

She didn't care what he was. She only wanted to feel him against her.

He turned his attentions lower. Fi tensed, only a moment to register the sight of claws slipping toward a place where claws *shouldn't* go, a peep of protest before—

Antal's palm pressed between her legs. One firm stroke curled Fi into another moan. No clawed fingers, but just as dexterous, dragging the heel of his hand across the most sensitive part of her. A bloom of energy fiercened his touch, not strong enough to burn or carve – heat that shuddered into her, sending every muscle taut. She had a few toys in her nightstand that employed similar Shaping.

Nothing as wild, as ruthless as daeyari energy. She wanted to melt into him, to rock her hips against his hand until it destroyed her. And his tail – that cruel, slender tail lashed around her waist, holding her dress up as he worked.

Merciless Void, why had she fought this for so long?

Fi's hands were everywhere. She scraped nails down his strong shoulders, across the collarbone she'd admired from a distance. Splaying his shirt open, she relished every hard line of his chest, hot and humming beneath her palms, energy coursing beneath his skin.

She tugged the buttons of his pants. Her fingers turned to putty as Antal ran a knuckle through her center, hot and slick with her eagerness.

'What do you want, Fionamara?' he whispered, cruel, against her hair.

'You know what I want.' She could barely speak through clenched teeth. Tight breaths.

'*Tell me.*' He stroked his palm slowly over her clit, making Fi writhe.

Her fingers were talons on his trousers. She pried open enough buttons to lay him bare, to take him in her hand. Her curiosity, finally appeased: daeyari did, in fact, have cocks. And Void, his felt *good* in her hand. Fi stroked experimental fingers down his length. Claws and fangs might be foreign weapons, but here was something familiar, maddeningly hot and hard in her palm.

Claws struck the wall beside her head. Antal leaned hard on one arm to steady himself, digging black sickles into the woodgrain. She ought to chastise him for the property damage. Fi was too busy devouring his reaction to her, all of him taut as he pushed against her grip, a low and hungry sound in his throat.

Fi was hungry, too. She angled his cock against her entrance, the pressure leaving her breathless.

'You,' she hissed. 'I want *you*.'

'How?' A rasp.

'Inside me. *Prick*.'

She cried out when he thrust into her, pressing her to the wall.

Fi's breath hitched through every delicious inch.

When she was early in her twenties, a very rude man in a bar told her good girls always screamed. Since then, she'd formed the resolute opinion that if anyone wanted to hear her scream, they'd better fucking earn it. It was with great difficulty, then, that she clamped her mouth shut against the unbecoming sound threatening to escape her throat.

She gasped as Antal moved inside her.

Slowly, at first, her thighs shuddering at how well he filled her.

His exhale, long with relish, fell hot against the sweat-slicked hollow of her throat. He worked in her with unhurried strokes, with ruthless purpose, until he found the angle that made Fi thrash between the pin of his hips and the wall at her back. She carved her fingers down his shoulders, fighting the moan in her chest.

'*Harder*.' She snarled like snapping teeth, an unbearable ache building inside her.

Antal's growl snapped fiercer. 'Can you ask for *nothing* nicely?'

'I—'

He thrust hard into her, and Fi lost her words.

His command broke her gasp into a pant, his claws tightening in her hair until she surrendered a whimper. And when she tilted against him, lifting one leg to wrap his waist at a better angle—

'*Antal.*' His name tumbled off her tongue, a wretched plea.

'There?' A wicked whisper, claws clamping behind the soft of her thigh as he buried himself into her.

'Yes.' Fi shuddered, her ferocity crumbling into purrs. 'Yes, *there.*'

Her fingers clawed through his hair, latching upon the anchor of antlers. She melted beneath him, bristles turning to liquid as pressure swelled in her core, teetering on one unsteady foot. And there he was to catch her: trapped between the wall and every hard line of him, his grip tight on her ass, tilting her hips to take him even deeper.

Fi scraped her hands against the wall.

His chest.

The unrelenting hold of his arms.

He hadn't fully removed his shirt, but she found the hot skin underneath, digging nails into the hard muscles of his back until he snarled something that might have been her name. Fi didn't catch it as she cried out, dizzy with the crest he pushed her over.

All of her went taut. One feral beast arcing against another, devouring every spasm as the climax swept through her.

He followed, fingers buried in thighs as he drove into her with one final, shuddering thrust, an exhale rumbling his chest.

Then, the slow fall. Still snared in his arms.

For the final time, their dance came to an end. Stillness again.

Fi slumped against the wall, gasping, muscles hot and spent. Antal's weight fell heavy against her, one arm supporting her waist, the other braced beside her head. They lingered there, breaths ragged in warring tandem, his warmth a lulling presence. His ozone, delicious on her tongue.

'You're good to your promise, daeyari,' Fi said when she could form the words. They slurred a little, her pulse too heavy in her throat.

Against her neck, Antal's mouth curled a grin. 'You're good for quite a number of things.'

His thumb brushed circles at her hip, a bloom of warmth beneath the pad – a shiver, at the tease of his claws. It was too easy to let him hold her, to let him nuzzle his nose along her jaw.

Pulling apart was harder.

Antal uncoiled his tail from her waist. Her dress fell across her legs as he released her, the smallest space between them like a breath of icy air. Fi leaned against the wall, hazy pleasure thick in her veins. He was *good*. Exactly what she'd needed after several days of tireless work. But as cold clarity crept back . . .

Antal studied Fi with head tilted, waiting for her to make the first move on this upended playing field. She looked him in the eye, unabashed beneath those burned-coal irises.

'That was . . . refreshing,' she said.

He hummed, a sound between agreement and amusement. Fi wanted to grab him by the antlers and make him hum against her throat, that intoxicating reverberation down into her ribs.

That swiftly, Fi realized she had a problem.

Her pulse quickened again. She'd enjoyed plenty of one-night stands, a fling of passionate fucking then a swift farewell. Quick. Clean. A clear head to focus afterward.

So why did Antal's eyes still leave a prickle everywhere they brushed? Why was she pressing herself against the wall, fighting the urge to fall into his arms all over again?

'We shouldn't stay up too late,' Fi said. 'We have a metal heist to plan.'

'We do,' he agreed. Too easy.

What was Fi thinking, letting him shove her against the wall?

They still had to work together. They still had to sleep in the same room together. How easy would it be to invite him into her bed? Test how warm he felt curled beside her. See what else the night led to . . .

Shit.

She had a *problem*.

'One time,' Fi reminded him. Or her. Or who the fuck knew.

Antal watched the scowl twist her face, his grin curled as if beholding the most amusing creature in all the Planes.

'Of course.' He laid a hand over where his heart ought to be. 'On my word.'

The taunt made Fi press her thighs together, hot and slick from what he'd done to her.

Antal backed away. Yet they couldn't flee too far from each other, could they? He went to her tub to wash. The moment he pulled off his shirt, that view of lithe back muscles and rolling shoulders, the scandalous taper of his waist . . . Fi made herself look away.

She had only one productive way to go from here: when Antal finished with the tub, she went about her nightly routine as if not a damn thing had happened.

She bathed the remnants of him off her. It shouldn't have felt so skin-prickling, being naked in the same room, after she'd just moaned for him. She dressed for bed behind the cover of her wooden screen. Antal drifted in her periphery, giving her the space requested. Only the twitch on his lips betrayed anything awry.

As the time came for sleep, the firmest line was drawn: Fi on her mattress, Antal perched in her rafters, a contented grin as his tail swayed beneath him. She risked one final glance up at him. One final flush to her cheeks.

It would be so easy. A few simple words to ask him to join her.

'Good night, Antal.'

He slitted one eye open, a glow of red in the dark.

'Sleep well, Fionamara.'

28

Let's pretend that never happened

Fi crouched on a snowy bluff, bundled in her dark coat with ermine ruff. The Bridge connecting the Winter and Autumn Planes stretched as a valley of ice and peat between two ridge-lines. Above the jagged peaks lay nothing but Void. No stars. No moon. A crimson aurora glinted over snow and metal rails transecting the valley floor.

Through her binoculars, Fi spotted movement down the tracks. The trans-Plane train departed Winter earlier that morning, shuttling passengers and cargo between worlds. Anticipation stoked her against the cold.

'It's coming,' she said.

'Odd,' Antal mused. 'You didn't give *me* that much warning.'

Fi couldn't flinch.

Couldn't blush.

The last dregs of her pride depended on keeping her lips flat, her shoulders steady, her brow delicately raised as she turned a bland look upon her heist partner.

Antal lounged against the slope, watching her with chin propped on one hand and tail swishing slow amusement. Daeyari weren't bothered by cold, yet the deep cut of his shirt was unnecessary, the dark fabric unbuttoned to reveal a swath of muscled chest. His pants seemed tighter than usual, framing the easy recline of his hips in a way that made Fi want to snarl at the utter unfairness of this new assault on her dignity.

Not a hint of that broke her facade.

'Do you often need partners to tell you when they're coming?' she asked, aloof.

Antal's grin curved wicked. 'How unkind of you, Fionamara. If I'd wasted over two centuries without learning how to satisfy a lover, I'd have to throw myself into the Void.'

'Bragging, now? How unbecoming.'

'You're right. I prefer demonstration.'

Fi hardened. 'You promised, Antlers. One time.'

'I agreed you'd only let me fuck you once. Not that I wouldn't talk about it. You ought to be clearer in your terms, mortal.'

Three days of suffering this. Three days of doing everything in her power not to stare at his stupid mouth, at his wretchedly tight pants, at that treacherous spot where he'd shoved her against the wall and . . . why did Fi already feel like she was losing?

'I think you're enjoying yourself too much,' she said.

'Tell me to stop, then.'

Fi fell quiet.

Definitely losing. Antal hummed in her silence, and it was the most smugly insufferable sound she'd ever endured.

She shoved the binoculars at him. 'We have a job to do. Take a look.'

He smirked at her deflection. Pride told Fi she ought to shut him down. A slicker part of her treacherous heart liked the game too much to call quits. Like holding a match, watching how close the flame could burn before searing her fingers.

Antal crouched beside her, too close, the heat off his skin brushing Fi's cheeks. A familiar taste of ozone laced her tongue. As he lifted the binoculars to view the approaching train, she did *try* not to stare, but the bare muscles of his forearms were right there. Hard not to imagine those hands pinning her down. The twist of his tongue against her mouth.

One time. Fi couldn't break this easily, or she'd slip headlong into the abyss. And with a creature like this? She had no idea what lay on the other side.

'We've got time before the train hits the first Curtain,' Antal observed.

'So we wait,' Fi agreed.

They settled upon the ridge, watching their target approach. Antal seemed half attentive, his gaze drawn to the abyss of Void overhead. He breathed deeper here than on the Plane, as if scenting something on the cold, empty air that she couldn't.

Since she'd learned to cross Curtains, since her earliest ventures off the Planes where her species evolved, Fi felt that undeniable pull from the Void. Impossible, to explain the feeling to other humans. Like that stomach-scooping allure of staring off a cliff, imagining the jump, how the fall would feel.

Antal looked upon the swath of black with the fondness of home.

'What was it like,' she asked, 'coming back from the Void?'

He tilted his head at her.

'That's where daeyari come from, isn't it?' Fi said. 'The stories say your mortal forms died, then your energy returned from the Void.'

Antal indulged her a chuckle. 'That's how the *first* daeyari became immortal. When Veshri died, his energy refused to cross to the Afterplane. He wove a new body from the ether of the Void, returning to walk the physical Planes, taught other daeyari to do the same. But that was millennia ago. Since then, we propagate the same as any other species. I was born. Like you.'

343

'You were born'—Fi swept a hand over him—'like *this*?'

'Our eyes changed when we became immortal, red irises and black sclera, the most noticeable relics of the Void. Our skin, colorless, from the Void ether. But the antlers, the claws, we had before, a body built as Veshri remembered himself. Now, all immortal daeyari are born with these traits.'

'So you get immortality, and you didn't even have to die for it?' She huffed. 'Unfair.'

'Perhaps. Though, our subsequent deaths prove more . . . problematic.'

Fi tried to picture a squirming baby Antal, claws scratching furniture and head crowned in nubby antlers.

'Do daeyari have velvet when they're younger?'

Antal gave her an appraiser's look, bright-eyed with a glint of teeth. 'Velvet?'

'Like when elk grow their antlers, they start off covered in velvet. Have to rip it off in a bloody mess.'

'Ah, yes. It's atrocious. A peril of daeyari puberty.'

'Ew. Really?'

'Worst part of the first few decades.'

'Still better than dying.'

'And you, Fionamara? How did you die?'

'*Excuse me?*'

Fi hated every time he made her stammer.

'Daeyari see Curtains innately,' Antal said. 'As do mortals who've died and returned, touched by the Void.' His voice lowered. 'You said you'd been to a daeyari shrine before mine. Did Verne . . .'

'No.' Fi spoke quickly, before those eyes could crack into her. 'Stupider than that. I fell into a river when I was a kid. Nearly drowned. Then I started seeing Curtains, and . . .' She clutched her knees, glaring at snow-crusted boots as the words bottled up on her tongue. She could spare a speck of honesty, couldn't she? Antal had told her about his father. Fair trade. 'I was supposed to be Verne's Arbiter.'

Antal's tail fell still. 'She refused you?'

'I ran away.'

Ran and never came back, like a coward. Left Astrid to take her place. That part stayed stoppered in her throat. Fi couldn't let Antal see that trembling creature locked inside of her. Not when she'd fought so hard to gain his respect.

'Verne took the vavriter instead?' Antal asked.

'Astrid.' The name settled bitter on Fi's tongue.

'You two were close?'

'We grew up together. Became friends, then best friends, then we were . . .'

A memory slipped back of the first antlers she'd gripped, shorter and wreathed in longer hair. The heat of Astrid's whispers against her neck. Long fingers tracing Fi's ribs.

She couldn't fight this blush, not when Antal's brow climbed to a knowing arc. It was low-hanging fruit. An easy place for a jab, soft flesh she'd been stupid to expose.

Antal didn't strike.

'Verne's Arbiter,' he mused. 'We would have met under very different circumstances.'

Fi doubted that. She couldn't imagine joining Verne's plans for conquest, but she didn't picture herself a hero, either. Most likely? She'd be dead, cast aside by an immortal who didn't abide inconveniences.

'Why don't you have an Arbiter?' Fi asked.

'Never needed one. I'd rather leave my people to their own devices.' Antal huffed. 'I suppose I have one, now.'

The drop of his voice twisted Fi's stomach. The silence between them hung with gratitude unspoken, a growing bond neither human nor immortal seemed capable of verbalizing, tied together by fate beneath the endless black of the Void.

Antal shrugged. 'And an Arbiter who moans well. Who could have guessed?'

Fi punched him hard on the shoulder. She hoped it hurt.

The train came into full view: a Shaping-powered engine charging down the tracks, three passenger cars with copper plating and lighted windows, another five cargo cars in back. Their target lay onboard: a shipment of conductive metal perfect for weapon smithing.

Antal perched at the edge of the bluff, tail twitching. Nervous? In their planning, he'd tried to explain to Fi the logistical difficulties of teleporting onto a moving object, but he'd assured her he could do it. Watching him now didn't fill her with confidence. He squinted at the train, eyes ticking back and forth, as if muddling through internal calculations.

He offered his hand. Did she trust him? Absolutely not. Did she have another option?

Also no.

The teleport passed in a lurch.

Fi slammed onto metal, the world roaring around her, momentum hitting her chest like . . . well, a *train*.

She Shaped a shield of energy over her arms as she tumbled overtop the speeding cargo car, wind whipping her hair, sleek metal roof panels offering no handholds. She flailed. Her fingers scraped rivets. Seams. Then at last, a rail, enough to latch on and stop herself slipping off.

Beside her came a scrape of claws. Fi saw a flash of Antal's wide eyes.

Then he fell over the side of the moving train.

'Antal!'

She lunged, grabbing his hand before he disappeared into

VOIDWALKER

oblivion. His weight hit her. Fi cried out, nails cracking against the rail as she fought to hold on, the single anchor for both of them as Antal dangled over the side of the car. Cold wind sliced her cheeks.

In her clammy grasp, Antal's hand slipped. She gritted her teeth. Panic sharpened her pulse as she realized she wasn't strong enough to pull him up.

'*Fionamara.*' Antal's shout fought the wind.

He sounded more . . . chiding than expected. Fi peered over the edge. Instead of finding a panicked daeyari clinging to her hand, Antal hung unconcerned, one foot braced against the train, a single brow arched.

He yanked his hand out of hers. Then vanished.

Static pricked Fi's tongue as he reappeared beside her, still with a wobble, but better poise than his first attempt.

'Fi. I can *teleport*,' he reminded her blandly.

Her cheeks lit on fire. She pulled herself into a more stable perch atop the train, hissing as she shook out aching fingers.

'Of course,' she said. 'I know that. Just got caught up in the moment was all.'

Antal studied her with face pinched. Then, a slow-spreading smirk.

'Were you worried about me?' he asked.

'No.'

'Were you trying to save me?'

'Why would I ever do something stupid like that?'

Fi blocked out his shit-eating grin and moved to the top hatch of the train car.

With the silver flash of an energy dagger, she pried open the lock, then she and Antal dropped into the dark interior. The walls rattled, metal rumbling over rails. She pressed a panel to activate overhead lights, illuminating a load of conductive metal

347

sheets wound into massive coils for transport. Not the side of a heist Fi was used to running, but she saw the thrill of it.

Fortunately, base metal didn't require a security detail. The greater challenge was getting a few coils off the train, but this was where Fi's plan came in. A scheme so brilliant, Antal and Boden had both gawked at her during the proposal: Boden in abject horror, Antal with a gleam Fi had devoured like candy.

She and Antal moved into position at the back of the car.

A *clack clack* sounded from the wheels, louder than the normal din. Any passengers in the cars ahead would probably discount the noise, but Fi noted her signal, grooves carved onto the rail line during their heist preparation. She braced her hands against a metal coil and readied a pulse of energy, carving heat from her forearms.

At the front of the car, a Curtain appeared.

It shouldn't have been there, nor anywhere close to the tracks. Fi spent the last few days cutting strategic openings for the train to pass through, invisible to normal passengers. As the train barreled forward, the Curtain flew toward them. Fi and Antal shoved a current of energy into the conductive metal coil then reeled back. Cold raked over her as the Curtain passed, leaving her on the Plane.

The coil of metal vanished, sent to the Shard on the other side.

'Fuck yes!' Fi pumped her fists above her head. She'd never tried passing objects through Curtains on their own, and though she'd practiced on smaller scraps of metal, succeeding with a full coil on a moving train ranked as a shout-worthy achievement.

'Ingenious,' Antal said. 'You have your clever moments, Fionamara.'

That impressed tone slipped out of him more often, little

chips of gold Fi snatched up and coveted for reasons she didn't care to talk about.

Another *clack*. Another Curtain. Another coil of metal passed through. They repeated the process three more times, sending their weighty contraband onto Shards to pick up later with Aisinay and a cart. With their quota met, Fi and Antal split apart.

'Check the rest of the cargo cars for anything useful,' she ordered. 'I'll pop up front, see if they've got weapons worth snatching near the engine car.'

'Be quick, Fionamara,' Antal warned. 'We shouldn't linger.'

'Yeah, yeah.' Fi hid her black-and-rainbow hair beneath a furry hat then pulled open the door between cars, heading for the passenger section.

For anyone not a Voidwalker – most humans – the trans-plane train was the only route of transport between worlds. The backmost passenger car was outfitted for cheap fares: wooden benches, minimal padding. Overhead, shelves rattled with the briefcases of accountants hopping between jobs, the stuffed duffel bags of travelers visiting long-distance family. Fi had only ever ridden trains for the purpose of meeting clients. She kept her head down, avoiding eye contact with the passengers.

The next car smelled of perfume. Wood polish. Benches faced one another in little alcoves with plusher cushions, relaxing panel lights. A carpet muffled the rattling beneath Fi's boots. Here, the passengers were entrepreneurs or wealthy families visiting warmer holiday residences. Little use to Fi, but most trains kept a security closet farther up, a chance to snag a couple of weapons for Nyskya. She pressed forward, finding an easier time avoiding glances as passengers sheltered in their private cubbies.

The ticket inspector heading down the aisle posed more

trouble. He wore a forest green suit with two lines of brass buttons. Young. Hopefully inexperienced.

'Check your ticket, miss?'

Fi put on a cheek-splitting smile. 'Oh, my seat's just ahead.' She pointed down the aisle and tried to nudge past.

The inspector blocked her way. Shit.

'Of course,' he said. 'I'll need to check your ticket first.'

Fi dug through her coat pockets. A dramatic frown. 'Oh no! I don't have it on me.'

'Passengers are required to have their tickets at all times, miss.'

'Sure, sure. Terribly sorry. If I could head back to my seat, I'm sure I can dig it up.'

Fi tried to sneak past the inspector again. He blocked her again, growing suspicious. She weighed her chances of fibbing through this, versus retreating to the back cars to rejoin Antal.

Then, a velvet voice sounded behind her.

'There you are, darling.'

Ice in Fi's lungs. Molten lead in her mouth. Splinters beneath her fingernails. Anything would be less agonizing than that spoiled-honey cadence, that purr that she recognized in the hollows of her bones.

Fi's chest tightened, all the world narrowing as she turned.

And faced Astrid.

29

Hello, darling, fancy seeing you here

The vavriter braced her hands on either wall of the aisle, willowy frame leaned into a posture of feigned ease. But Fi saw the asp underneath, caging her in. Astrid's grin revealed too many teeth. She perched on the balls of her feet, coiled beneath the guise of tight trousers and a shirt of loose maroon silk. Her eyes didn't glow like Antal's. The ruby irises pooled like blood fresh-spilled from an artery.

Astrid.

Her Astrid, wearing those eyes Fi had met at Verne's chateau, that vengeful spark trying to burn her alive. The foreign look threatened to render her numb, but Astrid's step forward snapped Fi back to her senses. She braced for attack.

Astrid slid to her side like a lover. Like what they used to be.

'Darling.' Astrid cooed, a brush of breath in Fi's ear and a nostalgic song that raked down her spine. 'You're always running off too soon. Forgetting important things.'

Cruelty. Fi stiffened as Astrid snaked an arm around her waist, that easy fit that came to them so long ago. The same warmth of Astrid's body seeping into Fi's bones. Yet wrapped at her side like the snares of an old vine, Astrid felt different. Harder. Sharper.

Something cold pressed the small of Fi's back. The hilt of an energy dagger, concealed in Astrid's affectionate palm.

The ticket inspector backed off, caught off guard by the vavriter, staring rudely at the twin points of Astrid's antlers. For his sake, Fi kept her grin.

'And yet you always seem to find your way back to me,' she said, mirroring Astrid's sugary tone. The words were razors on her tongue.

'You must have gotten turned around.' Astrid pressed the dagger hilt to Fi's spine. 'Our seat's back the other way.'

'Of course. Silly me.'

'Apologies,' she told the inspector. 'I'll keep a closer eye on her.'

He let them go, less concerned with their wanderings so long as they kept to the cheap section of the train. Astrid led Fi down the aisle with a hand too intimate on her back, into the rear passenger car.

They'd played games like this before. One time at a traveling fair, they'd come together beneath garlands of purple peatberry and string lights, spent the night pretending they didn't know each other. Astrid had slipped sweet whispers into Fi's ear as they competed for carnival prizes. Slipped hands into daring places. When no one was looking, they'd snuck away into the back room of the distillery. Fi sank her mouth between Astrid's legs and made her moan until she'd confessed to loving her.

A dagger hilt to the spine had never been a part of the act.

'Good to see you again, Fi,' Astrid whispered, thorns on every word. 'Always getting yourself into trouble.'

'I seem to recall *you* being the one who always got us in trouble,' Fi hissed back.

'Sure, Fi. I got us grounded. I got us yelled at. I got you that scar down your thigh, the one across your knuckles.' Astrid hardened. '*You* sent me to a daeyari.'

Fi couldn't argue that.

They passed through the last passenger section, into the privacy of a cargo car. Fi scanned the darkness for Antal, but he must have moved on.

'How did you find me?' Fi asked.

Astrid punched her in the jaw.

The blow sent Fi staggering. She caught herself against a crate, fighting dizziness and an ache through her teeth. Copper bloomed on her gums. She spit blood, then Astrid had her by the coat collar, shoved her to the wall. Cold metal rattled Fi's back.

'It was the strangest thing,' Astrid said. 'A Voidwalker working for the rail line ran an inspection yesterday. He reported several new Curtains had appeared. On the tracks, no less.'

Fi hissed a curse. The rail company employed a small army of Voidwalkers – one of the more boring career options she'd considered after running away from home – but they typically worked at the stations, guiding passengers on and off the Plane. To have caught one out on line inspection was rotten luck.

Astrid's eyes were black in the dark, a glint as she surveyed the rest of the train car. 'Where's the daeyari?'

'What daeyari?'

Astrid had her dagger out in a flash. No longer a bare hilt. A blade of mauve vavriter energy pressed Fi's throat, casting cruel shadows across the crates.

'Oh, Fi.' Astrid spoke honeyed words as her dagger seared Fi's neck. 'We've been apart a long time. Don't assume you still know how to push my buttons.'

Was it the harsh light, making Astrid's face look so foreign? The shadows under her eyes were too deep. Her lips were too rough, chapped, marred by the silver slip of a new scar on her chin. Fi had spent so long trying to bury this guilt, fleeing rather than facing the phantom holding her by the throat.

Fi did this to them. Fi was the coward who ran and never came back.

But.

A creeping, kindling *but* had been burrowing in her skull ever since Cardigan's villa. Cardigan, who had a Voidwalker all along. One who could cut Curtains. Astrid must have known. But she'd still cornered Fi in Thomaskweld to make her a part of this.

Fi had abandoned Astrid, left her on her own for a decade, *but* Fi had every reason to believe Astrid would survive. In return, Astrid had put Fi in mortal danger. Multiple times.

It didn't seem fair.

'Are you here to kill me?' Fi said. 'Or just reminisce over old times?'

Astrid's scowl was fierce, but after learning how to stand her ground with a daeyari, these teeth didn't seem so vicious.

'Verne's not happy with your skulking,' Astrid said. 'You're going to tell me what Antal is planning.'

What *Antal* was planning? As if Fi was some pawn.

A pent-up snarl finally slipped free, drawn out by scorching pain at her jugular and the red-hot audacity of this bitch she used to love. Fi felt sick at the thought of becoming Verne's Arbiter, yet Astrid seemed to stomach the work just fine.

'I see.' Fi puffed air from her mouth, playing with a stray curl. 'Counter offer?'

She struck a palm at Astrid's arm, hoping the dagger wouldn't strike lethal.

It didn't.

Astrid snarled and slashed for Fi's shoulder, a fraction off in the jostling train, lighting the space with mauve sparks as her blade dragged across the metal wall. Fi drew her sword hilt. Silver light flooded the car as she cracked an energy capsule into the pommel. Then, a warring scarlet as Astrid brandished a daeyari capsule and Shaped it into the blade of her broadsword. Fi had a single daeyari capsule in her pocket. She wasn't sure she wanted to burn it yet.

'I waited for you,' Astrid said as she advanced. 'I looked for you in your room. At the river. At that Curtain under the cedar grove where we always hid away for stargazing. You never. Came. Back!'

Astrid charged with a crushing strike at Fi's shoulder. Another at her side. Incapacitating blows, not lethal, but Fi would rather keep her limbs. She parried, struggling for space to maneuver with cargo tight on either side.

'You've gotten better with that sword,' Fi observed grudgingly.

'I *had* to.' Astrid swung again.

Static pricked Fi's tongue. Astrid tensed.

Antal appeared between them. He grabbed Astrid's sword on the downswing, a coat of red energy shielding his palms from the blade. Claws screeched down the length as Astrid shifted her stance. Daeyari and vavriter locked gazes over their grapple, but the dance of red light across her face betrayed no fear.

Of course Astrid had learned how to face a daeyari properly. Another place she was miles ahead of Fi.

'Antal,' Astrid greeted through clamped teeth. 'You ought to consider better company.'

Antal growled in reply.

Astrid twisted her blade free. Antal slashed with energy-coated claws, but a parry held him back in the tight space. Fi, trapped behind him, scoured the car for a way around.

Then came a slip in Astrid's swing. Antal lunged.

355

Fi shocked herself when her arm shot out. When she had to clamp her teeth to keep from shouting at him to stop.

As the two combatants crashed to the floor of the train car, an unexpected terror spiked Fi's chest. Terror for Astrid. She was *still* Astrid. She was still Fi's friend, falling beneath the claws of a daeyari, ripping Fi's heart in two directions.

Yet Astrid got her feet under her. She jabbed an elbow to Antal's throat before his teeth found hers, then a kick to the ribs shoved him off. As the daeyari skidded, Astrid stood unscathed, sword ready.

An impact shook the train car.

Fi steadied herself as the tremor faded. Another rumble of movement followed from the roof, accompanied by a scrape of metal and . . . claws. The fighting paused as all eyes looked up. Of the three of them, Fi had backed closest to the hatch she'd cut open for entry, a porthole view into Void sky and crimson aurora.

Then, one giant red eye.

'Fuck—'

Fi's curse clipped to a shout as a massive white paw scooped into the train. The claws dug mostly into her silviamesh, yet the pressure knocked her breath away. The world spun as she was wrenched upward, back into the roaring wind outside the train.

Then down again.

The slam of Fi's back atop the roof of the car left her aching for air. She found little, a paw pinning her in place.

The Beast – the *daeyari* – hunched over her, saliva dripping from sickle teeth.

Knowing what it was made the form even more grotesque: the way pale skin stretched this starved and pantherine body, the violent jerks of its tail, the gnarled antlers. The creature tilted its horse head, shadows pooling in the skeletal hollows

356

of its eye sockets as it looked at her. Those pupil-less red irises burned with nothing but hunger.

Nothing like Antal's.

Never in Fi's life had she reached for an energy capsule faster. The daeyari magic seared her palm. She adjusted, pulling for a less painful current, condensing red energy into a projectile that hit the Beast's jaw. It lurched off her, snarling.

Antal sprang out the train hatch. A heartbeat passed as he took in the scene – Fi on her back, a sizzle of red static, a derived daeyari reeling above her. He threw himself at the creature's throat with claws and teeth. The Beast snarled deeper, gripping Antal's smaller body in one rake of claws then hurling him against the train car with a *crack*. He rolled to a kneel as the creature retreated, black blood staining his chin, a grimace as he spit out a mouthful.

Then, he was at Fi's side.

Her thoughts spun circles, struggling to understand why Antal cupped her cheeks in both hands. Why his eyes went wide. Why he scoured her head to toe.

Worried. He was worried she'd been hurt.

'I'm fine, *I'm fine*,' she said. Some bruises beneath her silvia-mesh, but thank the merciless Void for nothing worse than that.

Energy crackled through the wind. At the far end of the car, the Beast lifted its ravaged throat. Sinew and skin wove back together as threads of sewing red magic, healing, just as Antal had when they'd faced Tyvo. Only faster.

They could win a fight against Astrid. But a fight against Astrid and this abomination?

'Let's go,' Fi said.

Antal snapped her a questioning look. An *'are you sure?'* look.

'We've done what we came for,' she said. 'Let's *go*.'

The Beast rose to full height, wounds nearly vanished, teeth bared in a snarl. Antal held out his hand. Fi reached for him.

'Fi!'

Astrid pulled herself through the hatch and found unsteady footing atop the train roof, wind cutting her short hair into obsidian shards. Her eyes burned ruby.

'Don't you dare run away from me again!' Astrid shouted against the wind.

The words flew like spears, crafted to skewer Fi's heart. To pin her down like guilt-laced hooks until she crumpled into another desperate decision.

What right did Astrid have to make such a demand?

Fi wasn't sure anymore whether friend or enemy stared back at her. She wasn't sure how much to blame her cowardice or Astrid's loathing for this tangle snaring them both.

But she wasn't running with that thoughtless abandon anymore. Fi was finally ready to fight – on *her* terms.

'Sorry, *darling*,' she called back. 'Catch you next time.'

Fi grabbed Antal's hand. As the world lurched, the last thing she heard was a roar of wind, and Astrid screaming her name.

30

This was supposed to be fun

'That's a dozen energy crossbows,' Kashvi reported, reading off a color-coded clipboard. 'Half as many sword hilts. Plenty of metal to make more. Good start toward a rebellion, I'd say.'

She wore a rare smile, dark hair drawn into a tail and eyes glinting mischief. Another late night saw the tavern empty, the copper light fixtures dimmed, Iliha gone to bed a half hour ago in preparation for morning baking. Boden had brought a crate of aurorabeast steaks for barter. In exchange, Kashvi set out three cups of hot mulled wine and a plate of butter cookies.

Fi wrapped her hands around the ceramic, grateful for warmth as the energy capsule in Kashvi's furnace burned low for the night. Boden accepted the drink but kept his attention buried in a notebook, brow pinched, a pair of the dorkiest reading glasses in the Planeverse perched low on his nose. After Fi's escape from Astrid then swift retrieval of the metal coils from the train, Boden had spent the following days cataloguing supplies for the weapon smiths.

'More than a good start,' he agreed. 'We have Fi to thank.'

'So we do.' Kashvi pulled up a chair and slid her cup closer, a soft scrape against the brass tabletop. 'You come through when you need to, smuggler.'

She spoke the tease with a tip of her cup. Fi stuck out her

tongue and joined her in a drink. The wine went down hot, a burn in her belly and a pleasant medley of spices coating her tongue.

Boden flipped the page of his notebook, callused fingers skimming over neat handwriting. Drink untouched. 'We've had ten volunteers for combat. A few more on the fence. I won't force anyone, but I'll check in over the next few days, see if I can convince some more.'

Supplies. Weapons. People. He'd talked of little else, drawing the shadows beneath his eyes deeper than their usual unhealthy shade.

'Bodie,' Fi chastised. 'Put that work away. It's late.'

'Listen to your sister,' Kashvi agreed.

The rare dual assault? Mayor Boden didn't stand a chance.

'We don't know how much time we have,' he said.

'Ten conscripts,' Kashvi said. 'On top of the three of us. You'll easily have five more once they see those gorgeous weapons Yvette's made. We'll have enough crossbows to put in everyone's hands. Mal has shelter and supplies lined up for any who don't want to fight. The rest, we work on tomorrow.' She held up a toast. 'Drink. *Now.*'

Fi liked Kashvi when she didn't have a stick up her ass.

Even worry-walrus Boden broke a grin. 'Nice to see you in a good mood.'

'Nice to be working toward something worthwhile.' Kashvi swirled her cup, distorting the curls of steam. 'And this . . . partnership with the daeyari is going better than expected.'

Fi would toast to that improvement in temper, however grudgingly Kashvi spoke the words. The three of them clinked cups then drank, the tavern silent apart from a groan of wind over the roof. Then, a sigh from Boden. He tilted his cup, studying the dark liquid.

'When we were little,' he said, 'Dad took us every year to visit the Nightglade Winery. Went on the haunted cart ride. Begged the winemaker for drinks. You remember that, Fi?'

'Yeah, yeah.' Fi studied her cup, voice low. 'I remember.'

She'd seen her first Void horse at that winery, dressed in strips of gauze like a phantom to spook visitors. Everyone else was enraptured by the animal's ghostly silver scales. Fi couldn't look away from its sightless eyes and black sclera – Void-touched. Like her.

'The owner gave us little shot glasses full of sparkling grape juice.' Boden laughed. 'We pretended they were wine. Swirled and toasted with our pinkies out.'

By all the Shattered Planes, what a memory. 'An excellent vintage.' Fi held up her cup, adopting the pompous appraiser's tone they'd played at during their childhood antics.

Boden sniffed his wine with a snobbish nose scrunch. 'Hints of bird nest and old moss.'

Fi laughed. 'Yeah, then Astrid would . . .'

Silence fell. Fi met Boden's pained stare, this hollowed haunt they carried between them, a fond memory they should have been sharing with one more old friend at their table.

'Astrid would steal the real thing for us,' Boden said. His finality wasn't just the end of the story. It was the end of the childhood they'd shared, ripped apart a decade ago and tossed to different corners of the territories.

Fi caught herself grasping at the scraps. Astrid's betrayal lived like a hot coal in her stomach, wrapped up in burning memories and burning lips that didn't easily extinguish. It was Fi's fault Astrid became an Arbiter. It was Astrid's fault Fi had nearly died in that explosion in Thomaskweld. Both of them striking blows they could never take back.

And yet . . . Astrid had hesitated on the train. She'd had a blade against Fi's throat, vengeance in her eyes, but refused to go for the lethal strike. Fi had still hurt to see Astrid in danger, even when they'd fallen too far apart to repair.

A mess. It was all just a mess in Fi's head.

Boden lifted his cup. 'To old memories.'

Kashvi joined. 'To a successful heist.'

'If we're doing that,' Fi complained, 'Antal ought to be here.'

Kashvi puckered as if she'd downed a shot of lemon juice. That exact look was the reason Antal had opted not to join the gathering inside, followed by the guilt-inducing qualifier that he'd wait nearby in case Fi needed him. He could bear the cold better than a human. He shouldn't have to. She hated the idea of him waiting alone outside while she celebrated the heist he'd helped orchestrate.

'Fi,' Kashvi warned.

'You could give him a chance.'

'He doesn't deserve a chance.'

On Fi's other side, Boden shot a discouraging look. *Drop it*, his weary eyes pleaded. Kashvi was in a rare good mood.

'You don't have to like him,' Fi said, heeding neither of them. 'But Antal helped us get metal for weapons. He repaired most of the village's conduits. He's held up his end of the deal.'

'So he can get his territory back,' Kashvi said.

'He cares about more than that.'

'You think you know what he wants? An immortal who's ruled this territory longer than you've been alive? Who's been eating people since before our great grandparents were alive?'

The things Kashvi claimed might be true, but Antal was more than that. He laughed at Fi's taunts and got that annoyed twitch to his tail when she pushed the upper hand. He closed his eyes when music played to let the melody carry him away.

He insisted on sleeping in her rafters out of stubbornness alone, she was fairly certain. All such normal things.

And when he said he wanted to make things better – that *he* wanted to be better – Fi wanted to believe him. She wanted to believe there'd be a brighter end to this than returning to the way things were before.

'We want things to change,' Fi said. 'So does he.'

'Why would he?' Kashvi shot back. 'He was the one in power. He could have stopped taking sacrifices before now, regardless of what he claims about "rules" for daeyari.'

Also true. Void have mercy, Kashvi could be stubborn.

'He has to eat something,' Fi said.

'My *sister*.' Kashvi slammed her cup. 'How would you feel if it was Boden?'

Fi stiffened. Across the table, Boden monitored their spat in silence, but Kashvi's low blow earned her a scowl of disapproval. What would Fi do if she never got to make fun of that furrowed brow again? Never got to hear that laugh that had grown from a nasal wheeze to a deep-chested bellow, as familiar as wind through the shiverpines?

'I'm not saying what Antal did was right,' Fi said.

'What, then?' Kashvi pressed.

Fi assembled her arguments: they needed to move on, they needed allies, they needed Kashvi to not be so Void-damned stubborn.

But none of that was enough, was it? Deflecting, pretending Kashvi's hurt wasn't there, would only make it fester. Just like with Astrid. Amends never made, allowed to grow into this fetid wound between them. Running was easier. Arguing was easier.

Here was a place to start moving forward. One simple enough for Fi to stomach.

'I'd be angry,' Fi agreed. 'If I were in your place, I'd hate Antal and all his kind. You're right to feel that way, Kashvi.' She leaned forward, resisting the jab at Kashvi's stunned look, keeping her voice level. 'But what are we going to do about it? You could scream at him, put a bolt through his head, and we'd still be exactly where we were before. *Or.* We can tell him he was wrong, make him do something about it. Stop other sisters from being lost.'

Kashvi didn't answer right away. The purse of her lips suggested Fi had finally said something right.

Boden's smug-ass grin, maybe she could live without.

'Listen to this,' he said. 'Fi's sounding like a diplomat at last.'

Fi scoffed through a chug of wine. 'I'm no diplomat. I just think we ought to treat our immortal partner more like a partner, less like a stray dog left outside.'

'Sounds diplomatic to me,' Boden said. 'My little Fi-Fi, finally growing up.'

Fi looked for something to throw at him, but tragically, she found nothing within reach except her wine and her cookies. Neither was worth sacrificing.

Kashvi slumped in her chair.

'Come on, Kashvi,' Fi said. 'What's the worst that could happen? Antal proves you right, and you get to rub it in my face?' She would. Fi had no doubt of that.

Kashvi grumbled, 'You're rubbing off on her, Boden.' She leveled a finger at Fi. 'He can come in. So long as he behaves himself.'

Maybe there was hope for Kashvi yet. Or maybe Fi's stubborn tick act had reached a new level of success. Nodding seemed the safest response, though Fi doubted Kashvi knew what behaving himself meant for Antal.

He'd better behave himself, after all the nice things she'd said about him.

She took another warming swig of mulled wine then scraped her chair backward.

Fi headed down the dark hall, through the kitchen with its cooling ovens and lingering smells of sage-spiced stew. Out the back door, a snap of cold met her. An energy lamp glowed over the yard, lighting fresh powder and heaps of shoveled ice.

The door drifted closed, leaving Fi in a separate world – that long, still moment in the deep of night, hanging like a breath caught in the chest. No movement on the streets. No sound until she crunched a boot to the snow. Not a cloud against the starry sky that draped Nyskya in diamond and velvet.

Not alone, though. The prickle on Fi's neck was so subtle, she might have discounted it as a passing chill, rather than the brush of unseen eyes.

'Hey?' she called out to nothing.

A soft scrape crossed the tavern roof. Fi looked up to find Antal perched on the eaves, his silhouette nearly indiscernible from shadow and moonlight.

'You'd better not scratch any of Kashvi's shingles,' she warned. 'Veshri himself won't be able to save you from her wrath.'

His chuckle danced on night air, twirling with the cold and the sigh of wind through the alley. Soundless, he slipped off the roof, catching himself on sure feet. Fi never tired of watching him move, the effortless motions of confident muscles.

Not that she should be looking so intently.

'Noted,' Antal said. 'Though I doubt I could make much worse of an impression.' He flicked a crimson eye to the door. 'Finished already?'

'Just getting to the good part.' Fi grinned. 'Join us?'

He tilted his head, scouring for hidden daggers or ulterior

motives. She had none, beyond the pleasant heat of wine in her stomach. Maybe a little had gone to her head.

Fi grew warmer as he circled her, slow and prowling strides, closing distance until their chests nearly touched. His tail arced behind her calves, trapping her against him.

An old intimidation tactic. She faced him with chin up.

'Scheming with Kashvi?' Antal accused.

'What makes you think that?'

'There are easier ways to have my head, Fionamara. A trap in your rafters, perhaps.' His grin flashed fangs. 'Or, you could ask nicely.'

This would qualify as not behaving.

He wasn't the only culprit.

'Please,' Fi purred. 'You'd be the one asking.'

A sluggish part of her brain warned she shouldn't tease like this, not when he stood close enough to fill her lungs with ozone, and definitely not with the buzz of wine dulling every thought. But if he insisted on taunting, only fair that she taunted back. Where was the harm? She still kept to her promise, and got to enjoy that delicious frown twitch his lips.

He pressed a hand to his false heart. 'Such confidence in a skill you don't intend to demonstrate.'

'Come inside,' she ordered.

His brows lifted higher. His voice dipped low. 'Will you make me ask for that, too?'

'Antal.'

He hummed. Despite his taunts, his smirk didn't return. 'A kind invitation. But I see little point joining where I'm not wanted.'

He stepped away.

Fi moved faster.

She grabbed him by one antler, holding him in place – holding him closer than they'd just been, his startled huff a warm blush against her cheek. No, she definitely shouldn't be this close, her pulse stoked by glowing red irises, that treacherous pull fluttering her stomach.

But standing her ground was the strongest weapon she had. No fear. No hesitation.

'*I* want you there,' Fi said.

The first time she'd refused to back down from Antal, his reply was annoyance. Perplexity. Now, his eyes smoldered on the hand holding his antler. A slower drift across her daggered gaze. Her mouth.

Antal tipped a finger beneath her chin, dragging his claw along soft skin with a slowness to still her breath.

Merciless Void, she'd pulled him too close. When he sighed, Fi caught his breath on parted lips, hungry at the tease. His mouth was soft. And perfect.

And what would she do, if he tried to kiss her again?

For a heartbeat, Fi wasn't sure. She tried to harden her usual bristles, her vow of resilience, that she'd not tumble for this beast a second time. But . . . the night was so cold. And he'd felt so good inside her. Fi drifted closer, tongue tracing her lip as she recalled how divine he'd tasted.

Antal inhaled, breathing her in – scenting her wine-spiced breath.

A frown soured his mouth.

'You're enjoying yourself,' he murmured. 'I'll only intrude.'

His pull away from her was agony. A shock of cold hit her cheeks, a shiver as Fi grasped for clearer thoughts, chastising herself for the slip.

'I'd enjoy you being with us,' she said.

'You're unusual.'

'How so, Antlers?'

He slipped his finger off her chin, twirling it on a rainbow curl. 'Should I list all the reasons? Or just that you're willing to stand this close to me?'

Fi wouldn't ask that tall order of Boden or Kashvi. 'I took time to open up to you.'

'Yes, you've opened for me in quite a few places, Fionamara.'

She swatted his chest.

He chuckled, knuckles brushing her jaw as he toyed with her hair. Still too close, but back to normal taunting, the refusal came easier.

One time.

Fi released his antler. She drew a deep breath of frozen air, letting it stoke her resolve as she stepped to the tavern door. 'Come.'

Antal's tail swished. 'You enjoy giving orders.'

'You enjoy me giving them.'

He growled. Fi devoured the morsel, still ravenous. Scraps would have to satisfy.

She returned inside with an airy feeling, that haze from the wine and a headier heat from Antal's quiet steps behind her. Mostly the wine, she insisted. She'd be back in fighting shape by morning. Tonight, she had a more awkward conversation to mediate.

'Behave yourself,' she hissed as they neared the end of the hall.

Fi had no clue what Antal's hum meant, compliance or frustration. Maybe both.

Kashvi had moved to the bar. She stood behind the brass and aurora-glass counter, perusing her liquor shelves with a spine rigid enough to make a daeyari envious. When she turned, the lock of her eyes with Antal's sent a shockwave through the room. Fi held her breath. Boden looked as though he'd been holding his even longer.

Antal stood a long moment in silence, trapped in their staring match. Maybe this was good. Maybe the best approach was to not say anything and let Kashvi warm to him like a panther drawn to her hearth.

'What was her name?' Antal asked quietly.

Kashvi froze with a handful of glasses.

Was it possible for Fi to *double* hold her breath?

'Emira,' Kashvi said, curt.

'Emira.' Antal spoke the name with slow purpose. 'Would you tell me something about her?'

Kashvi's fingers curled against the countertop. 'She was brave. But you know that already. Also funny. Kind. She collected succulent plants from the Summer Plane, built a special growing lamp to keep them alive through Winter.'

'She looked like you?'

A muscle feathered in Kashvi's jaw. She said nothing.

'I remember her,' Antal said, painfully quiet. 'She spoke well. Afraid, but she was brave. As you said.'

Kashvi's hand twitched at the counter's edge. Fi shifted between them, ready to intervene should she have to split apart a cat fight. Antal, she could handle, no worries. But she didn't know where Kashvi hid all her weapons and—

'Did it hurt?' Kashvi asked.

A crease wrought Antal's brow. 'No. I never hurt them.'

Kashvi's eyes went black as Void sky. Fi had never seen such a vicious look for her own antics, not for the rowdiest patrons, nor even that time a bear had tried to break into the kitchen. Kashvi probably had a crossbow stashed under the counter, right?

Instead of reaching for it, she nodded. A bitter reply, but final, her motions militant as she collected her cups and retrieved a liquor bottle from the shelf.

Fi breathed again. When she returned to her seat at the table,

Boden met her with a '*did that go well?*' stare. Damn if she knew. Kashvi went about her tasks like a disgruntled vole.

Antal pulled out a chair. Studied it. He sat on the edge with a stiff lean, and not until that moment did Fi realize what a hassle mortal chairs posed for a creature with a tail. She stifled a laugh, grateful for any distraction from the tense atmosphere.

'Do you drink, daeyari?' Kashvi set glasses on the table.

'Actually, I'—Antal snarled when Fi kicked his shin—'would be glad to join. Thank you.'

Kashvi sat. Poured. The liquor was light blue, wafting a smell of juniper and cinnamon.

The room quieted to the trickle of liquid. The groan of wind on the roof. Kashvi distributed glasses, even sliding one to Antal with a begrudging flick.

'Glad you could join us,' Boden said, proffering the olive branch. 'I had doubts about this plan. We all did. But we appreciate all you've done to bring the pieces together.'

'I've done what I can.' Antal swirled his glass. 'What I should have done earlier.'

Kashvi's laugh came humorless. 'Look at that. Finally, something we agree on.'

Fi and Boden swapped looks. Her pinched lips said, '*Can you believe this bitch?*' Boden's hard stare was a familiar one. '*Don't make this worse.*'

'Fi has a knack for finding interesting company,' Boden said, keeping the tone light. 'She's outdone herself this time.'

'She leaves quite an impression herself,' Antal said, too low.

Fi's stomach tightened into hot little knots. Void save her if anyone realized what an impression Antal had left on *her*. Or in her.

'To good impressions.' She raised her glass.

The liquor went down like a crossbow bolt, a spike in Fi's

stomach and a cinnamon fuzz coating her mouth. She winced, savoring the swift buzz. Boden finished his drink with more of a pained pucker.

Kashvi drew a rasping breath. Her liquor, she handled fine, but silver veins stiffened her arm. She leaned back in her chair, taking slow and intentional breaths until the tremor passed.

'Void alive,' she said, hoarse. 'Don't suppose you daeyari have a secret cure for silver sickness hiding up your claws?'

Antal had downed his drink without expression. He stared at the empty glass. 'No. Your bodies are . . . different from ours. More easily damaged by energy. Silver sickness is a mystery to us.'

Kashvi huffed to clear her throat. 'So you give us secondhand technology. Teach us magic that burns us from the inside out. You ever done anything *nice* for a human?'

'Hey, now,' Fi said. 'Rude. He's had human friends before.'

'Friends?' Kashvi squeezed the word.

'Yes, Kashvi, friends. Of the non-dinner variety.' She faced Antal. 'You said you even had one really close human friend?'

'So I did.'

Somehow, Antal turned stiffer. Fi frowned, studying the tap of claws against the table, his downcast eyes. Odd. He'd never lingered on this subject long, but . . .

'A close friend?' Kashvi said, skeptical.

'He was,' Antal replied.

'Was?'

There came the silence. The understanding.

Kashvi's chair creaked as she leaned back. 'How'd he die?'

'Kashvi,' Fi chided.

'What? He wants us to trust him?' Kashvi glared at Antal. 'Tell us what happened to the last human who befriended you.'

Movement caught Fi's eye – the flick of Antal's tail beneath the table. She'd meant the topic as a vote of confidence, not a hidden dagger. When they'd spoken about this before, she hadn't pressed, had assumed the flat plane of Antal's voice meant his friend was lost to age or sickness or some other human deficiency. Nothing anyone would want to talk about.

'He's done plenty to earn our trust,' Boden said. 'Repairing conduits. Getting materials.'

'All of which serve his ends as well as ours.' Kashvi pressed her hands to the table. 'What happened to your friend, daeyari?'

Fi shouldn't have brought this up. She shouldn't have—

'My family ate him.'

31

Ask me in the morning

Antal's words sank in slowly.

Fi replayed them. Tasted. Swallowed.

She stared at him, painfully aware she wasn't breathing properly. Painfully aware of him looking anywhere but at her.

He'd never wanted to talk about this. She'd never pressed. His *friend* had . . .

'Antal?' she forced out at last. And still, he wouldn't look at her.

Kashvi's reply came louder, a humorless laugh slicing the quiet. 'Well. At least daeyari are predictable.'

Fi didn't believe that. She couldn't. 'Surely, there's an explanation—'

'No.' Antal cut her off. 'It's as she says. Predictable.' He tipped his glass upside down on the table. 'My apologies for the intrusion. I won't bother you further.'

Before he could stand, Fi clamped a hand over his wrist. His claws splayed, wicked black tips scraping the brass table.

'*Fi*,' Antal warned with a flash of teeth.

'I swear by the endless black of the Void, Antal. If you walk out of here after a comment like that, I will snap your antlers into tiny twigs and hang bells on them.'

373

He bowed over the table, eyes closed. 'You think it's such an easy answer?'

'Don't give me that aloof bullshit.'

'*Fionamara*. Don't make me talk about this.' His voice cracked. 'Please.'

The facade vanished. Every facade vanished, his icy composure melting to bowed shoulders, chin low with the bitter weight of something daeyari weren't supposed to show. Pain. A visceral remorse. Even Kashvi squinted at the unexpected sight.

Fi softened her grip on Antal's wrist – less demanding, more entreating.

'Please,' she said. 'I want to understand.'

Antal's breath hissed through his teeth. He pulled his hand away from her, still no eye contact, but he made no move to leave. His claws clamped the edge of the table.

'On the Twilit Plane,' he said, 'Daeyari live alongside fewer humans. Your kind were brought to our world long ago as food. Those who remain are kept as workers or . . . *pets*.'

The word grated like cracked glass.

'Is that what your friend was?' Kashvi accused. 'A pet?'

'*Never*,' Antal snapped. 'He tended aurorabeasts for my family, a supplemental food source. I used to hide in the barn loft when I needed to get away from my parents. He found me there once, let me stay. We started talking. He . . .' Each word came softer, slower, a seeping ache as cold as the morning after fresh snowfall. 'He knew every animal in his herd. Not just which ones came easy to the barn and which loitered farther afield. He knew the kind ones who'd heed the softest whistle. He knew which ones he had to grab by the horns to keep in line.'

Fi listened in a stupor. How were there still so many pieces to this creature? Shards and splinters, hidden away behind that wretched mask of ice.

'He served our family for years,' Antal said. 'Work, in exchange for safety. That was what he'd been promised. Until my father realized I'd been sneaking away. In his eyes, we'd grown too close. He summoned me to our dining room . . .'

Fi didn't want to hear it – she *had* to hear it, from his lips. Antal was ashen.

He'd worn that same expression when Kashvi first confronted him, witnessing her anguish over a lost sister. At the time, Fi had assumed he'd never faced this side of grief.

She'd been wrong. That hollow carve to his eyes wasn't ignorance.

It was recognition.

'He was tied up like an animal.' Antal spoke through clenched fangs. 'Still alive. "*These creatures don't last,*" my father told me. "*They're a distraction. You have bigger things to accomplish.*" He didn't even beg. And I watched as . . .' His claws creaked against the table, gouges that Kashvi would never buff out. 'I watched my father slit his throat, then let him bleed out on the tile.'

He finished to silence.

Boden's mouth had fallen open. Fi stared at Antal in unveiled shock, this creature she'd once thought heartless, listening to his voice shake.

'Did you eat him?' Kashvi asked.

'I could *never*,' Antal snarled, baring fangs. 'I fought my father for the next fifty years, trying to convince him not to treat an intelligent race like cattle. He told me this was the way things are, that I was too young to understand. Then this territory opened up. He sent me here to learn *responsibility*.' The word seethed. 'His form of punishment. He always had loftier aspirations for me than foreign Plane governance. Even so . . .'

Antal sank back in his chair. His claws curled softer against the table.

'I came to love it here,' he whispered. 'The view of Thomas-kweld at night. The smell of the wind off the cliffs. And the freedom, finally away from those old ideas. A chance to be anything different.'

Fi had wondered. She'd asked Antal why he acted so unlike other daeyari, why he saw humans as more than food. He'd pushed. He'd deflected.

Here, at last, was a reason. A friend lost. A family splintered.

It wouldn't be fair to say he understood the flaws of their world the same way a human did – living in fear of being eaten wasn't the same as watching secondhand. Yet there was common ground in their grief, that glaze to Antal's eyes as he played through memories he wished desperately to change.

Fi knew that ache. Too well.

'You're right, of course.' Antal spoke with head low, eyes on the table. 'I could have done more as your territory lord. I've been complacent, indecisive . . . just as I was for him. Now you've given me a chance to do better. I know you doubt my intentions. But I *am* grateful.'

Fi wanted to comfort. To tell him she understood. Taking his hand again seemed too intimate with other eyes watching.

Instead, she slid her leg beneath the table, a brush against his. Antal didn't look up. His face betrayed nothing at her gesture.

Slowly, his tail wrapped around her, resting in a soft curl at the bend of her knee.

In the silent room, a stopper popped. Liquid bubbled as Kashvi poured another round of drinks. She, too, seemed changed, softer-eyed and less bristled.

Not forgiveness. Something closer to understanding. A first step.

'What was his name?' Kashvi asked.

Antal hesitated. 'Razik.'

The name came off his tongue like something disused, stashed out of sight collecting dust. Kashvi spun an impatient finger at Antal's overturned glass. He flipped it over. She poured.

'When my sister and I were little,' Kashvi said, 'we visited family on the Summer Plane. This sunny peach orchard that seemed to stretch forever, and at the end of the day, we each got a cone of peach ice cream. I dropped mine in the dirt. Cried like a blubbering fur seal. Emira picked me up, smiled and handed her own ice cream to me. Always selfless. Always looking to help others. The same reason she came to you.'

Kashvi set the bottle on the table.

'Do you understand, daeyari?'

Antal considered. 'Yes.'

'I want you to remember her. Every single person you've ever eaten had a life, a future. Just like your friend. Just like Razik.'

Antal let out a stiff breath. Nodded.

Kashvi raised her glass. 'To Razik.'

Fi and Boden lifted their drinks like wary hares. They looked to Antal. Waiting.

He took his glass in delicate claws. 'To Emira,' he said softly.

They all drank. This toast came smoother than the first, fewer glares. Fi gulped the fire down her throat then slammed her glass to the table.

'Enough of this,' she ordered. 'So Void-damned morbid. This is no way to celebrate.'

Boden ran a hand over his face. 'Well fuck, Fi. *You* started it.'

She had. Time to make amends.

'A drinking contest,' she proposed to clear the air. 'That's a proper way to celebrate. You in, Bodie?'

He eyed her. His empty glass. 'Um . . .'

'Glad to hear it. How about you, Antlers?'

Antal blinked. 'Excuse me?'

'You. Me.' Fi pointed between them with command – and a little waver, after the mulled wine and two shots. 'Drinking contest. Bring it on!'

A somber grin touched his mouth, gone so fast, she might have imagined it.

'Fionamara,' Antal chided. 'That's a horrendously bad idea. Even by your standards.'

He set his glass on the table, ready for another pour.

Fi hated when that smug ass daeyari was right.

Boden slumped into a groaning mess after three rounds of their drinking contest. Fi wasn't such a lightweight, and though Kashvi's cinnamon and juniper liquor packed a hot punch, she emerged from that first onslaught with the room spinning only slightly.

Antal's unphased posture, she took as a personal insult.

Three more rounds and an onset of nausea later, her confidence flagged. Another two rounds of 'would you rather fight one Beast daeyari or a dozen miniature Void horses?' and Fi's head hit the table. She groaned as her vision swirled. Her stomach vacillated between flaming hot and trying to somersault out of her abdomen.

'You can't get drunk, can you?' she accused in her most vicious slur.

Antal propped his head on one arm, studying his empty glass with a mild look.

'I can,' he said. 'Just not with this human excuse for liquor. Burns off too fast.'

'Prick.' Fi hiccupped. Antal's grin was punch-worthy.

At least he was grinning again.

'Fi-Fiii,' Boden moaned through the cradle of his arms. 'I've got to feed aurorabeasts in the morning.'

She rolled her head for a glare. 'Whose fucking fault is that, Bodie?'

'Your fault. Why have you done this to me?'

'Well *excuse me* for helping you live a little.'

He groaned and clutched his head. 'I'd rather be dead.'

'All right,' Kashvi interjected. 'Let's get you two home.'

Miss Brooding Buzzkill had abstained from the entire ordeal, warming her stiff hands on a mug of hot tea instead. This left her with the unenviable responsibility of grabbing Boden before he fell out of his chair. Pushover.

Fi stood on her own. A little wobble. Nothing serious. Had the tavern always looked so . . . tilting? One moment, she faced a wall. Next, the ceiling.

Her backwards careen stopped against something hard. Fi's flailing hand found no floorboards. Instead, fabric. A brush of cool skin. Antal's chest. He locked an arm around her waist to stop her slumping to the floor.

'I'll take Fionamara home,' Antal said. She could hear his stupid grin. And something buzzing.

'Forget it,' Kashvi said. 'I'll grab her after Boden.'

Antal scoffed. 'What do you think I'm going to do to her, Kashvi?'

'Yeah, Kashvi, *relaaax*.' Fi swayed with the words, nearly toppling out of Antal's grasp. 'He's fine. Plus, if he tries anything, I'll . . . I'll stab him, or something. I don't know.'

'I'd like to see you try,' came a whisper in her ear. And with the press of his arm at her hip, his chest at her back . . . Fi shuddered, a new heat blooming in her core.

Kashvi looked ready for protest, until Boden wobbled and nearly took them both to the ground. She squared her stance, supporting his weight. His angry mutters turned incoherent.

'I'll stop by in the morning,' Kashvi warned. 'She'd better be well and whole, daeyari.'

So angry all the time. Fi gave Kashvi her best pout.

'Of course, Kashvi,' Antal said, flat. 'Void save me from your wrath.'

His arm tightened on Fi.

'No, no, no!' Shouting made her head throb. 'Don't teleport. I'll throw up if you do.'

He tilted her a skeptical look. 'You're probably going to throw up anyway.'

'Antaaal.'

He sighed, holding her upright enough to stagger out the door.

Outside, the deepest chill of night had set in, making Fi shiver. She mumbled good night to Kashvi and Boden then clutched her arms in her coat and stared at her boots, focused on walking straight. Mostly straight. Not very straight, judging by Antal's growl as he tried to keep an arm around her. She tripped on something . . . it might actually have just been the ground. Fi tipped forward.

Antal caught her.

She yelped as he scooped her legs, lifting her into his arms as if she weighed nothing.

Fi squirmed, indignant in his grasp, but swiftly found herself more comfortable than expected. Less dizzy. She felt . . . safe. His bare arms, cool at first, grew warm against her.

She scowled. 'Can you change how hot your skin is?'

'It's just energy,' he replied.

He carried her out of Nyskya, through the Curtain at the edge of the trees and into the quiet of a Shard, pale trees reaching toward Void black and a dim red aurora. The gentle rock of his gait lulled Fi. She rested her head against his chest. Just for a moment. Just to stop her head spinning. His smell of ice and ozone turned her thoughts foggier.

'You did great tonight.' Fi patted him like a well-mannered dog. 'Good progress. Very tolerable.'

'And I only had to bare my heart. How easy.'

Fi puffed her lips. 'Kashvi's so mean. Acting like she still expects you to devour me or something. Rude.'

Antal quieted. 'Thank you.'

'For what?' Fi slurred.

'For thinking better of me.'

Sappy piece of shit daeyari, making Fi's chest flutter. She couldn't afford any kind of chest fluttering with her stomach struggling to stay down. Where did he get off on being so thoughtful? So considerate, to carry her home. So handsome, in the dim Void light.

'Teach me how to cuss in daeyari,' she demanded.

Antal glanced down, brow raised. 'What do you want to know?'

'Fuck.'

He laughed. 'A fine place to start. We have two versions. Oyzen is meant for insult. Oysen is more . . . intimate.' The words sounded nearly the same, the second a softer roll of the tongue.

'That's so weird,' Fi complained. But versatile. 'What about fuck you?'

'Oyzen yzru.' The sharp syllables danced off Antal's tongue. If Fi remembered any of tonight, she'd have to ask him to speak more daeyari to her.

'Fuck me?' she asked next.

He hesitated. 'In what context?'

'Fuck me, an insufferable daeyari is carrying me home because I can't walk straight.'

He grinned. 'Oyzen yzri.'

Fi mulled the mini linguistics lesson, trying to make it stick to her few active brain cells. 'So the other version is more literal. Fuck me. Oysen . . . yzri?' She rolled the softer 's' on her tongue, like he had.

Antal said nothing. Fi jabbed an insistent finger to his chest. '*Antlers*. Is that right? Oysen yzri?'

'Why do you want to know?'

Fi spread her arms in a grandiose gesture. He lurched to keep balance.

'Antal.' She waxed philosophical, even as individual syllables proved hard to disentangle. 'The spirit of fuck unites us all. A connection across language. Cultures.'

'If you say so.'

Fi scrunched her face at his dismissive tone.

'How many mortals have you fucked?' she asked.

A growl rumbled Antal's chest. Rumbled Fi. He considered her with lidded eyes, but it was the slow trace of his tongue across his lips that set her ablaze.

Merciless Void, she'd loved the taste of him. The brush of that tongue against her. A desperate ache tightened Fi's belly, the same she'd fought for days, unbearable now with his arms around her.

His mouth so close.

She brushed a finger along his jaw. One time. *One time.* What was wrong with one *more* time? Her breath shallowed as she tipped her head up.

Antal's claws clamped around her, holding Fi down.

'Ask me in the morning,' he said.

She blinked. 'What?'

'You can't ask me these kinds of questions when you're like this.'

'Like what?'

'Shitfaced drunk.'

'Pff. I'm not that—'

'*Fionamara.*'

The command stole her breath. He stopped walking, the two of them alone with the Void, holding her close and leaning closer. So lethal. So soft.

'Ask me in the morning.' Antal's mouth brushed her temple, a tease of heat that drew a gasp through Fi's lips. 'If you're still interested, I'll be happy to oblige.'

Fi fell silent the rest of the walk.

That didn't stop her staring at him, studying the lines of his face as her eyes drooped. Drifting in the glow of his irises. When they passed back onto the Plane, the chill of the Curtain drew shivers across her skin.

'How do you know which one goes home?' she murmured. 'If you teleport everywhere.'

'I can smell it.'

She frowned. 'What does it smell like?'

'It smells like you, Fionamara.'

'What . . . do I . . . smell like . . .'

Before he could answer, Fi drifted too far, lost in warm arms and the sweet abyss of sleep.

32

One cure for a hangover

Fi slept like the dead and woke little better.

Her first awareness upon waking was her mouth, the inside of which seemed to have been replaced by some manner of juniper-laced sandpaper. Fortunately, she didn't have to dwell on that sensation long, distracted by the throb in her head. She groaned a hoarse, crackling sound. At least she was somewhere soft. Warm. Dark. Cracking open crusted eyes, she found herself safe in her bed. Dim light slipped through curtained windows.

As was becoming a morning habit, she looked up.

Antal stretched along a rafter, tail dangling a lazy sway.

'Good morning, Fionamara,' he greeted drowsily. 'How did you sleep?'

Fi groaned liked a depressed walrus.

He chuckled. 'As expected, then.'

In a snarl of bedsheets and bad decisions, Fi scrunched her eyes shut and massaged her temples. Her headache laughed at the feeble attempt with a throb like an ice pick through her brain. The previous night, source of her agony, came back in fragmented pieces, a memory of too many shots and Antal carrying her home. She wiggled bare toes, her boots stowed by the door, but otherwise she wore the same clothes. A relief.

Because Fi vaguely remembered trying to kiss him. He'd stopped her.

A *tap* landed on her floorboards. Next, a clink of glass in her kitchen. Through slitted eyes, she watched the shadow glide toward her, a smolder of crimson irises in the dim room.

Antal paused an arm's length from her bed. Her rafters, her tub, her sofa, he'd made use of without qualm, but here was one place he'd avoided. A boundary never breached.

He offered a glass of water. Fi grabbed it and downed the liquid in too few gulps, leaving her mouth feeling more mud than sandpaper. She groaned again.

'How can I help?' Antal spoke low, gentle to her headache. Fi still winced.

'I don't suppose you have some magical daeyari cure for hangovers?'

'A cure, no. But perhaps some relief?'

'Please.' She'd take anything.

He came closer, another line bent, a shift in her mattress as he sat upon the edge. Fi tensed, wary but curious as he gestured for her to lay back down. Tenser still as he cupped a hand beneath her head, tender claws sliding through rainbow curls.

'Don't mess up my hair,' Fi grumbled. 'I'm sure it looks awful already.'

'It's always gorgeous.' His voice roughened. 'And I prefer it messy.'

What an unnecessary, uncalled for, delicious thing to say. Fi's huff of protest cut short when he touched her temple. His cool fingers made her sigh.

Then, a bloom of energy. The current flowed into her like a cleansing flush, cold water trickling through snow, a similar prickle to the mind-altering magic he'd worked before. Yet gentler. This version left her thoughts unmuddied, relaxing the swell of her throbbing head, a wave of relief that had Fi leaning into him. This creature of shadow and death whose touch could soften like silk. Immediately, her headache receded.

'I'm sorry about last night.' She lay on her back as he leaned over her, lulled by his touch, chewing her lip. 'I didn't realize talking about your friend would be so hard. I shouldn't have pushed.'

'You have an uncanny ability, making me speak of things I wouldn't normally.' He spoke softly, not accusing, more mulling the words. 'There's no need to apologize. I haven't spoken of him in a long time . . . Too long, perhaps.'

Antal moved his fingers through her hair, massaging the roots. The soft scrape of claws against her scalp produced a tingling, mesmerizing sensation that shuddered down her spine. Fi's exhale verged perilously close to a moan.

Smoldering looks and lustful dalliances were one thing. No one had touched Fi like this in . . . too long. Not since Astrid. Her old defense mechanism bristled, the urge to raise her guard lest weakness damn her.

A glimpse of Antal's contented grin kept her still.

A deeper warmth bloomed low in her belly, remembering the heat of his mouth on her temple the night before. To Fi's equal dismay and outrage, a full night's sleep hadn't diminished her desire to taste him again.

Here they were now on her bed, close as lovers, his ice and ozone scent heady on the air.

Still too few buttons fastened at his collar. How easy it would be, to reach out and run her fingers across his collarbone, down the hard plane of his chest . . .

'He was much like you,' Antal said.

Fi's guard slipped further, too curious not to ask. 'How so?'

'Bold. Not afraid to speak his mind, to stand his ground. Even with me.'

Her lips twitched a smile. 'So you're telling me you have a type?'

'I suppose I do.' Antal returned her grin, though strained, his words stretched oddly thin. 'It's not easy, finding humans who see me as more than a monster.'

She frowned. 'You're not a monster.'

'You've seen what daeyari become.'

'Verne's Beast is nothing like you.'

'It is.' He kept speaking, despite Fi's mouth open in protest. 'That Beast is part of me, Fionamara. Part of *all* daeyari. With reason stripped away, that's what remains. Only hunger and claws. What separates me, then?'

The question sounded rhetorical, but he paused anyway, shifting his soothing magic to her other temple. Fi waited, relishing each soft brush of his fingers.

'My actions,' he said. 'My choice to be more than a predator. Razik helped me see that.'

She huffed. 'Glad someone could kick your ass into shape before me.'

'He did.' Another small smile, frayed at the edges. 'But beneath all that bristle, he was fiercely caring. The same as you. I think the two of you would have gotten along.'

'I'm honored.' Truthfully. Beyond Boden, she'd rarely grown close enough to anyone for them to see beyond her bluster and bravado, those defensive facades. 'I guess I . . . hope your memories of mortals aren't all bad. That you have some good ones, too.'

Antal's eyes met hers, that piercing hold like he could see clear through her ribs.

'I've added quite a few recently,' he said, low enough to stop

Fi's heart. Then, with a smirk. 'Though, I still question how overconfident drunk Fi was in your ability to triumph over an army of small Void horses.'

His touch on her temple lightened. Receded. When he released her, it seemed too soon.

Fi sat up, and though the remnants of a headache lingered behind her eyes, the sharper pain had vanished. Her thoughts felt clearer than ever.

One time.

That was what she'd told herself, unsure how deep she was willing to plunge with this creature of fangs and eternity. Unsure how much she'd risk being devoured.

Was she a fool, that such qualms frightened her less and less?

He'd let his guard down only briefly, yet now Fi could see nothing else. She could see how meticulously the bluff was crafted, the cape of carnivores and myth, how necessary he had to flaunt teeth and claws to walk alongside his deadly kin. But there'd always been more to him. Since the first time he'd pinned her to the snow, it had been a snarl sharp as knives and claws soft as feathers. For every glare, there was a grin. For every taunt, there was a moment he'd spoken her name with the softness of a plea.

He swept a curl of hair off her cheek, tucking it tenderly behind her ear.

'Feeling better, Fionamara?'

Fi pushed forward and kissed him.

She met first with resistance. A stiffness of surprise. As Antal softened to her, Fi scraped her fingers across the shaved sides of his hair, along the smooth lacquer of his antlers, devouring this taste that had haunted her lips. First, came the spark of ozone on her tongue. Then that cold, crisp, hard-to-place *something* that called to her like a siren's song. She pressed deeper, sampling every curve of his mouth, so close to putting her finger on it.

Foreign, yet familiar. An endless sky without stars.

The Void.

He tasted like the Void.

Antal pulled back as breathless as she was. He cupped her face, eyes molten, yet he studied her with a frown.

'What happened to *one time?*' he said.

Hopeless from the start. Fi couldn't pull away from him, couldn't stop lidded eyes drifting back to his mouth.

'I guess I must be one dumb little rabbit,' she breathed.

Antal traced a thumb along her cheek, down the curve of her parted lips. Slow. Reverent. 'You were never a rabbit.' His chuckle brushed like velvet. 'You've always had sharp teeth.'

Fi was more interested in *his* sharp teeth. One time, be damned.

With a lunge, she was on top of him, straddling his lap as he sat on the edge of her bed. Her hands clawed his shoulders, pulling him into a deeper kiss. He cradled her cheeks, frustratingly light. Holding back.

'Fionamara,' he growled. A warning.

She stopped. Through speeding heart and shallow breaths, she registered him too tense beneath her, his tail flicking her bed, claws a whisper against her waist.

'What's wrong?' she goaded. 'I thought you wanted to have me again?'

'You made me promise. One time.' The words strained his teeth, a hiss of heat as he brushed his mouth to her jaw. 'I need you to be more explicit.'

'Explicit?'

'About what you want.'

He spoke in anguish, dripping every ache she'd suffered this past week. Fi leaned back. Stunned. After all his taunts, all his lewd comments and rakish looks, here she sat in his lap.

And he wouldn't touch her without permission.

The power was fire in her blood, more intoxicating than ten rounds of juniper liquor. All those years of Fi's life she'd spent terrified of daeyari, and now she had one dangling at her fingertips, watching with the keen eyes of a starving panther.

At last, she knew exactly what game they were playing.

She brushed her mouth to his. Not a kiss, but a whisper.

'Is this not explicit enough for you, Antlers?'

A growl rumbled his chest. His claws flexed, pricks against her waist, rigid with restraint. All those snarls and teeth, hiding a teddy bear underneath.

'No?' Fi dangled the question between them, innocent. 'How about this?'

She pulled their hips together, moving the soft between her legs against the hard of him – and he *was* hard, a bulge tight against his trousers. Antal sucked in a breath. So did Fi. The last time they'd collided had passed in such fervor, she'd had no chance to drink this in, the way he arced his back to drag against her. The corded muscles of his neck as he tipped his head, eyes half-closed.

'Vicious woman.'

Anything in that desperate hiss would have the same effect: turning Fi's insides to flame. She held her words steady.

'I told you I'd make you ask for it.'

She hooked a finger beneath his chin. Rolled her hips against him. Antal returned bared fangs, but she'd never seen his eyes so bright, so hungry. Not after she'd watched him eat. Not after the last time he'd fucked her.

'Fionamara.' Again, her name. This time like a plea.

'Yes, Antal?'

'Let me touch you.'

'Hmm . . .' She dragged her finger down his throat, splayed a palm over the swath of chest he'd left bare to taunt her. Energy simmered beneath his skin, a now-familiar current prickling her fingertips. 'You'd like to touch me? I feel like you're missing something.'

He growled again, crumbling into a groan as she pressed against him.

'*Please*,' he gritted through clenched teeth.

Fi shuddered, imagining the things she'd do to hear him speak like that again. She pulled him close, lips brushing as she spoke.

'Touch me,' she ordered. 'Anywhere you'd like. Any way you'd like.'

He snapped on her like a triggered snare.

Fi cried out as his arm locked her waist, dragging her hips against his. Even with loathsome fabric in the way, the hard press of his cock between her legs spiked a shiver clear up her sternum. Claws raked her spine. Dug into her hair. He kissed her like she would save him from starving, teeth sharp on her lips, his tongue pushing rough and greedy into her mouth.

As much as she'd delighted in holding control, she thrilled to pass it back, drowning in his need for her. Her need for him.

His fingers tightened in her hair, tipping her head back. Fi gasped at the jolt of anticipation.

'You'll pay for that,' he threatened.

Fuck. She wanted to.

'How do you plan on making me?' Fi taunted. 'All these bared teeth, yet under the surface, you're all snarl and no—'

She yelped as he pushed her back against the bed. A tug of her shirt exposed soft stomach, that pang of survival instinct turning to a thrill as he pinned her beneath splayed claws. The sable tips pressed the edge of comfort, not quite pain, stilling Fi's squirms as her breath tightened.

His free hand hooked her pants and pulled them down her thighs, laying her bare.

Without preface, he licked her.

Fi clamped her mouth against a shout as his tongue swept between her legs, slowing with a languid sweep across the pinnacle. He dragged a lick across her aching clit. The rough texture of his tongue against her own slickness, disintegrating. She fought for composure, but another sweep of his mouth turned her molten, desperate to press against him.

She couldn't, with his claws against her belly.

He stroked her with his tongue. Sucked her softly against his teeth. Fi needed more than this cruel taunt, this too-slow demise. She grabbed his antlers, pulling him against her.

Antal didn't budge. His tongue rolled over her in another slow, teasing caress.

'Want something, Fionamara?' Amusement curled his grin.

'*Fucker*,' she spat.

A month ago, if someone had asked Fi's opinion of daeyari teeth between her legs, she'd have shrieked. She nearly shrieked now for a different reason, his fangs skating her inner thigh. He teased one canine over the sensitive swell of her clit. She made a pitiful sound, aching for more.

He held her at his mercy. Her hips bucked as he worked, a slow build of that too-light tongue that would ruin her.

'Please,' Fi moaned. 'You smug-ass daeyari. *More.*'

She *felt* his grin against her.

'Ask nicely, Fionamara.'

'*Fuck you. I—*'

Her breath caught as his tongue slicked over her opening, so close to what she wanted, her thighs shook. Her hands tightened on the hard roots of his antlers, indignant at how quickly he'd turned this against her.

Delighted by her own desperation. Some things were worth begging for.

'Antal.' It was wretched, how soft she said his name. '*Please.*'

At her command, claws tightened against her stomach. His tongue pushed into her, a shallow delve, a spear of heat splitting her core.

'More.' The plea came out ragged. It shivered through her like a vice.

Every muscle tensed as his mouth pressed harder. His tongue stroked deeper.

Deeper.

Deeper.

Fi gasped, 'How fucking long is your *tongue*?'

Antal laughed against her, paralyzing. She pooled like liquid beneath his claws, lost in the feel of him and the building heat inside her, wondering how she'd ever stood a chance against this self-destructing inevitability.

Until he stopped.

The abrupt end made Fi whimper. Antal pulled back, head tilted over her as she shook with unfinished need.

Fi would destroy him. She'd skin this insolent immortal alive and mount his antlers on her mantle. She'd—

A knock pounded her door.

Fi's eyes widened in terror. In anguish. She looked to Antal. To the door. Back to him and his shit-eating smirk.

'They'll go away,' she begged the Planeverse.

'Hmm . . .' He cast her beneath lidded eyes, a brush of his thumb between her legs that coiled her into an arc against him. She bit her tongue against a shout.

The knocking came again, louder.

'They'll go away,' she whined. 'Keep going.'

'*Fi!*' came a shout from the porch.

Kashvi. Fi would disown that woman.

'Get your hungover ass out of bed,' Kashvi called from out-side. 'Or Void help me, I'll take this door down.'

Fi doubted she was bluffing.

'You should see to that,' Antal purred.

'Don't you dare,' Fi snarled back.

Her breath caught as he snared her in a bruising kiss that tasted of sweet and salt. The traces of her on his mouth.

'Until later?' he taunted, a promise sealed by a nip to her ear.

He pushed off and vanished. Fi sucked the static on her tongue.

At the telltale creak of wood, she looked up. Antal settled in his usual sprawl upon the rafters, a languid sway to his tail, watching her with too much smug satisfaction. His mouth curled, a flash of teeth as he stretched several inches of long black tongue to clean his lips.

That tongue was a cruelty.

Another barrage of knocks hit the door.

'By the wide black Void, Kashvi, I'm coming!'

Just not in the way she'd hoped.

Fi took a moment to gather her breath. After fixing her clothes and combing a hand through her hair, she stalked across the room, spitting curses about poor timing and *painfully* aware of eyes tracking her from above. She yanked her door open.

'*What?*'

Kashvi stood on the porch in snow-crusted boots and a maroon coat, brow scrunched as she looked Fi over from head to toe. Let the hangover take the blame for her disheveled appearance. Fi gulped frigid morning air, begging it to ease the ache Antal had left in her.

Boden's boreal horse snorted beyond the porch. Kashvi must have borrowed it for the ride up.

'Making sure all's well this morning.' Kashvi tipped a skeptical look into the dim interior of Fi's cottage, scowling at Antal in the rafters.

'You see, Kashvi?' he called down in a droll tone. 'I didn't eat her. As promised.'

Liar. The tease sparked in Fi's belly.

'Get yourself together,' Kashvi said. 'We need to go.'

'. . . Go?' Fi said.

'*You* suggested we start training recruits today. And don't go giving me hangover excuses. That was your idea, too.'

Fuck. Fi *had* agreed to this. She silently cursed her past enterprise.

'Get dressed,' Kashvi ordered. 'Iliha will have breakfast ready by the time we get back to Nyskya.'

'Yeah. Sounds great.'

Fi slammed the door shut, leaving Kashvi on the porch.

Gifted with privacy, she slumped against the wall and shut her eyes. She took several slow breaths as adrenaline and lust loosened their hold. The heat between her legs took longer to abate.

'A shame,' came a taunt from her rafters. 'I suppose we'll have to pick this up later.'

Fi would skin him with her teeth. Splay him like a pelt across her bed. That thought threatened to make her ache again.

But he was right. She shouldn't leave Kashvi waiting, or risk the woman barging in on something hard to explain.

That didn't mean surrendering to Antal's barbs. Fi drew herself up straight and locked eyes with the beast in her rafters, unflinching as she strode across the room. She pulled her shirt over her head in one swift tug, baring naked skin from the hip up.

Antal's tail swayed to a halt.

His rapt attention kept a coal burning in her, a flame to harbor against the cold. With similar nonchalance, she removed her pants, ignoring the slickness Antal had left between her legs. She opened her dresser and strapped her breasts into a bra. Next, a pair of slim black underwear with lace frill, barely enough to cover her ass.

When she looked up, Antal sat utterly still, claws curled against the rafter.

'What's wrong, Antlers? See something you want?'

His grin came wicked. 'Such sharp teeth.'

He dropped down in a flash, a tap of claws on floorboards then a rush of air from Fi's lungs as he grabbed her into a kiss. She sank into him, fingers knotting behind his neck, one final moan as his hands caressed the bare skin of her waist. She wanted to fall against him. Let him take her back to bed and ignore whatever obligations lay beyond her door.

'It will have to wait,' he said, chuckling as he pulled away from her hungry grasp. Then, in a low that would rumble through her the rest of the day. 'I need time to devour you properly.'

Fi tried not to crumble at the thought. Reluctant, she reached for a shirt.

They arrived in Nyskya by late morning, sky lavender as the Winter sun struggled to crest the surrounding cliffs. Fi inhaled a breakfast of grouse eggs and crisped boar belly at Kashvi's tavern. Tried to ignore Antal's burning looks every time she met his eyes.

Then it was time. The fruits of their labors, finally coming together.

They met Boden in a snowy clearing near his ranch. However

shitty Fi felt that morning, her brother looked ten times more bedraggled. With him stood crates of energy crossbows and sword hilts, delivered from Yvette's forges.

And there to learn how to wield them: fifteen volunteers from Nyskya's bravest, humans come to face the impossible in defense of their home.

They all knew by now of Antal's involvement. The sight of the daeyari still drew wide eyes, a nervous murmur through ice-sharp air.

'Gather up,' Boden announced, drawing them together like a faltering herd.

He looked to Fi. With a deep breath and steeled nerves, she stepped forward.

'Ready, hunters,' she announced. 'Today, you're learning how to fight a daeyari.'

33

Feast, fair beast

Silver energy snapped through Winter air. Then, a crack of crimson.

In a frosted field outside Nyskya, a baker's son wielded an energy sword for the first time. The blade – more substantial than the kitchen knives he was accustomed to Shaping – rippled silver as he struggled to hold its form. He gathered his nerves. Charged.

Antal evaded the strike like a slash of shadow. The baker turned into another swing, parried by red-coated claws.

On the sidelines, Boden scowled, his beard coated in frost, eyes shadowed after a long day, and a lingering hangover.

'Maybe we should—'

'Not yet,' Fi said. 'By all the Shattered Planes, and you say I'm impatient?'

Her crossed arms fought a shiver, cold seeping through her wool and ermine coat as twilight dimmed toward night. For humans, the scant light of their energy weapons would let them continue only a little longer in the dark. Fi would rather be moving, warmed by the swing of her sword, but others needed practice more than her.

The baker adjusted his stance. Antal hung back, waiting on his opponent. He moved slower than Fi knew he could, a cat batting the mouse between its paws, letting it test its swings against dulled claws.

'Do you think we stand a chance with this?' Boden asked quietly.

Fi had spent all day wondering that. They had weapons, they had determination, but most of their volunteers had never wielded anything more than a knife or hunting bow.

'They're only support,' Fi said. 'Antal and I will take the lead in combat. We only have to topple one daeyari. One Beast.'

'And Astrid,' Boden said.

Fi sucked in a breath, cold in her chest. 'And Astrid.'

They could do it. They had to do it. Even as the baker's sword sagged in his hands, swings failing to find their mark . . .

Boots thudded frozen ground. Antal spun, narrowly avoiding a second sword. Yvette joined the fray, silver braid flying as they swung, a sword more familiar in their hands. Antal deflected the strike, but his attention on the new opponent left his back open. The baker charged with a shout. Antal blocked. Yvette gave no reprieve.

Their match ended with Antal holding the baker's sword at bay, Yvette's blade hovering at his neck.

They had numbers. They had a home to fight for. From the sidelines, several trainees clapped at the completed match. Across the clearing, the other volunteers practiced target-shooting with energy crossbows as Kashvi strolled the line, bellowing orders to brace stocks and fire on an exhale. However slow, things were coming together.

In the sparring ring, the baker laughed in triumph. Yvette grinned, congratulating their partner with a pat on the back, then a lecture on better sword grips. The day began with most recruits too petrified to face Antal. It finished with nods to the daeyari, a grin from him in return.

'Is he still behaving for you?' Boden asked.

Fi would absolutely not blush. She was better than that.

'He behaves surprisingly well. Once you know how to ask.'

Boden laughed. 'My sister, the daeyari tamer?'

She didn't *hate* the sound of that.

Fi yelped when Boden snared an arm around her shoulders, pulling her into his chest. He chuckled as she squirmed, followed by a kiss to her forehead.

'*Eww*,' she complained. 'What are you doing?'

'I'm proud of you, Fi.'

She fell still.

Fi had spent so many years honing defenses. All bristles and barbs, all snarling in the face of any challenge. Her first instinct was to fight, at odds with the crushing comfort of her brother's arm holding her to his coat. His familiar smell of hay and aurorabeasts.

'It's the least I could do,' she muttered.

'What's that mean?'

'I told you, Boden. I'm not leaving you this time.'

He shifted her in front of him, gloves heavy on either shoulder. Fi met his eyes with scrunched nose and puffed lips, a slippery defense against that too-earnest gaze.

'Fi-Fi,' he chided.

Her nose wrinkled fiercer.

'That's all in the past,' Boden said. 'You know that . . . don't you?'

It wasn't.

Just a few days ago, when he wasn't padding his punches, he'd told her it wasn't in the past, that she was still clinging to old ghosts. And he was right. Fi had spent seven years building walls around her coward's heart, but never daring to inspect the cracked foundations.

'But I don't want—' she began.

'We don't need to talk about—' he said at the same time.

He stopped. Like he always did. A thousand words hung unsaid on the air between them, but he avoided every single one of them.

So did Fi.

She wanted everything to be fine between her and Boden. But by the merciless Void, had she ever actually apologized? Fi raked her memory, searching for a single time she'd swallowed her shattered-glass pride and said sorry for running, sorry for leaving him, sorry for making him wrangle her like a beast who'd broken out of pasture. She'd been too terrified of what he'd say. She'd survived this long by deflecting, never strong enough to ask the true depth of his disappointment in her.

That wasn't enough.

She'd never told Astrid she was sorry, either. Fi saw now how that hurt had swollen. Festered to something irreparable.

Boden deserved better. She wanted to do better.

She almost fucking said it.

'We're going to fight,' she told him. 'We're going to win.' A shrug. 'That, or we all end up Void ghosts and have to haunt Antal when he reincarnates as a dumb little antler seal.'

Boden laughed. Too easy.

Could she tell him sorry, if she hadn't earned it yet?

All Fi had now were promises made, none yet fulfilled. But she would. Once Verne was gone, and they had their home back, and she'd unknotted this mess she'd helped create, Fi would finally have a victory to hold up and say, 'look, I'm better now, I didn't run away this time'.

Boden hugged her. She was glad for his silence, space for her to wrap her arms around his back and smile into his sleeve, a tiny thing, safe and hidden from the cold, the prospect of finally working toward a future rather than merely fleeing the past.

As night fell in earnest, Kashvi dismissed her archers. Volunteer fighters trickled back toward the windows and hearths of Nyskya. Savo, the energy foreman, stopped by to update Boden on conduit repairs. While they spoke, his daughter swayed at his heels, her hair a puff of black against the fur ruff of her coat.

When her father wasn't looking, she inched closer to Antal. Stealthy, an inquisitive hand reached for his tail.

When the tail flicked away, she puffed her cheeks. Fi stifled a laugh, noting Antal's sly grin as he watched the small human with one eye.

The girl froze when she saw him looking. She stumbled back, but before she could retreat in earnest, Antal's tail swayed toward her. Wide-eyed, her tiny fingers poked the tip, soft as if cradling a fragile bird. She smiled.

Was this how their world could be? Peace between their species, rather than terror? Fi saw glimpses of something larger than her or even Nyskya, almost close enough to grasp.

Boden hugged her goodnight. Kashvi parted with a glare for the daeyari, a sliver less vicious since their night in her tavern.

Then, Fi and Antal were alone again.

He didn't offer his hand to teleport. As they set off walking through the snow, she honed her claws for a different kind of duel.

'I think you made some friends today,' Fi said.

'If by that you mean no one genuinely tried to take my head off.'

'You were the one playing nice with them.'

He hummed.

They reached the forest edge. The stone-faced daeyari at Fi's side wound her with as much tension as their early meetings, though for a different reason now. A spark cracked the air between them, a promise made that morning before they were rudely interrupted.

Would the thought have lingered on Antal's mind all day, as it had for Fi?

They passed through the gossamer cool of a Curtain. The golden lights of Nyskya vanished, replaced by the pale trees of a Shard, the silvered terrain and endless Void sky.

'Don't play coy,' Fi teased. 'I saw you grinning. You enjoyed your sparring matches?'

'It is . . . pleasant. Being amongst my people at last.'

'Not having humans flee from you in terror, you mean?' She swooned a dramatic hand across her forehead. 'The fell ruler of Thomaskweld, gracing us rural folk with your tutelage. I told you they'd warm up.'

He grinned again, that disarmingly earnest gesture. 'I suppose I *am* enjoying this.' Then a rumbled, 'Though, not as much as I'm going to enjoy *you*.'

His gaze cut sharp enough to rend her open. Fi relished the promise.

As his tongue traced his lip, her own hunger fiercened, eager to have his mouth on her again. To finish what they'd started. Yet it wasn't the beast that drew her breath short, so much as the man, the slow sweep of eyes and the softening of his features to something unguarded, something raw and reverent and just for her.

'You have your work cut out for you,' she said. An invitation.

He didn't pounce. Just a wicked grin. He offered his elbow as if for a stroll.

Fi tipped her chin up. Her best defense was the long-honed act, pretending to be fierce, unruffled by the flash of fangs.

Except sometimes, with Antal . . . it didn't feel like an act. Fi felt like another creature entirely, metal in her bones and an unbent spine. Perhaps she'd faked the facade so long, some had genuinely rubbed off on her.

'Do I look like the kind of woman who needs to be walked home?' she challenged.

'Would you rather I carry you again?'

Fi wouldn't mind that so much. For the sake of pride, she wrapped her fingers around the crook of his arm.

And they walked.

Antal's gait was glass, gliding over the frozen shale of the Shard, beneath gossamer leaves. Yet there was always a command to him, steady as the Void. What an odd shift, from once fearing the thought of this daeyari knowing where she lived, to him now leading her back home. Back to her bed. That would make a smoldering end to a story. Or a tragic one.

'Do you know any daeyari folktales?' Fi asked.

He cocked his head. 'The kind my people tell? Or yours?'

'The kind my father told a misbehaving little girl to stop her wandering into the forest.'

A grin. 'Did it work?'

'Not very well.' Fi had always been a difficult creature to wrangle. 'There was one about a woman, collecting flowers in the woods. She wandered too far. Became lost. In the cold, she stumbled upon a house of stone and tree roots, home to a creature with antlers.'

Antal listened with a tight line to his brow. Were daeyari the villains in their own folktales? Or was it a human convention, born out of millennia as prey?

'The daeyari offered gifts,' Fi continued. 'She asked for better clothes, and he spun her a dress of moonbeams. She asked for warmth, and he summoned music for her to dance. She asked for food, and he laid out a feast. But he didn't touch any himself. After eating her fill, the woman asked the beast how she could show her thanks. He said he'd have her. Then he feasted.'

At the tale's conclusion, Antal huffed. 'Blunt. Is this common in your stories?'

'It's a story with a moral: always ask the terms of a deal beforehand. Most stories end with the daeyari eating the foolish human.'

'That seems uncharitable.'

Perhaps it was. Or perhaps there was reason to keep one's heart guarded. Fi, arm locked with a predator, kept her tone mild.

'What do you suppose the daeyari sees in the lost mortal wandering his forest? A curiosity? A plaything?'

Antal's arm tightened, a low chuckle in his chest. 'To call you curious would be an understatement, Fionamara.'

'And what spares her from his teeth?'

They stepped through a second Curtain, back onto the Winter Plane. Familiar shiverpines screened the night, a whisper of wind through needles, a glimpse of Fi's cottage ahead.

Antal slipped her out of his elbow. 'You asked me a question last night. Do you remember?'

He tugged her along, grip light on her fingers. Fi followed the tether.

'I asked several things,' she said. 'Not all of which you gave me.'

'You wanted to know how many mortals I've bedded. The answer is: very few. Some daeyari enjoy playing with panicked prey, but I've never found that to my taste. I only dance with those who can hold their ground.'

In a step, they were doing just that – dancing. His leading hand found hers, his arm around her waist to guide her home. Fi fell into his tempo but kept her own strides, bold as she'd always been. Bold as he wanted her to be.

'I ran away from you,' she pointed out. 'When we first met. I fled like a startled hare.'

He flashed a sharp grin. 'Not your smartest move. But understandable. You found your feet quickly.' He slowed, dipping to brush his mouth across her jaw. 'Perhaps I do find you a curiosity. Is that such a bad thing?'

'That depends on how the story ends.'

'How would you like it to? A dress made of moonbeams? A spin beneath the Void?' He sent her out, a slow twirl across the clearing. Then back into his arms. 'Yet how odd, you assume all your folktales of devoured mortals end in death? There are other ways to enjoy flesh, Fionamara. Types of devouring that don't work well as cautionary tales for misbehaving girls.'

There could be truth to that. Certainly, Fi wasn't the first human to risk this plunge. Once again, she asked herself whether it was lust, or foolishness.

Or simply that she trusted him.

They reached her porch. Fi pulled away, backing up the steps to her door.

'Now you have me at a disadvantage,' she said. 'I've only had one immortal.'

Antal followed, claws soft on the boards, eyes glowing. 'How was it?'

'Satisfactory.'

He pressed a hand to his chest, a theatrical reel at her blow. 'You call my kind beasts. Yet you never miss the chance for a bite.'

He made the taunts too tempting. Too addicting.

Yet tonight felt different, something settled between them, not the spur of the moment spark that had drawn them together before. Fi's back bumped her door. As her fingers closed on the handle, she stood up straight, needing every shred of pride to deliver what he deserved.

Honesty.

'You're intoxicating,' she whispered. 'You make me feel desperate, but not like that fleeing hare. Like I'm scenting fresh air. Like I have claws. Like I could topple head-first into the Void just to bask in the abyss. Every second is vicious, and soft, and I never want to be anything else.'

Fi wished she could bottle Antal's reaction, measure out every minutia of stunned silence as he hung at the edge of her porch. She tipped the door open.

'Fair beast,' she said, 'would you care to come in from the cold?'

Antal swept her inside like a gale. Darkness wrapped them, the only light a trickle of moonbeams and aurora through the windows. The ember glow of his eyes. Claws brushed her hair as he pulled her into him, an eager rise to her breath, a desperate hitch to his.

'You're fire in my hands.' He kissed her. 'Unyielding.' Another, teeth hungry on her lips, ozone sparking her tongue. 'I can't seem to get my fill of crashing against you, just to see how you'll surprise me next. Yet that's not when you're most dangerous. When you soften for me, when you trust me here against you. I don't feel like I have claws.'

Fi swallowed fire in her throat. 'Claws aren't such a bad thing. The way you use them.'

Void save her, maybe she *was* the witless maiden from a story, lured to the predator's teeth not by moonspun dresses but velvet words.

But this felt different. In Antal's arms, they were two hunters tossed into a cage, pacing the grounds, each testing the sharpness of the other's fangs. Until they finally came together.

Antal pulled her hips to his, tail wrapping her calf in a possessive arc. 'You have hunger in your eyes, mortal. What would you ask of me?'

Fi wanted to melt for him. The fight was a sliver more thrilling.

'A dangerous proposal,' she returned. 'When I've just shared a cautionary tale about asking favors from daeyari?'

'Perhaps we can negotiate.'

'Is this a matter of negotiation?' She ran her hands up his chest, fingers carving canyons into soft fabric and hard muscle. 'Or passion?'

'One can be a play on the other.' His breath brushed her ear, a nip of fangs against her chin. 'I think you'll find my request . . . attractive.'

'That being?'

'Stubborn woman. I want to know how loud I can make you scream.'

Oh. Was that all?

Each time he stole her breath was a defeat. Fi would take the loss a thousand times if it meant this fire through her veins, this snare of his mouth as he drew her into a fiercer kiss.

'You want to hear me scream?' she warred. 'You'll have to earn it.'

He hummed a sound of delight. Of anticipation. 'You enjoy giving orders. Tell me what to do to you.'

Fi needed no pause to think. She'd weighed this moment a dozen times.

'Bite me.'

He hesitated. Delicious. Fi devoured the sweep of his eyes, Antal trying to read what she wanted. She'd never loved victory and defeat so much in equal measure.

'How?' he asked.

'Like you did before.'

He dipped his head, a questioning brush of teeth along her neck.

'Yes,' Fi rasped, heart hammering her throat. Pulse quick beneath his lips.

At the first press of fangs, she gasped. He moved too soft, caressing nips along her neck. Playing gentle? Fi was no fragile thing. She clawed fingers into his shirt, pulling herself into the heat of his mouth.

'You can do better than that,' she said. She *begged*.

At her urging, he fiercened: fingers dragging knots in her hair, a clamp of teeth on her neck. With it, a spike of adrenaline that threatened to buckle her legs. The ache was everything she'd wanted, that pleased growl in Antal's throat, the growing hardness where his hips pressed hers.

He pushed her onto the bed. Antal's claws ran the curves of Fi's ribs, a knee slipped between her legs. She pressed against him with a moan.

'Oysen yzri,' she pleaded, the strange syllables delicious on her tongue. 'Fuck me.'

A delighted grin curled Antal's lips.

'Yzi ex oysi yzu,' he purred against her. 'Va yzu na sansu.'

Void. Let him talk like this more often. Even without translation, the words tumbled like music through Fi's chest.

Deft claws removed her sweater. Next, the lacy bra she'd tempted him with earlier. Fi shuddered as warm palms brushed down her waist. In the dim light, she could barely make out the silhouette above her, yet of course he could see every detail.

His rough tongue traced the line of her collarbone. Down her chest. Around the curve of a breast. Too soft.

'Harder,' Fi urged.

The clamp of teeth to such a tender place made her writhe.

One brush into pain, a jolt that sent her arcing against him. She cried out and dug fingers through his hair, bracing against the base of his antlers. A lighter moan, as he swept his tongue over her tender nipple.

Again, Antal paused. He weighed her beneath him with devouring eyes, arms caging her head, tail swaying like a cat eager to pounce.

'Fionamara. Should I fuck you like a human? Or like a daeyari?'

Fi's lust-dizzied thoughts weren't coherent enough to dissect what that meant right away. She dug back to a conversation they'd had weeks ago, a tense walk through the woods when they'd barely known one another.

Daeyari don't fall easily onto our backs, Antal had told her. *We fight, to see who will end up on top.* Fi's breath was a shiver of anticipation.

'You'll win,' she complained.

'Most likely,' Antal returned with a grin.

Let him have her. This daeyari was as dangerous as all the stories said, just in no way Fi was prepared for. In no way she wanted to avoid. An abyss to tumble into.

She wouldn't go down easily.

Fi gripped both his antlers and heaved. It took all her strength to roll him, a flail of tail and lean muscle, claws seeking purchase against the furs of her bed. Even once she sat atop him, thighs straddling his waist, aware of every tense muscle and harder anatomy between her legs, Antal looked up at her with an insulting smirk.

'A spirited start,' he praised. 'Though lacking finesse.'

'Are you offering to teach me?'

A mistake.

He gripped her bare waist and twisted. Fi braced a knee,

fighting to hold her high ground, but he pinned her on her back. Her legs kicked futilely against the furs, Antal's mouth a blaze as he dragged commanding nips down her neck.

She realized too late, this wasn't a contest of strength. And Antal fought dirty.

As Fi wriggled free of his grasp, he ran his hands down the length of her, fingers prickling with energy, not missing an inch of tender stomach or hip. As she tore off his shirt, he pressed her down into the bed, the bare skin of his chest hot and flush against hers. She nearly managed to top him again – only for the beast to rear beneath her, a nip to her breast that sent her sinking back to the sheets with a moan. His hands like vices. His mouth like a weapon.

The hazard wasn't fighting him. It was fighting herself from giving in.

Fi loved it. She loved the rasp of Antal's breath, the fervor of their tangled limbs.

His fangs clamped the soft curve of her waist. *Hard*. Fi shrieked at the pain.

Antal jerked back immediately. He looked her over with wide, worried eyes, breaths heavy. After her surprise abated, Fi laughed at this creature, so soft beneath his facade of claws. She seized the distraction, launching herself into a snarling tackle. He fought, but she held him down, thighs pinning his hips, hands tight on his antlers.

'Don't worry about me,' she goaded. 'I'll take whatever you can throw at me, daeyari.'

She'd thought his eyes were molten before.

Fi cried out as he pitched her, a traitorous gasp as he pulled down her pants – as he ran his tongue between her legs, that slow and covetous motion that had nearly ruined her earlier. Nearly ruined her now. As he sucked every slick and needy piece of her, a desperate sound escaped her lips, aching to concede.

She rallied for one last push. Fi twisted her hip free of his wicked mouth, seeking to snare a leg around him.

He pounced too quickly, pinning her arms above her head. Antal hovered over her, both their breaths greedy, a finality to their game.

A burning question in his eyes.

'*Yes,*' Fi gasped.

She nearly perished in the seconds he took to remove his trousers. When his hard cock brushed her thigh, Fi tipped impatient hips up to take him, to sate the anguish aching between her legs.

His thrust sent her falling.

Fi arced off the bed, desperate to feel all of him as he sank into her. They came together as wrought iron. Muscles tensed and her fingers carving the unyielding slopes of his shoulders.

As he moved, she softened. She melted into the clasp of his arms, breath falling to shallower pants with each thrust. This seemed to be what he wanted, a growl rumbling his chest as he buried fingers into her hair, wound a hand beneath her back to angle her against him.

This wasn't like last time. That desperate, quick thing that had flared between them.

Not that Fi wasn't desperate now. But she wanted to feel him, to revel in each stroke he carved inside her, even as she longed for the finish. She surrendered with legs wrapped around his waist, climbing to a peak that had her clawing his back.

He bit down on her throat, pinning her to the bed as he pushed her over the edge.

Fi did scream. Their pact satisfied.

Again, when he refused to yield, working her to a second

climax that left her throat raw, every muscle hot and spent and shattering as he held her.

Yet even as the waves of her pleasure ebbed, even as Antal finished inside her with a shuddering thrust of his own, claws snared into her sheets and a fractured exhale shaped like her name, he didn't pull away like before.

Neither did Fi. Swathed in sweat and moonbeams, their breaths a warring tempo in the aftermath, she held him to her in the warmth of her bed.

Unwilling to let go.

34

Better than the rafters

Fi woke to sweet ozone in her nose. Coating her skin.

She shifted, groggy muscles reaching for a pleased stretch. Her naked body was draped in pre-dawn light, a mess of fur blankets, and something else, a warm weight she wasn't used to. Antal lay atop her like a panther possessive of his quarry: his arm and head pillowed on her chest, leg wrapping her waist, tail curled around one ankle.

The Plane's fiercest predator looked surprisingly docile as he slept, his breaths deep, claws light against Fi's side. And how had she never pieced it together? He slept on his stomach to avoid bumping his antlers. The revelation made her chuckle.

At her stirring, the daeyari woke. A sigh rumbled through him as he rolled the muscles of his shoulders. His head tilted, hooking her with one eye of drowsy, half-lidded crimson.

'I thought you preferred the rafters?' Fi said.

His gaze narrowed, a lazy drift across her dawn-lit face, swirls of bed-mussed hair, the swell of her breasts beneath him.

'This is acceptable,' he mumbled.

As temperamental as a house cat. Fi tried to move, but claws tightened on her waist, holding her to the bed. He shifted against her, brushing his nose along her neck. Heat kindled up her thighs. Not sharp like the night before, but deep, lulling.

'Stay,' he entreated, the word warm and heavy with sleep.

'Can't say you struck me as the cuddly type,' she teased.

'Small moments,' he muttered back.

He'd used the same phrase when they'd danced together, that simple moment she'd thought would be a passing triviality to an immortal. Small moments to differentiate one day from the last, one century from the last. Fi wasn't so ageless, but it had been a long time since she'd woken up alongside anyone. Longer still, someone she wanted to linger with in the morning.

She settled against him, drawing in deep breaths of warmth and ozone.

'This is an elaborate plan of yours, daeyari. All this effort of getting on my good side, just so you can eat me in the end?'

Antal chuckled, a rumble through her heart. 'A long game. I might have to keep it going a little longer, if you don't mind.' He traced a claw along her collarbone, voice dipping low. 'You were brave last night.'

'You were holding back.'

'Human bodies are more fragile than daeyari.'

His hand brushed the dip of her waist, a swirl around her hip. At the rise, teeth marks showed against pale skin, blushed red imprints and purpled bruising, tender to the touch. The pain had been sharp when he'd bitten her. Fi loved the shock of it, the jolt of adrenaline.

'Just as hard next time,' she said.

Antal's brow tipped up. 'Next time?'

'If you remember how to ask nicely.'

His smirk could spear her through the lungs. She ought to feel vulnerable, laying naked against him, all her soft parts exposed. But there was soft to him, too. The soft hollows of his throat beneath her fingers. The soft rise and fall of his abdomen with each breath.

Fi trailed her fingers along his jaw, perfectly smooth, no hint of stubble.

'You really don't have any hair on your body? Not even . . .' Fi glanced down.

Antal's gaze followed hers. Then, a laugh. 'Neither do *you*.'

Fi pressed her thighs together. 'Sure. But that's a war between me and my energy wax strips. Yours is natural, isn't it?'

She studied his other features with the benefit of this new proximity: the blush of his mouth, the tapered ears, the rim of black sclera gazing back at her like an abyss to slip into. As he leaned into her touch with a contented sound in his throat, she slid her hand over the shaved side of his head, through the thicker blue-black hair on top, landing on the roots of his antlers.

The designs adorning them were works of art – lines so thin, so precise, they must be energy carved. Though the antlers glinted lacquer black, the grooves were painted in contrast, a gradient from midnight blue to aurora green.

'What do they mean?' Fi asked.

Antal's gaze fell bemused upon her bold hands. 'The marks of my life. Added each century.'

Fi ran her finger over the ridges. Two wider bands divided the antlers into sections, two centuries fully filled, the third ongoing. At the base, nestled against the ink of his hair, carvings of flowers bloomed with tight swirls of petals.

'Midnight dahlia,' Antal said. 'The flowers have grown on my family's lands for five millennia. Petals crisp as ice. Deep blue as a moonless night.'

Surprisingly poetic, for a daeyari. Fi shifted her thumb to the next designs, a set of sigils she didn't recognize.

'The Planes I visited during my travel years,' Antal said. 'During the end of their first century, any self-respecting daeyari must travel, experience life among the shattered worlds.'

His haughty tone made Fi suspect the words weren't his.

'Not a fan of far-off horizons?' she teased.

'A glorified field trip. All Planes within daeyari control. Not far enough abroad to risk derived daeyari or other immortals.'

Fi stilled. 'There are . . . *other* immortals?'

'There are many dangers across the far Planes, Fionamara.'

A world so much larger than her. Too large. Though a Voidwalker would have no trouble venturing beyond the Season-Locked Planes, the vast unknown of Shards and Planes beyond had always daunted Fi. Give her an adventure on a snowbound rail line, an Autumn-kissed glade. She looked forward to the quiet comfort of returning home.

Antal's second section of carvings began with teal lines like waves, paired with . . . were those lines of energy conduits?

'A short time at an academy by the sea. I had aptitude as an engineer, I was told.'

'An *engineer*?' Fi jabbed his chest, giggling as he dug his leg tighter around her waist in retaliation. 'You've been holding out on me, Antlers.'

'It wasn't much,' he said. 'Basic conduit design. Energy theory.'

'That's how you've known how to repair the conduits in town? How you fixed my gramophone?'

'Conduits are simple circuitry. Gramophones, even more so.' His grin wavered. 'I . . . haven't worked on anything more complicated than that for a while.'

'Why not?'

'My father insisted on loftier aspirations.'

Well, look at that, another daeyari to add to Fi's slap-worthy list. Not a new development, considering what little Antal had mentioned of his parents. He tapped a claw to the next design: a constellation of stars.

'The Daey Celva. The . . . *Dusk Council*,' he said, translating the name to seasonspeak for the first time.

Fi logged her growing list of words. 'Daey means *dusk*? So daeyari, are . . .?'

'People of dusk,' Antal said.

How fitting.

'The Daey Celva is the governing body of the Twilit Plane,' he went on. 'The center of daeyari administration across the worlds. My family helped found it. My father has served for over six centuries. He set me on an apprenticeship. Until . . .'

The image was hard to picture. Antal, the brooding racoon who'd haunted Fi's rafters, apprenticed to the governing council of his species? He sounded equally dismal about the prospect. As for what ended that career, Fi could guess.

Upon his antlers, the latter half of his second century had no carvings. Utterly blank. Fi touched the smooth, Void-like space, struck by the emptiness. The grief.

'This is for the friend you lost?'

Antal's arm tightened on her waist. 'Yes.'

Half a century. Longer than Fi had been alive, vanished in one chunk of blank antler.

'A long time to grieve,' she said.

'My father didn't want me to forget.'

The pit in Fi's stomach deepened. The same father who'd slaughtered Antal's friend in front of him, no better than an animal.

'Is it such a bad thing?' she asked. 'For a daeyari to care for a human?'

'I'm my parents' only child. All their expectations laid on my back.' Antal's scowl showed fangs. 'I've long been a disappointment.'

A disappointment? May the Void stop Fi from strangling his

ungrateful parents if she ever met them. Not a wise proposal. They'd killed their son's friend, sent Antal to this Plane as punishment. Beyond the blank patch on his antlers, the first mark into his third century was a carving of Winter Plane conifers and aurora. His story up to now.

Antal could have kept this from her. Instead, he offered honesty. Vulnerability. The night before had been intimate, yet this was something else, a glimpse behind the icy mask. On the other side was an entire *person*. Not a creature of folktales or a ruler upon a throne, but a man. One who could have been an engineer, who'd suffered loss and betrayal yet still held his ground here, working toward a better future.

Fi didn't know what to say.

That was a lie. She knew words that would be kind, supportive. She didn't know if those were the *right* words, whether they'd push a step too far.

'I don't suppose your parents would approve of how you plan to rule your territory?'

He laughed, humorless. 'No.'

'Or of me?'

Fi meant it as a tease. Antal refused to look at her, tail twitching against her ankle.

'One time, maybe,' he said. 'Not . . . this.'

He didn't say what *this* referred to. Fi could only infer: the way he'd purred against her last night, waking up tangled in her bed. She wanted to live in blissful simplicity a little longer, concerned only with how her heart raced when Antal's claw swirled her hip, not the deeper question of what this meant.

The plan had always been to set things right. Antal back in Thomaskweld. Fi here with Boden. A simple plan, growing blurrier. The line between them, somewhere buried in snow.

His claw circled her stomach, leaving gooseflesh in its wake. 'It doesn't matter. I stopped caring what my father thinks of me long ago.'

'Sure.' Fi traced the tattoos down her arm, focusing on her own dahlias and bellflowers so she wouldn't have to look at him. 'Except parents . . . you always care a *little* about what they think. Right?'

Antal's hand slowed. Not a push, but an obvious question.

'My father tried to give me to Verne,' Fi said. 'And I still . . .'

She still wished she could speak to him one last time. That he could forgive her.

Where did *that* come from? When had Fi's barbs abandoned her? She didn't know where the line lay between her and Antal, but she wanted to give him something. She wanted him to know she understood.

'After I nearly died,' she said, 'when I told my father I could see Curtains, I'd never seen him so grim. Then . . . so hopeful. He said when I got older, Verne would want me. Voidwalkers make prized Arbiters for daeyari.'

Antal huffed. He'd known she was a Voidwalker soon after they met, yet he'd never used that as the reason she was useful. He'd been more interested in . . . her.

'Everyone in town told me I should be honored.' Fi frowned, recalling their condescending smiles, the way they talked over her qualms like pine needles swept beneath a porch. 'But I was afraid. I knew I wouldn't be good enough, that Verne wouldn't spare me. My father was afraid, too. He still handed me over when the time came.'

She had nowhere to hide from the scrutiny of Antal's eyes. Already, she lay naked beside him, yet baring herself like this felt more raw.

'Did you ever forgive him?' Antal asked.

'Forgive him? I'm the one who ran away. I didn't even say goodbye. Not to him. Or Boden. Or Astrid.'

'You didn't want to go to Verne,' he said, too calm.

'I should have been ready!' Fi flashed her teeth, a daeyari gesture, but it suited her needs. 'Our father put everything we had into making me an Arbiter. Said I needed to learn sword-play, but he couldn't afford lessons, bartered a couple of useless sessions by making me and Boden scrub the blacksmith's floors. Made us listen to his stories every night as if they were sage wisdom.' Her voice cracked. 'He couldn't scrounge enough energy chips to keep our furnace going some nights, but always enough to buy liquor, to slump into a chair and tell us how much better things would be if our mother was still there. But we could have been a family without her. We could have been . . . *something* . . . if he'd let us . . .'

Fi had clung to these words so long, moldy and wretched. She clung to Antal now, her fingers so tight in his hair that it must hurt, but he didn't flinch. Why was she telling him this? Because he'd told her about himself, a fair trade?

No. More than that. Because he looked at her like he under-stood, too.

'And then I ran,' she said, quieter. Smaller. 'I thought I'd work up the courage to go back one day, but a few years later . . . he was gone. Boden's the only family I have left.' She huffed. 'Now here I am. Still a coward.'

Antal's laugh made her flinch.

It came so sudden, so deep, echoing in her rafters and muffled against her bedsheets.

Fi drew herself up onto defensive elbows. 'What?'

'You, a coward? Don't be ridiculous, Fionamara.'

His flippant tone dispelled some tension, the cobwebs of old memories. Fi kept on guard.

'I ran away.'

'One moment of self-preservation. What about everything after? Since we met, I've seen not a scrap of cowardice. A coward wouldn't have stood her ground against me. A coward wouldn't seek revenge against an immortal who could rip her to pieces.' His smirk sharpened, a wicked look that raked the length of her body and left a shiver in its wake. 'A coward wouldn't have had so many *demands* last night.'

Fi slumped to the bed, feigning annoyance. Pretending his praise didn't stir her heart.

'Yeah, well,' she grumbled, 'you aren't a disappointment, either.'

Antal's eyes took on a luminous glint.

Oh no. Fi was losing again, wasn't she?

'Please,' he purred, 'tell me *all* the ways I've failed to disappoint you.'

She couldn't stop herself. Fi's gaze drifted over the lean body stretched beside her, fully exposed. Fully confident. A treacherous tension wound her belly at the very non-disappointing view of his chest, the muscles of his abdomen, the lines of hard thighs. And between those legs? *Definitely* not disappointing.

'I fear that might go to your head,' Fi said, bland.

'Certainly, it will.'

Antal leaned over her, a blanket of Void, a tease of teeth at her lips.

'You would have been wasted on Verne,' he said.

Fi reached for him like a lifeline. 'But not on you?'

'Have I wasted you yet?'

He shifted a leg between hers. A moan escaped her teeth, an ache beneath his pressure. Then, startled stillness as he nestled his nose to her throat, breathing her in with a relishing inhale.

Fi welcomed the touch. Their conversation hung heavy, but

here he offered an escape. A comfort. A joining in their wrongs and how safe she felt beside him.

'You have an intriguing smell, Fionamara.' Antal's words danced, a sparkly lure.

'How so?' she breathed, drawn to the hook.

'How to describe it . . .' He brushed his nose up her neck, breath warm on her skin. 'Like crackling firewood. Hot on every inhale. But then, the slightest chill at the end. A kiss from the Void.'

Void-touched. 'Like you?'

Antal considered. Grinned. 'Like me.'

Maybe that was the unerring pull between them, two creatures who felt equally at home beyond the Plane.

Fi's composure cracked, a needy sound in her throat as she surged to kiss him. His lips met hers with a hungry press, his teeth tugging her mouth open, his tongue slipping into her. She drank him in parched gulps. Antal kissed like he could devour her very essence, yet last night he'd employed this weapon surprisingly little during their wrestling.

'Daeyari aren't big on kissing,' Fi asked, 'are they?'

'Less common for us than for humans. But I can enjoy something different now and then.'

'Two can play that game, you know.'

Fi broke from his lips and bit into the soft beneath his jaw.

The sound Antal made verged on feral. Every muscle tightened against her, shaken by a moan in his chest, sharp with the claws curled against her ribs. A dizzying heat bloomed between Fi's legs, the delight of how desperately he reached for her. The thrill of discovering these intimate pieces of him.

'Careful with that.' His voice came rough.

'Why?'

'It's how daeyari give consent.'

424

Fi thrilled at this shiny new toy. At Antal, coiled against her. 'You mentioned a next time?' he rasped.

'I had conditions,' she returned, barely more composed.

'Please.' Antal pulled her against him and nipped her jaw – delicious, now that she knew what it meant. 'Please, Fionamara. Let me taste you again.'

'You've started tasting me twice now, daeyari, and never finished the task.'

She returned a bite to his chin, hard enough to draw a hiss through his teeth, to tell him exactly what she wanted.

His mouth was on her neck. Her chest. Down the plane of her stomach then a drag of fangs across her thigh.

'Fast?' he asked with bewitching severity. 'Or slow?'

'Slow,' she ordered on a shivering breath. 'Make me beg for it.'

And he did.

35

Just ignore the bite marks

It took too long for Fi to drag herself out of bed.

Longer still, the arduous process of dressing for the day ahead, slowed by subtle looks of appreciation as Antal tugged a pair of dark pants snug at his waist, his less subtle nips to her neck whenever she strayed too close. Watching him dress was torture, alleviated only by the view of taut back muscles as he slipped on a shirt, the delicious tension in his forearms as he rolled his sleeves to the elbow.

An otherworldly beauty, as alluring as whispering her fingers across the edge of a blade.

Antal smirked when he caught her staring. Insufferable bastard.

At last, Fi pulled on her coat and boots, bracing for the cold and a long day away from the bed she very much didn't want to leave. Before she opened the door, Antal snared an arm around her waist, nose nestled to her cheek.

'A shame we have business to attend,' he said. 'I'd enjoy you all day.'

Fi didn't need that temptation.

'Are you sure you aren't just hungry?' she said.

He hummed. 'Perhaps . . . some of that. Don't worry, Fiona-mara. I can enjoy my tastes of you without biting any harder.'

Fi wasn't worried for herself, surprisingly. She worried for him. Whatever hunger she'd helped satisfy last night – and this morning – was the easier of the two. Days ticked by since his last meal.

'We'll find something,' she said. 'Before facing Verne. Need you in fighting shape.'

Another logistic weighing on her mind. This morning, though? None of that felt as daunting. Training recruits, feeding a daeyari, planning to topple Verne – Fi stepped out of her cottage, took a breath of lung-chilling air, and felt she could accomplish anything.

Antal's steady presence at her side certainly helped.

They traveled into Nyskya, back to the training grounds. The recruits wouldn't appear for another hour, but Kashvi and Boden arrived early, sorting weapons and setting up targets. Kashvi, murderous scowl notwithstanding, agreed to let Antal teach her to use daeyari energy capsules when Shaping her crossbow bolts, testing small doses to determine what she could safely handle with her silver sickness.

Fi wandered to the far side of the archery range for some practice of her own. Yvette's crossbows were swiftly made but elegant, metal mechanisms that weighed heavy in Fi's hands. Several yards ahead, a copper disk hung from a tree.

She Shaped a silver energy bolt onto the track. Squared her stance. Aimed. Breathed.

Her victorious whoop echoed alongside the clang of the target, spinning from a direct hit.

'What's got you in such a good mood?'

Boden stood at her side, a crossbow looking as natural in his hands as a hare wielding a broadsword.

'Do I need a reason?' Fi returned, fully aware that the reason involved the surprising length of a daeyari's tongue – and fully committed to *not* telling Boden about it. Yet. Maybe after things got quieter.

Boden's huff billowed steam. He lifted his crossbow and spent several seconds aiming. When he fired, the bolt zipped past a tree and disappeared into the forest.

Fi laughed. It was cruel, but her sworn duty as a little sister. 'Having trouble, Bodie?'

'I wasn't made for this,' he grumbled.

'You were made for financial ledgers and aurorabeast snot? Noted.'

He muttered under his breath while fidgeting with the cross-bow. Armed with a suitably condescending grin, Fi stepped over to help.

'I'll get it,' Boden said.

'Sure you will. But you've got to fix your stance first.'

'I don't need your pity.'

'You need every ounce of it.' Fi kicked his legs wider in the snow. 'Brace the stock to your chest. Like this.'

She put her hands over Boden's and nudged the crossbow into alignment. He rolled his eyes. Void have mercy, was this the smug satisfaction he got from lecturing her about budgets?

'I seem to recall coming here to practice on my own,' he argued.

'I seem to recall you being a stubborn little shit,' Fi returned. 'Breathe in. Aim. Fire on the exhale.'

'That's what I've been doing!'

'Breathe *better*. A real target won't wait around for you to . . . what's wrong?'

Boden fell silent. Ashen. Staring at her. Fi entertained a hope that he might be staring at some monstrosity behind her, but when she turned, there was only an empty field.

She flinched when he cupped her cheek. Slow, cold fingers

brushed her neck, lowering the collar of her coat to . . .

Fuck.

'Fi . . .' Boden breathed.

Bite marks. She had bite marks on her neck. Fi had tried covering them with a collar, had banked on keeping her distance from prying eyes.

'*Fi.*' Boden's hiss grew urgent. 'What are these?'

One morning of peace. Was that so much to ask for?

'Nothing.' Fi willed her cheeks not to burn. She felt herself failing.

'Did Antal do this to you?'

Fi's energy fled her body. Gone to the Void. Bury her ashes in the frozen ground.

'I said it's nothing, Bodie.'

'Is he *hurting* you?'

Fi blinked.

Then again.

He thought that . . .

'Oh, Bodie. My sweet, innocent little boy.' She cupped his bearded cheeks in her hands. Took a deep breath. 'It's consensual.'

Boden's eyes shot wider. '*Consensual?*'

'As in, I gave him permission.'

'I know what consensual means, Fi.'

'I asked for it, more specifically.'

Fi wasn't ashamed. Not for an instant. But this was her own damn business, and she didn't want to have this conversation, mostly because the reaction she expected was . . .

'You're kidding,' came Boden's flat reply. 'You *let* him bite you? And then . . . Fi . . . please don't tell me you . . .'

Right. There it was.

'Why do you care?' Fi pleaded.

'I'm your brother, Fionamara.'

Shit. Pulling out the full name? Fi scoffed. 'You've never cared about the people I fucked.'

He winced at her blunt words. 'Those were people. Not a daeyari!'

'*He* is a person.'

'He is a *carnivore*.'

'That doesn't mean he can't—'

'Is everything all right?' came a wary voice behind them.

Fi and Boden froze, grappling over a crossbow like a pair of magpies with a shiny toy, turning in unison to see Antal staring at them.

Void, no.

Fi's molten gaze snapped back to Boden. No words. Just a clenched jaw and a mental scream. *Drop it, Bodie. I'm fine.*

Boden's glare came back defiant. *Not a chance.*

Boden. Fi's look promised death if he said so much as a word. 'Hey, Antal?' Boden said.

Fi tried to disappear. Where was her transport stone when she needed it? Thrown into the Void by Cardigan's damn assistant. Neither did she have a Curtain to leap into. Antal's eyes darted between them, visibly confused.

Boden yanked the crossbow from Fi's numb fingers. Propped it on his shoulder. The attempt at looking intimidating would have had her in stitches, if she weren't weighing the pros and cons of tackling him to the ground.

'Do you have any siblings?' Boden asked the daeyari.

Antal's eyes narrowed to baffled slits. 'No . . . daeyari are wary of overpopulation. Single children are most common.'

'But do you understand a brother's responsibility to make sure his sister is safe?'

'I . . . suppose.'

'Taken care of?'

Antal's head tilted. When his bewildered gaze slid to Fi, she gave him a withering look and tugged down her collar, displaying the bite marks.

Antal's entire demeanor changed. Not for the better, Fi was mortified to see. The bloom of his toothy grin had her bracing for battle.

'I see,' Antal said slowly. Practically licking his lips at Fi's discomfort. 'You worry I'm not taking care of her?'

Void no. Fi could use a Void right now to swallow her.

'I want to know you aren't going to *eat* her,' Boden said.

Fi saw the response coming a mile away. Too slow to stop it.

'Well,' Antal drawled, 'not unless she asks me to.'

Fi wondered what he'd look like reincarnated. After she murdered him, of course.

The blow struck Boden to mortified silence. He looked to Fi, and when she managed a tight nod without perishing, he dropped his attention to fidgeting with the crossbow.

'I don't need to know these details,' he muttered. 'My life is stressful enough.'

Antal laughed. Fi shot him a barbed glare.

'You're insufferable,' she said.

'Thank you,' he returned.

He held her gaze, but when Fi refused to back down – when she stared hard enough to drive a mental crossbow bolt through his crass skull – Antal's grin wavered.

'Boden,' Antal said, softer.

Boden waved a hand. 'I don't need to know specifics, please. I just want to know—'

'I promise you. I will never harm her, nor willfully allow harm to come to her.' Antal touched the highest point of an antler. 'As Veshri watches from the Void.'

432

That silenced Boden *and* Fi. His sincerity struck as a shock – and, if she was honest, a little flutter in her chest.

'You mean that?' Boden, once again, looked to Fi.

'I'm fine, Bodie.'

'Fine is a strong word, Fi.'

'Stop making this weird.'

'Weird? I've hardly ever met a daeyari, much less someone willing to fuck one!'

'She's doing *what?*' Kashvi's shrill voice sliced into the fray.

Fi's newest inquisitor stood with mouth open, crossbow more intimidating in her hands than any of Boden's attempts. Too busy arguing, Fi hadn't noticed her creeping closer. She pressed a hand to her temple, ready to combust.

'Maybe we should talk about this later?' Boden offered, finally mollified by her discomfort.

'You think?' Fi snapped.

'Oh no,' Kashvi said, 'don't stop on my account. I'm eager to hear what kind of insanity you're up to now. With a daeyari? With *this* daeyari? I knew you were on his side!'

Fi threw up her hands. 'Why in the far-reaching Void is my private time so interesting to everyone? There's nothing to . . .'

She trailed off.

Antal stood rigid. Not the mortified, soul-withering rigid Fi was enduring, but something taut. Alert. He lifted his head, scenting the air.

'Antal?' Fi asked.

His lips pulled into a snarl. 'There's another daeyari here.'

The air creaked, boots shifting on snow, grips tightening on crossbows.

'A daeyari?' Fi said. 'Who? Where?'

Before Antal could answer, a roar sounded from the village.

Part 4

The daeyari worship no gods that we know of.

Objectively, the beginning of the pact between mortals and daeyari marked a new exchange of knowledge, the end of the old pantheons once worshipped by humankind. Daeyari, with their wider grasp of Planes and the Void between, put stock in no divinities. Why should we?

But, although the daeyari acknowledge no official theology, they do all speak of Veshri, the first immortal. Veshri, the weaver, who created his body out of nothing.

Veshri, who watches from the Void.

— Excerpt from a doctoral thesis, Summer Plane College of History and Antiquities, *On the decline of the Great Beast pantheon on the Season-Locked Planes*

36

No one invited you

Let Fi stay in that dawn-lit training field outside of Nyskya. Let her worst worries be Boden's critique of her love life. Let her be back home in bed, wrapped in arms and furs, the cruel world kept at a safe distance a little longer.

But she recognized the roar that went up from the village. It sank into her chest like a Void-deep chill.

Fi emerged from a teleport with a gasp, Antal's hand clasping hers, boots slipping against snow in disorientation and haste. He'd brought them near the center of town, a pathway between residences. Cold hung sharp in the alley. Frost curling Fi's breath. She and Antal pressed themselves to the closest wall of snow-chaffed timber to watch and listen.

The roar didn't come again. Nyskya lay silent.

Too silent.

Like a forest gone quiet in the wake of a predator.

Antal sniffed the air. Here was another side of him Fi rarely saw: the hunter stalking prey. He dropped to a crouch, all tense muscles and swaying tail as he peered around the corner. At his nod, Fi followed.

She didn't have a daeyari's phantom footfalls, but she'd spent a decade avoiding sight when needed, careful steps to skirt trade warden patrols. They slunk behind the dark windows of the general store, into a yard hectic with ice-crusted scrap barrels and tarped firewood. Fi crouched behind a fence and peered through the slats.

The village 'square' was a generous name for an avenue at the heart of Nyskya, cut a couple of strides wider than other roads in town and kept better shoveled. A staging area for visiting merchants or drunken revelry during the sunless months. Even at this early hour, some residents ought to be trudging the path, off to open shops or check traps. Yet the expanse was empty.

Nearly.

Through the gap in the fence, Fi caught a heart-stopping glimpse of white skin against snow. Black antlers more twisted than wind-wracked pine boughs. A hairless, pantherine body.

Venom pooled in her stomach.

It was here. Verne's Beast was *here*.

The derived daeyari was a nightmare in any setting, yet to see the creature stalking Nyskya's main avenue, to watch its hollow red eyes sweep familiar windows and silent doorsteps, speared panic through Fi's sternum. Not here. Not now, when all their preparations had been going so well.

'Oyzen,' Antal cursed, snarling at the sight of his deformed kin.

The creature didn't come alone.

Astrid led the march, a crossbow propped on her shoulder, slow strides entirely too insolent for someone with an immortal Beast at her back. Yet the creature heeled to her like a trained hound: skeletal head hung low, steps measured to her pace.

'What's this bullshit?' Fi craned her neck, trying to get a better view. 'Both of them? Working together again? How's that fair?'

'An insult,' Antal said. 'Commanding that Beast like a trained animal.'

Fi quirked a brow. 'I thought you hated that thing?'

'An abomination, but it deserves dignity. It was a daeyari once. An immortal child of Veshri, lost to the Void.'

Fi didn't care what it was. She wanted both interlopers out of her home.

Astrid paused in the square, between the general store and Kashvi's tavern. While the Beast loitered at her heels, she surveyed silent streets, hair a black curtain down one side of her face, antlers frost-kissed. A long-sleeved blouse tucked into her trousers, hanging from her willowed frame like sheets of silken blood.

Fi and Antal stayed hidden. Astrid wouldn't find her quarry. She'd have to leave empty-handed, like last time.

'Fionamara,' Astrid called.

Her own name struck Fi like an ice pick through the chest. Of course, a friendly visit was too much to ask, considering the crossbow. And the deranged horse demon.

'I know you're here,' Astrid said. 'It's time to stop hiding.'

How dare she. Fi was a runner, not a hider. Bitch could at least get her insults right.

'She can't *know* we're here,' Fi hissed at Antal. 'Right?'

Fi adored his grimace when her teasing was the cause. She hated it now, the way Antal tipped his head to scent the air again. In the square, the Beast did the same, saliva glistening against curved teeth as it huffed.

'You've got to be kidding . . .' Fi said.

'Fionamara. If I can—'

'Yes, Antlers. I realize that if you can smell it, it can smell you. Thanks.'

The panic in Fi's chest carved deeper, splintering her ribs.

Panic was the enemy. When decisions needed to come swift, panic dug into the brain with hazy fingers. When hands needed to fly to weapons, panic locked the joints and shivered the grip. Fi knew she couldn't give in to those bitter pangs.

But looking at that Beast daeyari. At Astrid and her granite-cut jaw.

'Don't do this, Fi.' Astrid spoke in a warning low. 'No one else needs to get hurt because of you. Not again.'

Fi noticed it then: the village not entirely silent. Across the square, a wide-eyed face spied out a window. From the path behind the general store, Fi heard a tramp of snow, a hushed voice, someone hurrying to the shelter of home.

If Astrid set that Beast loose on Nyskya, no one would be safe.

She wouldn't. Would she? Fi rocked on her heels, anxious energy leaching heat from her arms and pricking her fingertips. 'What do we do?'

Antal had the audacity to sigh. 'They're your people.'

'They're *your* people too, Antal!'

'They . . . they are. I know they are.' His eyes closed, a slump as he rested his antlers against the fence. 'If we fight, people will be harmed. Those who didn't want to fight.'

And those lives would be on Fi's hands. She'd chosen to stay in Nyskya. She'd convinced the people here to fight for Antal.

Astrid shifted in impatience. She set a hand on the Beast's shoulder, stilling its pacing.

'Navek,' she told the creature. 'Vu yzu lavary?'

The words tumbled off Astrid's tongue stiffer than Antal's, but equally breath-stealing. Since when did she speak daeyari?

Of course she spoke daeyari. Such a useful Arbiter, whatever her mistress needed.

'What did she say?' Fi asked.

Antal made a low growl.

'*Antal.*'

'She asked the Beast if it's hungry.'

Fi gaped in horror. Astrid wouldn't do such a thing. *Her* Astrid would never do such a heinous thing. Whatever their quarrel with each other, the people of Nyskya were innocent.

But no matter what move came next, innocent people were in danger. Fi watched their plans breaking apart, weeks of sneaking and plotting and cobbling weapons together. They were supposed to have more time than this. Nyskya wasn't ready.

She sucked in a breath, cold against her teeth. They had to be ready. No other choice.

'I need to go out there,' she said.

'Those two didn't come for a pleasant chat,' Antal warned. 'The moment we show ourselves, there'll be no going back.'

'Not both of us. Just me.'

He snapped her a bone-peeling look. When Fi didn't back down, his lips flashed fangs.

'That isn't funny, Fionamara.'

She sure as the endless Void didn't think so. Panic climbed acrid up her throat. She swallowed it, willing herself to be level as ice. She knew how to negotiate. She knew how to stall a buyer out when the stakes turned dicey.

And she wasn't running anymore.

'We need more time for Boden and Kashvi to warn everyone,' Fi said. They'd split up at the training field, her and Antal to track the Beast, Boden and Kashvi to alert the waking village. 'Astrid knows we're here. And believe me, she's every bit as stubborn as I am. We can't let her get desperate, or who knows what that Beast will do.' She smacked a hand to her chest. 'If I go out there, I might be able to talk her out of the village. At the very least, I can stall her.'

'*Alone?*'

'If Astrid sees you, she'll come out swinging! I'm less of a threat. And I was practically crafted by the Void to distract that woman.'

'Or you could be ripped open by a derived daeyari.'

Antal seized her cheeks in his hands, too quick a motion . . . his eyes too wide. Fear. The same as that moment on the train, that panicked gaze sweeping over her when he'd thought she might be hurt. Fi fought a lump in her throat. A Void-born immortal shouldn't be capable of such terror-hollowed eyes.

Much less for her.

He was afraid. Afraid to send her out alone. That made sense, didn't it? From a logical standpoint: they were partners, their fates hinging on each other's survival. Yet logic didn't fit the fierce crease of his brow. Desperation whispered in the brush of his thumb across her cheek.

Fi placed her hands over his, fingers soft against claws.

'Stop looking at me like that, daeyari.' She forced a grin. 'I'll think you've started caring what happens to me.'

Too long a pause. Too still, his breath. 'Would that be such a terrible thing?'

No. And yes. For all the same reasons.

'You won't let me get hurt,' she said. 'I trust you. If anything goes wrong, you'll be at my side in a blink.'

Antal's tail formed a tense curl. 'I can only move so fast.'

Not faster than a crossbow bolt. Maybe not faster than a Beast's lunge.

'Astrid could have blazed in here full force,' Fi reasoned. 'She didn't. She wants me alive.' Fi hoped that was true with every strain of her shredded heart. 'Stay here. I'll buy us more time.'

Slowly, reluctantly, Antal released her. 'I'll be ready.'

'But, you know,' Fi added in a nervous pitch, 'if it looks like it's going bad, you don't have to wait for the dramatic entrance. I can handle myself. Sure I can. But if it's a choice between my stupid pride or getting my ass eaten, I trust your judgement to—'

Her breath hitched as Antal pulled her into a kiss. The heat of his mouth snared her, an ache in her chest that lulled away panic, if only for an exhale. With a parting brush of fangs against her lip, he rested his forehead to hers.

'And you call yourself a coward?' he said. 'Your teeth are as sharp as any daeyari.'

So he claimed. Time to test it. For the second time that day, Fi pulled away from arms she didn't want to leave.

She backtracked, quiet steps and a circuitous route to not betray Antal's position, boots heavy with a too-familiar weight. Here came the same spike of fear as when she'd marched to Verne's shrine. The same numbing dread as when she'd been dragged to Antal. Once again, she set her path toward a daeyari. This time, hopefully, not as prey.

The square opened ahead. Fi kept her steps even, pulling on her cloak of barbs to keep her spine straight. She drew courage from muffled footsteps beyond the street, Nyskya quietly rousing. She imagined Boden and Kashvi, hurrying through back alleys after they'd parted ways at the training field, warning villagers of the threat on their doorsteps. She imagined Antal, watching from the shadows.

This time, she wouldn't run. This time, she wasn't alone.

Her silviamesh bodysuit would have been nice. She'd passed on armor that morning, not anticipating she'd need it. Snowy boots and a frayed fur coat made for a less intimidating ensemble than she'd have liked.

The Beast noticed her first.

Fi had no sooner stepped beyond the shadow of a building than pupil-less red eyes latched onto her, the swivel of a skeletal maw with too-tight skin and too many teeth, a long and lashing tail. Claws dug into frozen soil. The Beast growled low enough to tremble permafrost.

But it was the snap of Astrid's ruby-cut gaze that shuddered down Fi's spine. She held out a hand, silencing the Beast at her side.

'Well,' Astrid said. 'It's about time.'

'Astrid,' Fi greeted.

'Fi,' came the venom-laced return.

Astrid. A wild creature, Fi's father had called her. Always the first to shoot when the elk hunt came into season. Always the first to dare a kiss with wine-sweet lips. Always the first to laugh as if the Void itself couldn't swallow her swagger.

Always the first to bury her doubts so deep, no one could see them.

Was that girl Fi used to know still there beneath the ice? That friend who'd held her hand when the nights dragged endless, only the stars to keep their secrets? Fi took the largest breath of her life and planted her feet, unflinching beneath two red glares.

'You wanted to see me?' She spread her arms, all smiles and false bravado. 'Here I am.'

Astrid looked her up and down, a twist on her lips, crossbow propped on her shoulder. 'I'm surprised.'

'That you found me?'

'That you're brave enough to show yourself. Well done on finally growing a spine, Fi. Only took you ten years.'

Always a honed blade, the edge cut perfectly to the curve of Fi's heart.

A few houses away, a door slammed. A dog barked, swiftly silenced.

'This doesn't have to happen here,' Fi said. 'You've found me.

Bravo. I'll listen to you gloat all you like – *outside* of Nyskya. Where no one else has to get involved.'

Astrid didn't budge. The Beast paced behind her, claws like sickles sowing snow.

'You're the one who brought us here, Fi. And after my last visit? Verne told me to disregard this place, that you couldn't possibly be stupid enough to stay here.' Astrid smiled too wide, no fangs like her daeyari ancestors, but just as vicious. 'I guess I know you better.'

Fi's hands curled into fists, frost-chilled tips and palms burning with energy. She'd left Astrid behind ten years ago, a coward's betrayal she could never take back.

But Astrid had betrayed her trust in Thomaskweld. Attacked her at Verne's chateau. Brought a Beast here to threaten dozens of innocent lives.

'No,' Fi said. 'I don't think we know each other very well anymore.'

'Harsh.' Astrid laughed once, a puff of mist on the air. 'Where's Antal?'

'Who?'

'*Fi.*'

'Oh. Him.' Bluffing was Fi's only defense, the only way to stop herself from screaming *why why why are you doing this* at Astrid until her throat turned raw. 'Who can say? I'm sure you know how daeyari are. So hard to pin down and—'

The Beast snarled her to silence.

It crouched on all fours, muscles taut, tail swishing the same way Antal's did when he saw something to pounce on. Its eyes weren't as focused, pupil-less irises hazed with hunger and molten energy, yet the way it stared . . .

Fuck. Did it . . . understand her?

'We're not playing this game.' Astrid's words snapped Fi back to focus, snapped her heart back onto a string. 'I know Antal's here. My friend smells him. So you can either tell me where he is, or we can go hunting.'

Fi needed more time. Footsteps crunched snow in a nearby alley. More people. Too close.

'Leave Nyskya alone,' she said. 'Then I'll tell you where Antal is.'

'So you can walk me into his teeth? No, Fi. I think you're better persuaded right here.' Astrid pressed her hand to the Beast's muzzle, silencing it once again.

And readied her crossbow.

'Where's the daeyari?' Cold metal glinted in Astrid's hands.

Only to intimidate. The same show of bravado Fi was putting on.

But Astrid hadn't struck lethal on the train. She wouldn't shoot now.

'You're better than this, Astrid.'

The crossbow settled in her grip, a musical note of clicking gears beneath skilled fingers. 'Why rope these people in with you, Fi?' Astrid's voice rose. 'Why get involved in this at all?'

'Some things are worth standing ground for.'

'But *I wasn't*?'

Ten years of cold snapped between them. Fi pictured Astrid returning from Verne's shrine alone. How still she must have fallen when she found Fi's room empty.

'You could have run,' Fi whispered. Then louder, 'You didn't have to stay, Astrid. You could have run, like me!'

'Someone had to stay behind. To protect our home when you abandoned us!'

Astrid raised the crossbow. Fi in the sights. A flash of maroon sparked her fingertips, an energy bolt Shaped onto the track.

The weapon trembled in Astrid's choking grasp.

She wouldn't shoot. Fi *knew* she wouldn't shoot.

'This isn't about what I did,' Fi said. 'This isn't about our fucking home. How can you use any of that to justify fighting at Verne's side?'

'You're helping a daeyari, too.'

'One who wants to change things! To be better than Verne!'

Astrid gritted her teeth, fingers like claws on the crossbow stock—a flash of fury in her eyes. 'Is that what's he told you? Don't be ridiculous. All daeyari are the same. All daeyari rule the same.' She squared her stance, stock braced to her shoulder.

She wouldn't shoot.

'You're wrong,' Fi shouted back. 'About him. About *me*. I'm not that person anymore, Astrid. I'm not running!'

'Neither am I, Fionamara!'

She wouldn't . . .

Fi flinched at the click.

At the flash of an energy bolt flying across the square.

37

Where's that smug grin, now?

The silver bolt cut through morning air, striking the Beast's shoulder. The creature's howl was ear-splitting.

Astrid spun, her own crossbow unfired, a flush of surprise as she watched the Beast reel, its wound healing in a sizzle of thick hide and black blood. Fi – once she'd recovered her heart out of her own damn throat – traced the bolt's trajectory, searching for the source of the attack.

Shouts filled the streets of Nyskya.

The quiet shattered, empty avenues unleashing a small battalion into the square: bakers' sons and forge daughters dressed in the quickest coats they could grab, armed with crossbows still unfamiliar in their hands. No less determined for it. This was their home.

Fi shook in relief. She'd done her job – bought Boden and Kashvi enough time to warn Nyskya of the intruders.

And more.

She ducked for cover as a volley of bolts loosed from every side of the square, quicksilver projectiles striking daeyari flesh, glancing off antlers, snapping against the ground. Their aim needed improving, deeper shots if they hoped to pierce that hide faster than it could heal. Even so, the sheer number of bolts had the Beast backing away, snarling as red energy sizzled over its skin. Astrid cursed and sought cover in an alley.

'Reload!' Kashvi led her ranks with crossbow ready, dark hair messy after what must have been a mad sprint through the village to raise their army. Her arm trembled as she raised it, voice rasped, but she didn't bend. 'Fire together on my signal. *On my signal*, you useless—'

The Beast lunged at its assailants.

'*Navek!*' Astrid shouted.

The derived daeyari paid her no heed. It bounded across the square, uncaring of energy bolts grazing its skull, latching onto a target. Feren, the gangly baker's assistant Fi had seen wield his first weapons just yesterday, screamed as teeth closed on his arm, a sickening crunch.

Static hit Fi's tongue.

Antal hurled himself at the Beast, sinking crimson-sheathed claws to the knuckles in the creature's throat. It reeled. Released its prey. Black blood drenched the snow, a crack of two warring red currents: one slicing, one defending. Watching those blood-stained teeth snap at Antal's head was harder than it used to be.

'Fi! Catch!'

Kashvi tossed Fi a crossbow. About time. She didn't want to fight here, didn't want to see Feren's face twisted in pain as he dragged himself to cover, but this was *her* home, too. Astrid wouldn't take it from her. Fi Shaped a silver bolt onto the crossbow track, struggling to aim a clear shot of the Beast's skull as it fought to shake Antal off. If she nicked the wrong daeyari, she'd never hear the end of it.

A zip.

A clang.

'Fuck!'

Fi threw her crossbow to the ground as energy seared her

fingers – an enemy bolt strike straight through the barrel. Her own bolt burst on the track, fireworks of silver that left the metal bent beyond use.

She spun on the culprit: Astrid, hunkered in an alley with a smirk.

New plan, then.

Fi screamed and hurled herself at Astrid.

They hit the snow in a writhe of limbs, Fi's fingers clawing the crossbow, Astrid's snared in the rainbow swirls of her hair. In the depths of Fi's memories, they were children tousling on an icy riverbank. Teenagers tangled in hot sheets. Astrid had always emerged the victor, a year older and fierce with slender sinew. Now, Fi held her own. After wrestling a daeyari, even Astrid's worst snarls didn't seem so harrowing.

'Call off your guard dog, Astrid!'

'He isn't listening, if you hadn't noticed!'

Useless. Fi couldn't fathom a bluff so brazen, Astrid parading that Beast around when she couldn't even—

A boot hit Fi's nose.

'Son of a bitch!'

Fi cradled her throbbing face, blood slick through her fingers. Astrid pushed to her feet. Raised her crossbow. With another curse, Fi lunged for cover behind the corner of the general store. An energy bolt snapped the ground where her leg had been.

What sick game was Astrid playing? This would be so much easier if she had the decency to aim for Fi's heart.

The Beast wasn't so discerning. A crack of bone drew Fi's attention back to the square, her breath catching as she watched the derived daeyari hurl Antal across the frozen ground. Antal rolled to a hunch, breaths heavy, black blood everywhere. The Beast lunged for him.

A crimson energy bolt sank into its temple.

Another howl pierced the square. Nyskya's recruits lacked for experience, but Kashvi held her crossbow at a practiced level, a daeyari capsule in hand, dark eyes glinting with focus.

Red energy snapped across the Beast's skull, repairing fractured bone and split flesh. Void be damned, how much would it take to kill the thing?

It lunged for a new target.

'Kashvi!' Fi shouted.

A flick of static. A snarl. The Beast's claws raked empty air as Kashvi vanished.

By the time the second spark hit Fi's tongue she was already running, toward the side of the tavern where she spotted Boden holding down a base of operations – where Kashvi and Antal reappeared in a haggard heap. Kashvi emerged from the teleport gasping, but unscathed.

Antal dropped to his knees, each exhale a string of curses. 'Veshri take my fucking bones, that Beast has teeth like bread knives!'

Fi skidded to his side in the snow, soft hands to keep him upright. 'Are you ok?'

'I'm *excellent*, Fionamara.'

The drip of sarcasm was a relief, though entirely inappropriate for how much black blood soaked his clothes. The wound was horrendous, a serrated slash down his arm, rent flesh and fabric stuck together. Boden pulled away from tending another injured fighter, a wad of gauze in hand, wide eyes as he realized gauze wouldn't do shit for Antal's horrific gash. Fi would have gawked the same, if she hadn't seen daeyari recover from worse. Red energy writhed over the exposed flesh, knitting Antal's skin back together.

Kashvi sat back on her elbows, a stunned look swiveling from the battlefield to their current position. 'You . . . we . . .

teleported?' She scowled at the daeyari. 'You *saved* me?'

Antal laughed through gritted teeth. 'We're on the same side, Kashvi.'

And for that moment, they were – Fi and Antal, Boden and Kashvi, all hunched together in the snow, drawn to common purpose in this reckless bid.

A roar rumbled the square. A snap of crossbows. No time to linger.

Fi looked to Kashvi. 'We need to—'

'Organize our fire. I know. *I know!*' Kashvi pushed to unsteady feet and ran to rejoin her troops, shouting orders to regroup. The Beast moved through their ranks like a sickle, felling another combatant as he tried to flee. A scream turned to rending flesh.

If that creature set after any of Nyskya's unarmed citizens, this would be a massacre.

'We've cleared civilians away from the square,' Boden said.

'Not good enough, Bodie. We need to get everyone out of the village.' Their plan had been to evacuate the residents *before* fighting broke out, not on such a crashed timeline, but they could still catch up.

Fi and Boden looked to Antal. The daeyari returned a sneer.

'Absolutely not,' he snapped.

'What if that Beast moves on the rest of the village?' Fi argued. 'What if Verne decides to show up? We have a plan, Antal, and we need to make it happen. *Now.* The fighters can stay. *You* need to get everyone else out to the safehouse we set up. You're the only one who can.'

'And leave you to fight that Beast on your own? I won't—'

'We're your partners, Antal!' Fi gripped him by the shirt collar. Faces inches apart. 'Trust us. Your people need you.'

She was close enough to hear his teeth clench. Energy raged

in his eyes, rippled hot under his skin. But there was no time
to argue.

'We're having words about this later,' he seethed.

'Bring your worst, daeyari.'

She kissed him hard, a taste of Void on her tongue and a
hammer in her ribs and everything moving in too-fast motion.
Antal sank against her, a drag of teeth against her mouth and
a snarl as he pulled away. Then gone in a blink.

Boden witnessed the display with flushed cheeks. Their entire
world crumbling around them, yet he found time to stammer,
'That's . . . really a fucking thing, then?'

'It's really a fucking thing.' Fi levelled a finger at him. 'And
you should be impressed.'

Antal would teleport Nyskya's civilians out of harm's way, a
hundred people or so, enough to keep him occupied for several
minutes. Kashvi regrouped their volunteer fighters at the edge
of the square, not fierce in number, but holding ground. Boden
squeezed Fi's shoulder then ran to join them, armed with a
medical kit. And Fi—

A mauve energy bolt crossed the square, biting one of Nyskya's fighters in the calf.

Fi sprinted toward where Astrid hid behind cover of a shop
porch.

Chaos worked to her advantage. Fi skirted the main skirmish
of bolts and claws, drawing her sword hilt in one hand, a capsule of daeyari energy in the other. Antal's energy. Where once
she'd balked at the foreign current burning her palm, now the
pulse bloomed familiar at her fingertips, a taste of ozone as she
drew energy to Shape into a crimson blade. Astrid leaned from
her cover, crossbow focused on another target.

She glanced sideways at the last moment, surprise sparking
ruby eyes.

Fi swung at the crossbow, her blade severing the metal track from the stock.

'I told you to get out of Nyskya!' she shouted. 'Out of my home!'

A decade of guilt and rage charged Fi's swing, catching Astrid across the shoulder. Astrid reeled, Shaping a cloak of maroon energy to shield the next strike.

'You *left* your home, Fi.'

'And I made a new one. Better than throwing my lot in with Verne!'

Astrid backed away, boots scraping the pitted wood of the porch, a gleam in her eyes like a cornered wildcat. 'I never threw my lot in,' she hissed. '*You* did it for me.'

You. You. *You.* It was always what Fi did, never the pit Astrid carved afterward. She couldn't bear this anymore, couldn't hold the full weight of their severed friendship on her shoulders alone. 'You could have refused her! You could have chosen anything else!'

'You think Verne would have let *two* of us walk away? She would have—'

The Beast's roar shook Fi's bones. She staggered, blade shifting to defense as she glanced to the larger fight in the square.

And saw the unthinkable. The Beast dropped to the ground, tangled in metal nets the local trappers used for heath boar. As it thrashed, Kashvi called for a volley. Bolts fired into haunches and neck, into the thick hide, the wounds seeping blood as they cracked with frantic red energy. Kashvi ordered her fighters to reload. To aim.

Fi couldn't believe her eyes. It was working. The plan was *working*.

Get fucked, Verne.

Static flickered on her tongue. Again. And again. Antal, in

and out of Nyskya, moving its people to safety before Verne could reap her vengeance. Her Beast was on its knees. Astrid watched the shifting battle with a ghostly pale to her face.

Then, the Beast bolted.

A flail of claws freed it from the nets, sending cords whipping around the square. While the fighters ducked for cover, the wounded Beast ran, black blood staining its wake as it stumbled out of the square, a panicked animal.

Astrid sucked in a sharp breath. Ruby eyes darted over the fleeing abomination, the surge of warriors regrouping. A sharper gaze locked with Fi.

Then, Astrid fled in the opposite direction.

That hypocrite. That conniving, craven snow slug. Fi hesitated, cold and bloodied, torn in two directions as Kashvi mustered her fighters to chase the Beast down the main avenue. As Astrid stumbled away down a side alley.

If the Beast daeyari escaped, it would return to Verne to heal, all their casualties for naught. Losing Astrid would mean the same, a warning to her mistress of what she'd found. Their enemies would return stronger, more prepared to crush Nyskya's makeshift rebellion, probably with a full daeyari at their side.

In the square, Boden pulled up the rear of the fighters, bandaging one last clawed arm before racing after the others.

He spotted Astrid. Then Fi.

She thanked the endless Void that they didn't need words. In an instant, Boden understood everything she did: that Kashvi and her fighters needed his help to take that Beast down, that Fi could handle Astrid. That Fi *had* to be the one who handled Astrid.

'Go!' Boden shouted. 'We'll catch the daeyari, don't let her get away!'

Fi ran.

38

Don't say I've never done you any favors

When Fi and Astrid were young, her father told them not to play along the riverbank. He said the ice was too dangerous.

Astrid insisted that was what made it fun.

If not for her, Fi wouldn't have fallen into the water that day. She wouldn't have died. She wouldn't have returned a Voidwalker, wouldn't have been groomed to become Verne's Arbiter, wouldn't have buckled then fled then hidden for ten years, only to come back with a bomb in a daeyari capital. Pebbles snowballed into avalanches.

But everything came back to Fi and Astrid, always running after each other.

Now, Fi followed a trail of trampled snow out of Nyskya, into the forest.

Did Astrid think she could outrun her? This was Fi's terrain, her boots easy over familiar slopes and snow-hidden ravines, her quarry's tracks haphazard. The chase wouldn't last long.

And once Fi caught up to her? What then?

Fi couldn't say if it was rage or despair pushing her to run so fast. Guilt or anger making her want to scream. Astrid had threatened Fi's life, had brought a monster into Nyskya, enough transgressions piled overtop each other that Fi knew her friend was gone. Knew what she had to do. Astrid brought this end upon herself.

But what if Fi hadn't left her behind? What if she'd swallowed her guilt and apologized all those years ago, not left this wound to rot between them?

Fi pushed on, following Astrid's tracks through the snow.

Until they ended at a Curtain.

The gossamer sheen rippled in the ice-still air, ethereal and taunting and utterly implausible. Astrid couldn't flee through a Curtain. She wasn't a Voidwalker.

Fi spun a circle, cold air burning her lungs, but the track didn't split off. No signs of broken branches or other escape.

Astrid *hadn't* been a Voidwalker. Ten years ago.

Fi's fury erupted as a scream. Ten years stolen from them. Ten years of change, too much to say how much of the woman she once loved remained. She drew her sword and charged into the Curtain, desperate for an end, to put this long-drawn agony behind her at last.

She stepped out onto a Shard.

And onto a slick of ice that nearly sent Fi to her ass. She skidded, catching herself with windmilling arms as a flat expanse of ice-coated lake stretched before her. The Void hung black overhead, starless, a red aurora humming some low register that almost sounded like a sob.

A slice of heat came for Fi's side.

Her sword parried Astrid's at an awkward angle, two red blades screeching against each other. They both pulled back, resetting. Astrid hunched, her shoulder wounded, scarlet light catching the sharp angles of her face and the points of her antlers.

Fi shouted, because it was all she knew how to do when everything hurt like this. 'And you criticize *me* for running away?'

'If we're keeping count, Fi, you're still several points ahead.'

'And since when are you a Voidwalker?'

Something tight coiled Astrid's lips, a knife slant to her brow. 'I do what my daeyari asks of me.'

'Aren't you precious? But to become a Voidwalker, you'd have to . . .'

Quiet. This Shard was too quiet. Astrid, staring at Fi with hollow eyes, was too quiet.

'You'd have to die . . .' Fi said. Too quiet.

Astrid charged with a war cry. Fi met her sword, a spark-strewn parry, a messy grapple as Astrid tried to pin her arm.

'Voidwalkers make more useful Arbiters,' Astrid snarled. 'Shouldn't you know that, Fi? It took a few tries. Not all of us get as lucky as you on the first go.'

Fi hated holding only half the cards. She hated that slipping feeling of catching up to something she should have realized sooner, as lurching as the slip of her boots against the ice. In their grapple, the sleeve of Astrid's shirt pulled back. Aurora light slanted against bare skin, milk-smooth when Fi had held it years ago, now coated in scars.

Slashes. And claws. And teeth.

Teeth. On *her* Astrid. So much rage in her friend's eyes. Fi had found a daeyari who didn't use his claws on her.

Astrid hadn't been so fortunate.

'Why did you stay with Verne?' Fi's words came out more plea than accusation. 'How could you help her do all this?'

'What else was I supposed to do!'

She swung.

'Verne would have hunted me down if I left her!' Astrid shouted.

Another swing, a spark against Fi's sword.

'She'd raze our entire town just to make a point, would spike my family from the gates of the power factory!'

Fi's parry slipped, the blade grazing her hand.

'You have no idea what I've had to do to protect the home you left behind!'

Astrid kept shouting. Kept swinging. 'The people I had to bring to her, Fi. Parents and dissenters and children. Fucking *children*!'

Fi couldn't hold her sword steady. She couldn't focus on anything beyond the rage cracking Astrid's words, the fractures in her heart.

A boot hooked Fi's leg.

She fell, smacking ribs to frozen ground. Then Astrid was on top of her. In a panicked scramble, Fi wrestled the sword from Astrid's hand, a hiss of energy on snow as it tumbled away. Astrid twisted Fi's arm, forcing her to drop her weapon with a shout. Fi dug nails into cloth instead, into the soft skin of Astrid's arms as she held Fi down by the throat.

A spark of maroon. Astrid raised an energy dagger, aimed at Fi's neck.

Then stopped.

They both fell still. Fi: wide eyes on the dagger, scarcely able to breathe past the clamp of Astrid's fingers. Astrid: straddled atop her, halted mid swing. The weapon trembled in her grip.

'You left,' Astrid hissed. 'You left, and I had nowhere to go. No one to help me.'

On the train, Astrid hadn't swung. In Nyskya, she hadn't shot.

'Astrid?' Fi whispered, a plea to a panicked beast.

Astrid's cracks turned to fractures, tears glinting her lashes. A dagger, shaking in her hand. 'It hurt, Fi. It hurt so damn much when you left. It *hurt* when Verne held me under the water.'

A tear spattered Fi's cheek. She didn't flinch, couldn't move as Astrid crumbled atop her. Her friend, used and broken by Verne, like so many others.

'*Why?*' Astrid shouted. 'After all this time. Why? Why can't I . . .' Her dagger fell limp. She slumped with it, tears staining her cheeks. 'Why did you leave me, Fi?'

She was still there. Burning eyes, scar-etched skin, but it was still *Astrid*. Fi reached out one trembling hand, soft on Astrid's arm.

'Astrid . . . please . . .'

Static snapped her tongue.

The impact slammed Astrid's side, knocking her off Fi and into a tumble across the ice. Air flooded into Fi's lungs. She coughed and rolled to her knees.

Her heart stopped at the sight of Antal pinning Astrid to the ground.

Astrid's retaliation came too desperate, sloppy with panic. She swung her dagger at the daeyari's neck. He caught her wrist, fangs bared. She punched, kicked, writhed against the ice, but Antal broke her guard with claws. Not soft, like he'd used on Fi. They sank deep into ribs, into the tender flesh of an arm. As Astrid screamed, his teeth lunged for her throat.

Fi shouted. 'Antal! Stop!'

He stopped.

Merciful Void, he actually stopped.

Astrid's chest heaved beneath him, lips quivering as her blood dripped from his claws. Without releasing his prey, Antal glanced sideways, one crimson eye to where Fi knelt with hand outstretched.

Fi's tongue was too numb to explain. The best she could manage was to shake her head.

Conflict warred across Antal's face, a tight mix of fury and confusion. But at Fi's urging, he obeyed. Astrid whimpered as the daeyari yanked his claws out of her. She rolled away from him, spitting blood and cradling her ribs.

Fi stood. Astrid tracked her approach.

Her laugh was a cruel thing, bitter and defeated and rasping with bloodied teeth. 'Prefer to end this yourself? Fitting.'

Fi stood over her.

Her friend. Her Astrid. On her knees beneath the Void – like they used to be. Like they'd never be again.

'Do it!' Astrid spat past a split lip. 'Or is this not enough?' Her glare followed the daeyari prowling the sidelines, watching the lash of his tail as he settled at Fi's side. 'I took you for better than one of *them*, playing with your food—'

'Do you regret it?' Fi asked softly.

Astrid's gaze snapped to her, brow furrowed.

'Do you regret what you had to do for Verne?' Fi said.

'Do I *regret* it?' Astrid hissed. 'There's not a single day I don't regret it. I didn't want any of this.' Her voice rose, echoing through the silence of the Shard. '*I never wanted any of this!*'

Astrid brought them to this end.

But Fi set them on the path.

Ten years of this. Ten years wishing she'd made a better choice. Even here, at the end, Fi chased poisonous thoughts of whether there'd been a path missed somewhere, a reunion in Thomaskweld where they fell grateful into each other's arms rather than clinging to old wounds.

But this kind of grief didn't heal when ignored. It grew. It festered. Fi would never be free of her guilt until she faced it head on, could never forgive herself until she did what she should have done ten fucking years ago.

Fi dropped to her knees and pulled Astrid into a hug.

'I'm sorry,' she said.

The silence was profound. Antal's tail twitched to a halt as he watched. When Astrid started breathing again, the motion hitched, a shallow rasp against Fi's neck.

'I'm sorry, Astrid.' Fi knotted fingers into her shirt, into her ice-damp hair.

Astrid stiffened. 'What are you doing?'

'I was young. I was so young and so scared, and everything was a blur as I ran, and even when I thought of going back, I couldn't *breathe* by the end of it. That doesn't begin to excuse what I did. You meant the world to me, Astrid. And I abandoned you. I left you to *her*. I know I don't deserve your forgiveness. I've been every bit the coward you've accused me of.'

'Fi. What are you *doing*?' Astrid's words shook.

Fi pulled back. She brushed a thumb to Astrid's lips, raw and chapped, but only fiercer for it. Hers, once. Never again. 'I won't be a coward anymore. I spent all this time wishing I could undo what happened. I see now . . . things can never go back to how they were between us.' She swallowed, a razor lodged in her throat. 'But we can do better than this.'

All those years ago, Fi ran because she was afraid – afraid of Verne, afraid of how Astrid would look at her when she learned what Fi had done. Could facing that fear have circumvented all this?

She could never know. She could only choose what happened next.

Fi stood.

'Go,' she ordered.

Astrid looked up at her with stricken eyes. Tears on her lashes. 'What?'

'Go. Walk away from this, Astrid. You're done fighting.'

Her lips quivered disbelief. And fear. 'But Verne . . .'

'You're done serving Verne!' Fi's shout rang across the ice like a crack of thunder. Then, softer, 'I got to run away last time. Now, it's your turn. Run away, and I'll stay behind to finish this. I'll make sure Verne doesn't hurt anyone else.'

Astrid stood with the resolve of damp paper, bent at the ribs. Bafflement was an uncommon pinch to her face, an unguarded glimpse of the person Fi used to know.

Warier, Astrid looked to Antal, appraising the daeyari's bared fangs and stiff tail with the tension of a snared rabbit.

'Don't look at *him*.' Fi grabbed Astrid's shirt in both fists, forcing their faces together. 'This is between you and me. It always has been. You called me to Thomaskweld. You dragged me into this fight.' Her grip slackened, breaths turned uneven. 'Let's finally be done with this, Astrid.'

Astrid didn't fight. Didn't pull away. Petrified, like granite.

Then, wide eyes and a whispered, 'You can't beat her, Fi.'

'Really? Because you look like shit. We drove that Beast out of Nyskya. Verne's next. Don't be a part of that, Astrid.' Fi released her. Pointed at the Curtain. 'Walk away.'

Astrid hesitated. Again, her glance cut to Antal, confusion growing when the beast didn't lunge, claws restrained by the command of the human at his side.

Antal scowled at Fi, tail an aggravated flick. She returned a glower that ought to make even an immortal tremble.

'Fionamara's offer is generous,' Antal conceded in a warning growl. 'You should take it, Arbiter. Swiftly.'

Astrid's eyes flicked between them, still confused. She swayed back a step. 'Fi—'

'*Go.*' Fi willed everything into the plea. All her hope. All her apology. 'Please, Astrid. Just . . . go.'

Those ruby eyes were made to chisel Fi's heart. She got one last look at them, wide and bright and straining with a thousand words unsaid.

Then, Astrid fled through the Curtain.

Fi counted the time in breaths. In the thrum of her heart against her sternum. In the soft crunch of ice as Antal moved to her side.

She waited long enough for Astrid to disappear.

Merciless Void, Fi hoped this was the right decision.

The aurora hummed overhead, a song for a starless night. In the distance, ice creaked upon the frozen lake. Antal brushed a thumb to Fi's cheek, inspecting dried blood and her swollen nose.

The tight line of his jaw said what he thought of her compassion. He let Astrid go, anyway.

'Thank you,' Fi whispered.

'Why?' There was an edge to his voice. And a slip of uncertainty. An unspoken question of *what in Veshri's mercy did I just watch, and why did we let her go?*

'I was supposed to be Verne's Arbiter,' Fi said. 'She took Astrid instead. She's only part of this because of me, and . . .' A steadying breath. 'Now we're even.'

Antal hummed. He licked his thumb, then gently wiped the crust of blood from her lip.

'If she ever touches you again,' he said, 'I'll carve her spine out, piece by piece.'

'Yeah. I'm sure she realizes that, Antlers.'

Fi gave a small laugh, grateful for the levity. For the comfort of his touch. Never long enough, before reality sank its claws in.

'The fighters in Nyskya,' Fi said. 'They went after the Beast.' She looked to Antal, hopeful he had more news since she'd left.

He shook his head. 'I came for you.'

Of course he did. Tender creature.

They pushed through the Curtain, back onto the Plane. Fi didn't look for Astrid's tracks in the snow, didn't want to know what direction she'd fled.

Antal offered his hand.

They emerged from the teleport in Nyskya's square. A wretched sight: snow stained red and black with blood, ground strewn with broken energy capsules, buildings marred by claws and stray bolts. And quiet. So quiet, with everyone gone.

Then, voices ahead.

Fi ran toward them. The haggard, human-shaped amalgamation of bloody coat and flyaway curls that was Fionamara Kolbeck ran because her heart felt like week-old pudding, her bones were barely strung together, and the sight of Nyskya's fighters returning down the main avenue seemed the only balm to hold her in one piece.

She grinned upon spotting Kashvi – actually *grinned* at that frazzled wolverine limping back with a knife-honed slant to her brow. And Boden . . .

Fi nearly lost her footing on the snow.

Nearly fell. Nearly screamed.

Ran faster instead.

Two fighters carried Boden between them, his arms draped across their shoulders. Head slumped.

Blood drenching his coat.

39

I already forgave you

Boden was fine.

He had to be fine.

Fi slipped underneath her brother's arm to take his weight, relieving the woman who'd carried him here with a limp of her own. Around her, people were speaking, a hum of worried voices. She hardly heard them.

There was so much blood soaking Boden's coat. His breaths were too shallow.

'Bodie?' she urged. 'Bodie, look at me.'

He muttered something, head slumped. The blood was heaviest at his stomach, but she couldn't get a clear look at the wound. Too much shredded fabric.

'—tracked the Beast out of town.' Kashvi's voice came hoarse. 'Then, gone. Must have fled through a Curtain.' She leaned heavily on Mal's arm, her own hands stiff with a glint of silver veins, barely gripping her crossbow.

'You let it get away?' Fi demanded.

'It fought like a cornered animal. We tried to box it in, but . . .' Kashvi licked chapped lips. She nodded to Yvette. The blacksmith supported Boden's other side, their silver hair dyed with two colors of blood, a deep cut down one cheek. 'Yvette took a fall, trying to get one of their smiths to safety. Boden ran in to help. That's when he got swiped.'

'Stupid, selfless man . . .' Yvette muttered, eyes bright with concern.

Fuck if that wasn't something Boden would do. Why hadn't Fi been there? Too busy chasing Astrid. Even when she tried to do the right thing, it still went wrong.

'Fionamara.'

Antal spoke quietly, tense eyes surveying their surroundings. 'We shouldn't linger. That Beast must be too degraded to remember how to teleport, but if it's coherent enough to use Curtains, it will find its way back to Verne.'

Fi didn't care about Verne. Boden needed help.

Void have mercy, there was so much blood.

Against Yvette's protests, Kashvi took Boden's other arm, ordering the smith to tend to the gash on their cheek. Then, Antal clasped their hands and took them away from Nyskya.

They'd known it would come to this, that if Verne discovered Nyskya's rebellion, the people would need a place to hide until the tyrant fell.

Fi and Boden's father had brought them to this mining outpost in Verne Territory when they were young, back when it was a bustle of metallurgy shops and energy drills carving conductive ore out of the mountain. Then the veins ran dry. The residents couldn't afford the daeyari sacrifice needed to keep the energy conduits running. The place was abandoned, buildings left to crumble in the craggy valley.

Vacant no longer. The residents of Nyskya huddled in the outpost yard, distributing the supplies Boden had toiled to prepare over the past weeks, hiding right under Verne's nose. Hopefully, her own territory was the last place she'd look for them.

At Antal's return, heads swiveled in the crowd.

A gasp went out, at the sight of their mayor in tatters.

'We need to lay him down.' Fi's words came breathless with barely-tamed panic. No need for that. Boden would be *fine*.

He coughed, a wet and crackling sound in his chest.

'Daeyari!' Kashvi said. 'Go back and get the rest of our people out of Nyskya.'

Antal spared too long a look at Boden before vanishing.

Fi and Kashvi brought him into a private room in the mining barracks. He cursed as they set him down on the bed. So much blood. The copper tang filled Fi's nose, mixed with a stink of bile. Pieces not where they belonged.

'Where's our doctor?' Fi touched an energy lantern on the bedside table, lighting narrow walls and dusty floorboards in cold silver.

'Overwhelmed.' Kashvi ran a hand through her bloodied hair. 'She's used to stitching gashes from stray hunting knives, not daeyari claws. That's why Boden was helping with triage.'

'We need her here.'

'No,' Boden mumbled. Another cough. Another distressing gurgle in his chest . . . blood on his lips. 'Let her tend to the others. They need her.'

Fi refrained from punching him. '*You* need her, Boden!'

Ignoring his protests, she unbuttoned his coat, pulling back matted fur to reveal . . .

Void alive. Her breath caught at the sight of flayed flesh. A mess of blood and dark body fluids. Exposed muscle and viscera, his entire abdomen shredded, the smell of it enough to close Fi's throat.

She couldn't stop to think about it. He'd be fine.

'Kashvi.' Damn it all, why was Fi's voice shaking? 'We need water. Towels. Anything to start cleaning this.'

'Fi-Fi,' Boden said.

'*Don't* call me that.'

'It's ok.'

'Stop it.'

'You don't have to do this.'

'Shut your Void-damned mouth, Boden!' Her fist clenched, hovering over his ruined stomach. Uncertain where to start. 'Just give me a minute to . . .' She didn't know what to do. Fi had *no idea* what to do. 'Shit. *Shit.* You've lost so much blood . . .'

'I know.'

Two words. Flat. Final.

Why did he have to talk like that? Like he'd always figured things out one step ahead of her. Anger tightened Fi's chest. Energy Shaping could cauterize the bleeding edges. It could pull flayed skin together. It could quicken natural healing.

Shaping couldn't regenerate tissue.

It couldn't replenish blood.

So much blood.

And that crackle in Boden's chest with each inhale. Something in his lungs.

He reached for her hand with cold fingers. 'It's ok, Fi.'

It wasn't. 'Stop talking like that Boden.'

'Sit down. Sit with me. Please.'

'*No.* I'll fix this.'

'You can't heal this, Fi. You know that.' Boden's head tilted on the pillow, heavy eyes looking over her shoulder. 'Unless the daeyari has a trick.'

Fi turned.

Antal stood in the doorway, motionless enough to be part of the frame, pale skin starkly ashen in the cruel slant of the energy lantern. He stared at Boden's stomach with hard eyes. A subtle flare of nostrils.

Could he smell a lethal wound that easy? Or did all the blood give it away?

'Daeyari flesh is made of Void ether,' Antal said quietly. 'We can regenerate. Mortal bodies . . . don't work the same way. Your flesh can't be rebuilt so simply.'

Boden nodded, as if this was to be expected. As if any of it was reasonable.

The crumbling started slowly. Cold in Fi's fingertips. Flame fracturing her chest.

'Kashvi?' Boden said.

Kashvi approached the bed, mouth clamped, eyes glassy.

Fi's ribs were too tight. Collapsing. Suffocating.

'How is everyone?' Boden asked.

'Antal got them all out,' Kashvi answered. 'Five fighters dead. Most of the rest wounded.'

'Go. Take care of them. Please.'

Kashvi was silent for a long moment. She placed a hand on his shoulder, a firm squeeze and a deep bow, touching her forehead to his. Floorboards creaked as she left the room, closing the door behind her.

Fi didn't remember how to breathe. How to push words past numb lips.

'Fi.' Her name was too hushed on Boden's lips. 'What happened with Astrid?'

She opened her mouth a few times before sound came out. 'Astrid?'

'You went after her?'

A lifetime ago. A matter of moments.

'I . . . let her go,' Fi said.

Boden's brow creased.

'I let her go, Boden. She did so many bad things. I know she did. To us, to other people. But Verne hurt her so much. Hurt her and used her, but even after all that, she was still Astrid. She deserves a second chance and . . .'

From too few words to too many. Fi gasped for air, but nothing was enough. Every breath, drenched with blood. Antal moved to her side like a phantom, tail curling around her leg.

Even that, not enough.

'You let her go.' Boden cracked a grin, bloody at the edges. 'I'm . . . proud of you, Fi.' Each pause, tainted by a wheeze. 'That must have been . . . so hard . . .'

No. No no no no no no no—

'Boden. Please. I'll get the doctor. We can *try*.' Fi had never begged like this: hands clenched against the bed, knees to floorboards, words quivering like pine needles in a gale.

Boden lifted a hand, smoothing his thumb over the crease of her brow.

'You always do this . . . when you get worried. When you're trying not to cry. Always so strong, Fi. Stronger than you think you are.'

Fi couldn't make her tongue work. Sandpaper in her mouth. Cotton swelling her eyes.

'And Antal.' Boden swallowed. 'I . . . give you permission.'

Her heart stuttered, a flare of indignant fury to cling to in the maelstrom.

'Are you *still* on about us sleeping together?' Fi snapped. 'My intimate life is none of your business, Boden!'

'Fi.' Her name again. Too soft.

'And even if it *was* your business, we've got more important things to worry about!'

'Fi. Not that type of permission.'

She didn't want to understand why her ears were ringing. Why her heart was thundering in her chest. Desperate for help, she looked up to Antal.

He fell still again. Wide-eyed again. Claws clenched and unclenched at his sides.

'Boden,' he said. 'I could never . . .'

'You're going to face Verne,' Boden said. 'Soon, most likely. You need to be at full strength.'

'Don't be ridiculous,' Fi said. 'You're being *ridiculous*, Boden.'

'This is the plan we agreed to!' Boden's raised voice shook through him. A wheeze in his chest, a bloom of blood on his lips. He hunched, silent a moment. Then, in breathy words, 'Feeding a daeyari without living sacrifices. That was the plan. Make it count.'

His words didn't make any sense. They rattled in Fi's teeth, curled barbs in her lungs. He couldn't be saying this.

Boden couldn't . . .

Antal knelt beside the bed.

What an odd sight. A few hours ago, Fi would have laughed to picture a Lord Daeyari knelt on drab floorboards, elbows propped on scratchy sheets, hunched over a human's bedside.

A dying man.

Her brother.

The finality in Antal's eyes struck her to ruin.

'Mayor Boden Kolbeck,' Antal said. 'You've taken excellent care of Nyskya. For that, you have my thanks.'

Boden grimaced. 'I want more than thanks, daeyari.'

'And you have my word. I'll see this through and see your people safe. As Veshri watches from the Void.' He touched the highest tip of an antler.

Boden's breaths grew shallower, more crackle than air. 'She's my only family, Antal. Take care of her. Please.'

'Boden, stop it.' Panic, now. Sharp edges to Fi's words. Tears stung her eyes, but she couldn't cry. She *never* cried. Not anymore. 'You can't talk like this. Nyskya needs you. *I* need you.'

'It's ok, Fi-Fi. I've done as much as I could. Just a . . . rotten stroke of luck. We always knew this was a chance, didn't we? But you'll take care of the rest.'

'You don't know that, Boden. What have I *ever* done right?' Fi was so cold. So hot. Like her shivers could rip her in two.

'You let Astrid go,' Boden said. 'Finally made amends.'

'I haven't made amends with *you*!'

'What—'

'I'm sorry, Boden. I'm sorry I ran away.' She'd planned this so differently, a bottle of whiskey between them, a warm hearth, a grin on his lips. 'I'm sorry I left you to take care of dad. Sorry I wasn't there when he died. Sorry I didn't come to the funeral, didn't help you build the pyre.' Merciless Void, there was so much. 'I'm sorry I made you go through all that alone, made you track me down and—'

'Fi.' Boden's hand fell upon hers. 'I already forgave you.'

He was lying. He was trying to comfort her. 'You didn't.'

His brow creased. 'Why not?'

'We never talked about it. You never wanted to talk about it!'

'Oh, Fi . . .' Barely a whisper now. 'I didn't know *how* to talk about it. When I found you seven years ago, you were so lost. My little sister, so hurt and afraid. I never wanted to force you back to that place. I thought if we just moved forward, put the past behind us . . . but I should have said all that.' He squeezed her hand. 'Fi. I forgive you. I forgave you years ago.'

'How?' Fi was shaking. She gripped his hand, so cold, so weak. '*I* brought this to Nyskya. I brought a daeyari to your doorstep. I thought we could fight Verne's Beast . . . now look at you!'

At the end, it was Boden's smile that stopped Fi breathing. That familiar way it spread across his face, crinkling lines around his eyes.

'And what about everything else?' he said. 'You stayed in Nyskya, helped me build it into a home we could be proud of, even when you were still hurting. You stayed to fight Verne with us, even when you were afraid. We're different people now, Fi. You're a different person. And I'm so proud of the person you've become. I forgave you. All that's left is for you to forgive yourself. Fuck . . . I'm so proud of you, Fi . . . Please. Make this count.'

He tried to move his hand again, to brush the tears that finally slipped down her cheeks.

His fingers fell still against hers.

All of him fell still.

The whole room, still.

The entire Plane.

Still.

Fi knelt at his side for a moment, a lifetime, until Antal wrapped an arm around her. She shrugged him off.

Then stood.

She backed away from the bed.

She walked out the door.

She stepped into the cold.

Inquiring eyes fell upon her.

She ignored them.

Tears streamed down her cheeks. She couldn't make them stop.

She crossed the yard.

She walked faster. Something boiling in her chest.

Into the forest with shaking hands.

Shaking teeth.

Shaking heart.

She walked faster.

She found a Curtain.

She pushed herself through.

She was cold.

She was alone.

She screamed.

Fi opened her lungs and screamed, not another soul to hear her on that barren Shard, a scream across flat ice and into the depths of the Void, every echo swallowed by uncaring eternity. She screamed until the sound cracked and the cold air cut her throat, until all the emptiness surrounding her filled with her anguish.

And that wasn't enough.

So Fi ran. Like she always did.

She pushed through another Curtain, onto the rock-cracked plain of another Shard. She screamed long enough to splinter stone, until the crunch of gravel beneath her boots grated like gnashing teeth. It wasn't enough.

Seven years, and she'd never told Boden she was sorry.

Another Shard. Petrified trees stretched stony limbs to the Void sky, barren of leaves. She screamed until her voice echoed through each twisting bough, was carved forever onto the white of the trunks. It wasn't enough.

Seven years of holding back, too terrified to tell him what he meant to her.

Another Shard. A lake like glass beneath a red aurora, a hum on the breeze like a funeral prayer. She screamed until ripples quaked the water's surface, clawed stones from the beach and hurled them to shatter everything around her. It wasn't enough.

This was how she'd always fled. Into nothingness, into the maze of dark mirror worlds beyond her cruel reality. Why was none of it enough this time?

He said he forgave her. How could Boden say he *forgave* her?

She screamed her way through another Shard.

Another.

Another.

As if the entirety of the Void wasn't enough to hold all the lament in her ribs.

Gone. Gone.

She'd waited too long, now Boden was gone.

She couldn't say what subconscious map led her to where the Shards became familiar. What desperate need pushed her through that final Curtain.

She emerged at the outskirts of Nyskya. Her home, in tatters.

Lavender morning lay upon the roofs. Blood and snow in the streets. Fi ran, tired legs trembling, searching for any movement, any sign of the Beast that had stolen her brother, so she could scream her fury into its soulless red eyes.

To no avail. The village was empty, silent and snow muffled.

They'd fought. They'd rallied. They'd been so close to victory. Fi should have been there. She should have been there with Boden, instead of running after . . .

Fi stumbled to the edge of the forest, to boot prints disappearing into the trees.

'Astrid!' she yelled to snow-laced boughs.

Nothing.

'Astrid! Come back!'

Maybe she wanted to lay the blame on Astrid's shoulders for bringing the Beast here. Maybe she wanted someone to tell her how to fix this. Maybe she just wanted to fall into the arms of someone, the only one who still remembered Boden the way Fi did, that bright-cheeked boy huddled over hot cocoa and counting stars wreathed in aurora.

It didn't matter the reason. No one replied.

Fi dropped to her knees in the snow, sobbing until she couldn't breathe.

Astrid was gone. Boden was gone. Their mother, fled in the night. Their father, burned on his funeral pyre. And Fi alone in the ashes of all they'd built. Her alone to move forward. How was she supposed to do that when she couldn't imagine standing? Couldn't fathom the strength to do anything but curl into the snow?

Static pricked her tongue.

Fi wiped a hand under her nose, slick with snot. She'd expected Antal to track her down before now. Trying to give her space? Fi didn't want him here. She didn't want him to see her on her knees with tear-soaked eyes, this shattered husk of a human who couldn't even save her only brother.

Antal didn't come closer. Didn't speak. Cagey bastard.

Fi stood with aching bones and aching heart. She wiped her face again, hoping to appear some sliver of presentable, knowing it was no use when her hand came back slathered with mucous and mascara. She turned with a scowl.

And found Verne staring back at her.

40

How do you like these teeth?

Antal had warned her that Nyskya wasn't safe.

It wasn't that Fi ignored him. The information had ceased existing, her mind too consumed by a grief she didn't know how to contain. Boden – her sweet, stubborn Boden – sacrificing himself to defend their village from a Beast.

Now, here was that Beast's master, come to inspect the aftermath.

Verne stood not ten strides from Fi. This daeyari was slimmer than Antal, not shorter in stature but sleeker in limb, an angular frame with ash gray calves bare to the snow. Gone were the silver ornaments that had tipped her antlers. Gone was the showy attire, her dress traded for leggings and a high-collared tunic, fabric glittering with iridescent inlays. Her raven hair was braided between her antlers, the loose sides swept from her face with silver pins.

She *felt* older than Antal, her added centuries shown not in wrinkled features, but something more lethal in her taut posture, those bright scarlet eyes. That same predatory sway to her tail, though. Fi's thoughts took up a new chorus, sorrow-labored breaths traded for a shaking exhale.

Run. Don't let her have you. Not after all this time.

'What are you doing out here, little one?' The question

479

rolled off Verne's black tongue like spoiled sugar. 'And all alone?'

Run run run run run.

Fi's legs shook. Her lifelong nightmare stood in front of her, alone with the blood-soaked streets of her abandoned home. Running would be easy. The rabbit's survival instinct.

Never run from a daeyari. Fi knew better.

At Fi's silence, Verne cocked her head, that animal-like tilt that captivated her in Antal. Blood-curdling now.

'Perhaps you can tell me what happened here?' Verne said. 'Where everyone's gone?' A carving edge slipped onto her tongue. 'Why my *pet* returned to me in tatters?'

Fi catalogued her weapons. The hilt of her sword in one coat pocket. A daeyari energy capsule in the other. Meager tools, and even if she'd been better outfitted, she'd balk at fighting a daeyari alone. This confrontation was supposed to come with allies at her back.

All their preparations, shattered in a single day.

'And my Arbiter?' Verne said. Flat as ice. 'What's become of her?'

The panic never left Fi, that instinct chiseled into her bones by a hundred generations of mortal ancestors carved beneath these creatures.

But fuck if she wasn't also angry. And grieving. And acutely aware that, despite ten years haggling with the seediest sons of bitches across the Season-Locked Planes, her fiercest negotiation tactics weren't going to cut it for Verne.

Verne. This monster who'd hollowed Astrid into a husk of her former self.

This tyrant whose conquest had stolen Fi's brother from her.

Verne stepped toward her. If Antal had taught Fi anything about these beasts, it was to hold her ground. She did so, even when the daeyari grinned, all blushed lips and sharp teeth.

Verne vanished, the teleport snapping Fi's tongue with telltale static. Petty trick. Fi tasted it against her teeth, tensing for the follow up.

Another prick.

Fi dove clear, hitting the ground at a roll, snow and rocks biting her shoulder. Verne lunged over her, black claws raking empty air. Fi palmed her daeyari energy capsule and Shaped the strongest current she dared, crimson burning her palm as she shoved a concussive blast.

Verne reeled backward, a scarlet shield snapping at her fingertips.

The daeyari emerged with no visible injuries, just a growl and flashed fangs. This monster Fi had always feared. This nightmare she'd let steer her life for decades. She gripped her sword hilt but didn't draw. Patience came harder when facing down a man-eater.

Another pulse of static hit her mouth as Verne vanished. There was always a pause. The briefest gap, enough time for Fi to draw her sword and Shape a current into the blade.

She swung as Verne reappeared.

Surprise flashed through the daeyari's eyes. Then, a dig of blade against flesh. Verne snarled and flinched away, clutching her arm, black blood dripping from shoulder to elbow.

The bitch wasn't untouchable. A strained laugh pushed through Fi's thudding heart, her haggard breaths.

After all Verne had taken from her? Fi would cleave her fucking head from her shoulders.

The wound healed quickly, gray flesh sewn back together by scarlet stitches. Fi would *have* to take Verne's head off, or none of this would matter.

The daeyari glowered at the blood on her hand. She lunged straight this time. No prickle of static. Just claws aimed at Fi's throat. Fi lifted her sword to parry.

Energy-coated claws sliced *through* the blade. Some fresh bullshit. The current sputtered. Fi clutched the hilt, fighting to Shape the weapon back to a stable state.

Belatedly, it occurred to Fi – she'd practiced fighting a daeyari who was, by his own admission, abysmal at Shaping. Verne was a better Shaper than Antal. More patient than Tyvo. No reason to panic. Fi just had to focus, plant her boots, and—

Verne clutched her hand into a fist. Fi felt the impact as if Verne had grabbed the sword itself, watched in horror as the blade flickered.

Then snapped out entirely.

She had time for half a curse.

When Verne lunged, Fi pushed another pulse of energy at her, anything to slow the daeyari down. Verne splayed her fingers against the blast, scarlet energy Shaped like sickles at her claw tips, slicing through Fi's attack with a *crack*. She struck Fi's chest hard enough to knock the breath from her lungs, the sword from her hand.

So Fi could stand her ground better against a daeyari.

Still not strong enough to defeat one alone.

Her back hit the rough trunk of a pine tree. Verne pinned her with claws around her arms, not gentle like Antal, the points only missing flesh thanks to the thickness of Fi's coat. Fi kicked. Twisted. Tried to break free.

A hand on her throat stilled her, claws digging against arteries hard enough to draw a warning trickle of blood.

A rabbit again. Fi loathed the feeling.

Verne cast her beneath appraising eyes, a hint of fangs through parted lips, tail flicking too quick for comfort. Fi steeled her nerves. She'd learned how to face daeyari these past weeks.

Except this daeyari looked at her in a way Antal never had. Like a helpless thing in her hands. Like a hare waiting to be skinned.

'You're Antal's pet.' Verne's accusation wasn't biting, but all the more stinging because of its flatness.

If anyone was going to call Fi a pet, it would be if she damn well asked for it. She bit her lip, a taste of copper on her tongue, a sting of claws at her neck.

'My derived daeyari returned alone,' Verne said. Less flat. A serrated edge of annoyance. 'So what have you done with my Arbiter? Where's Astrid?'

The name was vile on Verne's tongue, spoken with all the empathy one would show a misplaced tool. A sliver of relief, though, knowing Astrid hadn't gone crawling back to her mistress. Fi hoped she was a hundred Shards away by now.

'Dealt with,' Fi said. 'She was stupid enough to fight me on my home terrain? She got what was coming to her.'

She'd spin any lie, weave any spite into her words if it meant keeping Astrid safe from this beast.

Verne's lips thinned, only ire in her expression, not a fleck of grief.

'Astrid told me *you* were meant to be my Arbiter, rather than her.' Verne's claw dragged Fi's throat, catching at skin. 'Maybe you should have been, if you bested her. What a waste.'

Not in a lifetime. Not if Verne offered Fi all the riches on the Winter Plane. She held her tongue, shaking at the thought of Verne's teeth on Astrid. The scars she'd left on both of them.

Anger was a hindrance. Fi had to think, had to get these claws off her neck. She shouldn't have come back here alone, stood a piss-poor chance of fighting Verne without help. Fi had to run. If she could reach a Curtain, she might get out of this alive.

But Fi knew Nyskya like the back of her hand. There were no Curtains close enough.

Verne leaned close, a smell like ice and burnt timber. 'You're little use to me on your own, human. Where's Antal?'

'Kicking him out wasn't good enough for you?' All this time, and bristles were still Fi's weapons. A shield when fear threatened to buckle her.

'I'd be delighted to never see him again.' Verne's claws pressed sharper. 'And yet, Tyvo tells me you and Antal paid him a visit. Astrid reports you've been gathering metal. Too stubborn to walk away. But if Antal insists on being a poor loser, I'll deal with him more permanently. Where is he?'

Fi spat in her face.

A solid hit to the cheek. Excellent consistency, plenty of mucous from sobbing her eyes out, mixed with blood from a split lip. Verne, disappointingly, didn't flinch. She wiped her cheek clean with slender fingers, eyes a flare of scarlet beneath dark lashes. Not even a panther with a rabbit. A lioness with a flea itching her hide.

'So simple, your kind. Simple insults. Simple fears. Do I need to give you more to be afraid of, little pet?' Her claw traced Fi's cheek. 'Or will you cooperate?'

Verne could go fuck herself. Preferably, with something sharp and uncomfortable.

'I don't know where Antal is.'

'You lie. You fight with his energy. I can smell him on you.' Verne's eyes narrowed. 'In fact . . .'

Fi went taut as Verne sniffed her jaw. Her hair.

'I smell him . . . *all over you.*'

Verne cackled. There was cruelty in her mirth, the sound like teeth with grated edges. She tugged Fi's collar, revealing the evidence of fangs taken willingly to flesh. 'By Veshri's sharpened antlers. That heartsick idiot never learns his lesson, does he?'

No. Absolutely not. Fi already raged to think what Verne had done to her. To Astrid. To Boden. Hearing her speak of Antal with similar disparagement was a jolt of fury down Fi's spine. He wasn't weak like Verne thought he was. He wasn't a failure.

But of course Verne would see him that way, so intent on using everyone around her.

Fi would see this daeyari carved into pieces.

She had to escape. Live to fight with better odds. If there was no Curtain nearby, she'd have to cut a new one. Fi would cut her way through a dozen Shards if that was what it took.

For that to work, she needed a Shard close enough to cut into. Stepping into the Void would be just as swift a death. Fi tried to soften her gaze, searching for the phantom outlines of a Shard nearby, but she couldn't see anything beyond the Winter Plane.

'Tell me where Antal is. We can do this the easy way . . .'

Verne brushed a thumb across Fi's temple.

Panic tightened Fi's throat, the memory of that mind-spinning magic daeyari could wield. Her palms went clammy at the thought of words not her own, of treachery drawn from her lips, selling out Antal and all the people of Nyskya.

'Though . . .' Verne grinned, a wicked show of fangs. 'I prefer the fun way.'

Fi writhed as Verne ripped her coat off her shoulder. Claws sliced her sweater, exposing bare skin.

The daeyari sank her teeth into flesh.

Fi screamed.

Pain exploded through her shoulder, fangs slicing deep into skin and muscle. Then, the tearing. Fi shrieked anew, a flare of white-hot agony spiking her vision as Verne's teeth clamped then twisted then *tore*, ripping a mouthful of meat.

The rabbit flailed. Fi kicked and clawed, desperate to push Verne off her. Heat welled in her arms, her torso, energy leaching from muscles and into a current at her fingers. She had no thought for a specific weapon. Just a blast of energy. A frantic bid to force this monster away.

At the strike, Verne released her.

The daeyari didn't stagger. Didn't snarl. As Fi dropped to the snow, blood hot on her neck and pain nearly blinding. Verne stood over her with a grin. Her long black tongue traced her lips, licking blood and gore with stomach-churning relish.

'What's wrong, little one?' Verne cooed. 'You don't enjoy daeyari teeth as much as you thought you did?'

This was a game to her.

Verne would eat Fi alive and savor every second, this monster everything she'd feared a daeyari would be – cruel, conceited, immovable. Everything Antal wasn't.

'He's better than you,' Fi forced out in a quivering hiss. 'The people of this territory deserve *better* than you.'

Verne laughed again. 'Is that the nonsense he's promised? That he'll be kinder? Gentler? I suppose you think yourself the hero. Fighting for the justice of your species.'

The daeyari stepped toward her. Fi pushed herself away, dragging knees through the snow. Again, she searched for a Shard to cut into.

'Naïve little thing,' Verne spat. 'The pact is a kindness to you. Would you rather go back to the days when daeyari hunted you through the trees? When you were little more than wild packs shouting at the dark?'

Fi saw nothing beyond the Plane. Even if there was a Shard

nearby, her heart was beating too franticly to see clearly, the pain in her shoulder too hot.

'We've been more than generous.' Verne kept advancing. 'You should be grateful for any compromise. For the gifts we've given you. For being spared our teeth.'

Fi had to take a chance. Certain death with Verne, versus a possibility of escape.

'Tell me where Antal is!' Verne loomed over her, blood painting her mouth, no mercy in her Void-and-scarlet eyes. 'Or I'll show you what your insides look like—'

Fi drew a current into her fingertips and slashed the air.

Verne's eyes widened as the gossamer of a new Curtain rippled behind Fi's hand.

She could do this. There would be a Shard on the other side. Fi would hit the ground running, find another Curtain or keep cutting, flee until the daeyari lost her trail.

She'd made her life as a Voidwalker, stepping fearless into the unknown.

It wouldn't fail her now.

Fi swallowed her terror and pushed through the Curtain.

Straight into black.

Everywhere, black.

Black, and the *thud thud thud* of Fi's heart.

Fuck.

41

Just a girl, no horse, and the endless Void

Fi saw no stars. No sky.

No rocky Shard landscape, nor sigh of shiverpines. An odd light fell upon her, dim like moonlight but without a source, barely enough to see her own outline. She flexed her fingers, relieved to find them intact. Beyond her body she saw nothing but black. And she was . . .

Floating.

Fi floated on weightless limbs, hair drifting around her face and nothing solid beneath her boots, as if she'd plunged into a dark ocean.

A cold dread curled through her marrow. She'd made her life as a Voidwalker, traversing Shards and Bridges like a second home beyond her Plane, always with the black of the Void looming overhead. She'd walked the edges of solid ground, had stood on the lip of reality and gazed into the nothingness beyond.

But what had Antal told her once? She wasn't a *real* Void-walker, if she couldn't traverse the Void itself?

There was no Shard waiting on the other side of the Curtain she'd cut.

In her desperation to escape, she'd stepped off the Winter Plane and into the abyss.

Fi gulped a breath, but found no air. She flailed, that taste of

Void emptiness sharp on her tongue. Was suffocating to death any better than being eaten alive by Verne?

Yet lightheadedness never came. No fire in her fighting lungs. Fi couldn't breathe, but . . . for the moment, she didn't seem to need air. Her entire body hung in stasis. Compressed. Cold and creaking at the joints. She'd never heard anyone describe how the Void *felt*.

She'd never heard of any human surviving a fall into it.

The plus side: no Verne. Either the daeyari couldn't follow here, or wasn't stupid enough to try. Antal had spoken like even immortals were hesitant to step fully into the Void, after escaping it millennia ago. Fi craned her neck to view the hideous bite on her shoulder. The throbbing had stopped, as if that, too, was frozen in time. Her heart thudded slower with each beat. That might not be a good sign. One life-threatening danger traded for another.

No need to panic. Just relax. Breathe – metaphorically.

Shards peppered the Void. Fi only had to find one and drag herself out.

How was she supposed to find *anything*, within an endless liminal space?

Ignoring that metaphysical headache for a moment, she tried to move, as a starting point. She floated, but unlike water, there was no mass to paddle against, no ground to push off. Fi thrashed in place, but couldn't tell if she was moving in any direction.

How had the daeyari done it? Pulled themselves out of the Void? Probably easier for them, made of energy and whatever Void pudding they'd built their bodies of. Fi's human flesh weighed like stones thrown into a lake, dragging slowly down, down . . .

The compression on her skin grew heavier. Her breathless lungs ached. A creeping instinct told Fi: she couldn't stay like this forever.

She opened her mouth to shout for help. No sound emerged. Of course, she'd need air to scream.

Who would even hear her?

With another flurry of arms and legs, Fi tried to move, to run, to push, to swim. Nothing. The longer she struggled, the tighter the swell in her throat. The cold seeping into her skin was something more than temperature, a haze at the edge of her thoughts.

Fi couldn't die like this.

One brash mistake. She was supposed to be better than this now.

The Void had touched her as a child and sent her back, a spark of cold on her skin even when she walked the Plane. She begged the blackness to do so again, to let her move. To let her free. Back to frozen riverbanks and starry skies. Back to people who needed her.

Back to make Boden's sacrifice mean something. If his energy lingered in the Void, Fi imagined him shouting at her, chastisement for being so reckless. For trying to run away again.

She shouted back.

No sound, just a scream in her head: *Please! I don't want to die like this!*

Cold raked down Fi's spine. She kept shouting out of stubbornness, just to keep from giving in to the surrounding black, even if there was no one who could hear.

I get it, this was a stupid idea! This place is stupid! I'm stupid! Just let me go back to being stupid in a place with air, and I'll never cut a Curtain without looking again—

Static pricked the back of Fi's tongue.

Baffled, she smacked her lips. It tasted like a daeyari teleport – but that was ridiculous. Desperation making her imagine things. No one could possibly be here with her . . .

493

... Right?

With a sluggish torque of her torso, she looked behind her.

Red eyes stared back.

Fi screamed with a gusto that would have been embarrassing, had it made any sound. Her gaping mouth was little more flattering. She lashed her arms, fighting to pull away. To no success. Faced with futile struggle, she had no choice but to fall still and confront the apparition in front of her.

It wasn't Verne.

It wasn't Antal.

There in the endless black of the Void, Fi faced a daeyari she'd never seen before. And she'd remember a face like *this*. Sharp-cut, cool gray skin over high cheekbones, eyes carved with age uncanny for an immortal. His irises glowed like backlit carnelian. His antlers, tall and curved and wreathed in ten sharp points each side, enough to make Antal seem a young buck, a crown of black lacquer and carvings too dense for Fi to parse, dark hair a wide plait between the antler roots and tied back at the sides.

The daeyari was upside down.

No ... *she* was upside down, floating, while he stood on nothing, staring up at her with head tilted.

If this was a hallucination, it was one of her more creative ones.

Fi tried to ask who he was. Couldn't. Of course she couldn't. For all the insults of this place, being unable to speak was the worst. Didn't matter. He couldn't be real. She gritted her teeth against the dulling beat of her heart, the creep of ice through bones and—

Calm.

The word filled her head. Fi didn't know where it came from. And how was she supposed to be *calm*? She stoked energy from muscle, fighting the cold, but her heat sputtered.

Calm.

Fi twisted to look around, but she saw nothing, no one – except the apparition staring up at her. Maybe this was her subconscious trying to tell her something, conjuring this strange daeyari.

And how had she learned to stand her ground with daeyari? Not by being passive. By being bold. Never giving in.

She couldn't give in now. The Void was part of her, and she'd find a way out. Fi had to believe that to that last thud of her heart.

She armed herself with all her bristles and faced the daeyari.

Hey, you! she thought hard at him.

His brow arched. A good start.

Get me out of here, Fi ordered. *Now.*

The daeyari's eyes flicked wider, motes of carnelian fire in the dark. So Fi could surprise her own hallucinations? She wasn't sure if that was something to be proud of.

He pushed off from nothing. For a moment, they floated together, Fi taut as a loaded crossbow, the daeyari drifting to her side in an effortless swirl of tail and black robes that wisped at the edges. Like fabric woven from the Void. He offered a clawed hand.

Why not?

Fi grabbed it.

Weight latched onto her limbs, yanking her down. She lurched as something solid hit her boots. Then, she and the daeyari both stood on nothing, black beneath her feet that felt like stone.

A *very* creative hallucination. Fi shivered, her hand anchored light in his.

Where do you want to be?

Fi couldn't place if it was a voice, or just an urge in her head, her desperation to be gone from here.

Whatever the source of the question, Fi didn't hesitate to answer. She pictured herself in bed that morning, wrapped in Antal's warm arms and soft twilight through the window. Ozone on her skin. Before everything went wrong.

The daeyari's brow lifted higher. A tail flick. As if Fi needed snark from her own—

More specific.

A voice. It was a voice, smooth as midnight in her head.

Fi thought of the quarry where Nyskya's citizens sheltered, the people who needed her now that Boden was gone. She shouldn't have run. She should have stayed with them, not fled this grief like she always did, should have stood to face it no matter how it hurt.

More specific.

A demanding voice. Fi glowered at the daeyari, but he stared back with a face carved of granite, tail a slow swish and robes drifting without a breeze.

If he wanted specific . . .

Fi thought of her cabin outside Nyskya, her home and safe haven for seven years. The home she'd built with Boden. She thought of the porch, of timber she'd felled herself and dragged to the mill on Aisinay's cart. She thought of the knotted grain of the wood. The dark stain dusted with snow. The gouges in the beams where she and Boden had gotten drunk off Autumn Plane cider, then challenged each other to an energy dagger throwing contest that ended with—

Fi was gone in a rush.

Falling, though she couldn't tell what direction, careening through black as blood roared in her ears. Her chest tightened to the verge of bursting. A rake of cold across her skin.

She slammed into something wooden.

Then sucked in a breath.

One deep, blissful, snow-cold breath.

42

Well, excuse me for almost dying

Fi blinked at hazy surroundings, her thoughts the consistency of algae: dense and floating, even with solid ground beneath her again.

She eased herself onto aching elbows, every muscle in her tattered body gone numb. Cold. Prickling, like that sting of human flesh exposed to too much energy. But then, a foggy glimpse of familiar shiverpines. The rough boards of a porch beneath her fingers.

Her porch. Her cottage.

She spent the last of her strength on a haggard, disbelieving laugh. Home. She didn't understand how, but she was home.

At the edge of her vision, a shadow shifted.

Fi's thoughts sputtered as the daeyari from the Void paced the base of her stairs, inspecting the trees, the stars . . . then her. Persistent, for a hallucination. She had no strength to shudder, exhaustion urging her to collapse against the porch.

Another shadow appeared. This one, horse shaped. Aisinay approached on cautious hooves, ears lowered and nostrils flaring at the scent of the phantom. He held out a hand. She sniffed. When she swayed her finned tail in agreement, he stroked her muzzle.

Fi couldn't stay here. Verne might still be nearby.

She snarled at the effort of sitting up. Pain spiked her shoulder, shredded flesh no longer in stasis, blood seeping into her coat. She clawed the closest beam for support, toppled down the stairs, caught herself against Aisinay's scaled flank. The horse sniffed her hair, warm breath against Fi's neck.

She hauled herself onto the creature's bare back.

Black spotted her vision. Fi slumped against Aisinay, cheeks bruised by the fins down her neck, hoping her mount knew where to go after all the supplies she'd helped shuttle. As Fi tumbled toward unconsciousness, cold in her bones and pain drowning every thought, she cast one last look to her side.

Her parting sight was carnelian eyes. A tilted head and slow, swishing tail. A convincing hallucination. Perhaps too convincing.

Then, into black once more.

This black was less smothering than the last.

Fi drifted in and out, cotton-thick thoughts registering fragments of a horse's gait beneath her. The cold of a Curtain. Another. Another. Warm hands. Worried voices. A throb in her shoulder then coarse blankets like a cocoon. She drifted again, deeper this time.

She woke slowly.

The world returned to her in pieces: pain in her shoulder, an itch against her skin, weight at her legs.

The pain of her bite wound, wrapped in gauze.

The itch of blankets, a simple bed and barren room in an abandoned mining outpost.

And the weight against her legs. Antal sat in a chair, head pillowed atop his arms at the foot of her bed, chest rising with the tempo of sleep.

Even taking all this in, Fi's thoughts were sluggish putting the pieces together. She remembered teeth in her shoulder. She remembered running. Running from what?

A bed like this one. Blankets soaked in blood and—

'Antal?' His name slipped out like a plea. An anchor, as the world around Fi swirled too fast again.

He blinked awake. Crimson eyes darted over the room, surveying for danger. When they landed on her, the well of concern broke Fi like a hammer to the ribs.

'Fionamara.' Her name fell soft off his lips. The slightest catch against his teeth.

Fi sat up, but . . . by the merciless Void, her shoulder *hurt*. Bandages tugged her skin, warmed by an energy chip to fuel the healing, numbed by twilight sorel ointment. She gritted her teeth and forced herself still, trying not to strain the wound.

Antal watched every grimace, tail taut. 'What happened?'

'I . . .' A haze of grief. Teeth. Blackness. And Boden. Her brother was—

Fi shoved the thought away, safe behind a hastily built wall, before it could shatter her all over again.

'You left,' Antal said. Then, harder, 'Here one minute, then gone. Your horse brought you back like this.'

Fi swallowed against the lump in her throat. 'I went back to Nyskya. Verne was there.'

Antal's tail fell deathly still. His claws dug trenches into the blanket.

'You ran back there alone?' he hissed. 'You faced Verne? *Alone?*'

Well sure, when he put it so bluntly, Fi sounded like a reckless idiot. She *was* a reckless idiot. Somehow, she'd survived, made it back here to him, this last safe harbor after so much had been stripped from her, after Boden had—

'Stop looking like that, daeyari,' She urged her words into a tease. A desperate grasp at levity, when everything else ached. 'I'll think you've started caring what happens to me.'

'Would that be such a terrible thing?'

Antal's words bit like fangs. Fi reeled at the assault of hard eyes and bared teeth, the daeyari's tail a sharp lash. Angry. He was angry at her? She clutched her fists into the sheets, drawing instinctive barbs she was too exhausted to wield.

'I didn't know she'd be there,' Fi tried to argue back. 'I held my own. Just . . . not enough.'

'She could have killed you.'

'She didn't.'

'A lucky chance!'

His venom sank into her like another wound. Fresher. Hotter. Fi fought a sting in her eyes. She already knew this was her fault, always her fault, hated herself for running without thinking. She didn't need Antal clawing the guilt deeper.

'What difference does it make?' she shouted back, baring her own teeth. 'We knew this was a risk when we decided to fight. Even when we face Verne together, I could die. *You* could die. Boden already . . .' She swallowed, tightness overwhelming her chest.

'And do you think that means nothing to me?' Antal snapped. 'That *you* mean nothing to me?'

Fi fell speechless at the crack in his voice. Like a fissure through ice. Chips from that marble facade he wore, crumbled and strewn to the floor.

'I vowed I wouldn't do this again.' Antal's words dropped low, cutting like a knife. 'Then, the first mortals in a century who let me into their lives? One dies by a Beast who came hunting for *me.*' His voice shook as it rose. 'Not an hour later, the other throws herself at a daeyari alone! Void and Veshri help me, Fi. What if you hadn't come back?'

Fi felt cold again, knuckles white where she clenched the covers. Antal had teased her with teeth and sharpened words. He'd tasted her raw, held her in his bare arms and whispered shivers against her skin.

None of that, as intimate as the sincerity breaking him now. This anger, a mask for an ache that terrified Fi even more. He was angry . . .

Because he cared what happened to her.

Because that was hurt, brightening his eyes.

'Antal. I—'

He stood. A curt dismissal. 'You need to rest.'

'But—'

'*Rest*, Fionamara. I'll keep watch, make sure Verne doesn't discover us here.'

He stepped out the door before she could speak, gone in a swirl of tail around the frame.

Fi tried to go after him. She managed to swing her legs off the bed before dizziness struck, pain in her shoulder as she slumped against the wall. Footsteps came down the hallway.

'*Fi?*'

Kashvi stormed into the room, hair a frizzed bob, tired eyes framed with darker circles than Fi had ever seen on her.

'What are you doing?' Kashvi demanded. 'Get back in bed, you stubborn woman!'

'But Antal—'

'Hasn't left your side since your horse dragged you back in a bloody heap. You *both* need rest.'

Fi relented to Kashvi's strong arms pushing her into bed, exhaustion dragging her down against the pillow. Kashvi pulled up a chair, uncharacteristic worry etched into stone-hard cheeks.

'You're awake. Good.' Kashvi's sigh came heavy, a hand grasping Fi's too tightly. All the past snarls and spats between them, vanished into heart-stilling sincerity. 'What happened? One minute you were here, then . . .'

She eyed Fi's gauze-wrapped shoulder. Damning evidence of a bad decision.

'I ran into Verne,' Fi said. 'She's every bit the bitch you'd think she is, in case you were wondering.'

Kashvi didn't laugh. Her grip on Fi's hand tightened. 'Fuck, Fi. We saw the bite, but didn't know for sure. How did you get away?'

'I . . .'

That was the haziest part. Fi remembered panic. Cutting a Curtain. Where had she gone from there? So much black. The cold emptiness of the Void.

Then . . .

'I cut a Curtain,' Fi said, too groggy to disentangle the rest. 'I ran.'

Kashvi didn't press for details. For that, Fi was grateful. She settled back while Kashvi inspected her bandages, trying not to shudder at the memory of the Void crushing down on her.

At the image of carnelian eyes, clear enough to send a chill down Fi's spine.

43

You'll survive this

Fi didn't see Antal for the rest of that day. Or the next.

By the morning of the third, she'd grown restless. The bite in her shoulder would take longer to heal completely, but drawing on energy capsules had sped the process, twilight sorel ointment to numb the pain and gauze to protect from cold. Against the doctor's wishes, Fi dragged herself out of bed and donned her coat. There were others who needed treatment more than her.

And Fi had a pyre to build.

Nyskya's refugees milled about the abandoned buildings of the mining outpost. Fi nodded to a woman cooking elk on a fire spit, to a man supervising his children playing in the snow. She didn't know what to say to them. Didn't know how to be the anchor Boden had provided this village. Kashvi had taken charge of the day-to-day management, ensuring everyone was fed and warm. But supplies were limited, and their presence wouldn't go unnoticed forever.

They had to confront Verne. Soon.

Fi grabbed the metal haft of an axe and headed into the forest.

A calm came with chopping wood. She Shaped silver energy into an axe head and let it sing against the pines, hewing branches from trunks. A rhythm came to her, the methodical swing, then crack, then drag of limbs, fuel for Boden's funeral pyre.

Merciless Void, it hurt. Every swing spiked pain through her shoulder. Call it a form of grieving. Or of penance.

Fi should have told him sooner. She'd had seven years to apologize, to clear the air between her and Boden. Would those years have been different, if she'd confessed at the start? Would things have felt easier between them? Fi could never know.

She should have told him sooner.

She shouldn't have chased after Astrid.

She should have been at Boden's side.

Fi had sworn to do better, yet here she was again, always making the wrong choice.

As her pile of lumber grew, Fi started stacking, building a bed for her brother's body to lay upon. She'd worked up to the third layer when the forest went silent. Even the foraging squirrels and songbirds, bickering over pine nuts all morning, quieted in the boughs.

She turned.

Antal watched from the edge of the clearing. Fi marveled at his stillness, rooted as if he'd stood there as long as the shiver-pines. He must be older than a few of them.

She braced, the bite of their last conversation still raw. Two days had given her time to cool, to admit how lucky she was to return alive. She didn't know what to expect from Antal. Would he have carried his anger while he'd avoided her, fed and stoked it into more snarls at her recklessness? This closeness between them was too young, untested.

'Would you like help?' he asked lowly.

Fi considered the axe rubbing blisters in her hand. The pile of logs, not half finished. 'No. I need to do this. But . . . you can stay. If you'd like.'

A plea, as much as a peace offering. She didn't want to be alone. She didn't want to go back to bared fangs between them.

Fi cut the current to the axe head and leaned upon the haft, resting weary muscles. Antal stepped closer, phantom footfalls in the snow. He kept a cautious distance. Reconciliation was a new dance, one whose steps they hadn't learned with each other.

And yet the worried crease of his brow disarmed her in an instant.

'I'm sorry, Fionamara. I shouldn't have been angry at you.'

'No. You were right. I was lucky to get away from Verne alive.'

They exhaled together, tasting clear air. An untested dance, but they fell into wary steps.

'When you disappeared,' Antal said. 'I was worried.'

He spoke without anger, though that low tone carried a different kind of bite.

And do you think that means nothing to me? he'd said, desperation hidden beneath snarls. *That you mean nothing to me?*

'I didn't realize you cared.' Fi caught herself. 'Not like that. I know you *care*, but . . .' Not just for her. Antal had carried every one of Nyskya's people to safety. He'd stood with her in that room that smelled of too much blood, eyes hollowed as they watched Boden—

Fi pushed it away. The memory of him. Her grief, fighting to bubble to the surface.

Antal humored her a mirthless laugh. 'I can't fault you for that, uncommon as kindness seems to be amongst my kind.'

But he'd always been kind to her. Even when they fought, even when he was angry. Verne had dug claws into Fi like a pincushion. She'd spoken with sharp teeth and sharper dismissal, as if Fi were less than a mouse in her hand.

'You never hurt me,' Fi said. 'Even in the beginning, when we were at each other's throats. You never made me feel like you would hurt me.'

Antal studied the snow. 'I've not always made the best decisions, Fionamara. I've been complacent. I've lost people who were important to me. But I have *tried* to be better than a beast. I'll keep trying to be better.'

That hitch in his voice would ruin Fi. She noted it now, Antal's eyes downcast. She'd noted it two days ago, when she'd put her life in danger, Antal clutching her sheets in desperate claws and snarling what it would mean to lose her.

She'd noted it every time he spoke of the last human he lost.

He was much like you.

Of course, Fi had suspected before now. She hadn't wanted to confront him about something so personal, so raw. But the pieces fit. Verne's cackle when she'd realized Antal had shared a bed with Fi. That blank spot on his antlers, fifty whole years of mourning.

'Your last human friend,' Fi said. 'You and Razik . . . you were lovers, weren't you?'

No matter how soft she spoke, it wasn't soft enough, the silence of a snow-muffled forest amplifying each word like the plunge of a dagger.

Antal straightened. A slow inhale, too deliberate to hide.

A few weeks ago, he'd have snapped on a mask. He'd have stood there, as still as the trees, and told her nothing was wrong, only the twitch of his tail to betray him.

'Why do you ask?' He spoke low. Didn't look at her.

'Because it matters,' Fi said. 'It matters who he was to you.'

Antal's reaction said enough. His words were salt to the cut.

'These things are frowned upon, among daeyari. Humans are

useful resources: food, labor. An occasional novelty to play with. Never anything more than that.'

'Your father didn't disapprove just because you were friends. You were . . .' Oh no. *Oh no.* 'And he killed him in front of you?'

Fi's fingers were claws on the axe. How could this be, another wound he'd hidden from her? How could he bear a grief like that?

Antal stood so very still. From the start, she'd noted that about him, had wondered if the defensive facade was a trait honed by all daeyari, or something more unique to him, a tool crafted to survive.

Just like her own cloak of barbs.

'I hid in the aurorabeast barn sometimes,' Antal said with deathly quiet. 'When I needed to get away from my father. Razik found me there. He didn't tell anyone.'

Fi heard it clearer this time: the ache and the fondness, inseparable.

'He was the first person to truly see me,' Antal said. 'The version I crafted for my family, the mask I wore to exist in that world. He saw through that and found *me*. The person I could be.'

Fi braved a step toward him. 'I'm sorry, Antal. I'm so sorry they took him from you.'

'He served a powerful daeyari house.' Antal's words hardened. He still wouldn't look at her. 'He was useful. He was safe. He would have lived a long life. If not for me.'

'Antal—'

'And now, *you*.'

'This isn't your fault.'

'Plenty of this is my fault, Fionamara. Verne acted because I was too weak. That Beast came to Nyskya looking for me. I put you and Boden in danger.'

Fi had locked her grief behind a wall. Boden's name chiseled through the mortar. She buttressed the cracks, setting aside her pain a few seconds longer. Giving Antal this moment.

She didn't know how to fix the loss, or suffocating expectations, or homicidal parents. She could only reach into the quiet space between them, cupping Antal's soft cheeks in her hands. And she saw him. The man behind the teeth, revealed in pieces, little cracks of vulnerability. She saw at last the depth of the grief that brought him here, saw it mirrored in the ache of her own ribs. Her loss, a different kind of love, but no less deep.

'We chose this,' Fi said. 'We chose *you*. And whatever lofty ego you have about your powers of seduction? Don't think for an instant you'd have gotten me on my back if I didn't want to be there.'

His laugh was a small thing. Fi took it as a triumph.

'I know,' he said. 'But . . .'

Antal reached out, timid, as if whatever he touched might crack. He cradled his hand behind Fi's neck and pulled their foreheads together, a small space to share in this too-big world.

'I was sent to this Plane as a punishment,' he said. 'Instead? I found an escape.' His thumb brushed slow across her cheek. 'But there's this tricky thing about time. It keeps passing. Whole lives come and go, and even grief grows distant. I made my peace with Razik's death a long time ago. Then I met you.'

His fangs were simpler to deal with, less breath-stilling than these quiet confessions.

'Me?' Fi said. Inside of her, a splinter. Crumbling mortar.

'You,' Antal returned. 'Such sharp teeth. So unyielding, but . . . kind. Again and again, kinder than I deserve.'

He'd told her all this before. But these weren't sweet nothings whispered in her ear. These were pleas, hollowed by the old grief he carried. By the fresher grief they shared.

'I don't want to do nothing, Fionamara. I don't want to stand still while the people I care about pay my consequences. You have your own path, your own battles to wage. But the next time you have a reckless idea, please. Let me be here with you.'

What if you hadn't come back?

Fi clawed fingers into his shirt, seeking an anchor. No more running. No more bottling apologies like they'd earn a finer vintage.

'I'm sorry I ran.' Her voice shook. She couldn't stop. 'I wasn't thinking straight.'

'I know.' His words only split her further. Soft. Blameless.

'I shouldn't have gone back. I didn't know what to do. And Boden . . .'

'I know.'

'Boden's *gone*, Antal.'

There it came, the wound they'd been dancing around – layers of reconciliation and grief bandaged around the freshest cut, trying to staunch the bleeding. There went Fi's mortar. There went her wall. Boden was gone, reduced to a memory of blood choking her nose and his hand too light in hers, of screams sent to the Void until her throat turned raw. What happened to that fierce woman she'd been, standing her ground against a daeyari? She could barely stand now, clinging to Antal with whitened knuckles.

'What do I do Antal? How do I make this stop hurting?'

Her chest tightened, scarcely room to breathe. Antal held her against him.

'You don't, Fionamara. It hurts a little less with time. Not right now. I'm sorry.'

She let him lower her to the ground, let him pull her into his lap so she wouldn't have to sit in snow, his arms warm around her. She pressed her head into his chest as tears stung her eyes.

Antal always lauded her bravery. She couldn't let him see her cry.

'Before he died,' Fi said. 'Boden said he forgave me. Did you hear?'

'Yes.'

'What the fuck am I supposed to do with that?'

Boden was selfless to the end, using his final words to free her. Fi didn't know what to do with freedom, with Boden gone and Astrid gone and only herself remaining. This persona she'd manufactured out of fear, finally unshackled from the trial they'd endured ten years ago, testing whether she could stand on her own.

Antal stroked her hair, light claws against her scalp. 'Do you regret the years you spent with him?'

Of course not. They were good years, good memories of building Nyskya into a home. Fi and Boden did their best with what they had.

'I wouldn't trade them for anything,' she said.

'Then your time with him wasn't wasted.' Lower, 'Razik looked me in the eyes as he died. My father's claws at his throat, he looked at me and said it wasn't my fault. That he'd choose me again. Then I watched him bleed out on the floor.' A heavy breath lifted his chest, lifted Fi as she burrowed against him. 'A century later, I'm still not sure I deserved that forgiveness. But it was given to me. Wasting it would be far greater insult.'

Fi clamped her mouth shut. She didn't trust her voice not to crack.

'It's ok.' Antal tipped her chin up – forced the motion when she resisted – exposing a rebellious scowl and tear-damp cheeks that stung in the cold. '*This* is ok.'

He brushed a knuckle beneath her eye, wiping it dry.

Fi only knew how to hiss. To fight. 'This has all been an act. I'm a coward.'

Antal scoffed. 'Impossible.'

'It's true. I pretend to be brave. I pretend to know what I'm doing.' The confession rolled out of her, evidenced by tear-stained cheeks. 'This is all I really am inside.'

'Have you ever thought less of me? The moments I've shown you vulnerability?'

Fi paused. Frowned. 'No . . .' His softness brought them closer. She respected him more for it. She shook her head. 'No, but that's not . . .'

'Not what?'

'That's *different*.'

It wasn't different. It wasn't different at all, and Fi's brain couldn't process the realization, that the trait she'd found so endearing in Antal was the exact same she'd warred against in herself.

'Strength is easy to fake, Fionamara. Vulnerability is hard. Yet here you sit.'

Fi's sight blurred behind tears, hot in her eyes, chilling her lashes. She'd felt less exposed when she lay naked beneath him, begging him to put his teeth on her. Yet Antal met her without derision.

Her walls crumbled.

Not just the wall she'd built for Boden, but all of them, every wretched brick she'd piled up when sorrow threatened to choke her, every smear of mortar when the cracks began to show. Down it came with a thunderous crash, and for the first time in ten years . . .

Fi let herself be vulnerable.

Utterly, shatteringly vulnerable.

She threw herself against Antal's chest and cried, earnest

tears that drenched his shirt, wretched sobs that stole her breath. Each time she gasped, he hugged her closer. She let herself cry, bleeding grief and curled nails against the soft hollows of Antal's skin. She cried because she needed to drain this anguish from her bones if she was ever going to stand up again.

And as he held her, as Antal mumbled soft words into her hair and stroked her back, Fi wondered if he'd had anyone to hold him when he'd broken like this a century ago. She gripped him all the fiercer for it.

For a time, her tears seemed endless.

But that was never the case, was it? Eventually, Fi's breaths calmed. Her eyes blinked back to focus. Her hands still clenched Antal's shirt, a hollow but sated feeling in her chest, composure enough to finally look at him again. The daeyari regarded her with soft eyes, lashes veiling irises of glowing crimson.

Bright. Fresh.

Fed.

There came a fresh pang.

'Was it hard?' she whispered. 'Knowing his name?'

Fi was grateful for his pause, the weight he gave her question.

'I think,' Antal said, 'I was glad to know his name. Maybe that should become a habit.'

And he'd be stronger for it, strong enough for their confrontation with Verne. Another parting gift from Boden. Not to be squandered.

'We have to see this through,' Fi said. 'We have to make this right.'

'We will. As Veshri watches from the Void, I'll see this through with you, Fionamara.'

A different chill ran down Fi's spine. A memory of endless black. Red eyes. She swallowed the remnants of her sorrow for now, sitting straighter in Antal's lap.

'Antal?' Fi's voice came swollen. Hesitant.

He tilted his head, face half buried in the Void roots of her hair.

'Is Veshri . . . real?'

Antal paused a long moment. Then a confused, 'Of course Veshri is real. He was the first daeyari to achieve immortality, by weaving a body of Void ether. He taught others of his kind to follow, millennia ago.'

'Sure. But what about now?'

'Veshri wanders the Void. When daeyari near the end of their first millennium, it's common to take a pilgrimage. They travel the Shattered Planes, hoping to intersect Veshri's path.'

'What does he look like?'

Antal shifted her to arm's length. 'I wouldn't know from personal experience, but . . . Veshri is the oldest of the daeyari. More at home in the Void than upon the Planes, antlers sharp and clothes spun from darkness. Why do you ask, Fionamara?'

She'd love to tell him. In a moment. After she remembered how to breathe.

'When I was trying to get away from Verne. I cut a Curtain into the Void – a *mistake*,' she added, noting Antal's alarm. 'I panicked and I made a mistake and . . . I was in the Void, Antal. I should have fucking died. Then a daeyari appeared. I thought I imagined him, but . . . he helped me get out.'

A ludicrous story, when Fi spun it all into one run-on, tear-muffled summary.

Antal's eyes went impossibly wide.

'You cut into the Void?' he whispered.

'It was that or get eaten.'

'You met a daeyari. *In* the Void?'

'He looked really old. And his robes did this weird . . . wispy thing.'

'Did he speak to you?'

'He . . . I think so. In my head? He told me to think of where I wanted to be . . . then I slammed into my porch.'

Antal inhaled. 'Voidwalking.'

'. . . What?'

'Fionamara. That's Voidwalking. Not just dipping through the Void like daeyari teleportation, that's *real* Voidwalking.'

He cupped her cheeks, beholding Fi with concern and no small amount of awe.

'No,' she insisted, for her own sanity. 'You don't think it was him? I thought it was a hallucination. Adrenaline. Air deprivation. *Anything*. You don't really think it was Veshri?'

Antal's smile was melting. His words, whisper soft. 'Fionamara. Daeyari spend centuries seeking a single meeting with Veshri. For him to come to you – for him to speak – there's no greater honor.'

'Why would he appear to me?'

'Veshri comes to those who seek knowledge.'

'But why would he come to *me*, Antal?'

It made no sense. The concept of a demigod roaming the Void? Sure. Why not. All manner of strange things existed across the Shattered Planes, and Fi had already bedded one immortal, been thrashed by two others.

But why bother with her? Why pause to help a lost human floating within the Void?

Antal frowned. 'What's so insignificant about you, Fionamara? You already have a gift for walking Shards.'

'I slipped into a river. I nearly drowned.'

'You survived Verne. Three times now.'

'I ran away. Every single time. That doesn't—'

Fi fell silent when Antal pressed a kiss to her temple.

'Do you know what I see, Fionamara? I see a woman who

was nearly devoured in the woods. Instead, she turned into a hunter. Death tried to claim her, but she returned to walk the Shards as if they were home. Now, even Veshri sees potential in you.' He chuckled against her hair. 'Or perhaps, he was as intrigued by this brazen human as I was.'

Fi recalled the lift in Veshri's brow when she'd thought of Antal, as if he'd glimpsed her memory of them tangled in bed. Surprised to find his kin with a mortal? If Fi ever ran into him again, she'd guard her intimate thoughts more closely.

'But what does it mean?' she pressed. 'I'm on some . . . divine mission?'

Antal laughed. 'Nothing that dramatic. Veshri's no god, only wiser than most of us. Take it as a vote of confidence.' He grinned, a flash of fangs too close to normal. 'And a story worth bragging about.'

That seemed more manageable.

Fi rested on Antal's chest, measuring the world in the rise and fall of her breaths. In the beat of his phantom heart. Her eyes were swollen but dry. Her grief burrowed, not gone, satisfied with her penance for now.

Antal brushed his fingers through her hair. 'You'll survive this, Fionamara. No matter how it hurts, you'll survive. I don't need Veshri's wisdom to assure me of that.'

She'd been given more second chances than anyone deserved. Fi had emerged from that icy river as a child. She'd evaded Verne's claws, then Antal's, turned that enemy to an ally. Now, she'd escaped the Void itself. She couldn't waste a demigod's favor, whatever it meant.

She started by standing up. Two solid feet on the ground.

Fi wiped tears from her cheeks then appraised her half-finished pyre of wood.

'On second thought,' she told Antal, 'I'd appreciate your help. It's more work than expected.'

That night, the residents of Nyskya gathered in a forest that wasn't theirs, come to honor the man who'd brought them together. They grouped around the pyre, snow blushed green from the aurora overhead. No energy lights. Candles flickered in gloved hands, golden hues catching misted breaths.

They wrapped Boden's body in oil-soaked cloth and laid him atop the platform. Fi moved through the procession with pine sap sticky on her hands, tar acrid in her coat. She'd not been there for Boden when he'd burned their father. He'd said he forgave her. She had to trust him.

Antal kept watch from the treetops.

Kashvi handed Fi a torch soaked in pine resin.

She snapped a current to her fingers, a spark to light the flame. When she tipped the torch against the pyre, the wood hissed. Lighted.

One by one, the villagers came forward. Each person tossed a candle onto the pyre, small flames of remembrance, building to an inferno.

Fi stepped back as the roar of burning timber filled the clearing. Flames wreathed Boden's body in gold. His ashes would return to the dust of the Plane. His energy, already gone to the Void. *Beyond* the Void, if the old tales were true, another land beyond the Shattered Planes, an endless forest to walk for eternity. Perhaps Boden would find a sunlit meadow there, sweet browse for his aurorabeasts.

He'd told her to see this through. He'd forgiven her.

More than that: he'd asked Fi to forgive herself. To stop dwelling on mistakes and finally move forward. She swallowed a scratch in her throat. Wood smoke clung hot in her nose.

Beside her, Kashvi stood equally still, dark eyes glistening in the light of the pyre.

'We need to move soon,' Fi said. 'While Antal's strongest. Verne knows we're coming.'

'We don't have many fighters left,' Kashvi returned. 'But those who'll join are ready. Give the word.'

Fi nodded. 'Tomorrow, then.'

With the plan set, Fi cleared a spot to sit in the snow, a sentinel to watch until the last ember of the pyre burned out.

44

Bait and switch with an immortal beast

Fi woke before dawn. Starlight and aurora filled the window of her borrowed room as she lay on her side, knees pulled to her chest, dreading the cold that waited beyond this bed.

Reassured, though, by warmth at her back.

Antal curled around her like a shield. His tail wound her calf, a knee anchored between her thighs, an arm draping her ribs. He was awake, too. She felt it in the subtle press of his hand against her chest each time she stirred. In the uneven tempo of breath against her neck.

'Everyone comes back today,' she whispered to the dark.

Antal clutched her tighter against him.

Now came the toil of rising, of untangling his arm from around her waist. Scratchy sheets aside, she wished they could stay. She wished she had a hot bath, a chocolate pastry waiting on her kitchen counter, and nothing to do all day except pester Boden and his aurorabeasts. She wished her coat didn't smell of wood smoke.

But Fi had a job to do. And what was step one of any successful job? Looking fierce as shit. She forced herself tall as she tied back her hair, stripped out of sleeping clothes.

Antal's arm wrapped around her bare waist, drawing her against his chest . . . though, not for the reason she assumed.

S. A. MACLEAN

He handed her the hilt of her energy sword. Fi brightened at the unexpected gift. He must have retrieved it from Nyskya while she was recovering.

'You need to stop losing this,' he said.

'Do I?' Fi taunted. 'But then you'd have to come up with a real gift for – *What is that?*'

She gasped at his second offering: a folded suit of slate gray silviamesh.

'Not as tailored as your last piece,' he said, quiet. 'But no rips in the stomach. I'm sure you'll look just as vicious in it.'

He laid the silken armor in her hands, cool material drinking her heat. Fi had been moping for three days, and he'd been up to this? Gifts to help her fight. To remind her she could be strong.

She shoved Antal against the wall and kissed him. *Hard.*

Fi pressed herself to every soft and rigid piece of him, bare chest to bare chest, memorizing the curves of his mouth against hers. She hoped her desperation wasn't too obvious, this gnawing in her heart that anything could go wrong today. The bruising reply of his lips said her worry wasn't alone. Antal pulled her against him, claws dimpling the skin of her hips nearly firm enough to carve.

Then, a slower drag of fangs across her lip, relishing the shared breath. Antal nuzzled his nose to her cheek. Fi looped her arms around his waist, holding him for just a moment longer.

'I'm glad you're here with us,' she breathed into the curve of his neck.

He hugged her tighter. 'Everyone comes back today,' he murmured back.

Fi would hold him to that promise.

Outside, all was silent. Wind brushed the tops of the

shiverpines. An owl hooted in the pre-dawn. Aisinay flicked her ears not at the forest sounds, but the hum of the aurora, green reflected in her blind eyes. Fi stroked the horse's scaled neck.

Then came a crunch of boots on snow. Kashvi arrived with crossbow in hand, followed by the rest of Boden's advisory council. Mal, the general storekeeper, his crossbow comically small in burly arms. Yvette the smith, their pale complexion turned paler since Boden threw himself at a Beast's claws to save them, a cut still angry red on their cheek.

Not as big a force as they'd hoped for, but unmatched in motivation.

No greeting passed between them. They knew the plan. They knew they only had one shot at this, to take back their home and avenge Boden's memory.

Fi and Antal led the way, guiding the others through a Curtain.

The group emerged on a snowy ridge, the first light of dawn touching the mountains. Above the shiverpines, the minarets of Verne's chateau loomed like black teeth in the distance.

They'd arrived far enough away that the resident daeyari wouldn't smell them. She wouldn't taste the static of Antal flitting through treetops, scouting the terrain.

Astrid was off the board.

Which made Verne's derived Beast the next target, attacking the queen only once her pawns were toppled. Antal had caught the creature's scent here, distant from Verne's abode, like a dog chained in the yard. Twisted, everything Verne touched.

Fi kept a hand on Aisinay's side, steadying herself against memories of forest shrines and claws at her neck. This time would be different. This time she came as a hunter, not a hare.

S. A. MACLEAN

At Antal's signal that all was clear, they set off walking through the trees.

He kept to the higher vantage point of the canopy, a shadow amidst dark branches, an occasional flash of crimson eyes. Below, the human troupe made slower progress, hiking against deep snow in grim silence, their labored breaths the only break in the morning quiet.

Fi dug a couple of daeyari energy capsules from her pocket, more gifts from Antal, offering them to her fellow rebels. Yvette and Mal considered, but shook their heads.

Only Kashvi grabbed a capsule, cradling the orb of glowing red in her palm.

'How are you handling the daeyari energy?' Fi asked.

'Burns like shit if you aren't careful,' Kashvi said dryly. 'But at a lower dose . . . it's not so bad. Hurts less than Shaping my own energy, even. Because it's a different kind of current?'

Fi had never considered: that silver sickness was a mortal body's adverse reaction to its own energy, that non-mortal energy might elicit a milder response.

'Maybe that's what you should ask the daeyari for,' Mal teased. 'Once this is all settled. More of those fancy capsules.'

Kashvi huffed. 'Let the bastard fill his first promises, then we'll see what else he's good for.'

That was, possibly, the least like a death threat Kashvi had ever spoken about Antal. A true moment of camaraderie, as they marched toward possible doom.

They reached the foot of a cliff. Halfway up the snow-crusted face, dark rock opened into a cavern. The edges were chipped, scarred by claws. When Antal dropped down beside her, Fi cut him a dry look.

'What is it with you Void-damned daeyari and heights?' she hissed.

Antal appraised the cliff with a tail flick. 'Instinct. We used to hunt from the trees.'

'Now your prey come on their knees.' Kashvi joined them, a squint on the cavern above. Then, back the way they'd come. 'You saw that clearing we passed? With the hemlocks?'

Fi nodded.

'We'll set up there. Give us half an hour.'

Kashvi, Yvette, and Mal slipped into the forest like phantoms. Fi and Antal crouched in a copse of firs to wait, hidden by dark needles pillowed in snow. She shivered. Antal wrapped an arm around her, a warm chest to lean into.

Aisinay stood with them, alert like a prey animal, ears perked toward the cavern overhead. Her soft snort spoke of perplexity, her nibble at Fi's coat asking what in all the Shattered Planes they were doing waiting outside the lair of a Beast.

The Beast who took Boden from her.

'The derived daeyari,' Fi whispered, 'do they know what they were?'

Antal's tail swayed against her leg. 'It varies. Reincarnation degrades cognition at different rates, depending on how well daeyari can maintain their energy within the Void before re-materializing. But in that Beast's state, it likely remembers little of what it once was.'

Perhaps slaying the creature would be a mercy. Fi's breath came out as a shudder of mist.

'Are you all right?' Antal asked.

Of course not. They could all die today, more bones for Verne to feast upon.

'In all my life,' she said, 'this is the first time I've come for a daeyari of my own will.'

The silence beside her was so pointedly thick, she could taste it. Antal scrunched his mouth.

'To a daeyari,' he said.

'What?'

'The first time you've come *to* a daeyari. You've come *for* one. Several times.'

Fi swatted him. 'This is a life-or-death situation, Antlers.'

'A shame to waste it dwelling on the death part.'

His grin was insufferable. Delicious. Despite Fi's best effort to keep a stern face, she shared a laugh, quiet as snow off a pine bough, pruning the dread from her joints.

Half an hour passed. Time to move.

She climbed onto Aisinay. Antal mounted behind her, his chest a steadying presence at her back, an arm wrapped around her waist. What a sight that must make, a Void immortal upon a Void horse, though Aisinay adjusted fine to the weight. She offered a fiercer prance of protest when Fi lay a hand on her neck, urging her toward the cliff. With swiveled ears, the horse complied, carrying them out of the trees and onto an open scarp.

Not as prey. Never again.

At the base of the cliff, Fi looked up. The cave loomed like a hungry maw – the den of a predator, an immortal Beast from the depths of the Void.

'Hey!' she shouted at the top of her lungs. 'Anyone home?'

Her voice echoed off the rockface, thunderous in the silent morning.

Antal stiffened behind her – not in the fun way. She felt his arm tighten first, heard him sniff the pine-laced air. Beneath them, Aisinay fidgeted.

Then came the eyes: two motes of pupil-less red, glowing at the mouth of the cave.

That wretched survival instinct knotted Fi's stomach as the Beast slunk to the edge, claws like knives and pale skin

camouflaged against snowy rocks. A growl rumbled over stone.
The sound reverberated through Fi's aching ribs, this creature
that took her brother from her. All their hard work in Nyskya,
the lives lost, yet not a scratch remained on its healed hide.

They couldn't let it escape a second time.

'Teleporting would have been safer,' Antal grumbled in her
ear.

Safe wasn't what they needed. 'Daeyari enjoy the chase, don't
they?'

The Beast's skeletal horse head cocked to view the intruders
below, dim light pooling shadows in smoldering eye sockets. As
horrific as the first time she'd seen it in Thomaskweld. Aisinay's
impatient hooves churned the snow.

Then the daeyari lunged, and everything set in motion.

Fi pressed a hand to Aisinay's neck, urging her to move. The
horse complied, eager hooves lurching back into the cover of the
trees. Behind them, claws clattered stone. A snow-muffled *thud*
marked the Beast's landing, followed by a splinter of boughs as
it charged.

Fi settled her hands on either side of Aisinay's neck. A firm
touch pressed her into a full gallop, pulses of energy steering
her through the maze of trunks. The blind horse snorted in
protest, uncomfortable with this speed upon the Plane.

They couldn't slow. Heavy paws thudded behind them. A
crack of claws against timber, far too close for comfort. Antal
twisted in the saddle.

'*Fi.*'

She didn't need him using that urgent tone on her when
she could hear the problem clear enough. Fi steered Aisinay
around a snowbank, past a fallen log, slips in their pace that
they couldn't afford. At last, she risked a look behind.

The Beast moved through the trees like a wraith, a flash of

white skin and gnarled antlers, frightfully agile for its size. It lunged over the snowbank they'd had to skirt. A *scrape* then *crack* as claws shredded the fallen tree in its path. It never slowed, hungry red eyes fixed on prey, mouth agape in a razor-toothed pant.

And definitely getting closer.

'A little farther!' Fi called to Antal, shouting over the thunder of hooves and branches.

A snarl raised gooseflesh down her neck, close enough, she could practically smell the Beast's blood-stale breath. She couldn't break her attention from the path ahead, Aisinay depending on her not to steer them into a tree.

Behind her, Antal swiveled, his knee digging into her back as he faced the creature.

The air crackled crimson. As Aisinay snorted, Fi tasted the snap of ozone on her tongue, a slash of Antal's arm sending a crude bolt of energy at the Beast. The monster yelped when the projectile struck its face, pace faltering.

A short reprieve. Even as writhing red energy knit the Beast's brow back together, it picked up speed again, each ravenous lunge more reckless than before.

But they'd bought enough of a lead.

The forest opened to a clearing, bordered by the weeping boughs of snow-heavy hemlock trees. Fi steered Aisinay into the open, trawling the Beast behind them.

Another crack of wood sounded. This time, from the sides.

Metal cord rained from the trees, a net pulled taut in the Beast's path. It charged into the trap with a snarl, stumbling out of its sprint and into a skid across the snow, claws and tail thrashing to free itself.

'Fire!' Kashvi shouted.

Three crossbow bolts loosed: two silver, one red. No rogue

shots this time. They'd had their practice in Nyskya. Projectiles sank into haunches, jaw, neck. The Beast's howl shook the trees.

That, Verne might hear, even at this distance. Their clock started ticking.

Fi Shaped her crimson energy sword and pushed Aisinay into a charge.

The barrage of bolts brought the Beast to its knees. Kashvi, Yvette, and Mal grabbed the edges of the net, heels digging into frozen ground, holding the creature down as it fought. Fi came in at a gallop, her blade aimed to cleave its neck.

Before she could strike, the Beast lashed out, scythes of red energy carving off its claws.

Fi wouldn't call it *Shaping*, more the instinctive flail of a trapped animal. Her allies reeled back from the net as metal cords snapped.

One struck Fi and Antal off the horse.

The cord hit her side with enough tension for a nasty bruise at best, a cracked rib if her current luck held. She hit frozen ground. Rolled to escape Aisinay's hooves as the horse bolted. Then, the claws. The Beast swiped for her, dragging a serrated nail against the silviamesh of her thigh.

Antal was at her side in a snap of static, pulling her clear of the creature's next slash. Fi decided it would *not* be appropriate to kiss him in the middle of mortal combat, much as she wanted to. He returned a beleaguered look, as if her brazenness was actively shaving years off his immortal lifespan.

The Beast lunged for them – then lurched to a halt.

Half the net snagged the gnarled crown of its antlers. Their allies regrouped, heaving to hold the cords as the Beast snapped at Antal. He dodged teeth and saliva, grabbing the creature's antlers to hold it down.

'Fionamara!'

She swung her sword, slicing deep into the Beast's neck.

It roared. Verne would definitely hear *that*.

Black blood slicked Fi's hands as the blade cut hide, muscle, stalling at a crack of spine. Not enough to sever. Curse this Void-woven flesh. Defensive energy surged through the sinews, hardening like steel.

A red eye latched onto her, rimmed in wide black sclera. There had been moments when Fi thought she saw intelligence in those eyes, some remnant of the daeyari it had once been. Now, the irises glazed with feral survival.

Claws flailed at her side. Fi pulled back, freeing her sword from the Beast's neck with a sizzle of energy against skin. Its head lolled but stayed connected. Not deep enough.

They were running out of time.

The Beast bucked, throwing Antal to the ground. Claws snapped the last cords of the net. Then it ran. It ran like a deer with a hunter's bolt through its lungs, painting the snow with black blood as it stumbled toward the trees.

Not again.

Not with Boden's ashes cooling in a distant forest.

Not with all of Nyskya waiting to return home.

Not with the teeth of Verne's chateau looming in the distance, the Lord Daeyari bound to arrive any moment, drawn to the wails of her captive Beast.

Fi reached Aisinay at a sprint and leapt onto her back. As they broke into a gallop, crossbows clicked behind them. Kashvi called to fire. The bolts loosed, biting into the retreating Beast and bringing it to the ground.

Fi's heart thudded with each beat of Aisinay's hooves.

Her sword crackled as she raised the blade, lining up the killing blow.

'*Stop!*'

Aisinay skidded to a halt, hooves churning snow.

The force nearly sent Fi off her mount. She grabbed Aisinay's neck, a frill of fin down the center, steadying herself as the horse snorted. Fi steered her straight, sword still raised.

Blinking.

Confused, because it made no Void-damned sense.

The Beast crouched in front of her, head low, teeth bared. Neck muscles twitched as it attempted to heal, a creep of regenerating red sinew hissing against cold air. And there in the blood-flecked snow, kneeling at the monster's side . . .

Was Astrid.

45

We can't keep meeting like this

Seeing Astrid here made no sense.

Those wide, ruby eyes made no sense. Her hand on the Beast's snout, urging it to sit still, made no *sense*. For a moment, Fi considered whether she had, without her knowledge, developed a remarkably impressive skill for hallucination.

How else to explain this ghost. One who always came back.

'Fi.' Astrid held up her hand. 'Wait. Please.'

Oh, good. This apparition sounded like Astrid, too. Which meant Fi was fully entitled to shout back at her, 'What the fuck part of *leave and never come back* did you not understand, Astrid!'

Maybe Fi hadn't used those exact words, but she felt it was strongly implied.

Astrid hunched beside the monstrosity, her black hair damp with snow, her dark coat less eye-catching than her usual showy attire.

'You don't have to do this,' Astrid pleaded.

Fi swung off Aisinay's back, sword clenched tight enough to ache her knuckles.

'What are you doing here? I told you to run!'

'I did run. I ran from Verne, just like you asked. Please, Fi, just—'

531

'Then why are you still here?'

'I couldn't leave him behind!'

Fi stopped. Struggled to swallow the word. *'Him?'*

The Beast bared its serrated teeth, drenched in blood and breathing labored. When it shifted, Astrid pressed its snout, mumbling something soft in daeyari. The creature leaned against her, skeletal horse snout tapping light against her shoulder.

What in all the Shattered Planes . . .

Kashvi, Yvette, and Mal approached with crossbows raised. Eyes wide. They looked to Fi. As if she had any fucking clue what was happening.

'His name is Navek,' Astrid said. 'Or . . . it used to be.'

It had a name. How could this monster have a *name?*

'It wasn't his choice to come here,' Astrid went on. 'Verne wanted an edge in the fight. She wouldn't tell me where she went, out to some Plane far away from here, and she came back with . . . him. Smart enough to understand orders. Too far gone to argue back. She's used him like an animal.'

'He *is* an animal,' Fi said.

'He's hungry. Confused.'

'He killed Boden!'

Astrid went pale as snow. She looked from Fi, to the other humans – Boden not among them. Her fingers trembled against the Beast's blood-spattered skin.

'Boden is dead?' she breathed.

As if she cared. As if she wasn't the one who brought this upon them. As if Fi hadn't given her the chance to run away.

'When you brought this Beast to Nyskya,' Fi said. 'It killed Boden. And five others!'

'I . . . tried to stop him. He was afraid. And *hurt*, when all the crossbows started shooting.'

'It would have eaten everyone in the village!'

'He's done what Verne ordered him to do, just like me!' Their shouts stirred the Beast. Astrid stroked its snout, urging calm. 'Please, Fi. I know what it's like to be at Verne's mercy. You've come here to face her? Do it. He doesn't need to be part of that.'

The monstrosity quieted, a whimper against Astrid's hand.

Fi couldn't feel pity. Not for this creature. She'd given Astrid the chance to run because of that haunt in her eyes, the teeth scarring her arms. This Beast was . . .

Also afraid. Trembling in the snow, eyes flitting over its attackers like a beaten dog.

In Nyskya, Astrid had tried to stop the Beast attacking. He'd fought back when fired upon.

A daeyari, once. Intelligent, once.

'Antal?' Fi begged, hoping for some answer to this insanity.

He stood uncomfortably quiet beside her. Antal watched the Beast with that usual horror, that low flick of his tail, as if he saw fragments of himself in taut limbs and gnarled antlers. As if its mere, wretched existence deserved pity.

'This far gone,' Antal said, 'it . . . *he* wouldn't have the same sense of a first-form daeyari. More instinct than intention.'

'I didn't know about Boden,' Astrid said. 'I'm sorry, Fi. I know that can't mean much anymore, but I'm so sorry. I'm sorry I ever brought Navek to Nyskya, but he doesn't *understand*. He's as afraid of Verne as everyone else.'

Fi didn't know. She came here to fight, to wield her grief as a sword – not forgiveness.

'Astrid. I—'

Static pricked Fi's tongue.

Disappointingly, Antal hadn't moved.

'Look at this,' came Verne's velvet cadence. 'A reunion, and no one invited me?'

Antal snapped taut, a spark of fury in his eyes. Terror, in Astrid's. A creak of mortal crossbows raised in unison.

Verne stood at the edge of the clearing. She wore a black shirt tucked into slim trousers, silky fabric with iridescent stars, cut deep for a show of ash-gray chest. Delicate silver chains draped her antlers. Her coat was black velvet embroidered with white quartz, the regalia of a queen come to greet her commoners.

True to form, Kashvi fired first.

Without hesitation, she aimed and loosed, sending a crimson bolt flying at Verne's head. The daeyari was a heartbeat faster. Verne vanished, leaving the projectile to zip across the clearing and crackle through hemlock branches.

Verne reappeared with scarlet lacing her fingers. Her Shaping came more elegant than Antal's, harnessing the energy at her immortal core into a long whip of red. She slashed, striking Kashvi's crossbow into two pieces, slicing up the woman's arm. Kashvi shouted and dropped to her knees.

Panic followed. Mal and Yvette fired their silver bolts. Mal's missed. Yvette's grazed Verne's ashen cheek as the daeyari dodged. Her searing whip caught Yvette by the ankle, pulling them off their feet then dragging them across the ground.

Antal teleported between mortal and immortal. He slashed with crimson coated claws, severing Verne's whip in a crack of rival currents, freeing Yvette to back away.

Verne tipped her chin up, red energy at her fingertips, but no move to attack.

'Antal,' she greeted haughtily. 'You look upsettingly well.'

While the daeyari glared at each other, Fi rushed to Kashvi's side. The woman cradled her arm, skin seared with silver veins and the long red welt of an energy burn.

'I'm fine,' Kashvi hissed. 'Fuck, that bitch is fast.'

Her crossbow lay ruined in the snow. Yvette and Mal raised

theirs with fresh bolts, hesitating when Antal held out a hand to stop them.

Fi didn't know why she bothered making plans anymore. They were supposed to face Verne alone, surprised and power-less. Instead, the daeyari came to them, the Beast *and* Astrid back on the playing field.

Antal stood between them, a shield of claws and teeth. He slipped into his mask: face chiseled, tail still. Commendable. Fi would have cussed her out.

'Verne,' Antal returned. 'You needn't inconvenience yourself. We'd have come to you.'

'Why wait, when you've made such atrocious noise so early in the morning? You and your impressive rebellion.' Verne's scarlet eyes slid unimpressed over the mustered forces. 'You've been slinking behind my back for weeks, and this is the best you could gather?'

'More than I see at your side.'

She laughed. 'You should have run home, Antal. You think your human pets change the odds?' Her fanged grin fell on Fi, sharp enough to spike a throb through the healing bite in her shoulder. 'So this one made it back to you, after all. I thought humans willing to suck daeyari cock were a rarity, yet you have a talent for finding them.'

Oh, Fi was going to *kill* her.

'Help me understand,' Verne taunted. 'What is it you enjoy about fucking your food? You get off on having them soft? Defenseless?'

Antal's growl rumbled low in his chest. Fi bared her teeth the same, which only amused Verne further. The daeyari lord stood with velvet coat and silvered antlers wreathed in the growing dawn, flawlessly confident.

Just like every narcissist who'd tried to swindle Fi over the years. Yet Verne wasn't fully relaxed: tail coiled, weight taut on the balls of bare feet. Bluffers, all these daeyari. Verne had avoided killing Antal from the start, suggesting she shared his hesitance for slaying rivals and creating reincarnated beasts.

'But you've neglected manners, Antal,' Verne said. 'You offer only teeth? No discussion of terms?'

Fi gripped her sword hilt. 'I've got her *terms* right—'

Antal waved a hand to quiet her – bold of him, to think she gave a shit about diplomacy, but Fi restrained herself long enough to give him a chance. He stepped forward, fierce as a proper Lord Daeyari, and if Verne touched him, Fi would grind her antlers into glitter.

'My terms,' Antal said. 'Return my territory, and I'll rule as I see fit. No more living sacrifices.'

This, at last, struck Verne's calm. Her expression melted from smug. To baffled. To a fang-sharp sneer.

'No sacrifices?' she said.

'I won't rule my people with fear.'

'That's what this is about? All this trouble for a naïve, point-less promise?' Her voice lowered. 'The Daey Celva will never abide that. You should know better than anyone.'

'Then I'll deal with the Daey Celva.'

'Do you want to hear my terms, then?' Verne hardened, that crack like early-morning cold. 'Leave. Never show your face here again. Or I'll send your energy back to the Void, and your antlers back to your father with a note of what a disappointment you've been.'

Never mind – Verne's antlers were turning into glitter regard-less.

Antal's tail flicked, claws curled into sickles. Two crossbows flanked him, and Fi with her sword. This wasn't how the plan was meant to go, but they still had Verne outnumbered. If Astrid could keep the Beast out of the fight . . .

'Astrid,' Verne said.

Astrid flinched when the daeyari said her name, scarlet eyes flicking to her Arbiter for the first time.

'It's good to see you.' Verne spoke viciously soft. 'I was concerned when you didn't come back. Perhaps this would be a good time to assure me of where your loyalties lie?'

Astrid stood with the slowness of a cornered hare. Fi watched a dozen tangled emotions ghost across her face: that glass-eyed fear of facing Verne's wrath. Shock, at how swiftly Antal stepped to Fi's defense. A calculation, gauging the distance he'd left between them.

'Astrid,' Verne snapped. 'You belong to *me*, not this sniveling coward. Come here.'

Ok. That was enough diplomacy.

Fi readied her sword with a snarl, red energy bright against her arms and crackling ozone on her tongue. She wouldn't stand idle while Verne insulted her. Insulted Antal. Insulted Astrid, after Fi had vowed to protect her. She lurched toward the usurping daeyari—

Astrid moved like the snap of a willow bough.

She snatched Fi's wrist, twisting the sword from her hand then pinning her arm behind her back. Fi snarled, confusion and outrage throwing her off balance as Astrid pressed an energy dagger to her throat.

Soft lips pressed her ear.

'Trust me,' Astrid whispered.

Fi's treacherous heart had never stopped trusting her.

But shit, Astrid, this wasn't the best time for a team building exercise. Antal pivoted, eyes widening on the blade held to Fi's neck, a snarl for Astrid that promised splintered bones. He'd vowed to rip the Arbiter's spine out piece by piece. Yet when he stepped closer, Astrid pressed her dagger, hot energy searing Fi's skin.

Antal froze. Verne grinned.

In that moment, Fi understood the plan.

'Call off your daeyari, Fi.' Astrid spoke with bravado, but Fi felt the trembling hand against her neck. Both of them, thrust into this world of teeth, forced to fight for survival.

'Antal, *stay*,' Fi said. Not a plea. An order.

Confusion slashed his brow, a look of distress that crept up on her heart faster than she could counter. He still looked like he'd peel Astrid into pieces. But he came no closer.

Verne cackled.

'Are you so easily tamed, Antal? One whimpering human, and your claws go dull?' She beckoned to Astrid. 'Bring her here.'

Astrid walked Fi forward, dagger burning her throat. Antal stayed rooted as if it pained him, as if Fi's commanding stare could slice out whatever phantom heart dwelled in his chest. How had she earned such trust?

She wouldn't waste it.

'Perhaps we can still barter,' Verne said as they neared her.

Behind Fi's back, Astrid twisted Fi's wrist until her fingers brushed a belt. Then, the hilt of an energy dagger. Who needed two daggers? Astrid, of course.

Fi gripped the weapon.

'Leave, Antal,' Verne said with condescending confidence, a victorious tilt to her grin. 'Leave in earnest this time. And maybe I'll let you keep your pet—'

When Astrid released her, Fi didn't hesitate.

She lunged at the distracted daeyari, plunging her energy dagger into Verne's chest, straight into whatever shriveled heart rested within her ribs. Astrid struck next, digging a blade into her Lord Daeyari's throat. Verne's snarl came out choking, blood staining her fangs.

A dagger wasn't enough to sever her neck.

Verne lashed with scarlet claws so fast, Fi barely drew a shield in time. The blast shoved her backward, red shards striking silviamesh, slicing across her cheeks. She hit the ground stinging. Too far away, Astrid fell to her knees, burns cut across unarmored arms and hands. Behind them, Yvette shouted as Mal hunched, clutching his face.

Verne backed away, throat healing, eyes like firebrands on her traitorous Arbiter.

When Antal lunged, she pulled a metal cord from beneath her coat. He snarled as Verne dodged his claw swipe, lashing the cord around his wrist with a flash of binding red energy, a kick sending him to the ground. Then, a glower at her Beast, still crouched on the sidelines.

'Daeyari!' Verne shouted, hoarse through blood. 'Ulk! Lemen yzrae!'

The Beast tensed at her command. Minutes ago, Fi had contemplated pity for the creature. But pity returned to horror as he stood to full height, fully healed, teeth bared and red eyes bright at the call of his mistress.

Mal hunched in the snow, injured but breathing. Kashvi grabbed the crossbow from his hands and aimed at Verne. Yvette stayed fixed on the Beast, all backing to a defensive huddle. No one fired, a gamble of which target to hit first, leaving an opening for the other to strike. This was why they'd planned to face Verne alone.

But it was Astrid who moved, pushing to her feet despite the burns on her arms.

'Navek!' She held up a shaking hand. 'Ijen! Wait!'

539

The Beast's skeletal head snapped to her.

And hesitated.

A mote of intelligence sparked in the creature's blank red eyes. He looked to Astrid, the woman who'd touched him with light hands. To Verne, her expression murderous.

'Useless beast!' Verne snarled. 'You're mine! Lemen yzrae!'

'Ijen, Navek,' Astrid urged. 'You're not hers. You don't have to—'

She shrieked as Verne fell on her, claws sinking into her arms.

'How dare you?' Verne spat at her Arbiter. 'You think you can betray me? You think you're anything to me, just because of those half antlers on your head? I'll—'

The *crack* was haunting – a little musical, if Fi was honest. The sound of the Beast's jaws closing on Verne's leg, bone snapping beneath teeth. He ripped her sideways, hurling her against the frozen ground with an equally satisfying smack.

Verne pushed to her good knee with a gasp, shock flashing in scarlet eyes as her Beast mantled protective over Astrid, black blood on his teeth.

A sharper shock, when Fi came at her with a sword.

Obviously, Fi had considered helping Antal. But he was a big boy, fighting furiously to sever the bindings Verne left on his wrists. Fi grabbed for her sword hilt, ripped it from the snow then ran at Verne, swinging for her head – disappointed, to slice across her chest instead. The daeyari was fast, even limping on one leg.

A silver energy bolt struck Verne's side. A second bolt of crimson hit her collarbone. She reeled, concern stark on her face for the first time.

Fi grinned like fury given form.

'You can still yield, Verne!' Antal shouted from his crouch in the snow, such a soft-hearted creature, even as Fi charged like a feral mongoose.

'Yield to *you?*' Verne spat. She stumbled, avoiding Fi's sword with a hasty shield of energy. 'You don't deserve this territory! You—'

She snarled as another crossbow bolt hit her arm. Immortal or not, Verne was injured, outnumbered.

Cornered animals were always the most dangerous.

She vanished before Fi's sword found her throat. Verne re-appeared next to Antal, a tackle sending them both to the ground, that flurry of claws and tails when daeyari came together. Verne struck with slashes of searing scarlet across his ribs. Antal hissed and fought to hold her down, struggling with his wrists still bound.

Kashvi raised her crossbow.

'Don't hit *him!*' Fi shouted, batting the weapon aside.

Verne yowled as Antal's claws raked her side. One last flail of a trapped wildcat. Fi ran to help, scouring for an opening as the two daeyari rolled.

When Verne sank her teeth into Antal's shoulder, he flinched. A split second for Verne to plant her foot. To grab him tight against her.

They vanished together.

Fi blinked at the empty space, marked by trampled snow and black blood. She waited for them to reappear. She waited for the prick of static on her tongue, the sounds of snarling daeyari.

Nothing came.

Kashvi spun her crossbow around the clearing, past Yvette crouched at Mal's side, past the Beast still growling over an injured Astrid. 'Where did they . . .'

'*There,*' Astrid said in a pained rasp, pointing over the trees.

In the distance, a snap of red lit the window of Verne's chateau.

Fi churned with too much molten rage for her tired, mortal

body. That coward. That vile beast of velvet-clad Void sludge. Verne didn't have to fight an outnumbered battle.

She could pick Antal off alone. Heal her wounds, then hunt down the rest of them.

Antal couldn't face her alone.

He'd begged Fi not to fight alone, to let him stand with her.

'Shit,' Kashvi hissed. 'Grab the nets. We need to move!'

'We can't run there in time.' Fi's voice shook. She'd seen how fast daeyari fights played out, how quickly teeth shredded spine.

'Then what do you propose—'

This time, Fi didn't hesitate. She grabbed her sword and slashed open a Curtain, not bothering to look where it led.

Straight into the Void with open arms.

46

Voidwalker

The black was more familiar now.

So was the stasis, cold pressure creaking Fi's joints as she floated, weightless.

Still terrifying, to feel the nothingness around her. No air to draw into her lungs.

She wondered if time flowed differently in the Void, the same way distance could bend on Shards. She hoped so. Antal was fighting alone. Last time he'd faced Verne on his own, she'd scraped the floor with him. Fi had to get there, had to help him.

Veshri!

She shouted the name of the first immortal in her mind, willing it to echo through every corner of the Void.

Veshri! Can you hear me?

What had summoned him before? Her panic? Her desperation? This time, she reached out with bristled resolve.

Veshri! You cryptic ass! I need you!

No shiver ran down her neck. No spark of static.

Only black.

Of course, nothing could be so easy. Fi had been stupendously lucky when the wandering daeyari paid her any attention the first time, too much to ask for a second salvation.

She hadn't charged into the maw of liminal space just to gamble on the whims of a fickle immortal. Antal needed her.

In cataloging her last journey through the Void, one detail stoked Fi's confidence. Veshri had come to her call. He'd drifted circles around her, had grasped her hand and woven solid ground out of nothing beneath her feet.

Then, he'd made her think of where she wanted to be.

Veshri comes to those who seek knowledge, Antal had told her.

Surely, the esteemed first immortal could have pulled Fi out of the Void himself. Instead, he'd made her do it on her own. She just had to remember how.

Fi closed her eyes. No sound around her, but it took a moment to focus past the weight of that silence, the drag of black nothingness against her joints. She thought of Antal and Verne tangled in a writhe of claws, what he'd risked to stay and fight his usurper alongside a band of humans. Not a detailed anchor. Motivation, rather than method.

More specific.

Fi pictured Verne's reception room, how the black stone raked a chill down her spine. She pictured the firepit down the center, logs aglow with red energy rather than flame.

Antal had saved her life. And she'd saved his. More than a trade of debts – a partnership. She couldn't fail him now.

She pictured half-moon windows overlooking a valley, views of conifers and a silver lake. She felt frigid air. Smelled that snap of ozone.

Her lungs ached without breath. Her fingertips sizzled, a pulse of cold.

She pictured rafters carved with folktale beasts and glowing eyes. Marble tiles beneath her boots. A crack in the stone, one she'd noted when Astrid threw her to the ground.

Cold brushed her skin and wound through her ribs, tangled in the enamel of her teeth.

Then, Fi was falling.

She plummeted through nothing, a roar of blood in her ears and no air to gasp. Terror and thrill raced through her as she tumbled through the endless space between realities.

Her first brush with the Void was a misstep on a frozen riverbank.

Her second, dumb luck.

The third made her a Voidwalker – a *real* one. Antal could never claim otherwise.

Fi pitched onto the Winter Plane with paradoxical momentum, having floated in stasis seconds ago. She fell, gasping for air as her elbows slammed the floor – black marble tile, a crack at the edge. Through spinning head, she noted the half-moon windows, the red glow of the firepit and carved rafters of Verne's chateau. Static itched her skin, the coat of the Void mixed with energy on the air.

Then, that tang of copper-less blood. Ahead of her, two daeyari tangled on the floor.

Antal was on his back. That useless fool was on his back *again*, shirt shredded, wrists bound in scarlet cord. Verne hunched over him with claws buried around his collarbone. Antal's knees braced her stomach, clawed feet digging into thighs, holding her back from his throat. Slipping.

A heinous amount of blood coated them both, black seeping from rends and punctures.

But for a moment, stillness.

The two daeyari froze from their scuffle, caricatures of mortal combat as they both gawked at Fi's sprawl upon the floor. Antal's head tipped back against the tiles, gaze glazed with pain, yet he stared at her as if beholding the most stupefying creature in all the Shattered Planes.

Verne's breath came heavy, eyes impossibly wide against her honed immortal face.

'How the *fuck*?' she hissed.

Antal lurched to bite her neck.

They rolled in a blur of tails and teeth. Antal pressed Verne to the floor, fangs digging for her spine. She clawed his stomach. In his flinch, she shoved him off, the leg the Beast had snapped already healed enough to support her weight. Red energy crackled at her fingers.

Fi Shaped her crimson sword and ran. Unafraid. This monster wouldn't take anyone else from her.

Her opening was brief, a split-second to appraise where to strike Verne and leave Antal unharmed. Pruning an antler would make a humiliating blow.

She swung for a hand instead. Her sword severed Verne's wrist, cauterizing ash gray skin and black blood. The dismembered limb fell to the floor with a clatter of claws.

'Heal *that*, daeyari!'

Verne shrieked. What a world-shifting sight, Fi's lifelong nightmare, hunched in pain on the floor and a whimper through her teeth, the pretty braids of her hair torn into a snarl around her antlers. Not just vulnerable, but pitiful. A wraith made to bleed.

Rage glinted scarlet in Verne's eyes. Antal lunged, but she swiped with her good hand, Shaping concussive energy that sent him crashing against the ground. Verne's fist clenched. A whip of energy caught Fi's ankle and threw her against a wall, driving the air from her chest.

'You think you're clever, mortal?' Verne shouted. 'You think you're powerful? In the time it takes me to blink, your bones will rot in the soil!'

Red sickles arced from her claws.

Antal tackled her, unbound, the metal cord finally ripped to shreds on the floor. They crashed to the tile, a snarl on Verne's bloody lips as she turned her claws toward his throat.

But this wasn't her game anymore. She couldn't winnow them in isolation, couldn't turn one-on-one combat to her favor because Fi was *there* at Antal's side, kneeing him out of the way so her sword had a clear strike. Verne's attack shifted to a shield, deflecting the swing.

Separated, Verne had bested each of them. Together, she couldn't get a blow in.

Uncertainty flashed in Verne's eyes. The confusion of a lioness who, for the first time in her long life, was forced to ponder the peril of the hare. Her movements turned defensive: parrying Fi's blade, kicking Antal in the ribs, trying to put space between them.

Before Verne could teleport, Antal sank his claws into her thighs, pinning her to the floor.

Fi drove her sword down into Verne's chest. The blade sank through skin and sternum and heart, lodging in stone beneath.

Fi waited for Verne to get up. She braced for the daeyari's next blow, a cunning play of magic or trickery to put her and Antal back on the defensive. Verne grabbed the blade in her good hand, energy shrieking against her claws. Her fingers closed. Slipped. No purchase. With neck rent, blood in her teeth, Verne's gasp came out wet and shockingly . . . mortal.

It seemed impossible, watching Verne's arm slump to the floor.

Her breaths shallowed, struggling around the blade in her chest. She didn't get up. She didn't pull the sword free. A strike to the heart didn't kill a daeyari, but it left Verne shuddering. She coughed a mouthful of black then looked to Antal.

'Do it,' she rasped.

The image seared into Fi's mind: Verne laid low, a sword in her chest, hand severed. In the folktales, daeyari didn't bleed out on floors. To see the monster broken left Fi as breathless as the Void.

Antal stood slowly. He looked haggard, arm cradling the half-healed gouges of his stomach, claw marks dragged across cheek and sternum, bites along his arms. Yet he had the nerve, the outright audacity to look at Fi, scouring her for injury.

But he was alive.

Fi was alive.

Which only left . . .

'Do it, you coward!' Verne shouted. 'Isn't this what you came for?'

Antal bared fangs at his fallen rival, breaths labored as sparks of crimson knit his skin back together. His tail swayed low. Uncertain. Here they stood at the verge of triumph, yet the hardest decision remained.

He looked to Fi with fear in his eyes.

'I'll be back,' Verne vowed. 'Whether it takes me a century or ten, I'll be back for you.'

Back with fiercer claws, longer fangs. Or would Verne's journey of rematerialization rob her of enough sense that she'd forget her vendetta and never trouble them again? The pinch of Antal's brow said he didn't know for certain.

Fi didn't know, either. She'd taken lives before, never out of malice, but when her own survival was threatened. Verne certainly threatened her survival, even if killing her would buy temporary peace at the price of future peril.

Fi and Antal were still standing there, neither willing to make the move, when footsteps scraped the stairs outside.

She spun to face the door, energy ready at her fingertips as the Beast daeyari burst into the room with a screech of claws

VOIDWALKER

on tile, lithe white limbs and . . . *Astrid* mounted on his back.
She hunched atop the monstrosity with burnt arms and bloody
coat, gripping gnarled antlers for balance. The daeyari dropped
to a prowl, growling at Fi and Antal through bared fangs.

Then, he spotted Verne on the ground.

The creature's eyes snapped feral as a wolf scenting blood.
With a curse, Astrid stumbled off his back, planting her boots
and grabbing antlers to stop the Beast from charging. He
snarled back at her but didn't fight.

'Astrid,' Verne called in a pitiful rasp. 'Help me.'

She reached a shaking hand toward her Arbiter. Her claws
curled as if she still held the leash choking Astrid's neck.
Astrid's knuckles whitened, eyes wide upon her fallen mistress.

'You did it,' Astrid said in a hush. 'By the merciless Void, you
did it.' She looked to Fi, bewildered. Pleading. 'What are you
waiting for?'

Waiting for courage, the resolve to act and live with the
consequences. Antal kept telling Fi she was brave. The way he
looked at her now, eyes bright and jaw set, said that confidence
never wavered.

'You decide,' he told her.

'*Her?*' Verne spat. 'You'd have your human pet make decisions
you're too afraid to?' Back to her Arbiter. 'Astrid. Navek. This
is the craven daeyari you'd throw yourselves behind? I brought
you out of nothing. I've given you everything you ever needed!'

Antal never looked away from Fi. 'My fight with Verne is
political. She's hurt you in far worse ways. What end do you
find just?'

Verne had taken so much – her home, her life with Astrid.
Her brother. Yet this reached beyond Fi. The people of Nyskya,
displaced from their villages. All the sacrifices Verne had glutted
on. And in this room, Astrid and her Beast huddled together,

haunted eyes latched to the Lord Daeyari who'd wielded them like tools.

If Verne left here alive, none of them would know peace. The alternative was a gamble.

Fi had never let a gamble intimidate her.

She looked to Astrid. 'Do it.'

Fear sparked in Verne's eyes. She squirmed, but her blood-smeared hand found no purchase against the sword.

'Astrid,' Verne said – a command, now. A threat. 'Don't be stupid. You think they'll let you leave here alive? After all you've done? Help me, and I'll forgive you for—'

Astrid released the Beast's antlers.

In one lunge, he was upon his prey. Fi wasn't surprised to find Verne a coward in the end, writhing in panic as the Beast caged her chest in his claws, a scream as teeth closed on her skull. The Beast braced. Tore. Verne's head came off in a crack of spine, followed by a jolt of energy that left a burnt taste on Fi's tongue. Tendrils of scarlet sizzled over the ground.

Then quiet.

Verne's body fell limp. Her energy fizzled like spent embers, leaving black blood and scorched lines across the floor. The Beast dropped her head then growled over the corpse, claws digging into inert flesh. Let him have it. Fi wouldn't have intervened.

Astrid did, urging the Beast off his quarry like a falconer with a mantling hawk. He licked blood off his teeth. Astrid inspected Verne's remains from a wary distance, as if the daeyari might still reach out and snatch her.

'It's done?' Astrid said. 'She'd dead? You daeyari can really *die*?'

Verne looked as dead as anything Fi had ever seen. And Antal, the stillest she'd ever seen, no flick to his tail, not even a blink as he stared at Verne's limp form. Fi wasn't convinced he was breathing.

Dead. Verne was actually dead.

Antal snapped back to focus. Crimson eyes sharpened on Astrid, fierce enough to make her retreat against the Beast. Belatedly, it occurred to Fi that Antal might not appreciate Astrid putting a dagger to her throat, even with good intentions.

'You had the chance to walk away from this, Arbiter.' He stalked toward her, tail a predatory swish. 'A gracious offer. Yet you've returned—'

Fi grabbed his wrist. At his growl, she stepped in front of him, cupping a hand to his cheek to remind him what soft was. That this was the person he could choose to be.

'That's enough,' she said lowly. No less of an order.

Enough blood on the floor. This victory came thanks to Astrid and her Beast staying out of the fight. Antal had the nerve to bare his fangs at her, but the sense to concede, settling with a huff and a soft tap of his nose to her cheek.

When Boden had realized Fi's entanglement with the daeyari, he'd reacted with shock. Kashvi, with ridicule. Astrid was the first to look impressed, a wide stare of ruby eyes.

'Void alive, Fi,' she breathed. 'It's true, then? You're braver than I gave you credit for.'

Both of them, braver than they'd started ten years ago. No matter how ashen Astrid looked as she studied Verne, still bracing for the corpse to move, she'd found the courage to finally strike against her mistress. Now, they could both be free.

As for this Beast . . .

Fi wasn't afraid of daeyari. Not anymore. Nothing but spitting cats, snarling and baring fangs as an intimidation tactic. This was how she reassured herself as she approached the creature, steps slow and unthreatening. Still, he growled. Astrid laid her hand on the Beast's head. He leaned into her touch, too gentle for his monstrous form.

Behind Fi, Antal followed with a whisper of claws on marble.

So many times, she'd mused what separated him from his monstrous kin. The mangled shape. The hunger. The hollow red eyes. But how could Navek be a monster, when he'd chosen to protect Astrid? Less monstrous than Verne, who'd only ever acted for herself.

Fi laid a hand on his snout. His skin was cool. He huffed her scent.

'Fionamara,' Antal said. 'He can't stay here.'

'He can't,' she agreed.

They both looked to Astrid.

'I'll take him away,' she said. 'Back to the Contested Planes. You'll never see him again.' Her fingers traced his antlers. 'It's . . . probably good that I don't stay, either.'

The best option for both of them. Astrid had done what she had to survive, enough to deserve a new start, not enough to clear her culpability as Verne's right hand. Not for Fi, with Boden's loss aching her ribs. Not for the rest of the humans in Verne's territory.

The best option, and Fi hated it. Saying goodbye was harder a second time.

Astrid laughed, a harsh and breathy sound. For the first time in a decade, Fi recognized the cadence, that show of bravado masking trepidation. 'Traveling is common for daeyari, isn't it? Maybe it's time I follow my roots.'

Fi noticed her nails biting into her palm, only because Antal squeezed her hand, a brush of his thumb against her fingers. The way his voice softened could only be for her.

'Do you know of the Starfall Plane?' he asked Astrid.

Wary, she nodded. 'That's still daeyari controlled. Not far enough.'

'No. But the closest gateway to the Contested Planes. Take care, Arbiter. You may have found common ground with this derived daeyari, but others of his kind won't be as docile.' Antal hardened. 'And there are more dangerous creatures in the far Planes, immortals who don't take kindly to anyone with antlers.'

Astrid's lips thinned. 'I've heard.'

What in all the Shattered Planes was this cryptic nonsense—Astrid pulled Fi into a hug.

Brave of her, with Antal so close. With Fi still barbed. In her mind, Astrid was holding her hand as Fi led them through their first Curtain. She was raising a sword, calling Fi a coward. She was kissing Fi with lips of honeyed balm and starlight in her eyes. She was leading a Beast through Nyskya, armed with a crossbow. Warring memories, all with weight of their own.

Fi hugged her back, a bittersweet thing, but as warm as she remembered.

'I'm sorry, Fi,' Astrid said into her hair. 'I didn't want us to turn into this.'

'Neither did I.'

The apology didn't fix everything. Wounds still festered between them, maybe some that would never heal. But here was the best resolution they'd get. A second chance.

'Make it count,' Fi said.

'You too.' As Astrid withdrew, she brushed a hand along Fi's cheek. Left a kiss on her temple.

Her glare for Antal was sharp as splintered rubies.

'She likes dahlias,' Astrid said. Hard. 'And everything with sugar in it. And you have to let her win arguments most of the time to keep her happy.'

'*Excuse me?*' Fi protested. 'I never—'

'I know,' Antal said dryly. '. . . Except about the flowers. Thank you.'

Rotten, both of them.

Astrid climbed onto Navek's back. A wild creature, Fi's father had always said. All the wilder now, messy with blood and hair tangled against her antlers, that stubborn tip to her jaw as she sat upon a monstrosity. Fi's last memory was a wave goodbye, the slink of a derived daeyari out of Verne's ruined hall.

But finally, the ghost of a grin on Astrid's lips, as somber as the ache in Fi's chest, as free as she'd always deserved to be.

47

Say it like you mean it

Without them, the room was too quiet.

The firepit hissed with energy, red veins dim like embers through the logs. Here came an ending to so many things. Unknown beginnings.

If Boden were here, he'd tell Fi beginnings were what made everything worth it, even if hers looked different without him. Without Astrid. But this wasn't her first attempt at starting fresh. Last time was a flight of fear, hiding and scavenging and hoping her past wouldn't catch up to her. This time, her past lay bloody on the floor.

Once the Beast's footsteps receded, Antal paced Verne's body, inspecting every angle with a grim set to his jaw.

'She's dead.' A trite observation, but Fi needed to say it out loud. 'She'll come back?'

Antal grumbled, 'Only pieces of a daeyari ever come back, whatever survives the Void. It will take time. She might be different, might not even return here. That's always the gamble.'

The weight in his words, Fi couldn't fully comprehend. To her, Verne was a vanquished foe. Antal studied the corpse like a calculation, a piece moved on the board a century from now. A lifetime for Fi. An eventuality for him. For the first time since they'd met, she felt small again.

Verne was dead. Antal's territory, his to reclaim. Suddenly, a more cavernous question opened before Fi, too daunting to glance at before now, a tightening of that old fight or flight instinct in her chest: where did she go from here?

'What will happen to Verne's territory?' Fi asked.

'A new daeyari will need to be nominated. Approved by the Daey Celva and all neighbors.' He rubbed his temple. 'There will be many politics to play in the coming weeks.'

'But you'll return to Thomaskweld?'

'Yes.'

'And you'll do better this time? That was the deal, daeyari.'

Antal's head tilted as he caught the edge to her tone. Lidded eyes swept over Fi's crossed arms, her bristled stance, appraising her with a hunter's wariness. His tail flicked.

'Are you not coming with me?' he said lowly.

'Am I?'

She'd never asked.

They'd entered this ring as a pair of panthers with hackles raised, teeth bared. How swiftly fangs turned to fondness. Antal had stood at Fi's side while she'd conquered her demons. He'd bowed to her forgiving Astrid. Had helped Fi forgive herself. He'd opened himself raw, gifting her more power than she'd ever thought to wield, enticing her to tumble into his arms.

But she'd never *asked* what came after. They'd been forced partners for this dance, had learned the steps and each other's tells. Now the song ended. They could part ways, leave these past weeks as a fond melody.

Or a new song could start.

Antal circled Fi on phantom footfalls. She recognized those cautious steps they'd spun at the beginning, now a honed routine. They better knew the length of each other's teeth. They knew the soft and vulnerable places. But this didn't taste of their game of bluffs.

This was a negotiation.

'I won't force you to come,' Antal said. 'But I extend an invitation. Come back with me to Thomaskweld.'

'To what end?'

'To help me make this transition. There's much work to be done.' His tail brushed her leg. 'And I'm overdue for an Arbiter.'

Fi's inhale hissed against her teeth. Her back went steel straight.

'No,' she said.

Antal scowled. 'No?'

He paused too close, ozone rich in her nose and tail hooked behind her knee, proximity wielded as a weapon. Fi ceded no ground.

'I won't be your Arbiter. I'm no servant of a daeyari, no tool to be wielded.'

Antal's fiercest weapons weren't his claws. Not his teeth. It was that spark in his eyes when Fi breathed fire at him. That devious twist of lips from scowl to smirk. He closed the distance between them, his next barter the brush of a knuckle along her jaw. His words, a purr.

'Will you return with me as Fionamara, then?'

A better offer. Fi was still dealing with an immortal, one who knew how to flutter her pulse. She weighed her terms.

'To what end?' she asked again.

He tipped her chin, finger nestling in the hollow beneath. 'To help recover my territory. Help me make the decisions we agreed to.' He leaned closer, breath warm on her cheek. 'To share my bed, if you will it.'

His mouth dangled close, a lure, inviting Fi to take what she wanted. She leaned into him. That firm chest. Those lean muscles fit to pin her down and make her shout ridiculous things into the night. She clutched the remnants of his shirt, pulling him close enough for lips to brush.

But when Antal tilted to claim her, she hovered out of reach.

'My bed is more comfortable,' she challenged.

He huffed his fluster, hot against her mouth. His veiled eyes were a study in indifference, but Fi wound tight enough against him, she felt the tension in his posture.

'You've only been in my bed once,' he said. 'I can't help but feel you weren't properly acquainted.'

'You've only been in *my* bed once,' she countered.

'Perhaps we can alternate. A compromise.'

A daeyari willing to compromise? There was a fine start. But not enough.

Because Fi wanted this. She wanted more than the cottage in the woods where she'd hidden for seven years. She wanted to fix her world rather than flee from it. She wanted Antal's scorching stares and the way he made her feel like she could hold her head as tall as an immortal.

She wanted *him*.

This type of want, though, was a desperate thing, too dangerous to leave any detail assumed. Antal's circling words and formal terms weren't enough.

Fi's fingers clawed his collar. 'Say it. No flowery language, daeyari. *Say it.*'

She measured the shortness of his breath. His arm tightening at her waist. 'Say what?'

'Say what you mean. Why should I go back with you?'

His frown was a delicious thing, frustration and worry chiseled into the hard lines of his brow. Then came the crack. Realization softened him to the lover who'd held her through the dawn, the confidant who'd brushed tears from her cheeks.

558

He pressed his forehead to hers. 'Because I *want* you to come back with me.'

Exactly what she needed to hear.

'More,' Fi ordered.

'I want you, Fionamara. I want you to be at my side.'

Fi fell into him until no space remained. She twined her fingers behind his neck, ozone mixed with a tang of blood. She didn't care. She only cared about his arms around her, his heat warming her tired bones, the promise in his words. And yet she'd never undignify herself by sealing a deal so easy.

'I have conditions.'

'I dare say, I'm coming to see how you smugglers operate.' Antal's tone was forcibly dry. Beneath it, a glint of amusement. 'Let's hear them.'

'I'll be a thorn in your side,' Fi vowed.

'You think I can't bear thorns, Fionamara? I haven't plucked you out yet.'

'I'll rip you to pieces.'

'Use your tongue half as often as your teeth, and I'll relish every moment.'

Fi bared those teeth at his smugness, at how fiercely it made her want to kiss him. 'Other daeyari will come. They'll see you as weak, like Verne did.'

'Let them come. And we'll prove them wrong.' Antal nipped the corner of her mouth, entreating. 'Please, Fionamara. Come back with me.'

Bewitching creature. Fi could devour him, every taunt and promise, every time he stoked her heart with that soft grin.

'I'm human.'

She whispered her final caveat, almost too daunting to confess. Could he truly ask her to stand beside him? Not a tool by another name?

Antal cupped her chin, a rapturous look as he met her gaze. 'And I shudder at any fool who'd dare doubt such a ferocious beast as you.'

That simple. As if he truly saw her as nothing less for what she was.

Fi dove into the kiss, no hesitation at the plunge, no fear at its depth nor how fiercely Antal's mouth moved to consume her. He cupped the back of her neck, a rumbling sigh as she caught his lip in her teeth.

She emerged for the space of a breath.

'Yes,' she said. 'I want to go back with you.'

Antal pulled her in this time, claws buried in the Void and rainbow curls of her hair, lips bruising. Every stroke of his mouth was a word of relief. The slick of his tongue, an acceptance. The claws bracing her ribs, a fire as desperate as the one he stoked in her. Fi pressed herself into him, hooked fingers between trousers and the hot skin of his waist, but she couldn't drag herself close enough. An imminent problem.

One that would have to wait.

Outside, footsteps climbed the stairs. Kashvi shouted, voice rough with fatigue.

Fi, breathless for a different reason, cursed and thanked the woman's doggedness on the same exhale. She pulled away from Antal, not fast enough to avoid a nip to her chin. She bit him back, drawing a growl.

'Stop that,' he warned. 'Or I'll have to steal you away before you can brag to your allies of victory.'

'Our allies,' she reminded him.

'No, Fionamara. This was your doing. I was merely claws at your side.'

Kashvi, Yvette, and Mal burst into the hall with crossbows drawn. Then, wide eyes. The moment was surreal – as if before now, these frenzied few minutes might have been a dream.

Kashvi's stunned silence, the slow creep of her grin both confirmed this was real.

Verne, dead on the floor. Fi and Antal, standing victorious.

He nodded, urging her to do the honors. She grabbed Verne's head by the antlers and held it up for all to witness.

'It's done,' Fi announced with a wicked grin. 'And we're just getting started.'

48

Yzi vali yzru

Antal insisted on a bath and a change of clothes before speaking to Verne's citizens. Fi maintained her opinion that he'd make a stronger impression shirtless and covered in blood, but that was his loss.

They spent most of the day in Verne Territory, informing the governor and attendants of their ruler's demise, setting buttresses to keep things running without their Lord Daeyari. Temporary measures. The full transition would take weeks, months, but for now, they had a higher priority.

That night, Nyskya's residents returned home.

Fi sat on the steps of the tavern, aching bones and a weary smile as she watched the town return to life: families gathering in the square and dispersing back to their houses. Mal serving hot cider and butter cookies from the porch of his general store, grinning despite the bandaged burn down his cheek. Kashvi and Yvette checking the roster. All thanks to . . .

Static pricked Fi's tongue.

Antal appeared in the square, hand clasped with Savo, the power foreman. Savo's daughter, Anisa, sat in the crook of Antal's arm, though she'd nearly summited his shoulder in a bid to tug at lacquer black antlers.

'Are they real?' she said, grabbing one antler hard enough to tip Antal's head.

'Of course they're real,' he returned with the patience of a martyr.

'Daddy, look! They're real!'

'Yes, sweetie,' Savo said. 'Let's not pull on the Lord Daeyari's antlers. There we go.'

Savo took his daughter, whose interest swiftly latched onto the prospect of cookies. Antal slashed Fi a *'we will never speak of this'* look, which guaranteed she was absolutely going to speak of this. Frequently.

Another prickle, and he was gone, off on the next trip.

'Leave, Kashvi!' Yvette hauled the resistant wolverine toward the tavern. 'That's nearly everyone. I'll handle the stragglers. Go rest.'

Kashvi must be exhausted, with how quickly she gave in. She approached with stiff strides, arm hooked with Iliha's for support. Fi stood to greet them.

'Break until morning?' Kashvi proposed.

'Kashvi,' Fi countered. 'I don't want to see your stubborn face until at least the day after tomorrow. You've earned it.'

Kashvi laughed. Gave Fi a firm hug then Iliha the softest kiss on her cheek.

'Two days' rest,' Iliha said sternly. 'At minimum.'

'Oh?' Kashvi cracked a hard-earned grin. 'Or else what?'

'I can be very convincing—'

The two of them retired inside. Fi waited as the last of the villagers returned.

She'd be lying to say she didn't catch herself looking for Boden amongst the crowd. Didn't feel a skip in her heart each time she remembered he wasn't coming back. He'd loved her enough to search for her seven years ago. To give her this safe place to build a home. She'd keep it safe for him.

Antal returned with a pair of metal smiths. Then a carpenter. Then a baker. At last, he circled the square to join Fi, shoulders sagging with world-ending fatigue, though his tail betrayed him, a low but contented swish.

'That's the last of them,' he announced.

Fi appraised his work with a nod. 'Excellent job, Lord Daey-ari. You've done well by the people of Nyskya.' Then, softer, 'Ready to go home?'

'Please,' he groaned. 'I'll be picturing that teleportation route in my sleep—'

He stilled as Fi wound her fingers into his. Confiding, she asked, 'Would you like to go back to *your* home, Antal?'

No more threat of Verne. No more Beast prowling the cliffs.

Antal blinked at her, a moment of surprise. A slow, tired smile.

Then they were gone.

Night lay upon the city of Thomaskweld.

Fi returned to stone beneath her boots. A groan of wind at the mouth of the cave.

Antal's quarters were remarkably as she remembered: a room carved into the cliff, a rug of black trees and silver moonlight, a sitting area with a low table and cushions. All of it, windblown. Dusted in snow. Whatever energy once laced the walls had dissipated, leaving the rock cold and dark.

Antal surveyed his abode with a scowl. He crouched, tapping a claw to one of those thin floor conduits, a hairline of copper in moonlight.

Crimson energy flooded the vein. It branched across the

ground to melt the snow, flowed up walls to set lanterns alight in soft twilight blue. Already, the wind quieted. The air warmed.

Fi slipped off her boots, relishing magic-heated stone beneath bare feet.

'You're installing this in my house,' she informed him.

Antal cut her a wry grin. 'I suppose I still owe you a favor, for your help.'

'Incorrect. You're doing *that* for free, because I kiss very well.' Fi tipped her chin up. 'I haven't decided what my favor will be.'

He moved to the window – so she wouldn't see his compromising smirk, Fi suspected. Last time she'd been here, she'd huddled in a corner, keeping distance like a trapped hare. Now, she joined the Lord Daeyari at the ledge overlooking his city.

At this height, the wind bit her cheeks and set her hair to flight. Invigorating. Below, the golden lights of Thomaskweld consumed the valley floor. Energy conduits branched like veins from the power factories. A beautiful city. Larger than any she'd lived in.

'How does it feel to be back?' she asked.

Antal breathed deep of the bracing air. 'I missed it here.'

'The infatuation with heights still baffles me. Though, the view is nice.'

Antal slipped an arm around her waist, nuzzling his nose to her cheek as the wind swept both their hair into knots. 'A better view than ever.'

Fi scoffed. 'Filthy flatterer.'

'Tell me to stop.'

Of course she wouldn't.

'Don't forget,' Fi said. 'You owe Boden a better governing council. Materials for Yvette. Strawberries for Mal.'

'Yes, yes, of course, all debts to be paid. A daunting list.'

Antal chuckled, breath warm against her jaw. 'Though, this homecoming, I can get used to.'

He offered a hand. Fi took it. He danced her along the cliff, swaying to their own imagined music, feet weaving the ledge. With his arm around her, she felt no fear, only reveled in the wind through her hair.

'You did well today, daeyari,' Fi said as he spun her. 'Fulfilling your promises. Yet you've another promise left unsatisfied.'

'Do I?' He caught her around the back, pulling her into a tighter turn.

She leaned in, grateful for his heat. 'You've assured me your bed is as comfortable as mine. And yet I've seen no evidence.'

'Ah.' He finished with a dip, swinging Fi low atop the crook of his arm, mouth against her lips. 'We should see to that.'

He kissed her.

He kissed her like each time was a new discovery, a secret to be untangled by the caress of his tongue. Fi languished in the slow strokes. The lack of hurry. Exhaustion weighed her bones, excitement and fear for the work still ahead: reclaiming Thomaskwcld, building something better. Tomorrow held more challenges.

Tonight, they held each other. Everything else faded away.

'I'm not easy to impress, daeyari.' Fi nipped his jaw. 'Take me to your bed. I'll judge it to my strictest standards.'

Antal bit back at her chin, a growl rumbling his chest.

He pulled her across the room, slipping off her coat. At the cold, Fi burrowed against him. Before, she'd slunk these chambers as a captive, shivering in clothes that weren't hers, ozone foreign in her nose. She craved it now, longed for the scent to cover every part of her.

In the hall, she unbuttoned his shirt, fingers curling into talons to tear it off his shoulders. Antal pulled her sweater over her head, claws feathering her ribs. Between the two of them, just enough bite.

He pushed her against the wall. Bare rock hit her back, cold and sharp against her shoulder blades. Fi hissed.

'Not *just* the height,' she complained, teeth skating his jaw. 'You insist this home of yours is comfortable, even with so many hard things?'

He purred, 'Don't pretend you won't be begging for hard things in a moment.'

'You're mistaken, daeyari. I won't be the one begging—'

She gasped as he hooked an arm behind her knees, lifting her to his chest. Fi dragged her fingers over the shaved sides of his hair, into the longer strands between his antlers, laying slow kisses along his neck as he carried her down the hall.

It must not be the first time, right? When he'd chased her from his shrine, when she'd woken in his room, he must have carried her here. They'd been adversaries, yet he'd made sure she was safe and warm.

His bed was as she remembered: a downy mattress set on a stone ledge. He dropped her into the nest of furs, silver fox and mink, her legs hanging over the side.

Then, he fell upon her with his teeth. Fi squirmed in delight at his fangs on her neck, scraping down the hollow of her throat. She sighed, as his mouth crossed her chest, slowing with relish around each tender curve of her breasts. He nipped her stomach. Traced every flower tattooed down her hip. At last, he sank to his knees off the edge of the bed, knelt between her parted thighs.

Merciless Void, he looked good on his knees, unlacing her pants with his teeth.

Once she lay naked before him, he spread her legs, pinned her down beneath splayed claws and hot palms. Fi didn't beg.

Her breath *did* shudder, as teeth traced the inner curve of her thigh. An arch into him, as his tongue found her center, legs trembling against his grip.

Her ruin began as a slow drag of his tongue across her clit. A brush of fangs that bloomed heat through her core. This beast's mouth would be the end of her – what a delicious demise.

'How's the bed?' Antal asked, breathy between strokes.

Fi contorted against the furs, fingers clawed into soft fox pelt. They smelled like him.

'I can't possibly . . .' she panted, 'make a decision so rashly . . . when you've hardly begun to . . . *fuck*.'

A firm suck of his mouth dragged a moan from her throat. Her hips arched off the bed, desperate for more.

'Fair enough,' he murmured, a grin on his lips.

Antal's tongue worked over her. Into her, those strokes mercilessly deep, that build of tension that had her rocking her hips to fill the ache, until at last—

She came with a shout, everything hot and shuddering and wonderful, writhing beneath the mercy of his mouth. This otherworldly creature. This wretched, wonderful predator.

Hers, to enjoy as long as she wished, as they built a new home together.

As Fi caught her breath, Antal climbed onto the bed, mantling over her. He combed claws through her hair.

Then, whispered against her ear, 'Don't look so content, Fionamara. I'm not finished with you.'

She cupped his cheeks with eyes lidded – grin wicked. 'Neither am I, daeyari.'

Fi grabbed him by the antlers, heaving the startled beast sideways.

Here, she didn't have to cower. Here, she didn't have to hide behind her cloak of bristles. Here, she was a creature of claws and fangs, her snarl as fierce as Antal's when she pushed his back to the bed. His tail wrapped her thigh. Claws gripped her waist, poised to throw her off.

'*Stay*,' Fi ordered.

Antal froze beneath her, breaths heavy. Concern creased his brow.

Then, eyes narrowed at the realization: her mounted atop him, thighs straddling his hips. Head tall. *Not* begging. Fi felt every muscle tense between her legs, Antal's fangs bared, tail swishing.

But he stayed, like a good beast.

Daeyari didn't fall easily to their backs, he'd claimed. So what was that hungry glint in his eyes?

Fi scraped her palm up his bare chest, a simmer of hot energy beneath fingertips. 'Do you enjoy being on the bottom, daeyari?'

'That depends,' he returned, rough.

'But you enjoy when I give you orders?'

'I enjoy *you*. The fiercer, the better.' He growled the words, but held still beneath the command of her palm. A new game to play.

She made swift work of his trousers, relishing the lean lines of his waist laid bare beneath her fingers, that long V dipping to his pelvis – relishing the *other* long piece of him that rose to greet her. Fi grasped his cock, a firm stroke of her palm from root to tip. Antal tilted his head back, groaning as he pressed against her grip.

'Kasek aza . . .' he breathed, a curse and a plea at once.

'*Kasek . . . aza . . .*' Fi formed the words slowly, trying to mirror how Antal made them sound. 'You've called me that before?'

'Kasek aza,' he purred. '*Vicious woman.*'

She grinned. Then mouthed the words anew. Fi liked the way

they sounded in her mouth – she liked the way they sounded in *his* mouth more.

She rose on her knees and guided him into her. They shared an exhale, hers verging perilously close to a whimper, consumed by the bliss of hard heat filling her, by taut muscles between her thighs and claws digging into the bedsheets.

At the first roll of her hips, Antal arced with her, eyes fluttering closed and tail wrapping her waist to pull her tighter against him. He ran a hand up her thigh. Between her legs. Fi gasped when his thumb stroked her, brushed in energy, a spark of heat that sent her smoldering.

But Fi was in control.

She set the rhythm. She set his hand on her hip, an anchor to move against, a brush of claws across her ass. She reined him back when he tried to press too quickly, reveling in the desperate hiss through his teeth. From this perch, she was unconquerable. This thrum of power as potent as the lust between her legs.

As Fi reached another crest, she tipped her head back in a cry of victory, all of her trembling as Antal moved beneath her, drawing out the waves.

Again, he tensed, hands hard on her hips.

'*Stay.*'

Fi's order came frayed. Antal heeded, strained as a starving creature beneath her.

Still heady with her own pleasure, Fi drank his need for her like spiced wine, his labored breaths, claws digging into her thighs. Dancing an edge, a silent plea in half-lidded crimson eyes. She tipped a finger beneath his chin.

'Don't worry,' she said. 'I'll bring you there. Don't you trust me?'

A pained sound scraped Antal's throat. 'Too much. You seem to relish tormenting me.'

Fi bent over him, close enough to savor each haggard breath against her neck. To feel him strain as she rocked with his cock inside her, building him toward his own end, her fingers tight on his antlers.

Antal tensed as he finished, burying himself between her legs with a shudder, growling her name into the curls of her hair. Claws gripped tight on her ass. Then slackened. Softer, he dragged his spent hips against hers with a rasped exhale.

When he fell ragged to the bed, Fi fell with him.

They tangled in the aftermath, all twisted legs and tail, sweat-dewed foreheads pressed together. Fi cupped his cheeks in her hands. She ran her tongue across her teeth, tasting every lingering trace of ozone, savoring the fading bloom of her pleasure and a satisfied heat settling in her core.

She drank in the beast at her side, so sated with *her*, he could scarcely keep his eyes open. Antal wrapped her in arms and tail, stringing breathless kisses along her temple.

'Kasek ava,' he murmured, affectionate, against her skin. 'Qess, ery yzu grelu.'

Fi frowned. 'Are you going to tell me what the rest of that means?'

'I suppose you'll have to learn to speak daeyari.' Fatigue dragged his words, pulling his lashes low as he settled her into the heat of his chest.

Fi burrowed against him. All of her was spent, warm, drunk on lust and the caress of furs.

'Teach me now,' she said.

'Hm?' His thumb traced circles at her hip.

'Teach me how to say . . . I love you.'

His thumb slowed. Fi watched herself measured in the smolder of his eyes, felt the weight of his breaths still shallow from tasting her.

'Yzi vali yzru,' he said. Then kissed her to seal it to her lips.

'Yzi . . . vali . . . yzru,' Fi said when he released her for air.

'Sharpen your consonants more.' He pulled her against him. 'Yzi vali yzru.'

Her leg wrapped his waist, fingers cradling his face. 'Yzi vali yzru.'

'Closer.' His teeth on her lip. 'Yzi vali yzru.'

'*Yzi vali yzru.*' It was perfect, her mouth tracing his to match the syllables.

'Not quite. Say it again.'

'Ass.' She jabbed his chest. 'You *want* to hear me say it again?'

'Is that such a terrible thing?'

Fi laughed and nestled against him. No. Not such a terrible thing at all.

'This bed is acceptable,' she admitted, drifting toward sleep. 'Though mine is just as comfortable.'

'We can visit whenever you'd like,' Antal murmured back. 'My clever Voidwalker. Some practice, and you might come to make the journey as easy as I can.'

Fi hummed at the thought. A human with two daeyari antlers as trophies. One who could walk the Void as easily as a creature born from it.

Wouldn't that make for an exciting folktale?

Epilogue

The rubble of the Thomaskweld capitol building was more impressive than Fi remembered. Not that she'd seen the aftermath before now, her previous priorities centered on fleeing for her life, escaping a Beast, then getting knocked unconscious by a pair of traitors.

Antal stood beside her in the chill morning, inspecting the carnage with a dry arc to his brow. Half the building remained intact. The rest, a mess of stone and glass. His tail flicked.

'How many energy capsules did you smuggle in here?'

'I didn't count them, Antal.' She crossed her arms, bundled in a new coat of maroon wool with a fox fur ruff.

He let out a long-suffering sigh. In the week following Verne's defeat, they'd both found little sleep, busy surveying the damage in Thomaskweld. The usurper had left the capitol building in ruin. She'd made no repairs of sabotaged energy conduits, coercion against rebellious citizens.

No more. The people of this territory would have what they needed, at no cost of blood.

'Do you know what I think?' Fi said.

'Oh. Let's hear it.'

'I think you never planned to eat me after all.'

Antal's brow slipped higher. 'Is that so?'

'*I* think'—she leaned into him—'your devious plan was to rid yourself of Fionamara Kolbeck, dreaded smuggler, bane of your territory.'

'A terror.'

'To save your economy, you had to tame me.'

Antal's arm wrapped her waist. His jaw clenched, a blatant attempt not to laugh. 'A clever theory. With one glaring issue.'

'That being?'

Fi stilled as his mouth brushed hers. 'Why would I want to tame you? I prefer you wild.'

Behind them, Kashvi cleared her throat.

The dawn glinted lavender across the inky crop of her hair, the double line of silver buttons down her midnight jacket. Her lips pursed, unamused. Doubly so at Fi's syrupy grin.

'Good morning, Kashvi,' Fi said in a goading lilt. 'Or should I say: esteemed Governor.'

Kashvi brandished a clipboard, looking as though she'd relish putting her pen through either of their eyes. '*Interim* governor. You have me until there's a proper election. Void knows how much of this mess we can clean up before then.'

She grumbled and flipped through her paperwork. Immaculate paperwork, every note color coded and organized in tidy columns. After Boden, Kashvi had been the beating heart of Nyskya. Trustworthy. Determined. An obvious choice to help get the territory back on its feet. And as much as she liked to complain, she'd taken the position with minimal arm twisting. Perhaps Fi wasn't the only one who'd grown restless in their quiet village. Perhaps it was Iliha's doing, eyeing empty storefronts along Thomaskweld's main avenue.

Or perhaps they both realized they could do more than keep Nyskya safe, by making all of the territory just as much of a haven.

When Kashvi had accepted Antal's offer, he'd asked if this meant a clean start between them. She'd told him it would give her time to think about it – which wasn't a *no*.

'Latest reports on energy conduits are in my office,' Kashvi said. 'Let's go.'

She led them into the intact wing of the capitol. They crossed over marble tiles and under ceilings painted in starlight and aurora, halls quiet thanks to a skeleton staff. Those humans who did cross paths with their returned Lord Daeyari swerved out of his way. Trust would take time, but Fi had faith it would come. He'd won her over.

The previous governor's office had become rubble during the explosion. Kashvi brought them to a repurposed meeting room with tall windows overlooking the capitol plaza, a long table of polished pine hidden beneath stacks of paperwork.

'Mail for you on the table,' Kashvi said. 'Get rid of it, I'm low on space.' She disappeared into an adjoining room, followed by a rustle of papers.

Antal inspected a stack of three letters, distinct from government paperwork in their thick texture and wax seals, sitting against a bottle of . . . wine? The liquid inside was dark, oddly streaked with silver that swirled even as it sat still.

Fi, too curious to not look and not reserved enough to feign disinterest, peered over Antal's shoulder as he popped open the first seal.

'Letters from my daeyari neighbors,' he explained, sounding profoundly unenthused. 'Proper etiquette, during any shift in power . . . oh good, this one's from Tyvo.'

The sharp text was inked in daeyari. Antal had peppered Fi with language lessons all week – mostly greetings, curses, and 'your ass looks magnificent when you bend over like that' – not enough to decipher a letter. Other than the curses, of course.

Antal read. Scowled. 'Tyvo says if I set foot in his territory again, he'll stake my head on top of a shiverpine.'

'Just with a lot more fucks than that?' Fi said, noting the familiar words.

'*A lot* more fucks than that. Hardly unexpected.' He tossed the letter to the trash bin and reached for the next.

'Ah.' He hummed, eyes darting over the page; no curses, this one. 'From Kyl, Verne's eastern neighbor. Well wishes on my return . . . her support as we review candidates to replace Verne . . . at least we won't have a territory war.' He discarded the letter and picked up the last, tied to the wine bottle.

Antal went so still, Fi nearly waved a hand in front of his face to check for consciousness.

The envelope was thick gray paper, Antal's name written in a swooping yet ruthless script. His tail gave a violent flick. He flipped it, revealing a seal of midnight blue wax. An imprint of a dahlia, same as the carving on the base of his antlers.

'Fuck,' Fi said. 'Antal . . . is that . . .'

He opened it with a slice of claw.

The letter was brief. Shortest of the three, two succinct sentences in glistening midnight ink. Then a name: Avroz.

Antal had never spoken his father's name to her.

'What does it say?' Fi asked.

He read it several times, eyes flicking across the page. At last, he ripped the paper in two and tossed the scraps in the trash.

'Antal,' Fi said, firmer. 'What does he want—'

'*Well done on not dying,*' he recited stiffly. '*Leaving her alive would have been preferable.*'

Fi blinked. 'Void . . . what an *asshole.*'

Antal hummed in agreement and picked up the wine, a swirl sending the contents spinning like a bottled blizzard. He seemed more annoyed than worried, an act he'd had two and a half centuries to hone.

His father was watching. Verne had warned that the Daey Celva – the *Dusk Council* – wouldn't be pleased with any changes in policy.

'Daeyari wine?' Fi asked. 'Is it any good?'

'It would possibly kill you.' Antal dropped the gift in the trash with a resolute *thunk*.

Fi agreed. A problem for another day, once their city was restored.

Kashvi returned, another binder in hand.

'Here are all the reports of faulty energy conduits within the city. *So far.*' Kashvi thrust the binder at Antal. 'Most urgent is the South River District. Replacement parts should arrive this morning, if our humble Lord Daeyari would be so kind as to help install them.'

Antal scowled at her condescending tone. Fi snickered.

They left the capitol, crossing the complex through stone plazas and gardens glittering with frost. A quiet morning. As the sun crested the valley, slanted rays caught on the plated copper and glass of the trade warden offices, on the green and silver dome of the courthouse. Then, the red stone of the perimeter wall.

The gates stood open, a path to the waking city.

At times, Fi had viewed Thomaskweld as a hostile place: the metal constructs and tight avenues, hustlers in smoky pubs looking to make lopsided deals. To say nothing of the capitol stuffed with law enforcement. The lurking eyes of an immortal with teeth.

Other times, Thomaskweld brimmed with possibility. There were walks down riverside parkways lit with energy conduits.

Music and dancing in cellar bars. The aurora reflected in windows of dark glass.

Today, she found a new perspective. In that maze of streets lay more than hostility. More than entertainment. Here was a new home, a chance to build something larger than her.

A pair of guards flanked the gate, dressed in midnight uniforms. They nodded to Kashvi, pursed their brows at Fi, avoided eye contact with Antal. He'd dressed casual, abandoning his embroidered finery in favor of rolled sleeves and loose buttons at his collar.

Most likely, even Antal's capitol guards weren't used to seeing him in person. Fi had never heard of a daeyari walking his streets like a lowly human.

Outside the gate, Antal paused.

'What's the hold-up?' Kashvi shouted several paces ahead. 'We've got *limited daylight* and it's burning fast!'

Fi moved to Antal's side. He studied the city beyond the wall, sharp eyes slipping over the manicured avenue and dormant streetlamps, the clack of a distant trolley. A murmur of voices sounded ahead, stores opening and smells of coffee wafting from the cafes.

'Teleporting to the energy factory would be faster,' Antal muttered.

Fi braced fists on her hips. 'Someone once told me walking is a sign of respect among daeyari. And it's a lovely morning.'

His tail curled an anxious arc. 'What if this doesn't work, Fionamara?'

She knew that tremor in his words. What chance did they stand of weaving this change they'd envisioned? Would the humans of this territory ever trust a daeyari after being culled as food for so long? Would another challenger come to crush their new order?

But Fi had vowed to not let fear rule her any longer.

'You want to stop hiding from your own people?' she said. 'To walk the streets of your city without them looking at you like a monster? This is how we start.'

'And what if I can't do what I've promised you?'

Fi pictured him alone in his cliffside abode, sprawled across pillows as he watched his city glisten far below. She pictured herself returning to an empty cottage, only music to keep her company.

As Antal had done for her so many times, Fi offered her hand.

'If we fail, we'll do it together,' she said. 'But I'd wager both of us are too stubborn for that, *Lord Antal*.'

He begrudged her a grin. 'You're certainly too stubborn, Voidwalker.'

'Sometime today!' Kashvi shouted.

Fi clenched her teeth. 'Also. I need you to be the responsible one. Otherwise, I'm going to hurl that woman into the river.'

'You've already cost me one governor, Fionamara. Let me get *some* use out of this one.'

Antal took her hand. No more hiding. Whatever lay ahead, they'd meet it with claws.

His.

And hers.

Daeyari Language Glossary

Daeyari	People of dusk
Daey Celva	Dusk Council
Ijen	Wait
Ka Voz grel ef yzru	May the Void smile on you
Kasek aza	Vicious woman
Maelvasi je yzir kezros	Welcome to my home
Oyzen yzri	Fuck me
Oyzen yzru	Fuck you
Qess, ery yzu grelu	Soft, when you smile
Ulk! Lemen yzrae!	Up! Eat them!
Vavriter	Half antler
Veshri vavrae	Veshri's antlers
Vu yzu lavary?	Are you hungry?
Yelz daeyari	Young daeyari
Yzi ex oysi yzu, va yzu na sansu	I'm going to fuck you, until you can't stand
Yzi vali yzru	I love you
Yz'vum en zhem jivvi	We're in no hurry

Acknowledgements

I wrote the first draft of *Voidwalker* in early 2022, before I had my first book deal, before I even had a literary agent. The story was a dream back then, a book of my heart that might never amount to anything. I'm astounded to look back at how much has changed in that time, and how this book has journeyed with me through all of it.

First and foremost, an endless thank you to my enthusiastic hype man (aka agent) John Baker. When you offered me rep, I was blown away by your love for my cozy phoenix book, but then you asked if I had any other projects in mind, and it was your (mostly) unflinching reply to 'so, how do you feel about monster smut?' that sold me on working together. Sending you this monster smut was one of my scariest moments as a writer, but then hearing you rave about Fi and Antal on the phone for 2+ hours, I knew we were ready to conquer the world.

If pitching my agent on monster romance wasn't scary enough, running it by my editor was terrifying. But Bethan Morgan, you signed me on bird snuggles, then went *all in* on the antlers without hesitation. Thank you, as always, for taking a chance on me, for being such a tireless and indomitable partner, for championing *Voidwalker* in ways I never could have imagined.

Thank you to Hennah Sandhu and Jenna Petts for your

marketing and publicity prowess, and to everyone at Gollancz who worked to hype up Team Antler. Thank you to Tiana Coven for bringing *Voidwalker* stateside, to Angela Man, Kayleigh Webb, and the rest of the fabulous team at Orbit.

Have you seen the phenomenal trade cover for this book? Just take a moment to flip back and bask in its beauty, and thank you to the extremely talented Fernanda Suarez for creating such a masterpiece of color and shirtless antler demon.

So many beta readers helped shape this story into what you're holding. Thank you to Ashley, Bori, Laura, Lauren, Lore, Nemo, Nina, and Virginia for sharing your feedback, and for all your encouragement in rooting for my beloved simp monster and his scary human girlfriend.

Finally, thank you to Monty and Perry. My cats. Somehow, your silly cat tails inspired the mannerisms of an entire race of carnivorous immortal creatures. I'm sure you imagine yourselves just as fierce (and, just like Antal, you'd probably be wrong).

Credits

S. A. MacLean and Gollancz would like to thank everyone at Orion who worked on the UK publication of *Voidwalker*.

Editorial
Bethan Morgan
Zakirah Alam

Copy-editor
Andy Ryan

Proofreader
Emily-Fay Lunn

Editorial Management
Jane Hughes
Charlie Panayiotou
Lucy Bilton

Audio
Paul Stark
Louise Richardson
Georgina Cutler

Contracts
Dan Herron
Ellie Bowker
Oliver Chacón

Design
Nick Shah
Rachel Lancaster
Deborah Francois
Helen Ewing

Finance
Nick Gibson
Jasdip Nandra
Sue Baker
Tom Costello

Inventory
Jo Jacobs
Dan Stevens

Production
Paul Hussey
Katie Horrocks

Marketing
Hennah Sandhu

Publicity
Jenna Petts

Sales
David Murphy
Victoria Laws
Esther Waters
Karin Burnik
Anne-Katrine Buch
Frances Doyle
Group Sales teams across
Digital, Field, International
and Non-Trade

Operations
Group Sales Operations team

Rights
Rebecca Folland
Tara Hiatt
Ben Fowler
Alice Cottrell
Ruth Blakemore
Marie Henckel